DISTRICT LIBRARY
49045

✎ PU ... ✎

SHADOW ...

Dear Reader,

A beautiful ballerina. A big bad wolf. And an angel who's made for sin. Sound like a fairy tale? It is, but not like anything your mother ever told you at bedtime.

With Erin Kellison's first book in this series, *Shadow Bound*, I knew we had something special. *Shadow Fall* proves that Erin is no less than exceptional.

She weaves a delicious blend of thriller, fantasy, and romance. With touches of mythical lore from various cultures, she creates her own spellbinding story that sounds so natural you feel as though you should have heard it somewhere before, and yet is so entirely new you never know where it will go next.

So turn the page to meet mermaids, wraiths, and shape-shifters, and delve into one of the most enjoyable stories we've ever had the pleasure to publish. After all, you have nothing to lose. If you don't absolutely love this book, we'll send you a full refund of the purchase price. See the back of this book for details on our Publisher's Pledge program.

For now, though, Shadowman awaits . . .

All best,
Leah Hultenschmidt
Editorial Director

FALLEN ANGEL

It had to have been the music that changed her. He'd gone too far, revealed too much. But that was the way with music; it demanded everything. No holding back. Denying what he'd played now was like trying to stop something that had already happened.

Fine, then. She knew. He loved her. He'd loved her since he first saw her dance in the Shadowlands.

But she had to understand.

He said, "I. Ruin. Everything."

Annabella's smile faltered, a dark glimmer of sadness far away in her eyes.

So she did understand. No matter how he felt, he was no good for her. He could play well and fight better, but that was about it. He was a thieving, murderous opportunist. Not too long ago he'd taken all he could get from her, and he would again tonight.

He dropped his gaze to get rid of Adam's cuff links. Everything borrowed, nothing his. Never his. He threw them on an end table, rolled his cuffs, and forced himself to look up again.

"You'll have to tell me what you're thinking," he said. She was smart; by now she had to have guessed that he'd quit trespassing in her head.

She pinned him with dangerous intent. "Fine then. You ruin everything? Ruin *me*."

Other *Leisure* books by Erin Kellison:

SHADOW BOUND

ERIN KELLISON

SHADOW FALL

LEISURE BOOKS NEW YORK CITY

Kel

For Mom and Dad
with love.

A LEISURE BOOK®

August 2010

Published by

Dorchester Publishing Co., Inc.
200 Madison Avenue
New York, NY 10016

Copyright © 2010 by Clarissa Ellison

All rights reserved. No part of this book may be reproduced or transmitted in any form or by any electronic or mechanical means, including photocopying, recording or by any information storage and retrieval system, without the written permission of the publisher, except where permitted by law.

ISBN 10: 0-505-52830-4
ISBN 13: 978-0-505-52830-8
E-ISBN: 978-1-4285-0857-6

The name "Leisure Books" and the stylized "L" with design are trademarks of Dorchester Publishing Co., Inc.

Printed in the United States of America.

10 9 8 7 6 5 4 3 2 1

If you purchased this book without a cover you should be aware that this book is stolen property. It was reported as "unsold and destroyed" to the publisher and neither the author nor the publisher has received any payment for this "stripped book."

Visit us online at www.dorchesterpub.com.

⁊/₁₀
B&t

SHADOW FALL

The Faerie have no concept of time, breath of life, or gift of death. They are Other, neither good nor evil, and therefore capable of both extremes. They inhabit the twilight Shadowlands, a *between* space that buffers mortality from the hereafter, where magic is thick, influencing human dreams and nightmares.

The greatest of the Fae, Shadowman, also known as Death, guarded the veil and couriered souls across the divide for millennia upon millennia.

One day, Death fell in love and abandoned his post. As a direct consequence of his actions, the boundary between mortality and the Shadowlands thinned and is now . . . *permeable* to beings on both sides.

—from *The Shadowlands Treatise*,
by Talia Kathleen Thorne,
The Segue Institute

PROLOGUE

A fist to his jaw snapped Custo's head to the side. His ear roared as a storm of broad heat spread across his cheek and behind his left eye. He shuddered with the swell of ache that followed, each beat of his heart searing a lightning strike of pain through his skull as dark clouds gathered in his mind.

Focus.

He flexed his hands against the bonds that cut into his wrists—not to escape, that was impossible—but to control the wicked-slick fear that might wheeze out of him in a weak moment.

He was going to die. The trick now was to die well. No sniveling allowed.

Spencer's face loomed into Custo's blurred view. His brown hair was close-cropped, just shy of a buzz. A black earbud connected him to the rest of his team, the covert government agency that investigated paranormal activity. They were supposed to be the good guys, but something had gone terribly wrong. Spencer had always been a bastard, but colluding with the wraiths made him a traitor.

"Just tell me where Adam is, and I'll let you go. There's really no need for this—we're going to find him anyway. He doesn't need to know it was you," Spencer said.

A wet, warm trickle found the channel beneath Custo's nose. The coppery smell filled his head.

Adam would know, and worse, Adam would forgive.

A rough scrape—metal on the floor. A coin of light pressure on his foot.

Custo cracked his eyes. *What now—?*

Spencer had positioned one of Adam's sleek chairs directly in front of his own and levered himself into the seat, close enough to bump knees. With Spencer's weight in the chair, the pressure on Custo's foot increased. A bone ached, burned, then snapped with a sizzle of white-hot sparks that shot up his calf. Reality slipped out of focus for a fraction of a moment.

Spencer sat back in the chair, a friendly smile on his face. "Really, I'll let you *walk* right out of here. Just tell me where Adam is."

Spencer loved games, loved winning. The only way to thwart him was to beat him into the ground, or not to play. There was no winning today. It was better to think of something else.

Custo focused beyond Spencer, scanning the bedroom for a distraction. The New York City loft was typical Adam Thorne—clean lines of modern, uncluttered wealth in industrial grays and blacks, accented by bold colors—a strong red in the case of the bedroom, which detailed the side table and the low Asian bed centered on the opposite wall. In the abstract painting above, the red deepened to a *sangre* splatter.

Sangre. Blood. Custo dropped his gaze to the wide-planked wood floor.

"You must know where he is." Spencer gripped Custo's hand, his urgency overriding his previous levity.

I thought he was here. We were supposed to meet here. Adam had brought Talia to the loft for safekeeping. Custo was to rendezvous with them, and together they would strategize an offensive strike on the wraiths' locus of power. Adam had even checked in with Custo several times over the course of the evening to monitor his progress.

Something must have happened, and Adam and Talia bolted.

"He tells you everything." Spencer found Custo's index finger. Lifted it away from the arm of the chair.

Draw this out, and maybe they can escape.

Custo's breath caught in his chest as his finger came to a

burning right angle with the back of his hand. He gritted his teeth—a molar had loosened—and waited for the—

Pop. Custo shivered under the break of his cold sweat, then surged against the bonds that held him to the chair. Too fucking tight.

He just had to hold out a little longer. Long enough for Adam and Talia to get to safety.

"So sorry," Spencer said, pulling the finger back into alignment. He twisted it this way and that. The little bones screamed. "I think it's broken."

Very funny. Only nine more to go.

"What about that freak Talia?" Spencer lifted the middle finger. Custo tried to pull his hand back, but the damn ropes held him firmly to the chair.

Talia. Yeah, she was a little odd. No doubt about it. One scream and her dark daddy Shadowman came to the rescue. Handy having Death for a father.

Death. Custo watched as a female wraith glided from the corner of the room and settled onto Adam's bed to lounge against the pillows, her hungry gaze meeting his. A thin, pale brunette. She looked human, and at one time she was, but something had changed her and made a monster of the woman. A soul-sucker. The Segue Institute, a private organization that had teamed with Spencer's government group, had been dedicated to discovering the source of the human-wraith transformation and curing it, if possible. The focus had shifted to full war when Talia deduced that wraiths were monsters by choice, forgoing humanity for immortality.

Pop. Custo's hand twitched in an acute spasm of agony, double that of the first break. He breathed deeply, lungs straining for control.

Spencer selected another.

Heart lurching in his chest, Custo ground his teeth together as the pressure on his thumb increased to liquid fire, but pissed himself anyway.

Spencer lurched back with a laugh. "Whoa, buddy! Ya scared to die?"

"Not as scared as you." Custo's voice was gravel, the sound rumbling from his chest.

"I'm not the one who peed my pants."

The sour-sweet smell lifted into the room and burned through the coppery scent of blood.

"You"—Custo put his tongue to his loose tooth—"you turned coward the moment you sided with the wraiths."

The wraith woman winked. "On the contrary, takes nerve to be in the same room with a hungry one."

Spencer ignored her. He gave a huge sigh and rolled his eyes heavenward. "You just don't get it, Custo. You never did. There's no fighting immortality. Adam and I have been over this a million times. What the wraiths do may not be pretty—feeding on the life essence of their human forebears—but it is a natural evolutionary step toward conquering Death. I merely read the writing on the wall."

"You got scared. I always knew you were chickenshit."

"I got smart." Spencer's tone rose with anger. "Who are you to talk anyway? I know what you've done."

What I've done?

"Heinrich Graf for starters."

Oh. The German bastard who'd had a contract out on Adam's life. A shot at long distance had taken care of him. "Scum."

"You seduced his daughter to discover his whereabouts. Scum, yourself."

"I didn't suck out her soul." Custo's gaze darted to the wraith.

"Splitting hairs. You used her to kill her own father."

A mistake, and not the worst of his wrongs. Some things simply had to be taken care of, and Adam couldn't do it. Didn't have enough of the dark side in him to see it through. But yeah, if there were a God, there'd be no mercy when this was through. Just more hell. Once there, at least, he could scream. Not here. Not for a piece of shit like Spencer.

Bad life. Good death. He'd settle for that.

"Where's Adam?" Spencer repeated. "You'll tell me before we're through."

Custo gave him his best, bloody smile. If Spencer and his wraiths hadn't found the emergency escape, he sure as hell wasn't going to tell him. Not even to save his own life.

Custo gathered the saliva and blood that coated his mouth and spat in Spencer's face. Got the asshole's chin and neck.

Spencer drew his sidearm. He touched the hard tip of the gun to Custo's forehead while he wiped himself clean with his other sleeve, a sneer of disgust stretching his face.

The wraith woman sat up on the bed and whined. "If you're giving up on your questions, let me finish him. I'm hungry."

Spencer's eye twitched. "No. He's mine."

He drew his arm back. Struck. Knocked the sight from Custo's eyes.

Pain wedged through his cheekbone to split his skull. Custo blinked hard against a thick film obscuring his vision, and yet, strangely, he was able to see perfectly: The room changed, brightened. Long fluorescent lights glared overhead where the bedroom had been lit by recessed cans. A sense of constriction bound his chest in a different, suffocating kind of discomfort. Thick, earthy smells of blood and fluid and sweat filled his nose.

A man masked in soft blue-green stared down at him and commanded, "One more push!"

Oh, dear God. His birth.

Then a cry, the squall of an infant, offered up from his own throat.

A nudge under his chin brought Custo back to the bedroom in the loft.

Spencer leaned in, and Custo could feel his breath on his face. "You can die fast and easy or slow and miserable."

Custo's heart labored while he refused to inhale—no used Spencer air for him, thank you.

"It's your choice," Spencer said. He scratched his cheek with the barrel of the gun.

"Schl—" Custo's jaw wouldn't work right. He tried again for *slow and miserable*. Give Adam time.

"Let me have him," the wraith complained. "Adam and the girl are probably long gone anyway."

"No. And stay out of my business," Spencer answered.

The wraith stood, hand on the doorknob. "What a waste . . ."

Spencer brought his gun-heavy hand down again.

A crush of blackness hit Custo and jarred his memory to sudden clarity a second time. A private library, wood shelves gleaming. A young man in a dark suit sat behind a wide desk, while Custo perched on a hard, striped sofa, feet swinging in the air above the floor, trying not to—what word had his mommy said?—fidget. One of his shoelaces had come undone again.

"I said I'd pay for his schooling, but that's it." The man's voice was cold.

"He's your son," his mommy answered. She was wearing the shirt that showed her bra today. Custo hated that shirt— why didn't she fix that top button?

"He's my *bastard*—it's a little different—and I want nothing to do with him."

Reality tumbled back into Custo's consciousness, Spencer slapping his cheek. Custo tried to lift his head, but his chin only bounced on his chest. His ears were full of the rush of ocean and wind, which made no sense in the middle of the city.

"Adam wouldn't do the same for you," Spencer said. "He has to know you're here and what I'd do to you. Last chance."

Not even if it were his first. "No."

"You can't save him, you know. Not even if he gets away today." Spencer leaned in to Custo's ear. "A little secret, just between you and me . . . there's someone else at Segue who sides with the wraiths. Someone you both trust. The minute Adam turns his back . . ."

Spencer reared back for effect, swung, and the world split again. Custo was in a school yard surrounded by wide white buildings and the strong scent of honeysuckle. That first day at Shelby Boys' School.

Some pansy blue blood planted a fist to his face.

Custo shook off the surprise of the blow and looked for the assailant. The kid was tall and skinny, face flushed, blue eyes bright with fear as a bunch of other boys egged him on.

"Fight! Fight! Fight!" the rest of the boys chanted.

This should be easy. Custo ducked to the side when the pussy threw a wild punch, then clocked him on the jaw.

The boy fell in a sprawl on the ground.

Custo stepped forward, shifted to plant a kick in the boy's gut—a reminder to everyone what would happen if they dared put their hands on the poor, stupid new kid again— and got hauled back by his collar. The fabric burned at his throat.

"He hit me first!" Custo yelled to whatever teacher had made it to the grounds in time to stop the fight. They couldn't expel him on the first day, could they?

"And you got him back. Enough."

Not a teacher. An older kid. Well, Custo could take him, too. He dropped his weight and spun. Buttons popped, but the other kid hung on.

"I'm Adam Thorne," he said, seemingly unperturbed, "and we're going to be friends."

Custo wrestled against Adam's hold. He stamped on the older boy's prissy loafer—a baby trick, but Adam was keeping him too off balance to do more.

"Best friends," Adam amended in grim, low tones. "The rest of you, move out. Not the time or place, men."

The skinny kid scrambled up from the dirt and milled away with the rest of group. Custo lifted his chin to their backward looks. *Just try me.*

Adam saved his life that day. Another expulsion would have sent him back to the streets. Permanently.

Spencer's earbud buzzed through the cloudy murk of Custo's memories.

"Repeat," Spencer said, "Adam's here?"

Custo's heart clenched. *Goddamn stupid hero.*

"Guess we don't need you anymore," Spencer hissed darkly in Custo's face. "This was way too easy."

No! Wait! He had to warn—

A white thunderclap of pain and Custo's consciousness spread like water running from a dropped clay vessel, his life falling in so many pieces around him. The expanse of the loft was laid open to his understanding, a sixth sense that strengthened exponentially in the sudden absence of all others.

In the great room beyond, Adam and Talia held their ground near the elevator, darkness billowing out in silken waves from Talia's position. She stood at the brink of Shadow, one foot in mortality, one beyond, compelling the Other darkness to obscure the room, to hide them from capture.

Custo's mind clouded with Shadow as well. The darkness flickered with lightning strikes of memory. His first lay, Janet Summerton, with her peachy breasts and ginger hair. University, still on his father's buck, dorming with a geek on scholarship. Adam's frantic call for help when his brother Jacob had gone insane—turned wraith—and killed their parents. The flashes of memory advanced with each trembling heartbeat toward the decision to enter the loft's building to meet Adam and Talia, when the place had so clearly been compromised.

And Custo would do it again. *My life for his.*

Spencer crossed the room and stood, his back to the bedroom door, gun ready at his chest, and utterly oblivious to the murky forest of dark trees that grew in place of the dissolving walls. Black trunks and skeletal limbs stretched into a violet sky through which brilliant stars blazed, each with a skittering comet's tail streaming the passage of time.

A gray wind lashed through the room just as Adam kicked in the bedroom door and plugged two bullets in the wraith's head. She went down with a wide-eyed thump, but she wouldn't, couldn't, die. That was her trade—a life of monstrous soul feeding in return for immortality.

Adam and Spencer spoke with angry gestures, but the words foundered on the hiss and whip of the crowding shadows. Spencer ducked out of the room when Adam caught sight of the ruined body in the chair.

Adam, there's another traitor at Segue, Custo said.

But Adam didn't signify he heard the warning. He fell on his knees before Custo's chair.

Adam! Listen to me!

The trees grew to maturity, their boughs forming a dark tunnel to God knows where.

Adam!

Custo looked back, one last time, into mortality. His body had been cut free and Adam was struggling to haul it to the bed, his face contracted with rage and grief.

Not necessary. Not worth it. Never worth it. But, of course, Adam couldn't hear him.

The blackness shuddered, shade upon shade. Something was coming.

From the deep, a gleam of silvery metal arched into a wicked crescent moon. A scythe. The harried shadows parted and a figure emerged, wrapped in a cloak of blackness. Shadowman was partially hooded, but his face caught starlight. His features glowed with fantastic beauty, but his eyes were wells of loneliness. And no wonder—his was an existence filled with solitary, grim work. Custo couldn't blame the tortured soul for stealing a human moment to love, even if that moment had allowed a demon into the world to raise an army of wraiths. If anyone could find a way to kill the demon, it was Adam and Shadowman's daughter, the banshee Talia.

I have to warn him. Please.

Shadowman was immovable, his expression as unforgiving as stone. Hand gripping the scythe, he slowly swung out his arm, as if opening a gate to oblivion.

Death. Then Hell. Custo gathered what was left of his courage, clamping down on the naked quake of fear at his core. No sniveling allowed.

He moved out of pain and into uncertainty, the tunnel of sharp branches lengthening to a bright point of light. Probably a white-hot fire to burn at the blood staining his soul for eternity.

On either side of the dark path, whispers. Eyes flashing. Magic gathering to lure strays from the way. The tunnel led to a primeval shore where a narrow skiff waited to carry them across a gray channel toward a high, great gate. The light of the surrounding walls shifted through the varied spectrum of the rainbow, at once blue and yellow, then azure and verdant green.

There must be a mistake—even Spencer knew the truth.

Shadowman delivered him to the gleaming portal, which opened in welcome. The light was blinding. A song of piercing joy rose to cheer an addition to the Host.

Custo turned to Shadowman, but Death was gone.

So not Hell. Worse. A cosmic joke. A bloodied soul to be numbered with the angels.

He was a liar, a murderer, a thief, but never a hypocrite. He didn't belong here.

The shining gate closed behind him, clanging shut like a Sunday church bell.

Custo braced his hands on the spectacular surface. There had to be a way out. A way to open the gate and a way to warn Adam.

Custo banged a fist against the entrance.

Or if not, *good* people died every day. Death would be back eventually, and damn if Custo wouldn't be ready.

ONE

ANNABELLA stepped *en pointe* into a soft arabesque, arms lightly crossed over her breasts, head bowed in a ghostly whisper of submission. With her arching movement, the skirt of her long practice tutu created a silent white wedding bell in the front mirrors of the studio. The moment stretched as the ethereal strains of *Giselle* filled the room. The first eerie whine of the strings . . . the second . . .

One soft breath and she inclined her weight forward just as her partner propelled her into a seamless lift.

"Stop. Stop. Stop." Thomas Venroy hit his cane against the floor for someone to shut off the music. The artistic director communicated almost everything with that sharp rap of his cane. In spite of the hugging, humid heat of the studio, he wore dress slacks and a button-down shirt. His nearly bald head was covered by a weak gray comb-over.

Annabella relaxed out of position, chest heaving, her hands braced on her hips. The air was stale with old sweat, but no one would think of opening a window to let the chill air in to cramp their muscles.

She looked over her shoulder at her partner, Jasper Morgan. He'd taken advantage of the break to snag a towel from his bag to wipe himself down. The rest of the dancers who made up the corps lounged on the barre or sat on the floor along the back wall of the studio. They'd been at this for over five hours, but tomorrow's dress rehearsal would be more about staging and costumes than fine-tuning the movements. The time was now. She'd stay all night if she had to—this was her debut as principal. Her Giselle had to be perfect, even if the company was only doing the second act for the gala performance.

Jasper flung the towel over his shoulder and crouched on the floor. Probably to stretch his back—hers was killing her, too. When she got home, she'd swallow a bottle of ibuprofen, take a hot bath, and bawl like a baby. But not now. Not with people watching.

"Annabella," Venroy said from his stool at the front mirrors, "your shoulders are full of tension. You are supposed to be a *wili*. A ghost. Like a puff of smoke."

Tension. Right. She was freaking stressed out of her mind.

She squared her shoulders. "I'll do better," she said. "My concentration slipped, that's all."

"Anna." Venroy waved away her words. "You're tired. Jasper is tired. Go home and—"

"No," Annabella cut him off. She winced at her sharp tone, took a deep breath, and pleaded, "I need to get this right. I've almost got it. I can feel it. One more time."

Venroy frowned. One of the girls in the back murmured *diva,* but Anna didn't turn her head. What they thought of her didn't matter, not really. She'd given up her life for ballet; she didn't expect anyone to start inviting her to slumber parties now.

She glanced down at Jasper. "Please?"

Jasper groaned as he stood, but he balled his towel and threw it to the side of the room. He'd been a principal for more than two years already, and he was just as invested in this performance. At six feet, he was the ideal height to partner her. His blue-and-blond good looks always showed well onstage, not to mention that he sure knew how to fill out a pair of tights. Too bad he was gay.

Jasper's grudging support had her spirits rising. She looked back at Venroy in question.

"Oh, all right. One last time." Venroy's gaze shifted to the dancers at the back wall. "Be ready."

Annabella backed up to her starting position again and

waited for the music to begin. One last chance for "perfect" before the big night.

Deep breath. Shoulders relaxed. Ready.

The soft music slid again from the CD player, and she let the ribbons of sound guide her. She glided through the intermediate steps following the pas de deux, the touch of her pointe shoes nearly silent on the floor.

She threaded the discrete movements together so that her step-step arabesque became the haunted shift of a forest sylph. She shed Annabella and let the magic of the ballet take over. Let the dance transform her into the ghost, the wili, of Giselle.

The arabesque. A breath. And Jasper's strong hands were at her waist to skim her body through the ether.

He set her gently on the forest floor, near her grave, then stepped forward to embrace her, to capture the spirit of his love. Too late, too late. The two-timing Prince Albrecht broke her weak heart and she died. Now he comes at midnight to grieve for her.

"Lightly! Don't forget your arms!" Venroy called.

Annabella corrected the angle of her port de bras so her arms were tentative, the tilt of her head mournful.

She floated back, on tiptoe, stirred by an errant breeze through the darkened trees.

"Yes! Don't let Jasper catch you!"

Jasper blurred in her vision as she took a light run upstage. If she looked at him, really looked at him, she'd lose the moment. The magical transport between here and the Otherworld. Her blood sparkled through her thrumming body, tingling at her fingertips in the sweep and twist of each extension. Darkness crowded the corners of the story, a forest of magic replacing the barrier of the studio walls.

"That's it! Beautiful, Anna!" Venroy raised his cane. "Ladies, be ready!"

The music rose and her wili sisters poured from the tree

line, circling her like a cauldron of mist before forming two straight lines at the edges of the clearing, arms crossed over their breasts, heads bowed, eyes hollow and downcast as in death.

The music hesitated, and then a single violin sang, the melody rising in tempo, yet still queer in tone. She sprung into a series of backward moving leaps, feet quick, body light, then prepared for her diagonal cross—

She brought her gaze up for her pique turn.

A pair of wide-set yellow eyes peered back at her from the murk of the imaginary trees. Feral eyes.

Her breath caught. She blinked hard and shook her head. She forcibly relaxed: *Shoulders down. Concentrate.*

The music rose—her cue—and she began her lightning-swift, traveling turns. Her feet were busy, fast with technique, while her upper body all but floated through the air. She was the ghost of a lovelorn girl; gravity had no power over her. She was as fluid as water, as dense as atmosphere. Magic and midnight alone could claim her.

A low growl rumbled through the wood . . . From the whip of her turn, her gaze found the yellow eyes again and now the hulking shadow of a wolf, crouched to spring.

Her balance shifted, faltered. Her foot slipped out from under her and . . . she fell with a body slap to the studio floor.

Wolf. Heart pounding, Annabella skittered away from the now-empty corner of the room. Her gaze darted around the studio, the lights suddenly bright and harsh. The wilis dropped their positions and shuffled out of line.

Anybody see that?

Their interest was fixed on her.

Just me then.

The thing was gone, as was the dark forest, evaporating into her imagination.

She finally brought her attention to Venroy, who was pinching the bridge of his nose, eyes closed.

Embarrassed heat swept over her. Maybe it *was* time to go home.

Mortal. Trespasser. *Woman*.

Bright like fire. Dancing like flame. A threat.

Her fecund scent burned in the hunter's nose. Earthy, musky, sweet. Hunger curled in his belly. His teeth sharpened for flesh.

The mortal light flickered, then doused, but the smell of her lingered. Drew him. He stalked the boundary of Twilight, his paws silently picking through the layers of Shadow to search her out. He cocked his head to sniff.

This way. The hunt was on.

"Anna, I'd like a moment," Venroy said. "The rest of you are done for the night."

Annabella pushed herself to standing. Her hip and elbow finally registered the ache of the fall. *Just great.* She shot a quick glance to the corps, who were leaving in twos and threes. A couple months ago, she'd been one of them. When the lineup for the new season had been announced, she'd had every expectation of being in the long line of wilis for the classical component of the schedule. Certainly not in front of them, as the lead.

And it had all started with those fateful words, "Anna, I'd like a moment."

This time she didn't think it would be good news.

Chin up. Dress rehearsal was tomorrow—she was Giselle whether they liked it or not. She strode forward. She prayed Venroy would keep his voice low. Falling on her ass was humiliating enough. Having the whole studio hear his rebuke would be too much.

Venroy's expression softened. "You are worrying me, Anna. I wonder if you were promoted too early. Too young. Your technique is strong, but others are equal, some better.

You certainly work hard, but everyone else here does as well."

Her stomach turned. She didn't want to hear the rest.

"And you have talent. Undeniable talent." He shook his head. "I am not talking about aptitude. I am talking about *the gift*. When you dance, the story comes alive. Do you know what I mean?"

"I know how I feel when I dance." Her voice was thick.

His gaze sharpened. "How?"

"Different. Wonderful. But strange, too. Like the world loses its grip on me and I can fly. Does that sound crazy?"

"No," Venroy said. "And yes. But that is ballet." He grew serious. "We can cancel the *Giselle* portion of the opening gala and substitute it with something else. *Serenade* is ready."

Her face burned. "I swear I can do this."

"You've been pushing yourself too hard. There is no shame in saying you aren't ready. We'll simply make the change." He stood and adjusted his pant legs. "But if you choose *Giselle* and become distracted like that during the performance, it will be your last as principal."

The heat in Annabella's face abruptly fell away. Her heart beat hard, once, registering his criticism and sending a fresh wave of mortification though her system. Her eyes pricked with tears. The very idea of Thomas Venroy disappointed in her made her chest horribly tight. She swallowed the lump in her throat and looked down at her shoes, concentrating on the worn peach satin so she wouldn't cry. She was a grown woman, for Pete's sake.

"What's it going to be?"

There was only one answer. "*Giselle*."

Venroy took her chin, raised her face to him, and gave her a little shake. "Anna, please. I believe in you. You shine so bright when you dance. Try to enjoy this moment."

She was trying. She was giving this performance every scrap of talent and soul that she had. This was her dream.

Sighing, Venroy picked his folded gray-brown sport coat off the floor at his feet, gave it a dusting, and then shrugged it on. "Go home. Get a full night of sleep. Trust yourself that the performance will be wonderful. Once you are on the stage, in costume, you won't be able to help yourself. Distractions will disappear. You will be Giselle, body and spirit."

Will that wolf still be there? She bit her lip so the question wouldn't slip out. She swallowed hard again and nodded. She couldn't have Venroy thinking she was losing it.

Wrapping an arm around her waist, he led her to the studio door, and then gave her butt a pat to nudge her toward the dressing room.

Jasper was leaning on the wall outside the studio. "What you need is a good, hard screw."

Annabella stopped and gave him a halfhearted smile. The sweetie had waited to see that she was okay. His towel was wrapped around the back of his neck, and both his hands gripped the ends. The rest of his fantastic body was on display under his sweaty tights and tank. Very impressive.

He grinned back at her. "You know, the kind that obliterates your mind and makes your body weep."

She mustered a laugh. "You offering?"

"I would if I could, honey. You need it." He took her hand and gave her palm a kiss. "But I think it would confuse my boyfriend."

"Lucky guy," she said and turned for the dressing room. It was common knowledge that Jasper and his boyfriend Ricky were as good as married.

Jasper released her hand. "Go find yourself a nice boy . . ."

"Ha!" she answered back, pulling open the dressing room door. A nice boy. He sounded like her mother. She had no time for nice boys. Or bad ones.

The dressing room door closed on, ". . . it works wonders!"

Annabella sidled by a group of dancers clogging the entry. If she hurried, she could be home in twenty minutes.

The showers beyond hissed. Most of the dancers were in a rush, too, calling good-bye and squeezing past half-naked bodies. Anna dropped to the bench. She kicked off her tutu, hung it on a peg inside a locker, and then worked the knots of her shoe ribbons loose.

"Anna," Katrina called. She'd been her friend since they joined the company together a couple years ago. They hadn't spoken much since Annabella had been promoted.

"Yeah?" Annabella leaned back on the bench to see Katrina pulling a tee over her head.

"Couple of us are going out for a drink to unwind. You want to come?" While grabbing some jeans, Katrina batted away another girl—Marcia, by her slick French twist—who groaned at the extended invitation.

A drink. Some laughs. Like old times.

Politically, yes, she should go. She knew that. Katrina knew that. Judging by the slight hush, everyone in the dressing room knew that, too.

But . . . her body hurt, her mind was reeling, and she really, really needed a good cry. The last thing she wanted was for her mini breakdown to be alcohol induced and public. She'd probably start babbling about wolves with yellowy eyes and . . . No. Drinks were definitely not a good idea right now

Katrina read the answer on her face, gave a cold shrug, and turned away.

Annabella caught a couple of the looks shared by some of the other dancers. One mouthed the word *diva*—the second time today that particular label had been applied to her. The insult smarted this time.

Diva? She didn't get it. Nothing about her had changed since her promotion to principal.

Anna ripped off her shoes and threw them in her bag. She rummaged to find sweats to pull over her tights and leo. She'd shower at home.

But *diva?* Okay, tonight she'd requested the extra run-through, but it only cost everyone maybe ten minutes. Fifteen tops. And she couldn't help it if she was too tired to go out for drinks—she'd been the one dancing all night. Not them. The corps mostly *stands* in the second act of *Giselle*, and Venroy had let them all sit for the majority of the time.

Diva? Please.

She tucked a light scarf around her head—no way on earth was she getting sick this close to the performance season—and was ready to go.

The air outside was sharp with the smell of crisp leaves mixed with lingering exhaust, underscored by a medley of city scents—a trace of spicy food, beer, old newspaper, mellow sewer funk, and fresh laundry. She breathed deep for a hit of the city's pervasive vitality, enough to get her back to her studio apartment. The sounds of distant traffic and sirens drew her into a brisk walk. The bus stop was only a block away. The sooner she was home, the sooner she could crash. She tightened her scarf under her chin and picked up her pace.

The darkened street wasn't completely deserted. Streetlights and buildings splashed enough light to see clearly four blocks in either direction. A couple strolled ahead of her, and a group of chatty smokers—young professionals by the looks of their day-wrinkled slacks and shirts—loitered outside a lit doorway. Nothing any city girl would worry about.

The bench at the bus stop was empty. Annabella sat, crossed her legs, and looked down the street again. No bus in sight.

Her mind wandered back to rehearsal. Tense shoulders—that's what Venroy had said. She'd try harder to relax. And he'd said to watch her arms. Maybe there was something off with her upper carriage altogether.

Stop. You're obsessing again. She stood to distract herself and leaned against a lamppost.

Still, it wouldn't hurt to watch old videos. She had
Natalia Makarova's *Giselle*. She'd seen the performance a
million times, but never concentrating on shoulders and
arms. Maybe—

Across the street, a dense well of shadow drew her attention. Something was moving in there. Make that prowling.
A big cat, maybe. Or a dog. Or . . . or . . .

Her heartbeat accelerated. She deliberately looked away.
This was *not* happening again.

If she had brought her iPod, she could've turned off her
mind. Between *Giselle* and the creepy wolf hallucination
from rehearsal, she was going to give herself a nervous
breakdown.

She took a shuddering breath.

There was no need to wait at the bench all night. She
could pick up the bus at the next stop. And she needed a
bigger distraction. She grabbed her bag, reaching inside for
her cell phone at the same time. She hit "1" and TALK to call
her best friend, who answered.

"Hi, Mom," Annabella said. She shouldered her bag and
lengthened her stride down the sidewalk, taking care to
stay where the streetlights were brightest. Paranoid, but
whatever.

"Oh, good," her mom answered. "I've been trying to get
a hold of you. I need an extra ticket for your brother's girlfriend. Apparently he didn't break up with her, so now she's
coming opening night."

Annabella's footfalls echoed on the sidewalk. A chill slid
down her spine, raising the hairs at her nape as her heart
worked her up to a fast stride. She tried to outpace the niggling
feeling that someone was stalking her, but glanced over her
shoulder anyway.

Nothing there but motley shadows, and a block away, a
pedestrian.

"Annabella?"

Oh. Brother. Girlfriend. Ticket. Right. "You think he's going to propose to her again instead?"

"I really don't know—" Her mom broke off. "Why are you out of breath?"

"Walking home." She glanced across the street and almost tripped to a stop.

A patch of skulking shadow traveled the opposite sidewalk. The shadow kept to its own, black on black, and was easy to lose if she blinked.

"Bell, it's late." Concern filled her mom's voice. "Get a cab. My treat."

"I would, but I don't see one." She kept her gaze trained on the layered darkness, her body stone-still waiting for the next movement. Everything seemed to be shifting ever so slightly around her. The buildings, the street lamps, the metal garbage bins. She was totally cracking up.

"Honey, what's wrong?"

"Nothing. It's stupid. I had a rotten rehearsal." But since she could tell her mom anything, she added, "And I think I'm being followed."

"What?" Her mom's voice rose. "Where are you? Can you find someplace safe?"

Damn it. Now her mom was worried. "It's just a dog, Mom. A dog is following me."

"Get inside."

"Businesses are closed. I'm waiting for the bus." Not a quarter of a block away was the next stop, an empty lit bench waiting. No shadows there. Annabella made for it.

"Is there anyone to ask for help?"

She glanced around. There was no one in sight anymore. Weird. It wasn't *that* late. "Not really."

"How can you be alone in the middle of New York City?" her mother demanded.

"I'm fine, Mom. Don't worry. The . . . uh . . . dog is staying on the other side of the street."

Even as she spoke the shadows organized again into the unmistakable form of a black wolf, his eyes shining from the deep pitch of his rough, triangular face.

This had to stop. She had to get a freaking grip.

She dropped herself onto the bench and closed her eyes while her body quaked. *There's nothing there. Just a figment of my imagination.* A part of her screamed *danger!* while the rest of her remained resolute. She was not cracking up, not now. They could check her into an asylum . . . *after* the gala.

"Annabella?"

She opened her eyes as the wolf began a slow advance across the street. Head lowered, ears pinned back, he picked his way through the darkest fall of shadow toward her. His growl was low with menace. His eyes were wild yellow, and locked on her.

"Mom, I'm scared." She sounded three, instead of twenty-three, but she didn't care. She crab-crawled upward to sit on the backrest of the bench. Her blood pounded in her ears as she clutched the phone like a lifeline. Her body loosened slightly, and she knew, tired as she was, that she could run if she had to.

"I'm calling the police on the other line."

Annabella's eyes teared at the urgency in her mom's voice. She shouldn't have called home in the first place, shouldn't have put her mom through this. The wolf crossed the midline of the road and she started to shake. A roaring sound filled her ears. *This isn't happening. This can't be happening.*

"Honey, it's going to be okay." Sure enough, her mom released a tirade of demands in the background. "Where is the dog now?"

"It's . . . uh . . ." Fear choked her answer. The wolf ambled closer, his paws silent on the pavement. As he drew near, she perceived that the blackness of his coat was instead a variable absence of color. The thing lacked substance, like a nightmare, and yet his intent was palpable enough.

"Honey?" Her mom's voice was high and harsh, frantic.

A scream built up in Annabella's throat, gathering into a tight kernel of fear.

But the wolf stopped there, at the edge of a circular pool of streetlight. He snarled into a series of sharp barks, loud as cracking thunder, but did not cross into the halo of light. The barks hit her like blows, but she kept her seat. Didn't run off into the dark.

The wolf satisfied himself with a slow prowl around the perimeter of the glow, his gaze fixed on her. Waiting.

If she could have wrapped the lamplight around her like a cloak, she would have. As it was, she fully intended to stay on this bench all night, until the sun rose and burned away the monster.

"Honey!"

"I'm here."

"The dog?"

Wolf. "Mad, I think." Her voice shook her words to pieces. "I'm not going to move. Or breathe. Maybe it will leave me alone."

"Oh, honey." Now her mom was crying.

"I'm sorry, Mom." The tears in her voice matched her mother's. The wolf finished its first threatening lap. "I should've taken a cab. I promise to take a cab from now on."

Her gaze followed the animal as it started a second circuit, somewhat larger to take him farther from the street bench.

The high-pitched squeal of a bus's brakes told her why. The bus had arrived, hissing to a stop, its interior bright as day. Salvation.

"What's that?" her mom asked.

The bus's door folded open. Annabella laughed as tears spilled down her cheeks, and she stepped from streetlight to safety. "The bus. I'm on the bus."

"Oh, thank you, God," her mom breathed into the phone. "You'll be okay now?"

With every light on in her apartment and a good night's sleep. "Yeah, I think so."

She glanced out the window onto the darkened street as she took her seat, searching for signs of movement. *I hope so.*

TWO

ANGELS. Custo couldn't stand them in his head, picking up his thoughts and casting theirs his way.

From each one, understanding, acceptance, and a convoluted explanation of how they were related to him through such and such crap ancestral line. One big happy family. He wanted to tell them all to piss off and leave him the hell alone. With all the fluid mind-speak going on, he was certain his opinion was more than clear.

The barrage of mental dialogue intensified near the elaborately carved marble passages of the Halls of Memory, each subtle detail telling the story of the world. Would it kill them to use their mouths to speak? Their incessant nonvocal histories and orations on the meticulous ordering of the universe made him want to knock the serene expressions from their faces. Who could possibly give a damn about creation when there was a war raging on Earth?

Humanity against the wraiths. A traitor within Segue, the world's only defense against the immortal soul-suckers.

But no amount of asking, shouting, or begging for aid would move them. Each passing moment was a moment wasted.

So Custo kept as far from the halls as possible, haunting the gate, waiting for that cold bastard Shadowman's return. Except, as often as Death approached, Custo had yet to catch him before he was gone again. Like the angels, the dark fae hadn't listened to his pleas when he died. And now Death was quick when delivering his souls, too quick thus far for Custo to catch and convince.

Yet there had to be a way.

Custo climbed the white stone steps of the gate's outer

wall, his fingers grazing the intricate carvings that decorated the massive boundary between the Shadowlands and Heaven. Some talented, very patient soul had rendered the ivory stone into a complex latticework interspersed with miniature carvings of animals, flora, and the faces and forms of generations upon generations of people, young and old, happy and despairing.

A growing warmth in Custo's consciousness alerted him that his lookout on the wall was already taken. He stretched his mind to isolate the identity and intent of the individual before he turned back and went the other way. He was really not in the mood . . .

Oh. His heretofore unknown cousin, Luca, come to baby-sit him again. Could be worse.

Custo joined Luca, leaning against the stone ramparts above the rambling expanse of the Shadowlands. His vantage looked down upon the diamond white shore, beyond that, the wide gray channel, and farther still, the Shadow forest with leaves dark and changeable as nightshade. The Shadowlands' only constant was the tempting question, *What if . . . ?*

Any moment now, Death would be back. From this angle and altitude, Shadowman's small boat would be visible. Custo's ticket out of here.

"Go away," Custo said.

Luca chuckled. "I thought you might want company."

"You know I don't." He had to get out of here. To find a way to return to mortality and warn Adam. Beleaguered by the wraith war, Adam wouldn't think to look for sabotage within his own ranks, even after Spencer's betrayal. Adam was just too trusting. Without Adam, The Segue Institute would crumble, and without Segue, the wraiths would eventually dominate the world.

Luca sighed. "If you went into service, you might find the time easier to bear. You might find purpose. There is great work to be done."

Not any work he was suited for. "I prefer solitude."

The saving grace of Heaven, the only thing that kept Custo remotely sane, was that in spite of the overwhelming—and in his opinion, slightly obsessive—order to the place, nothing about *him* had really changed. At least that he could tell. He was himself, and if he wanted to wait at the outer wall, no one tried to force him to do otherwise. For that reprieve alone, he gave Luca his attention.

Luca had died in his late forties, but he appeared youthful and fit, as if twenty-five. He was casual in jeans and a white tee, where Custo wore black. Luca's dark hair was longish and curling. Almost femme, if his black gaze weren't so intense.

"You might find your memories less bothersome," Luca said.

No thank you. His memories—the good, the bad, and the very bad—were all that he had left. All that defined him. He didn't want to become something else. Someone else.

"When you're ready, then. I'll always know where to find you." Luca put a hand to Custo's shoulder briefly, and then descended the stairs.

Custo dismissed the good-bye and turned back to his watch. There were no good-byes in Heaven, only unwanted, endless hellos.

A blink or an eon, and the boat appeared. Custo gripped the wall to contain a rush of anticipation.

How much time had passed while he'd been waiting, he couldn't guess. A minute? A year? A millennia? Impossible to tell.

The narrow vessel carried two passengers: an old man, white hair glowing with the light of the gate, and tall, grim Shadowman, wrapped in his seethe of darkness. The old man passed, Heaven burst with jubilation and welcome, and the gate clanged shut against the potent throb of the twilight Shadowlands.

But this time Death didn't leave, though divine light pierced and tore at his cloak, snapping it back toward the darkened tree line. Likewise, the shining black strands of his hair lifted, whipping from his broad shoulders in the streaming brilliance of the gate. His bared torso was defined with muscle, his fae-tinged skin flecked with gritty black, burning with Heaven's brightness. As quickly as the light eroded the tip of his nose and wore away at his flesh, Shadow renewed him. Death's expression was severe, the high slashes of his cheekbones growing prominent with his effort, but he showed no inclination to retreat.

At last.

"Kathleen!" Shadowman raged at the wall, his voice thick, deep, and cracked. His anguish shook the gate, the walls shifting to deeper hues.

So he'd come for her at last, the woman who'd tempted Death to fall for love. Why now, after all this time? Had something happened on Earth?

Custo needed to get home. Not knowing was torture.

"Kathleen!" Death called again, louder, resolute. His free hand fisted in defiance at his side; the other clutched the staff of his scythe, knuckles mottling with black. His body flexed, as if he faced into a violent, blasting wind. A law of Heaven, one of God knows how many, prohibited the faerie within the walls.

Maybe . . .

Custo reached with his mind to locate Death's lost love. Maybe he could make a deal with a lord of the Shadowlands in return for a favor. Custo cast his consciousness out like a net, but came back empty. He cast again and sifted more carefully. Nothing. Damn.

Kathleen was not in Heaven.

"Kathleen!" Death threw his scythe into the water, as if repudiating any continued, willing concert with the divine. The light of Heaven tore his cloak to ribbons.

Custo's mind darkened with subtle purpose, proof positive that Heaven was no place for him either.

"Hey!" he shouted from the top of the wall.

Shadowman looked up. His eyes were all black, glossy with power.

"Trade you," Custo offered. Was such a thing possible?

No answer, just a throb of soul-deep, intense inspection.

"You want in or don't you? Heaven's no place for me, and I'm not hanging around until they figure it out." Right about now it would become overwhelmingly apparent that he didn't belong.

Custo glanced over his shoulder. No one coming for him. Yet.

"I do." Shadowman spoke the words like a vow. The sound carried and penetrated to chill Custo's marrow. He was glad he wouldn't be here when Death discovered Kathleen was elsewhere.

Custo grinned. "Meet me at the gate."

Custo took the steps by twos and threes. He kept his eyes from the grassy plains that led to the Great Halls. He didn't want to lose his nerve. His chance.

He felt along the carved surface of the gate, and his hand warmed, burned, as it passed over the intricate figures of a couple entwined in an embrace, marking the lock to Heaven. Funneling every ounce of will, he pushed.

The gate cracked open.

Custo found Shadowman's blistering hand mirrored his. A spark of light, and their positions were reversed. Custo was delivered.

Segue.

Without a backward glance, Custo set off at a run across the beach. He dived into the channel, aiming for the drifting boat. With any luck, there'd be an oar inside. A shock of wet cold stunned, but didn't slow him. The stuff went in his mouth—salty—and his ears and nose. He blinked the drops

out of his stinging eyes, urgency pushing him to stroke and
kick a path across the water.

As he swam, he extended his mind for signs of pursuit.
His consciousness broadened to find Luca back at the top of
the wall with a host of others, looking out, tracking his
progress. And below, he perceived how the sandy shelf fell
away and the water rapidly deepened.

Something sinuous grazed his leg as he reached Shadowman's slender gray boat. The side pitched as Custo swung a
leg over and heaved himself inside, accomplishing the feat
with a wet body roll that nearly capsized the vessel. He knelt
immediately and looked into the water.

The shadow of a large creature—not a fish—broke the
surface. A mermaid, if he had to put a name to it, with
greenish skin that went blue over defined cheekbones forming the features of a water goddess. Her hair twisted in
thick, frondy pieces like Medusa, and her black eyes blinked
rapidly, regarding him. She lay on her back so that the water
lapped her full, tight breasts.

Oh, sweet beauty. His mind clouded, Adam and Segue
and Earth receding from his consciousness. Adam would
understand . . .

The mermaid smiled and teased one of her nipples.

A wave of desire flowed over Custo, painfully gathering at
his groin. His sudden need washed away everything except
the mermaid's glorious undulating body. His gaze roved over
her slick form, looking for a place to plug himself in and
drown in ecstasy. Now that would be a good death!

A tremendous bellow snapped his attention again to the
great wall. Shadowman's low-pitched shout of rage shook
the sandy shores of Heaven like an earthquake, the grains
settling into fine, tiered ripples.

Uh oh. Seemed as though Death discovered that his love
was not in Heaven.

The water rose with Shadowman's anger, the boat perching

precariously on a wave as the channel water retracted with a great sucking noise away from the forest's shore.

The mermaid screeched and bared pointy piranha teeth before diving into the choppy waves.

Custo reared back—not the kind of kiss he'd been looking for.

A tsunami was building, the latent energy of the waters swelling beneath the boat. Custo looked for an oar. Nothing. An oar couldn't save him anyway. He sat in the boat bottom and gripped the sides.

With a sudden rush, the boat was propelled toward the Shadowlands. He sailed through the air like a spear until the water hit the tree line and he lost his hold, tossed into the grip of a tree. He clung to the branches as water tumbled beneath him. The boat careened away, shattered nearby, and showered him with the splinters of Shadowman's bitter disappointment.

Custo shook his head clear, the mermaid's seduction receding with the water. She had utterly enslaved his mind, subsuming his purpose to her will. If her power over him was any indication, the Shadowlands was one seriously dangerous place.

He stayed in his nest until the water ebbed, rattling the branches in belated shock and scanning the density of the wood below for danger. Finding nothing, he picked his way down to the sludge. It was tight work. His jeans were plastered to his legs, restraining movement, and his shirt ripped under his sleeve on a bony branch, but he made it to the bottom and ran through the squishy mire into the darkness.

Mortality had to be on the other side of the forest, didn't it? Through the deep trees and a bright crossing, Earth would just have to accommodate this no-name bastard again. Then Segue, and the message for Adam. After that, he had no idea.

The damp sent a chill running over his body, which he

ignored as he pushed himself deeper to evade capture. There was no path, only shadow layered with black trunks, illuminated by a soft glow that had no discernable source. A woodsy smell predominated, not that he could ever guess the variety of the tree, nor care to. The rich earth below was layered with dead growth and cragged over with rambling tree roots.

He was much better suited to civilization. Give him a fight in an alley any day over a walk in the woods.

He stretched his mind again, but that sense had grown dumb in the forest. He couldn't tell what was ahead or behind, not for sure. But there had to be a way to get back. Adam's institute had documented ghosts. Segue was simply going to have to find room for one more haunt.

Bright red drew his attention to succulent berries hanging heavy and fat like grapes on the branches of a nearby bush. Custo's mouth watered with their sweet, wet scent. His stomach felt suddenly, miserably hollow. How convenient that these should be right here when he needed them. He reached for a cluster, licking his lips in anticipation, but stopped himself.

He didn't need to eat. He was dead.

Still, the berries promised a succulent burst of flavor in his mouth. Just one bite—

No. After the mermaid he couldn't trust anything. Every story, every fairy tale he'd ever heard, counseled against eating something in the Otherworld. He couldn't trust anything in Shadow. Custo turned away.

A small creature skittered through the trees, something like a rabbit. It stopped on its haunches and craned its head to regard him with too-human eyes. Strange. The animal perked up its head, as if sensing danger, and bounded off again.

Custo listened as well, but he heard only the shift and sigh of the trees. An occasional crack. An eerie whine.

No. Not a whine. Sad, slow violins.

He turned around, his gaze searching the trees. Ahead, a scrap of white light glowed, partially obscured by black trunks. The light dimmed and then grew again.

He moved forward to investigate and discovered a clearing surrounded by wicked, wintry trees. In the center of the clearing, a woman danced. She was made of light, her figure slight, long and waifish, her skin pale and glistening. Her dark hair was pulled into a knot at the back of her head, like a fairy or a ballerina. Likewise, she floated on tiptoe and defied gravity with the stretch and arch of her body. The haunting music was part of her, yet it scored him.

More faerie magic? He didn't care.

She kept her eyes downcast for the most part, so terribly sad, but when she raised her face to twirl, shining like hope, he knew he would never be the same.

She had to be his. He knew it with every broken fiber of his being.

The soft curve of her jaw, her full young lips and her storybook eyes were his perfection. A momentary pang of reservation struck him hard: The woman—little more than a girl—was everything that he wasn't. Where he was coarse, she was all silky lines and smooth dips. While he was grasping and gritty, she moved with the sweetest magic, like a dream. Where he was tainted and used, she was bright and new.

Custo pushed his hesitation aside. So he was a selfish bastard. Too bad. He had to catch her or he knew he'd be soul sick forever.

He concealed himself behind a thick tree, tensed, ready. He didn't want to scare her, but if she'd just move this way . . .

A growl rumbled across the clearing.

Custo's attention snapped to the darkness of the opposite trees. A huge black wolf bared his teeth, his body crouched and ready to attack the woman.

The dancer stiffened slightly, but continued to move. Why? She obviously knew the wolf was there. A deeper pallor to her skin told him she was afraid. Why didn't she back away?

The wolf spotted Custo and altered his stance, ears pinned back for attack.

Custo felt a wave of electric anger burn through him. He could not let the wolf harm her.

He stepped out of the trees slowly, his arms raised and open. His attention was divided between the shock of the woman, finally coming to a skittery stillness, and the redoubled menace of the wolf, his lips retracting to the gums, his teeth sharp as blades.

Custo moved into the center of the clearing. The woman's gaze flitted from him to the wolf, to something beyond them in the trees.

"Oh, no. Not again," she murmured. Then louder, with false brightness, "No, Jasper. Just a slick spot on the floor right here. Anybody have some rosin?" Her nervous voice was oddly warped and distant. The glow of her skin dimmed, her magic shifting.

The wolf charged her, two great bounds. Custo threw himself between them and pushed her out of harm's way. He felt the weight of the wolf crush his back and they fell.

The air burned like white lightning.

They landed on a hard surface, but he felt no impact. The girl jumped out of the way, quick on her feet, and the wolf jumped over Custo's head. It leaped out into a great void, filled with empty red velvet seats, row upon row with balconies above, and was lost in the darkness. A theater.

"I've got some, Annabella," someone said.

The dancer didn't answer; she kept her gaze on Custo, unblinking, fearful, and yet so lovely. The other mortals disregarded him as if he weren't there, though he stood up, center stage.

He was back. Somehow he was back, returned to Earth. But as what?

Then he began to burn. He had no substance, but he was on fire regardless. His body screamed with pain, and he ran.

"No, wait!" the girl called.

He'd have answered, but he couldn't bear the heat. Every nerve was quivering, sizzling. He passed through the layered curtains at the side of the stage and felt the dust from the corners rise to chase him. He felt the dirt and moisture of the air whip into a frenzied, pursuing swarm. Every stray mote and drop gathered to him.

He ran, though he had no feet to touch the floor.

He fled down a winding corridor, out the exit, and past a smoker's propped doorway into the night of the city. On the sidewalk the cloud of earth and wetness descended upon him. The earthen tornado drove him down onto the ground to inundate and . . . reform him.

He could sense the atoms of his mass rearranging, recombining, the zap and snap of molecules configuring cells to create organs, flesh, and bone. The crack and pull of sinew stringing him together had him quivering in terror. He felt the moment the fluid thickened to blood, and then its first rush through his new veins, charged by the slam of a heartbeat. With his first breath, he screamed his agony, arching his back on the concrete. Then he wept, gulping and hoarse.

"Call the police," somebody said.

Custo swiped at his running eyes and nose and scuttled back toward the building. The concrete scraped his butt, so he knew he was naked.

"Just stay calm," the man said, arms extended, palms down. He was youngish, in sweats and running shoes. "Help is on the way."

Help? He had to be out of his mind.

Another voice echoed off the building's walls. More people coming.

Custo's breath came in harsh pants, but he managed to stand. His knees buckled, but he caught himself on a rusty railing and held himself up. A wild shiver ran over him. Damn, it was cold. So damn cold.

"Stay back," the man said, retreating a few paces himself.

Custo looked around. Where the hell was he? Tall buildings rose around him, most of them gray, but one had a shiny mirrored surface.

He turned and lurched into a jog, his hand skimming the building for support. When he found his balance, he picked up speed, ducking into a service alley when he heard the *twerp* of a police car. He waited there, shaking with shock and a strange sense of vertigo.

Custo held up his hand, stretching the dark lines of his palm, then flipped it over. It appeared to be his own, minus the ragged scar across his knuckles. He closed his fingers into a fist and squeezed until his hand burned. Strong again. He wasn't a ghost, that was for sure. Angel? He had no idea. Maybe he should have asked more questions of Luca when he'd had the chance.

He tried his angel's trick and opened his mind. Humanity crashed into his consciousness, soul after soul, their inner voices crowding out all coherent thought. Too much, too much. He tried to disengage, but couldn't find himself in the chaotic press. A last gasp, and he sought *her*. He reached for her like a lifeline and felt a blissful tug. Sanity returned with the knowledge that the girl was safe, inside. And?—he touched her mind—she was getting ready to head home and she was arming herself for a fight.

His new heart clenched. What did she fear? Where?

The wolf. Had to be.

Custo recalled the wolf's attack. The collision. The fall. Sickening guilt rushed through Custo's veins. He was responsible for the beast's cross into mortality. She'd somehow opened the way, but he brought the wolf through.

Well, the wolf couldn't have her. Soon all of Segue would be searching for it, and the girl wouldn't be bothered again. He'd just have to move fast.

Custo waited behind a Dumpster until some poor slob walked by alone. He grabbed him and dragged him into the alley with an arm around his neck and a hand over his mouth. The man bucked against him, but he was too short and light to do any damage.

"I only want your pants," Custo growled in the man's ear.

Three minutes later Custo staggered out of the alley fully clothed. He made for the nearest corner. The street signs read W FIFTY-SIXTH and AVE OF THE AMERICAS. New York City. Midtown.

Then he knew where to go. The Segue Institute had safe houses globally. New York City had four that Custo could think of. Four and one more, the last a secure location that only he and Adam knew about. Once there, he'd have access to supplies, cash, food, and weapons. Most importantly, he could find and warn Adam.

But not without the girl.

THREE

ANNABELLA gripped her brand-new jumbo flashlight while she exited the heavy bronze door of City Center onto West Fifty-sixth. The flashlight was heavy, designed for camping, but there was no way she was going to be caught in the dark without her own source of light. Not with that freaky wolf on the loose—on the streets or in her head. She kept her finger on the power button, like a trigger. And when she got that silly-girl shaky feeling, she imagined turning on the light and smoking the monster.

Take that, you growling son of a bitch!

Her heartbeat accelerated as she stepped into a night of crackling energy. The one-way street was hissing with traffic, punctuated by the occasional blare of a horn. She headed directly to the curb to hail a cab. Her plan: carry her own light source everywhere, make it home safely, preferably with yummy takeout (she was starving), turn on every light in her studio apartment, all three of them, and sleep in the very brightest patch. She wasn't about to let any real or imagined wolf take this chance away from her. Tomorrow she would debut as Giselle.

And then everything would go back to normal.

A cab drew alongside her. So far so good. She threw her bag along the backseat before sliding in herself, flashlight in her lap, choking for a second on a breath of strong Far Eastern incense.

Just as the driver pulled away from the curb, the opposite passenger door opened with a blast of thick exhaust. The cab jerked to a halt and Annabella startled, flicking a fat beam in the intruder's direction.

"Cab's taken," she said when she recognized that it was a man—or at least, the lower half of one.

The man pushed her bag to the floor, got in anyway, and slammed the door. "West Thirty-sixth and Fifth," he said. His low voice was rough with authority.

Jerk. "Hey, I was here first—"

The man turned his head and she swallowed her words.

Him.

In the partial illumination of the cab, his hair and skin washed to monochromatic shades of gold. His eyes were fair, direct, and tense, and he was slightly out of breath. A current of dark trouble ran along his barely controlled surface as he looked at her. Or rather, looked her over. His gaze settled on her flashlight and his brow furrowed in thought before one side of his mouth tugged up.

Heat flooded her body and burned her face.

"Lady?" the cabdriver asked over his shoulder.

No way. She got here first. And besides, she had to go straight home, have a nice dinner, relax, and get some rest for the gala tomorrow. Not to mention something was very wrong about this guy. His face might have been gorgeous, but his clothes were too small, clearly not his own. He'd rolled up the sleeves, but his shirt still didn't fit across his broad shoulders. His pants were a joke, short by inches and straining across his thighs. One grand plié and the seams would rip.

Only one thing could make her change her mind, and she didn't care if she sounded stupid. "You see a wolf lately?"

The man gave a short nod. "In the middle of your dance, onstage."

Crap. She'd kinda been hoping she was crazy. She gnawed on her bottom lip. The least she could do for the man who put his body between her and a charging wolf was share a cab. Maybe he could even tell her what was going on.

She eased her grip on the flashlight and met the driver's gaze. "It's okay."

The driver turned his attention to the road with a shrug and the cab pulled away from the curb.

The stranger didn't relax, didn't settle into his seat. His interest was focused on her—the weight of it had her clutching her flashlight again. The light might not hurt him, but she could brain him with the casing if she had to.

"What's your name?" he asked, his words short and clipped.

"Annabella," she answered, wary. "Yours?"

"Custo." He darted a glance out the rear window, then came back to her. "You're a dancer? A ballerina?"

"Yes." She couldn't help adding, "A principal with the Classical Ballet Theater. And you are . . . ?"

". . . taking you somewhere safe. Somewhere we can talk." He winged his arm along the backrest.

Not likely. He could share her cab, but nothing else. No need to tell him that, though. He was keyed up enough already.

"What day is it?" he asked.

"Friday."

"The date," he clarified, his forehead tensing.

"October twenty-second." October twenty-third was the gala performance, the start to the season. Her big day.

He frowned as if that still wasn't the answer he wanted, but didn't press. "Do you have a mobile phone?"

"Um . . . no, I don't." A white lie—she just hated loaning it out. Besides, that was her lifeline number two. Not that she'd call her mom again and take another ten years off the poor woman's life. No, if she had to call anyone, she'd call the cops herself. Maybe for this guy.

Custo grabbed her bag off the floor, unzipping it before she had a chance to object. She snatched at the strap—where did he get off searching her stuff? He pushed through some of her sweaty dance clothes, warm-ups, shoes. Oh, shit, her backup tampons. She yanked the bag away from him.

And anyway, the phone was in her sweatshirt pocket. "What the hell are you doing? It's not in there."

"Give me your phone." He held out his hand. "It's an emergency."

She needed her phone. She wasn't about to give it to this aggressive lunatic. Sharing the cab was clearly a mistake, but she could correct it. She looked out her window to figure out what part of town she was in. Just past the New York Public Library. She had her flashlight; she could grab another cab.

"It's an emergency, damn it," Custo insisted.

When she still hesitated, he reached for her.

"Okay, okay." She recoiled and groped in her pocket. She threw it at him. "Just stay back."

He fumbled the catch, and she addressed the driver. "I'll get out here."

The cab began to slow.

Punching in a number, Custo said, "Not a good idea. The wolf is undoubtedly tracking your movements."

The wolf. The memory of its dark hulk, eyes glaring, had her heartbeat tripping. Tracking her?

"Never mind," Annabella said to the driver.

Custo groaned frustration. Ha! He must have gotten voice mail.

"Adam, surprise—it's Custo. I'm back. Remember that time at the Shelby School when we cut the power to the compound long enough to stop the clocks? Don't trust anyone at Segue until you speak with me." Custo paused. "I'm headed now for our New York storage cache. You can reach me at this number, or there shortly."

His message made her head hurt. What kind of cryptic crapola was that? "Excuse me . . . ? I'd like my phone back."

Custo handed it back to her, slightly smiling, as if her irritation amused him. "If it rings, answer immediately."

She wasn't about to let him boss her. She let her finger

linger on the power button. Off. No more calls for the crazy cab moocher.

They turned off the main road and shot down a smaller side street lined with cars already parked for the night. Must be getting close.

She had her own questions, and she only had a few more minutes to get the answers. "That wolf . . . it's been stalking me for days. I haven't slept. I'm so hopped up on caffeine I don't think I'll ever sleep again. And I have to be my best for tomorrow night. My *best*. Can you please tell me what is going on?"

"I have to hear your end of it first to know for sure." A tremor ran through him, and a muscle in his jaw twitched as he mastered himself.

Maybe he was on drugs. "I just told you my end of it."

"When it began. How the wolf found you."

Annabella threw up her hands in frustration. "I don't know when—" No, wait. She did. "Rehearsal. Last night, when we put the second act together. We'd been rehearsing separately, working on one bit one night, another bit another. This was the first time that we had the full company there."

"How did it happen?" Passing headlights coasted over his features and accented the golden flecks in his amber-green irises. So pretty, too bad he was . . . unbalanced and rude.

"I was dancing one of my solos—I thought I had it right. Felt good anyway. I looked up and saw the wolf. Heard him growling at me. I don't know how he got there or why. I thought I was just super tired and stressed. Is he for real?"

"Very much so," Custo answered. "You see him only when you are dancing?"

"No. He followed me last night to my bus stop."

He frowned. "You were alone?"

"Yes."

"How did you escape him?" His questions kept coming, rapid fire. When was he going to start answering some?

"He's afraid of light," she explained, lifting her improvised weapon. "He stays in the shadow."

Custo frowned and cursed, "Damn it."

"Are you going to tell me what is going on or not?"

He held his breath, then expelled all his indecision. "The wolf is a creature of Shadow, of that I am certain."

"A creature of wha—?"

Custo looked down at his hands, fisting and flexing them strangely, as if he'd never seen them before. "He is a creature of Shadow, bound to Shadow, but he crossed into this world with me tonight, you understand?"

Okay, the man was deranged, and she was going crazy right along with him. Crossed from where?

The driver looked in the rearview mirror. "You got an address, mister?"

Custo glanced out the window. "Here is fine."

The car pulled over to the curb, and Custo opened his door. Panic rolled over Annabella. What now? She couldn't go off with a stranger. He could be psycho or a murderer, or, or . . .

Custo climbed out, turned, and grabbed her bag. He dropped it on the sidewalk and reached in to her, his fingers sharply beckoning. "Come on."

This was so not what her mother intended when she offered to pay for the cab. Annabella shrank back, though her body perversely thrilled all over at the prospect. The man was certifiable, but damn hot anyway. "I don't even know you."

He bent to make eye contact. "You know you're safe with me."

From wolves, maybe.

"Annabella?"

Oh, this is stupid. But she slid across the seat dragging the heavy flashlight, took his hand—warm, strong—and climbed out of the cab. He reached into his pocket and produced a wad of bills, handing the driver a twenty.

As the cab pulled away, Annabella had the strangest sensation that everything normal in her life was going with it. What the hell was she doing?

"Let's get off the street." Custo put an arm around her waist and pulled her close to his body. Her heart thumped, but she didn't fight him. She fit snugly, tucked alongside him, and his tight hold somehow made her both more and less nervous. He smelled dark and sharp. Sweaty, but still very good.

His body against hers was rigid with tension. He hurried them down the block and across the street to a doorway tucked into an alcove. A keypad was affixed at eye level. He punched in a code, and the lock released on the door, almost inaudibly.

She felt the tug on her waist as he tried to draw her inside.

"Um . . ." she said, her stomach suddenly knotting with nerves, "I do have to get back to my apartment soon. The gala is tomorrow, and if I don't get some sleep—"

"You'll be staying here now," he said.

She pulled back against his forward momentum. Staying here? Tonight?

Custo took her shoulders, dipped his head to catch her gaze with his marshy eyes. The back light from the interior lit his dark blond hair into a soft gold halo. "Annabella, there is a Shadow wolf stalking you. It sounds absurd, I know, but the creatures of Faeric know no reason. You can rest here. Sleep. You'll dance better for it tomorrow night. I'll see that nothing touches you."

She narrowed her eyes at him.

"I won't touch you either." He lifted a brow, making fun of the direction of her thoughts, but the deliberate guttural rumble of his assurance had her mentally pinning on the word *yet* after his statement.

Her gaze drifted to his mouth. His lips curved up slightly

in response. She lifted her gaze just in time to catch the wicked gleam, lit by humor, in his eyes. She tried to look away but couldn't. The air around them hummed with energy generated by his intensity, her nerves, and the electricity of their closeness.

What to do . . . What to do . . . Annabella's body hummed with painful indecision. Go off with the psycho, hot man in the short pants or brave the wolfy night alone? Groaning, she gave a reluctant nod—last night's vigil had been fueled by strong coffee. It might be early for anyone else to think of bed, but there was no way on earth she could keep her eyes open for long. This man seemed to know what he was talking about, in spite of his ridiculous clothes.

Custo must have seen her acceptance, because he pulled her inside and led her down a long, low hallway. The white paint on the walls had cracked with age and time as the building settled. The place had a dusty smell, as if it hadn't been aired in forever. The only window in the interior was narrow and high with a dirty view of concrete. The main room was filled with stacked army green plastic cartons, blocky lettering identifying them as the property of something called The Segue Institute. A storage room.

Okay . . . so maybe she could be safe here, but she'd be excruciatingly uncomfortable. Her dance bag made for a rotten pillow—she'd tried that in rehearsal enough times. Maybe they should go back to her place. Or get a hotel room. Correction, adjoining hotel rooms.

Custo hefted a carton out of the way. Judging by the strain of his bunched muscle against the too-small fabric of his shirt, it must have been heavy. With his efforts, however, the top of a doorway was revealed, so there was a little hope.

She watched as he moved the rest of the cartons out of the way. The man had a tight, sculpted ass under those ridiculous navy khakis. When he was done, his shirt was damp with sweat. Another numbered panel was attached to the wall. Custo punched in a code, and the lock on the door released. The successive containment of the place reminded her of a prison. She had to be out of her mind.

Custo opened the door and used one of the cartons as a doorstop. A phone warbled within the room. Probably that Adam he'd called earlier.

Oh, shit . . . her phone was still off.

Custo darted inside and left her to follow. She fumbled to get out her mobile phone and hit the power button. As it turned on and searched for a signal, she peeked in the room. The air was similarly stale, but the space was open, meticulously clean, and—thank goodness—furnished. Every corner of the place was brightly lit. A wraparound desk edged one wall, topped with a computer, the monitor blank. Another door led to a tidy modern bathroom. And beyond a gray partition, she spotted the foot of a low queen-size bed. One bed, huh?

He'd be on the floor.

"I swear it's me," Custo was saying into the phone. "Who else would know about the Shelby clocks?"

A pause.

"But I didn't turn wraith. You know I would never—"

Another pause.

"Stranger things have happened, Adam. Hear me out."

Custo dragged out a chair from the desk and sat. "We'll be here. We'll wait for you. And, uh, we've got a situation."

He frowned again, and then lifted his gaze to Annabella. "Me and a friend. I'll tell you when you get here."

Annabella raised her eyebrows after he hung up. "Well?"

"Adam is on his way."

Another crazy person. She leaned against the open doorway, sighing. "He thinks you're a wraith?"

Fan-freakin'-tastic. The past couple of years wraiths had been all over the Internet and occasionally on the news, though she had never seen one (or wanted to) herself. She didn't know much about them except they were murderous, insane, and really strong. One Internet clip showed some wicked-looking teeth as well. But what they really were and where they came from, she had no idea.

Annabella sized up Custo. He was definitely crazy enough and strong enough. She didn't want to think about the murderous part. At least his teeth seemed normal.

"He's entertaining the possibility." Custo stood and moved toward a cabinet. He rummaged inside a drawer and drew out some kind of anorak, which he dropped on the floor. He dug deeper and retrieved a pile of black clothing. "I want to grab a quick shower. Do you mind? I'll answer all your questions when I get out."

Her list was growing longer.

Annabella glanced around. The place was bright and the flashlight was heavy in her hand. No shadows here. Plus the message light was blinking on her phone. Probably her mom. "Yeah, okay."

Custo disappeared into the bathroom, but he left the door cracked.

Annabella retrieved her messages. She had one strange hang-up—Adam, most likely—and, sure enough, a call from her mom. Annabella called her, soothed her worries—no mad dogs tonight, lied about an impromptu date with a cute guy, and finished with a "can't talk now," heavy with meaning. Her mom was so happy she was on a date that she agreed to hang up on the provision she'd get details later. That conversation would be interesting.

Annabella ended the call, done and done, then reconsidered and dialed her own number. The call went straight to voice mail. "I am out with a slightly imbalanced man named Custo, who . . . uh . . . might be a wraith. He is tall, about six three, well built, with green eyes and dark blond hair. He has taken me back to a place owned by The Segue Institute, whatever that is. He had the codes to get in anyway. It's on the ground floor of a brick building near West Thirty-sixth and Fifth. Oh, and he placed a call to a man named Adam from my mobile phone. If I should disappear or wind up dead, start there."

"Smart girl," Custo said from the bathroom doorway. "Next time, get a building number, even if it's next door or across the street. Or any identifying marker of some kind."

"Well, you can't blame me for playing it safe." She pocketed her phone and stepped back, hitting the desk with her thighs. *Uh . . . Wow.* Custo in ugly, too-small clothes was good-looking. Custo in a form-fitting, long-sleeve black tee, each ripple of his body hugged by the soft cloth, was devastating. And she knew good bodies. He wore black fatigues, but she couldn't help imagining him in ballet tights. She almost laughed: This man? In tights? Wouldn't happen in a million years.

"I wasn't blaming you, I was commending you. I like that you can think on your feet. I like that you had the foresight to get that flashlight. Must be awkward to lug around. I assume you have extra batteries?"

She tilted up her chin. "In my bag."

He grinned at her, and she stopped thinking altogether. The smile finally reached his eyes, brightening them with humor. A superscary wolf was stalking her, and this man was *happy?*

"Everything is going to be fine now. I'd tell you to go ahead and bed down, but Adam will be here shortly. Good thing he was in New York. He could have easily been back in West Virginia . . ." Custo's smile faltered. ". . . unless they abandoned that facility after the attack."

"What facility? Who is Adam?"

"Adam Thorne. He runs The Segue Institute. It's a research facility whose chief focus is the growing wraith population, though it occasionally extends to include other paranormal phenomena as well."

"Wraiths again." And paranormal phenomena. The guy was loco, but then again she was seeing imaginary wolves, so she couldn't exactly point any fingers.

"Predators that look like you and me," Custo explained. "But inhumanly strong and immortal. They feed on the souls of their human prey. I've been working with Adam to control their spread for . . . over six years."

Sounded to her from Custo's call that his employment was in question. She bit her tongue on that one. She didn't seem to have very many options. "This Adam will look into my wolf?"

"Yes. Absolutely."

"Tonight?"

"We'll do what we can tonight. Segue has a significant intelligence operation, we should be able—"

Custo tilted his head, as if listening. Then he moved in a blur, grabbed her arm—the flashlight had her wrist twisting painfully—and pulled her behind him. "It's going to be fine," he said too calmly.

"Where is it?" Annabella's heart jumped. She grabbed his waist to steady herself and peeked around his trunk, flashlight on, searching for the hulk of the wolf.

She couldn't see anything but crates.

"Hold your fire. I am unarmed," Custo yelled, "and I have an innocent woman here."

So not the wolf. She kept the flashlight pointed at the door anyway.

Custo glanced down at her. "Don't resist. I expected this. Adam is only being careful."

"On the floor," a gravelly male voice called back.

Custo nodded, as if he thought that was the right course of action. "Down," he said. "They won't hurt you."

"But I thought—" She didn't know what she had thought. Maybe that they'd be spending the night here. Maybe that he'd have some quick fix to her problem, like Jasper's hot screw. Maybe that she'd be safe enough to rest so she could be ready for her performance. If she didn't put her head down soon, she was going to fall down anyway.

"On the floor now!"

Custo pushed her to her knees as he lowered himself. "No sudden movements. Just lie on the floor. Everything is going to be all right."

No sooner had her cheek touched cold linoleum than several pairs of black combat boots ran into view. One pressed on Custo's neck, the tip of a gun at his head. Other boots had him at his arms, the small of his back, his legs.

"No, no, no," Annabella yelled as her body trembled with fear and anger. This was a mistake. A mistake to share a cab. A mistake to trust a strange man. A mistake that might cost her *Giselle*. "He called *you*! He called *you*!"

Custo had the perverse nerve to attempt a smile at that, boot rubber in his face, but he remained silent, the rest of him still.

Rough hands hauled Annabella up from under her armpits. Her flashlight clattered to the floor. From the corner of her eye, she spied a soldier dumping the contents of her bag into a messy pile and dissecting her stuff. She was driven up against a wall, held with her arms twisted behind her. Whatever idiot was doing this to her probably thought the arm hold hurt, but he'd be wrong. She'd been dancing since she was four; flexibility was no problem for her. She could have gotten out of it if she wanted, but she took her cues from Custo.

Let it happen.

A hand roved her body, dipping between her boobs, as if they were big enough to hide anything. Then the jerk swept the juncture at her thighs. Totally humiliating. He located her mobile phone—didn't take a genius to put a hand in her pocket. Then suddenly she was yanked back and propelled out the doorway. "If he twitches," her captor called, "shoot him."

"He was helping me," Annabella said, finally getting a glimpse of the infamous Adam. Dark hair, chiseled face, clenched jaw. Might be good-looking if he weren't such an asshole.

"I doubt that very much." Adam directed her to a black SUV idling in front of the building.

The street was otherwise dark, shadows shifting with her quick glance. If she couldn't have Custo, she at least wanted her flashlight, though she doubted Adam would run back in and get it for her. Someone inside the SUV opened the side door.

"No, you don't understand," she said, "he's a little crazy, but I swear he hasn't done anything wrong." She tried to twist out of Adam's cruel grasp while he propelled her into the vehicle.

"No, *you* don't understand, Ms. Ames."

How did he know her name?

"That couldn't be Custo Santovari." Adam's eyes were flinty, his mouth cruelly twisted with strong emotion. "The Custo I know died over two years ago."

FOUR

BLOOD ran off Custo's arm into crimson splatters on the cold concrete floor of his holding cell. His forearm was a scream of pain from a deep diagonal slice through skin and muscle—a parting gift from one of Adam's men, and a test: wraiths heal rapidly, humans do not.

Not that Custo had expected a welcome parade; Adam had to take all due precautions. Custo leaned against the cell wall—his butt was already going numb from his seat on the hard floor—and rested his lower arm on his knees in plain sight. His sleeve was bunched over his elbow. Easiest way to safely ID a wraith was to watch him regenerate, a bracing combination of nightmare and miracle.

Custo was more than a little curious himself. Did an AWOL angel heal rapidly, too?

A long two-inch sliver of thick Plexiglas broke up the monotonous gray of his prison. No way to get food in without unsealing the two-foot-thick steel-reinforced door. No place to piss. Aside from the metallic scent of blood, the air had a wet earth smell, as if he were underground, but laced by the peculiar funk of the walking dead. A wraith's cell.

Custo knew the three Segue facilities in the northeastern U.S. by heart—he'd been involved in the construction of them all—but this place wasn't familiar. Had to be new, and if it was new, then the wraith war continued and at least several months had passed since his death. Actually, since he'd picked up from Annabella's thoughts a general awareness of wraiths, the threat had to be public as well. He did a little mental math. Probably over a year had passed. It made sense that Adam was so suspicious.

"I'm not a wraith, Adam," Custo called. His voice bounced back at him.

As expected, no answer.

Custo stretched his consciousness to locate Adam. He was there, on the other side of the cell. Custo touched his mind: his friend was determined to wait out the test. Custo pushed harder, trying to unlock Adam's deeper thinking, but as always, only immediate intent was discernible, and even that was unreliable. People changed their minds all the time.

He extended himself further and found Annabella, not far away. Her thoughts were a muddle. Probably scared, worried, angry. But safe. There was no better place for her than Segue, both for her protection and for the resolution of her problem. The sooner he settled the wraith question with Adam, the sooner he could put her at ease. He didn't want her frightened any longer than necessary. She was feisty, which he liked, but too delicate to fight a creature of Shadow. He'd take care of everything.

An image flashed in his mind: Annabella wrapped around him while he was buried deep within her, the heat of their friction, hearts pounding against each other, his mouth on the apple of her shoulder, the sweet taste of her skin . . .

A sharp sizzle, white-hot, brought Custo's attention back to his arm. Pain cleared his fantasy from his mind. He blinked hard and examined his wound.

The deepest layers of rent tissue were obscured by congealing blood, the gape in his skin cracking slightly like a wide, lipless mouth. The shallow edges of the cut, however, had gone from scarlet to pink as the skin came back together, sealing with the pucker of a scar. It was a miracle of millimeters, but Custo had no doubt he was healing—fast.

Shit. His heart tightened like a fist.

Adam would have only one conclusion—wraith. And on the subject of wraiths, Adam had always been blindly resolute. Kill them, kill them all. Custo couldn't blame him. Adam's own brother, Jacob, had made the choice to become a wraith, trading humanity for immortality, then murdered Adam's mother and father, fed on them to make himself stronger, and mocked Adam for being too human, too weak to stop him. Jacob should have known better, should have known Adam wouldn't break and would never forgive the destruction of his family. The Segue Institute was born with a single clearly defined purpose—find a way to end Jacob.

The heat in Custo's arm was now bone-deep, aching with the weave and knit of his flesh. The healing wasn't nearly as fast as a wraith's, who could recover in minutes from what should've been mortal wounds, but it far exceeded a normal man's. Therefore, damn it, wraith.

Custo lifted his uninjured arm, licked his thumb, and cleaned away the dried blood at one edge of the wound. It was obvious now that he was healing supernaturally. No point hiding the truth.

He turned the closing wound toward the slit in the wall, so there would be no mistake. "I'm not a wraith, Adam. I'm—" He broke off. Still couldn't say the ridiculous word out loud. He groaned inwardly and took a deep breath. Tried again. "I'm an *angel*."

Silence. Not even a flicker of a question from Adam's mind.

Custo sighed. "I know. I know. Sounds absurd. I don't expect you to believe me when I don't believe it myself, but there it is. The only way you're going to know either way is to trust me. I'm asking you to trust me."

Silence.

Jacob had loved to play games with Adam's memories, to trick him into painful recollections of times when life was full and whole. Custo refused to do the same—to pull out their shared past to manipulate his friend. Not that Adam would be moved. He had learned to turn a deaf ear to the insidious ramblings of a wraith in a cell, the clever pleas for release, though the wraith had the voice of his brother or long-lost friend.

Dropping his arm back on his knees, Custo sighed. He could feel Adam's presence on the other side of the concrete, a bright condensation of identity. Adam couldn't afford mistakes. If the world were anything like it had been before, there was no way Adam could take a chance on him.

Adam's mind came to a decision.

Custo brought himself to standing as the lock released on the cell door.

"I want a lawyer. You've got no right to hold me against my will!" Annabella yelled at the slit in the wall of her weird holding cell. It was worse than the prison cells she'd seen on TV—cold, nondescript gray, like an awful basement, with only a shitty folding table and a shitty pair of folding chairs. At least the room was somewhat lit. If she stayed near the door, she should be fine. The dim corner on the other side was out of the question. It seemed like the kind of place the wolf would hide. She wanted her flashlight to burn him out.

She slapped the palm of her hand on the table to make some noise. In the concrete room, the slap was like the report of a gun.

"Hello, damn it! I'm frickin' exhausted in here!" Her voice was rough and shrill. She was terrified out of her mind, cringing at the least little thing. If she were getting sick from all this Custo crap, she was going to kill him. Kill that Adam bastard, too. She should have never agreed to share that cab. "I want a lawyer!"

Annabella dragged a chair around to the bright side of the table. The damn thing started to collapse into itself and she had to fight with the seat to get it properly unfolded again. She banged it on the floor when she got the seat open, and lowered herself carefully onto it.

"I. Must. Chill," she said aloud. Obviously no one was listening to her. "I must chill. I must stay calm. I perform in"—she calculated the number of hours before she'd be onstage—"twenty hours-ish. I must keep it together. Deep breaths." She inhaled until her lungs were bursting, then let out the air slowly. And again. Much better.

She glanced over her shoulder at the slit in the concrete. Screw it. "Get me out of here!" Her screech broke on *here*, the type of sound that shattered glass, but it didn't do much to the concrete. She'd have to try harder.

This was *so* not happening. She looked around herself again.

"Maybe I've gone completely insane." Sure seemed more plausible than any other explanation. "That's it. I'm insane. This is not a prison cell; this is a padded room in some very low-budget hospital. I am not being hunted by a wolf—that's only a manifestation of all my fears and stress. And that man Custo is . . ." . . . *my hottest fantasy come to life. See? Crazy.*

Concrete scraped loudly against concrete. Annabella stood, knocking her chair onto the floor. The huge, thick door retracted. She felt her anger rising again. Whoever was responsible for her unlawful imprisonment was going to get an earful from her. And charges filed with the police. And a civil lawsuit for attempting to ruin her performance.

"I want some ans—" Annabella began. She broke off when the door finally retracted enough to reveal her jailer.

A short, very pregnant woman. If Annabella was exhausted, the woman looked ready to pass out. She was deathly pale, dark circles under her eyes, both aspects accentuated by white-blonde hair pulled back in a day-old ponytail.

Annabella fought to hold on to the outrage and obscenities she planned to hurl at whoever came through that door for kidnapping her and locking her in a creepy basement.

Not to mention she was starving to death. She'd just danced for four hours.

The woman gave her a little smile.

"Oh, damn it," Annabella said, surly. "Let me get the chair for you." She turned to offer it, but, of course, the damn thing had fallen in on itself again.

The woman chuckled and waddled forward. "I appreciate it."

"Well, you look ready to pop," Annabella grumbled, getting the metal chair unfolded again. "Here."

"Not for another two months. Twins." The woman used the table to lower herself down. The metal door slid closed and locked with another loud scrape.

"Uh . . ." Annabella looked at the door, her body flushing with anger again.

The woman squeezed her hand. "Don't worry. I'm Adam's wife, Talia. We won't be in here long. He's spying on Custo now, but he checks on me all the time." She sighed heavily. "All the time," she emphasized with a roll of her eyes.

Annabella wrestled with the second chair. "Where is here? And why the hell am I being held hostage?"

"You're not a hostage. And you are just north of New York City, at one of Segue's holding facilities."

"This is criminal."

Talia shrugged. "The president himself has granted us the authority to apprehend and hold wraiths."

"I'm not a wraith," Annabella shot back. *The president? . . . of the United States?*

"But you believe it anyway." Talia flashed that tired smile again, pulling her hand back with a satisfied sigh. "Want to tell me why?"

Why? Like she'd have any clue why the world suddenly became crazy-scary. First the wolf, then the surreal encounter with Custo, and then the soldiers dragging them both away from that hideout in the city.

Talia lifted her eyebrows in friendly interest. "How about starting with how you met Custo?"

"How about letting me out of here?"

"Custo first," Talia said. "Besides, I promised Adam that I wouldn't release you from the cell."

In spite of her anger, Annabella felt herself crack a smile. "But left out the fact you planned to join me?"

Talia shrugged again. "He's a little distracted with Custo's return, and I took advantage."

"Will you catch hell?" The woman seemed so whipped already. It would be just like that SOB Adam to stress her out some more.

"Adam will want to yell at me so bad the little vein on the side of his head will bulge, but he won't. Poor man has it tough these days."

"Poor man? He frisked me! As in . . . *everywhere!*" Annabella lifted her brows to make sure that Talia got her meaning.

"Lucky. I wish he'd frisk me." That tired smile again.

Annabella gave Talia a once-over. "Looks like he frisked you just fine seven months ago."

Talia's smile lifted further and lit her eyes. "He did at that. Our belated honeymoon to Paris was very good to us. Tell me about Custo before Adam gets back or someone tattles on me."

Custo? What about a little freedom first? A little due process?

Annabella met Talia's steady, weary gaze, and felt the last of her anger crumbling. "Oh, fine."

She thought back to the moment she first saw him. It was only a flash really: The dress rehearsal had been typically good and bad. She'd barely started the final solo when the wolf appeared. She'd ignored the animal, figuring that if he were real, it was already too late to run, and if he weren't, she didn't have anything to worry about. She'd spotted Custo on the other side of her, hidden behind a bit of scenery.

"He came out of nowhere," Annabella said. "One minute I was dancing alone onstage, the next Custo was with me, tackling my hallucination of a wolf."

"I beg your pardon?" Talia's brow furrowed. "A wolf?"

"Yeah. You're not going to believe me, but I swear it's the truth." Custo believed her; maybe this woman would, too. "There is a huge wolf . . . in the city . . . that is made out of shadows, and he has been stalking me for two days."

Annabella sat back in her chair and waited for Talia's response. If the woman's face showed one iota of disbelief, contempt, or amusement, then pregnant or not, she was going to get a piece of Annabella's mind.

Talia's face tightened, her mouth thinning. "Is the wolf made out of shadow, or does it exist in the shadows?"

Her serious expression had a chill sweeping over Annabella, prickling at her scalp as all the blood dropped out of her face. "He's real?"

"It's definitely possible."

Two people believed her. Which meant the wolf was real and was stalking her. Annabella put her head on the table as the room spun.

"You're safe here," Talia said. Annabella felt a comforting hand on her shoulder. "Why don't you start from the beginning?"

The hunter crouched in a corner of darkness, panting with fear. Foul scents of industry, sharp and acrid, filled the air. Foreign sounds jarred him, echoing in a world of harsh, cold gray. His claws scrabbled and scratched on a firmament of flat, unnatural stone. No trees, no magic. Just large, wide caverns upon caverns going deep into the earth.

Not his territory. Not his realm. He was the trespasser here.

The hunter braced in meager earth-shadow. A high whine scraped up his throat. Back. He had to get back.

Mortals clumped with heavy, telling footfalls. Controlled violence hummed in the air around them. Fighters, all. The bright man, the one who'd faced him in Twilight, was worse, but they'd caged him.

The woman was here somewhere, too, her scent faint, yet threaded through the passageways she'd traversed.

She could get him back to Twilight. She could open the way to the never-ending forest. His running grounds.

A fighter stomped near, coming closer. A man, steamy and ripe with life.

The hunter bared his teeth, ears pinned, ready to strike.

The man walked the passage as if he belonged, his presence permitted everywhere in these caverns. Closer and closer. Fat with mortal juices.

This fighter could approach the woman. Perhaps he could compel her magic to open the way back.

The hunter sprang to take him.

The door retracted, and Custo stepped into the center of the cell—not too close to the opening as if to attack or escape, but not remaining on the far side, as if to draw Adam away from the door and the safety beyond.

Adam strode in anyway, the door grinding closed behind him. Custo could tell from the loose, but ready set of his shoulders that he was prepared to tangle, if necessary. Though they'd often handled wraiths together, Adam had taken on a couple of wraiths solo before.

"I'm not a wraith." Custo sat on the floor to prove it. If he were a wraith, he'd be moving in for an Adam treat.

"An angel?" Adam's tone was flat, concealing his true attitude.

Custo scratched his chin like a movie mob boss—an old private joke—and shrugged.

"From God?"

Custo winced slightly and dropped the act.

"Then from whom?" A touch of sarcasm there.

Custo cleared his voice. "I'm . . . uh . . . absent without leave."

Adam frowned slightly, then sat on the floor and crossed his legs, mirroring Custo's position, his gaze coolly assessing. "Let's have it then. The story."

There was too much and too little to tell, but at least he had an obvious place to begin. "Well, Spencer killed me." Custo left off the torture part.

"I remember," Adam said. His jaw tensed. Angry. But his mind betrayed nothing.

"What happened to him by the way?" Custo mimicked Adam's surface composure, but he was angry, too. He had a score to settle.

"You mean you weren't looking down from your cloud in the sky?" Full, bitter sarcasm now. Very angry.

"Doesn't work that way." Custo kept his tone deliberately light. "Did you kill him?" As far as Custo knew, Adam had never killed anybody. Custo didn't think he could take it.

"Wraith beat me to it."

Ah. "Fitting. He was colluding with them." Spencer had been the SPCI liaison to The Segue Institute. SPCI, the Strategic Preternatural Coalition Initiative, was a covert government agency attempting to police the wraiths while Segue studied them, trying to discover the catalyst that changed them from human to monster. SPCI mostly mucked things up.

Custo drew a deep breath. "By the way, Spencer told me that you had another traitor at Segue. Another wraith collaborator. Someone you trust."

Just like that, his message was delivered. A grasping knot of acute worry released. Adam had been warned.

How could you know that? Adam's mind asked, but he said, "When did he tell you that?"

So Adam already knew. That was good news.

"Before . . . you know . . . he offed me." It was utterly galling that that Spencer piece of shit had killed him. No pride in that. "Have you had any suspicions about another traitor?" Custo asked, though he knew the answer from Adam's mind.

Adam shrugged. "We've had some intel leaks over the past six months or so and lives lost because of it. Talia killed the demon who created the wraiths soon after you died. The remaining wraiths number in the thousands and are nested all over the world. For a while we were able to aggressively track and . . . *dispatch* them, but they've become better at hiding and coordinating their attacks. Their target is Segue—me and Talia, specifically."

"Is that why you're in these charming new digs?" Custo cast an eye around the unrelenting gray of his cell. "Not your style, Adam."

"This place isn't mine. It's the U.S. Army's, who has, by the way, become very cooperative with our efforts."

Custo held up a hand to stop him. "Oh, please not SPCI. If there is one rotten egg, there are sure to be others."

"SPCI was disbanded. The wraiths' existence is public knowledge now, and we have full military support."

Custo glanced down at his now-healed arm, trying to process this new information. Spencer was dead, a personal disappointment. The government had granted full cooperation, which was excellent progress. And the war with the wraiths was status quo. He flexed the muscle of his forearm and the crusted blood cracked.

Adam spoke his thoughts, exactly as they came. "So I have an unknown quantity in you . . ."

Custo smiled. That was putting it mildly. He brought his gaze back up.

"And a traitor within Segue."

Custo nodded, his grin widening. "No thanks necessary. I only escaped from Heaven, eluded a piranha mermaid with huge tits, and fell to Earth to save your sorry, purebred bottom."

Adam gave half a chuckle, then sobered. "You're not a wraith?"

"An-gel."

Adam lifted an eyebrow. "Mermaid?"

"With huge tits. Bluish ones." Custo cupped his hands a foot away from his chest to demonstrate.

Adam laughed outright. "And what was Heaven like?"

"Boring. Clean. Nice." Custo shrugged. "You'd like it, but it's not so much for me."

Adam inclined his head. "Not for me either if Talia can't go." *Banshee.*

"Oh? You've been busy." Seemed Adam had fallen hard for his half-fae, half-human researcher. And yes, the laws of Heaven did bar the fae from entering. Could a banshee, able to rend the boundary between mortality and the Otherworld with her scream, enter the gates of Heaven? Custo guessed it depended on which side of her heritage won out. Definitely problematic.

"I'm going to be a father—twins." There was a deep pool of happiness in the simple statement, and then he sobered, eyes direct. "It's because of her pregnancy that the wraiths are redoubling their attacks. Hunting us. I can't afford to take any risks."

"I want to help. I know what family means to you." *I was there when your first one was ripped apart.*

Silence stretched.

Finally, Adam cleared his voice, cleared the past, too. Custo felt the shift in his mind, could almost sense him packing away the memories, and let the matter drop. Some things were simply unbearable to revisit.

"I've got an extremely irate young woman in another cell.

One Annabella Ames. She threatened to dismember me if I didn't reunite the two of you. Colorful vocabulary."

Atta girl. "We have to make certain she's protected at all times."

"That's why we put you in here."

Very funny. This was serious. "You know that trick with the dark that Talia can pull? The one she used to hide from the wraiths?"

Adam tilted his head.

"Well, I know what she was doing. She was thinning the boundary between mortality and the Shadowlands, pulling on the darkness there. And believe me, there's a lot of darkness to draw from." Custo paused again, giving Adam a chance to affirm or refute his statements.

Adam didn't comment, vocally or mentally.

"Annabella can't thin the boundary, but she can almost cross when she is dancing. She's got some kind of magic to her—it's . . . it's . . . captivating." The image of her glowing form moving among the darkened trees came to Custo's mind. Exquisite. "Anyway, a creature from the Shadowlands, a wolf, tried to attack her. I got in the way, and somehow we both followed her back into the world."

Adam's brow furrowed. "So you want me to protect her from a wolf?"

"Us. I want *us* to protect her. And it's a Shadow wolf."

"How's that different?" Adam pushed to standing. *Time to go. Hope Talia didn't cave to her soft heart.*

Custo followed suit. "It's made of Shadow. It exists, thrives, in Shadow. We need to keep her guarded at all times."

Adam signaled toward the slit and the lock on the door released with a deep click and scrape. Custo stepped forward, but Adam stopped him with a hand to his chest. "I'm not entirely convinced." Adam's tone and expression were stone serious.

What was it going to take? Although it seemed odd for a

68   ERIN KELLISON

dead man, Custo was hungry. He wanted something to eat and a beer to wash it down. He wanted a chance to be alone with Annabella. See if her skin was as silky as it looked.

"You always had exceptional control," Adam said. "I wouldn't expect any less, but I can't in good conscience let you out after a five-minute chat."

"What kind of proof do you need?"

"What have you got? I don't see any wings."

"Myth."

Adam smiled, glancing over his shoulder at the now-open door. "Talia would say that the truth has its roots in myth."

That sounded like her.

Custo sighed. "I don't know how to make you believe, and I don't have all the time in the world like Jacob."

Custo wanted to get back to living. Needed to get back to living. In fact, life-affirming acts were first on his to-do list. He'd been waiting for too long.

Adam leaned slightly forward. "Jacob is dead, as are hundreds of wraiths like him."

"Shadowman?" Custo remembered the moment the wraith war started, the day Talia discovered her scream. The wraiths had attacked the West Virginia Segue compound. Escape was impossible. Until Talia . . . The sound was like nothing he'd ever heard before, beautiful and terrible, serene and shattering, contradiction unified. She'd ripped a hole in the sky through which Death entered, his scythe swinging, cutting scores of wraiths out of the world. She'd fainted before her father had reached Jacob.

But if Jacob was dead, then she'd called on her father again.

Adam made a show of looking around the concrete hole, his face lining with pain and grim determination. "We capture wraiths, hold them here while we prepare, and then . . ."

And then Talia and her trumpet call for Death.

Adam exited without a backward glance. *I'll do what needs to be done. I found a way to kill my brother. I can kill you, too.*

Fisting his hands, Custo remembered. Shadowman had passed over the human men and women that day. Would he pass over an angel?

What about the angel who betrayed him?

FIVE

ANNABELLA'S stomach growled while she waited for the two lovebirds to finish their spat and get her the hell out of the concrete prison. Tall, angry Adam made a good effort to keep his voice soft when it was obvious he wanted to shake Talia, whose very pregnant stomach jutted alarmingly from her middle. Two babies, and the poor woman still had a couple months to go. Wow.

Sure enough, the vein at his temple pulsed as he stared down at her. "What could you possibly be thinking?"

Talia postured back, nudging him with her big belly. "I'm pregnant, not an invalid."

Annabella eyed the open door; maybe she could make a run for it.

"That's not remotely the point, and you know it, Talia. Segue has protocols for a rea—"

"—protocols for *wraiths*," Talia interrupted. "She's not a wraith, so there is no need to keep her locked up."

"You touched her?" Adam's voice dropped a few octaves.

Annabella wondered what touching her had to do with it, but she wasn't about to exacerbate the situation and ask.

"And what if she had been?" he pressed.

"She's not."

Adam closed his eyes, his lips silently forming the words, *one, two, three, four* . . . When he opened them again, the weight of his attention fell on Annabella. She took a step back.

"Apparently," he said with effort, "you're not a wraith."

Talia grinned as if she'd won a battle and wrapped an arm around Adam's waist. Annabella watched them in reluctant appreciation. They balanced each other. Dark, angry Adam and light, small Talia.

"Let's get you comfortable for the night," Talia said. "You have a big performance tomorrow and need your rest."

Wait a minute . . . "I'm not staying here." They'd dragged her by force and stuffed her in an airless cell, and now they thought she was going to sleep in this hellhole? Nuh-uh. "No way. If you'll kindly return my flashlight, I'll head home."

"If a creature of Shadow is stalking you, this is the safest place for you to be." Talia's eyes were tense with concern.

Adam's steely gray gaze softened as well, and he shrugged somewhat reluctantly. "And your involvement with Segue may have made you a target for wraiths."

"Great. So you're saying that because I accepted the help of *your* friend, I am actually in more danger." Freaking fantastic. "I want to talk to Custo."

"That's not possible." Adam's voice was flat and uncompromising.

"Oh, I think it is," Annabella said, so livid a quaver entered her voice. She might not have the nerve to yell at the pregnant woman, but Adam could take it. "I want to see Custo, and I want to see him now."

"He's not safe."

"He treated me a whole lot better than you."

Adam's eyes glittered. "Custo is in lockdown and will remain there. Wraiths are permitted no visitors."

Frustration had Annabella's body warming. "You seem like a smart guy, and yet you're not getting it."

Adam's eyes narrowed, but she didn't care.

"He. Saved. Me." She enunciated each word in case he was hard of hearing, too.

"Custo will remain in lockdown. You are welcome to stay here while we investigate your problem, but you are also free to leave." Adam gestured toward the door.

Poor Talia. The man was impossible. Annabella turned on her heel to exit the cell. Free to leave? Well, that's exactly what she was going to do.

"Stay," Talia said, reaching out to catch her arm. "Just for the night."

Annabella tried not to scowl at her. "I don't want any of this. I want my old life back."

"I don't think there's any going back," Talia said with a slow shake of her head.

Obviously, Talia knew nothing about the power of avoidance. A lot of problems went away if Annabella ignored them and thought of something else, something better. It was a gift.

"One night," Talia repeated.

Annabella took a deep breath and sighed, her rage and bluff evaporating into the air. She needed the sleep—she couldn't avoid that. And if they could help her get rid of the wolf as Custo promised, then okay. She didn't like it, but okay. "One night."

Talia broke out of Adam's hold and moved to the door. "You'll be comfortable in the infirmary. There are a couple of private rooms, and it is always staffed, so help is close. I doubt any wolf, Shadow or otherwise, could bother you there."

Adam gestured, *ladies first.*

Annabella exited the cell behind Talia to find herself in a long concrete corridor of several similar cells. Uniformed guards stood sentry at regular intervals, armor molding their upper bodies and helmets stretching down over their faces. Some kind of machine gun was held at their chests, ready to fire. Good thing she hadn't tried to run. Where the hell was she?

"Don't mind them," Talia said over her shoulder as they walked the length of the passage. "They're the good guys."

Good guys, right. If those were the good guys, then the bad guys must be seriously scary.

The three of them came to an enormous retractable door

made of riveted metal both wide and high enough to accommodate a vehicle. Adam tapped a coded panel at its side, and the door shuddered open, an earsplitting screech of metal on metal echoing through the space. Beyond, the corridor resembled a long, lit tunnel, like an industrial subway. Broken yellow lines on the floor dictated two-way traffic, though it was empty now. The concrete ceiling was high, yet the passage had a cavernous feeling, as if she were far underground. In spite of all the space, all the air, Annabella had to work to breathe against a mounting press of claustrophobia.

"The place was retrofitted from a government bomb shelter," Talia said. "It's built to withstand anything, which is great for wraith control, but I hate it anyway."

"I think I hate it, too," Annabella answered with a thick swallow. She was all about creature comforts—soft pillows, Egyptian sheets, warm colors, cuddly throws flung over the arm of the sofa, and knickknacks cluttering every surface. This place was as cold and harsh and empty as a grave. "You live here?"

Talia laughed, but it sounded forced. "Temporarily. The Segue Institute's main facility is in West Virginia, recently renovated and very comfortable."

Annabella doubted it.

They came to and boarded a massive yellow cargo lift, an open-air vehicle elevator. Annabella mimicked Adam and Talia, standing back from the edge and grasping the railing. Talia leaned into Adam's chest, and the elevator rose slowly through an opening in the high ceiling to another floor.

Traffic on the upper level was brisk: a tram of sorts, engine whining, slowly transported crates of equipment. Tunnel pedestrians in lab coats walked with purpose, badges flapping at their waists and on their chests. Armed sentries stood post, as they had on the level below. Sweaty, muscled men in tanks and shorts jogged the length of the space, feet falling in perfect rhythm to an outlying soldier who set the pace.

Adam looked down at Talia. "You didn't take a cart?"

"I felt like walking," she said. "I've been sitting all day."

"You *should* be sitting."

"Don't boss me."

Annabella followed the bickering pair, turning from the corridor down a low, modern hallway, busy with a smattering of determined-looking people in lab coats and white shirts going about their work—whatever that was. Custo and Adam were right about something: She couldn't see the wolf infiltrating this place. It banished imagination, even nightmares. The security of the codes, badges, and soldiers made the very idea of a Shadow wolf silly.

They came to a set of glass doors marked INFIRMARY and were about to enter when Adam was stopped by a harried man, who murmured something in his ear.

Adam listened, then turned back to Talia. "Mind if you get her settled? I need to take care of something."

"Not at all. I'll meet you back in our quarters later." Talia reached up, grabbed his shirtfront, and brushed her mouth against his. Adam's hand went to her hair and his nostrils flared as if he were inhaling her, and when he pulled away, the lines of stress on his face had lessened. The simple gesture made Annabella ache inside. However Adam and Talia might argue, there was something very real and solid about their connection. Not the fairy-tale brand of love, saccharine and schmaltzy, but the enduring kind. The kind that saw a couple through the ups and downs of life. It had been missing from Annabella's parents, from any relationship she'd had the opportunity to examine, and she'd concluded it was a myth. But here it was. Now. In this soul-smothering basement bunker. Real. If ever a "true love" existed, this was it.

"Please don't tire yourself out," Adam said, tone long-suffering, and moved down the hall.

Annabella swallowed hard, packing away the newfound knowledge for examination later, and followed Talia's waddle inside the infirmary. The sliding doors hissed closed behind them. Centered in the entryway was a long white counter, staffed by a tall and broad-shouldered male nurse. "Dr. Thorne, are you feeling well? Those babies giving you any trouble?"

"I'm not here for me, Rudy," Talia answered. "I'm here for Ms. Ames. She needs a private room and a good night's sleep. Can you help us accommodate her?"

"Fifteen is open," Rudy said. He looked at Annabella. "Do you need a sleep aid?"

She hadn't thought of that. Maybe taking something was a good idea. A sleeping pill could put her under for eight to ten, and then she could wake refreshed and ready for the biggest day of her life. Without it, her rest was bound to be rotten, all things considered.

"Yeah," she said. "Is there something light I could take? Knock me out, but not put me in a coma?"

"I'll see what I can do. Fifteen is right down there." Rudy gestured down the hall. "Do you need anything else for the night? Contact solution or any personal items?"

Annabella looked at Talia. "Not if I get my bag back." Which incidentally had an old, smushed chocolate brownie protein bar in there. Some dinner.

"Of course. Adam would be thorough." Talia heaved a big sigh. "You go on down to your room. I'll make some calls and have it delivered right away. We'll have you tucked in and asleep in no time."

"Thanks," Annabella said. The word felt funny in her mouth. Why on earth was she thanking her? For returning the bag they had confiscated when they kidnapped her? Crazy. But then again, Talia had shown her nothing but kindness. And what about Custo? Was there any kindness for him?

Annabella shook her head to clear her thoughts. She was too tired to think, and there was nothing she could do anyway. She'd sleep and then deal with everything tomorrow. She turned and made her way to the room with the number "15" on a flap above the door.

She gripped the lever and entered. The room was small and tidy. A hospital bed fitted with white sheets was centered on the opposite wall, a beige blanket folded across the end. Another door, kitty-corner to the entry, was ajar, the gleaming edge of a toilet promising a private bath. Nothing fancy, but clean.

Okay. She could rest here for one night. Rudy, the linebacker-turned-nurse, wouldn't let anything get past him. Maybe this was the best solution after all.

The console above the bed had an overhead light, and Annabella moved forward to find the switch to turn it on for a little extra protection. As she was fiddling with the switch, the door closed behind her.

Her sleeping pill? Her bag?

She turned and found a soldier. His hair was buzzed, jaw square. Bulging arm muscles, bronzed by the sun, were displayed by a tight army tank. He wore baggy camo pants tucked into black boots. No bag.

When he didn't say anything, she was forced to ask, "Yes?"

He cocked his head at a sharp, oblique angle, chin tilted slightly downward. Gaze fixed on her.

Maybe the guy was confused. "Rudy, the nurse out front, assigned this room to me," she explained.

The soldier took a predatory, silent step forward. Light from the bed lamp broke over his features, softly highlighting old acne scars across his cheeks and his yellow eyes.

A chill skittered over Annabella's skin as her heart fluttered. She let her hand fall on the hospital bed railing and pressed the call button for the nurse.

The soldier took another stealthy step, shoulders slightly hunched as he approached.

Her heart clutched hard over two gulping beats before accelerating into a rush that pounded in her head. The soldier was familiar, but her mind refused to recall how.

He sniffed at the air. "I can't smell so good now."

Annabella flattened herself against the wall and console, and the light cascaded over her shoulders, bright at the edges of her vision. Her consciousness sparked at last, though she had known from the moment she saw him. "Wolf."

He skulked forward again, upper lip curling to bare teeth. The yellow of his eyes became consumed by black, the irises swallowed by deep and shifting shadow.

"Who—? How—? I don't understand." Hysteria rose like bile in her throat.

"What are you?" the wolf asked, his voice soft, husky, and low, rumbling from his chest. He tilted his head again, moving in closer.

Annabella gripped the bed railing, torn between climbing over it and staying beneath the light, her place of protection. Not so much protection anymore—the wolf now stood in the dim illumination of the room. "What are *you?*" she asked back.

He considered her question.

"I am the hunter." He bent his head to the exposed skin at her neck. "You and the other one trespassed in my territory."

She craned her head away, but he brushed his cheek there anyway. Nuzzled, his hot breath in her hair and curling around her ear.

"I don't know what you're talking about. What do you want from me?" Sobs clogged her question. Though her body was painfully tense, a deep shudder had her trembling beneath him.

He groaned, almost a growl, before answering. "This body wants to be inside you. To fill you. Is that where you keep your magic?"

"Oh, please, no." Tears slid down her cheeks. Her knees threatened to give.

"Then how do you glow? Why does magic obey you? How do you light Shadow?" His low voice was full of wonder.

"I don't know what you're talking about," she gasped.

Hot, slick teeth pulled at her earlobe. "Show me again."

"Show you what?" she whined, insinuating her arms between them to push him away.

"Bridge our worlds." His hand found her ass and he ground his pelvis against hers. "But you feel so good, I almost don't want to go back."

"Please go back," she begged. "You don't belong here."

"I could stay a while longer, like this, with you." He growled again. "Feels so good."

"Go back."

His other palm skimmed up her waist. He cupped her breast. "I'll stay. I think I can bridge our worlds a little myself."

Annabella's next breath released in a frightened whimper, high and weak. A sound somebody else would make. Somebody who let bad things happen to them. Somebody who didn't think to fight. Not her.

The realization was a spark of cold anger in her head that spread down her body to tighten her stomach. The muscles in her legs warmed with her new resolve. Trembling, she shifted slightly to fit her body to the wolf's *just so*. He squeezed his approval. Then she brought her knee up fast and hard, with a lifetime of strength and technical accuracy behind it.

He yelped and recoiled, stumbling back a few clutched steps, hands at his groin. When he lifted his face, it was devoid of color, the faint veins around his eyes bleeding inky black with pain and surprise.

Annabella ducked out of her corner, but he blocked her passage to the door. "Somebody help me!" she screamed. They said she'd be safe here. Where was Rudy?

"Why did you do that?" the wolf ground out, straightening slowly.

"Stay back, or I'll do it again."

His eyes turned sad, confused. "But we could be so good—"

If he said "good" one more time, she was going to rip his "bridge" off him and shove it down his throat.

A light courtesy rap on the door, and it opened, Talia peeking her head in. "I've got your bag."

Damn, not Rudy. Pregnant Talia. Annabella couldn't have the one nice person in this place, and her babies, harmed because of her. "Get out, Talia. Now."

The wolf's head snapped toward the door.

Fear flickered over Talia's features, a hand on her belly, but she didn't run. Her expression hardened as she pushed the door open all the way.

"It's the wolf, Talia, run!"

But Talia didn't listen, her gaze fixed on the soldier. "You're a creature of Shadow?"

"Yes," he said, voice a murmured undertone. "What are you?" He drew the *you* out into a wolfish croon.

"Banshee," she said.

Banshee? What the freak was that? Nothing made sense, and there was no time for an explanation. Not with him prowling toward Talia.

"Wolf," Annabella called sharply, "you want me."

"And I'll have you," he answered over his shoulder.

The room darkened perceptibly, the shadows gaining substance and thickness, layering the room. The bed light dimmed to a faint glow. Annabella's breath caught and held until her lungs screamed.

"Go back to Shadow," Talia commanded. Darkness whipped and snapped around her, the room filling with a kinetic energy.

"No!" the wolf barked, the sound ripped from a human throat.

"I said," Talia's voice took on shattering intensity, painful to the ears, "Go back!"

The wolf staggered, contracting as if sucker punched, then burst into a splattered cloud of flickering darkness, like a swarm of chattering moths. The shadows gathered into a dark, dense pulse, then rushed past Talia to skim the hallway out of sight, blending in the deep patches formed by obstructed light.

Annabella's mind blanked for a moment. Her body complained for air and she finally exhaled, grabbing the wall for support and gulping deep. She almost crumbled to the floor, but Talia beat her to it, her knees cracking with impact on the linoleum. Annabella darted forward to catch her before she fell onto her swollen belly.

"Oh God. Are you okay?" Annabella put her arms around her, thinking to get her to the bed, but Talia groaned. The floor would have to do until help came.

"Con"—Talia choked on air—"traction."

Not good. Not with two months still to go. "Help!" Annabella yelled down the hallway. To Talia she said, "It's going to be okay."

Talia brought a hand up, fingertips scarlet with blood. Her gaze turned to Annabella, fear in her soul-filled eyes.

"Deep breaths," Annabella said with an exaggerated inhalation and exhalation in case Talia had forgotten how. "You're going to be fine."

"My babies."

"They're going to be fine, too. You're already in the infirmary." Annabella eased her to sitting on the floor. "You're probably just in for a nice long rest. And a whole lot of bossing from your husband."

Talia smiled weakly. Her eyes darted down the hallway. "You said he was a wolf."

"I thought he was."

"Talia!" A man's voice.

Annabella looked up to see Adam pelting down the hall. He was on his knees at Talia's back before Annabella could blink.

"The wolf's in Segue," Talia gasped. "Gone for the moment."

"Where are you hurt?"

"The wolf didn't touch her," Annabella said. "I think it's shock."

Talia shook her head, tearing. "I used Shadow, but I'm not as strong pregnant. I couldn't completely banish him."

Shadow again. Annabella had thought Shadow was a place, but now it seemed like more. Something that could be used, manipulated. It was a crazy conclusion, of course, but she'd seen it with her own two eyes: Talia had darkened the room, filled it with churning shadows that obeyed her, and then drew on a strange power when she had yelled at the wolf.

"Shhhh." Adam put his mouth to her hair, obviously struggling for control. "Love, you're going to be fine. The babies are going to be fine." He shifted her in his arms and stood. Annabella backed away so he could carry Talia to the bed.

Beyond the room, Annabella could hear the shouts of people, a rising commotion in the entrance to the infirmary.

A doctor. Talia needed a doctor.

Annabella tore down the hall, grabbed the first person in a white coat. "We need a doctor for Talia."

"I'm in research." The man craned his head around. "Where's Powell?"

"I'm here," a female voice answered. A middle-aged woman dressed in slacks and a bright satiny-pink blouse stood abruptly from the behind the nurse's counter. Annabella looked over to find Rudy collapsed on the floor, eyes open but fixed, sightless. Dead.

SIX

CUSTO paced his cell, his hands gripped behind his neck as he strained for control. Shouting wouldn't help. Kicking at the steel and concrete door would accomplish nothing. Reasoning with the guards he detected outside his cell was useless. Their minds were fixed. Each one had resolved to follow orders. He expected no less; Adam only picked the best.

Custo groaned and leaned into a standing push-up on the door to expend some of his energy. If a wraith couldn't break out, he sure as hell couldn't. Heaven was a lot easier in that regard. With his mind he traced Adam and Annabella, caught them for a shred of a moment, but then lost them again in the maelstrom of humanity. Maddening.

Mind reading was a handy trick. It had helped him avoid all sorts of uncomfortable encounters in Heaven, and in theory, it should have made him all but invincible on Earth. The problem was twofold: Locating an isolated individual was difficult to begin with, but then, as soon as a shard of clear thinking cut through someone's consciousness, it was swept away, flotsam in a tidal wave of other thoughts. Custo had barely caught someone's inkling in his mind's grasp before it was no longer relevant.

Of this he was certain: Something was happening. He caught two sustained, desperate resolutions in the sudden thought frenzy in the building. Annabella intended to defend herself, and Adam was determined to save Talia's life. Both objectives were clear, edged with absolute purpose. Neither boded well, but taken together, something disastrous must have happened. Wraith attack? Wolf?

He dipped into another push-up, then thrust away from the wall.

"Let me out!" He could do nothing locked in this prison. "I can help!"

Time passed, serene, while painful tension gripped him.

He was sitting in a corner, head in his hands, when the door thudded and screeched, retracting. He leaped to his feet before the edge parted with the wall.

Adam stood beyond, a smudge of blood on the waist of his shirt.

"What's happened? Are Talia and Annabella all right?" It took all of Custo's will not to approach Adam, not to push him out of the way and find the women for himself.

"You're an angel?" Adam's voice was absent, hoarse. Desperation spoke.

Cold dread seeped into Custo. "I think so."

"You were sure before," Adam said, each word sharp and cutting.

"I was an angel in Heaven, but I left. I don't know what that makes me now. Not really."

"Damn it." Adam put his hands on his head, shoulders hunched, staring at the floor as if it might hold answers. Custo touched his mind and found only a cyclone of confusion. Adam had no idea what to do.

"Let me try," Custo said. Talia had to be in great danger for Adam to be so shattered. Custo remembered the babies, twins. What if he couldn't help? What if he couldn't save her? He wasn't going to think about that, not with blood staining Adam's shirt.

"And if you're a wraith sent to kill her?"

"I'm not."

"But what if you are?" Adam glanced at Custo's now-healed forearm.

Custo let him look. "I'm not."

"How can I know for sure?" Intensity lined Adam's face. "Can you prove it? Please?"

"Is it so hard to trust me?"

MONROE COUNTY LIBRARY SYSTEM

Dorsch Memorial Branch Library

YOUR INFORMATION DESTINATION

Checkout Check outs summary for BASILE, N
Thu Jul 26 2018 09:37 EDT 2018

BARCODE: 31298016900302906
TITLE: Shadowman / Erin Kellison
DUE DATE: Aug 16 2018
STATUS:

BARCODE: 31308002277006
TITLE: Fire kissed / Erin Kellison
DUE DATE: Aug 16 2018
STATUS:

BARCODE: 35101512360302402
TITLE: Shadow fall / Erin Kellison
DUE DATE: Aug 16 2018
STATUS:

Thank You!

Renew Online at http://monroe.lib.mi.us
or call us at 1-800-462-2050

"This is my wife were talking about." The anguish in Adam's voice brought Custo back to the night Adam's parents had died, murdered by Jacob. If Adam lost another family, he'd lose himself, of that Custo had no doubt.

Gently, then. "I'm not asking you to choose between us."

Adam's mottled face blanched with feeling. "If you hurt her . . ."

". . . then lock me away forever."

Adam grimaced, aging with the necessity of a decision, but Custo knew he'd made up his mind. Felt the harrowing leap of faith.

"Come on. And fast." Adam turned and darted out the door, around the corner. Custo sprinted forward to catch up. He asked no questions while Adam cursed at a slow-moving security door. A small army green vehicle was waiting, bigger than a golf cart, but smaller than a commercial car, and before Custo was seated, Adam had it accelerating through a concrete tunnel. They drove onto a lift, and while the mechanism slowly elevated them, Custo caught sight of Adam's white knuckles.

Custo tried to read the events from Adam's mind, but it was moving too fast to discern particulars. He could feel Annabella drawing closer, which was some measure of comfort. "What happened?"

"Wolf."

Custo's own grip tightened. "He got in? How?"

Adam didn't look over to answer. He kept his gaze fixed on the slow slide of concrete wall as they rose. "He somehow took on the form of one of my soldiers, who is now dead. The wolf then escaped after Talia . . . used her voice."

Adam's tone was flat, but Custo could guess what roiled beneath the surface. Segue was vulnerable. The lives they were responsible for—Talia, Annabella, all the rest— vulnerable. If the wolf could shape-shift, he could probably look like Adam or Talia or even himself and have them questioning each other more than they already were.

Custo reached for Annabella's mind again and caught the trace of a thought—something about going home. He couldn't sense her feelings, but knew she was scared. He had to ask. "Annabella?"

"Fine. Tough." A grudging respect.

The lift jolted to a stop. "Talia?"

"In labor."

Two guards flanked the entrance labeled INFIRMARY, and inside each doorway another grim-faced man was posted. Stance wide, guns at their chests, they were ready for literally anything.

Adam was moving fast, but Custo caught a few details. The place was anachronistic for a Segue satellite compound, ceilings too low for comfort. Fixtures outdated, but utilitarian. There was an age spot on the wall in the entryway where a circular clock once had been, and an odd, rounded sink circa the sixties was attached to the back wall. Definitely out of date.

Custo followed Adam down a hallway, stopping at an open door labeled "15." Talia lay on her back, slightly tilted to the side, a white sheet pulled up to her waist. Her face was chalky next to the white-gold tangle of her hair. Custo had known her in his past life—she'd been a pale, pretty thing with intelligent eyes. There was something different about her now, or rather, different about the way he saw her. The pallor of her skin had a strange sheen to it, a black-light luminescence that made the tilt of her eyes less exotic-human and more, distinctly, *Other*. Looking at her now, on the flip side of mortality, there was no doubt she was fae.

Dr. Gillian Powell, a longtime member of Segue's staff, examined a strip of paper printing from a machine to the left of the bed. Gillian was good, thorough. She'd stitched

him up more than once in the Jacob days. She'd save Talia
and the babies if they could be saved.

Talia winced, straining her head to the side as Custo
came through the doorway after Adam.

"More contractions?" Adam asked as he rushed to the bed
and knelt on the floor, eye level with Talia.

"They'd stopped, and I thought I had it under control, but
now . . ." Gillian trailed off. She frowned at another machine, her mind saying, *That's not right.* A rapidly blinking
heart accompanied escalating numbers, but the doctor put
her stethoscope to her ears and checked Talia out for herself.

Talia groaned, squeezing her eyes shut. "Too bright."

Adam leaned in closer. "What is, honey?"

"Custo," she gasped.

Custo took a step back. Suddenly this didn't seem like such
a great idea. A banshee and an angel in the same room—
something about the combination felt inherently wrong.
Fundamentally at odds. Maybe the barrier between their
worlds was there for a reason. Maybe light and darkness
were exclusive by necessity. Maybe he was hurting her.

Talia whimpered. Custo gripped the doorway. He wanted
to help if he could. He was a goddamn angel. He should be
able to do something. Ease her. Heal her.

Adam looked over at him, confusion and alarm on his
face. "What's happening?"

Talia shuddered and Custo backed into the hall. "I don't
know." When she next groaned, he took himself out of the
infirmary altogether.

In a long, thin, windy tunnel between two rooms, the hunter
collected himself. The darkness deepened here, almost to
pitch, and fed the slow reformation of his body. Shadow
condensed, thickened, to form a twitching ear, a sharp claw,
burning eyes. Air blew through the tunnel, rippling with

the shudder of his new fur. He trembled, still variable, still weak, but growing.

Smell came first: bland and acrid, and over it all, the heady scent of a mortal woman, filling his Shadow mind. Then sight: the tunnel terminated near the top of a room, where a bright square patch gleamed, reaching like flame. And sound: a woman wept with choking sobs.

Finally understanding, born of walking human steps and stroking exquisite skin: Mortal. Woman. Magic. A harsh, vicious longing twined with his new awareness, stoking his animal hunger and transmuting it into something else, something almost human, and thus unbearable.

The hunter wanted it all. *Mine.*

Now, how to get her?

Custo raised his head as Adam approached. He'd been sitting on a stack of crates and, God help him, praying. Not that he expected an answer; he'd been an utter fool.

"So you're an angel," Adam said. He was stating fact, echoing the realization in his mind, not mocking, not questioning. Finally. "You deserve it. You were . . . *are* the best man I've ever known, after my father."

Custo steeled himself against the unwarranted comparison. What could he say to that? Adam didn't know about some of the bloody things he'd done. Couldn't possibly guess what he was responsible for. "I'm sorry I endangered Talia, your children, Segue. I had no idea that the wolf would or could follow."

"Gillian gave her something to stop the contractions." Adam sat heavily next to him. "It's working for now, and her heart rate dropped when you left the room. She's on strict bed rest and will be until she delivers."

Custo nodded. The contractions had stopped. He had to repeat it a couple of times to himself before the anxiety in his blood, heavy and poisonous as lead, thinned enough for him to breathe.

"I think I hurt her by just being in the room."

Yes, Adam agreed. "I would appreciate it if both you and Annabella would stay away from her until this is resolved," Adam said slowly, without recrimination. "I don't want to stress the pregnancy more than it has been already. Talia told me to say hi, by the way, and not to beat yourself up about being so 'shiny.' Her word, by the way."

"Of course. Annabella and I will go, find somewhere else safe." He braced his hands on his knees. He definitely couldn't stay at Segue. His very presence endangered Talia. Light against Shadow.

"That's not necessary. Segue is the best place for the two of you, and you know it. It's a big place." *Plenty of room.*

"And if the wolf comes back in the meantime?"

"We'll fight." Adam gave him an exhausted half smile.

Custo cleared his throat to ease the tightness there, but guilt and worry still strangled him. "Can I see Annabella now?"

Adam waited a beat, gaze meeting his. "Yes. I stuck her in the lab, under guard. She's pretty shaken up. I haven't had a chance to question her, so I've only had Talia's side of the story. Call me when you get Annabella's. I'll assemble a research team."

"In the time I've been gone have you seen anything like the wolf?" Custo rose and followed Adam to a set of doors on the other side of the concrete tunnel.

"Paranormal phenomena have jumped dramatically in the past eighteen months. Hauntings and poltergeists mainly, but here and there I've heard of incidents that are *Other*. Something like the wolf was bound to happen. Feel free to access my files. I'm not leaving Talia's side for a while, so you can sleep in my place tonight—we'll get something fixed up for the two of you tomorrow. Our living quarters are two floors up. I have the whole floor."

Fitting back into Adam's life, just like old times. It didn't feel right this time either.

Adam tapped a code into the security panel. The door slid open and Custo immediately spotted Annabella. She'd risen from a stool at a brushed-steel worktable in the center of the room. Her eyes were swollen, mascara smudged in a line out to her temple, and her nose was pink. When she saw Custo, she let out a harsh sob, ducked under the table, and crossed the room as fast as her stagger would allow.

Her mind was full of jumbled words . . . *hunter, territory, bridge, banshee.*

Custo opened his arms, ready to take her in, to comfort her, to promise to protect her from further harm. She approached, arms likewise extended, but instead she shoved him into the door. Hard. Knocked off balance, Custo nearly fell, but caught himself, palms flat on the glass.

"You said Segue was safe!" Annabella's eyes were wild, her face flushed. "You said these people knew how to deal with scary shit! You said I could get some sleep. Sleep!" She broke into a hysterical laugh that turned into a sob.

"Shhh . . ." Custo recovered and wrapped his arms around her in an attempt to restrain her, but she bucked against his hold. Her body would fit perfectly, amazingly in the circle of his arms if she'd just calm down enough . . .

"Don't fucking shush me!" She hit his chest with the heel of her hand, yet clutched his shoulder for support. "Talia— *Talia!*—had to save me." Tears ran freely down her face. She swiped at her eyes and sniffed. "This place is frickin' Fort Knox and a pregnant woman had to save me." Her expression hardened. "If that woman loses her babies, I swear I will kill you."

Custo glanced over at Adam, who met his gaze. *Good luck,* Adam thought. He gave a short nod and exited the room. The guards followed, though Custo was sure they'd be on the other side of the door.

Alone now, Custo shifted his grasp on her, controlling Annabella's jerking body at her hips. "Talia is going to be fine. Her contractions have stopped."

Tears ran down Annabella's cheeks, her fight subsiding into steady, drawn-out tremors. "But what about the blood?"

"Under control." He assumed, or Adam would have still been in a panic.

Annabella hiccuped. For all her trembling, she felt cold in his arms. "What if he comes back? The light didn't work. I thought it would—light worked before, that time on the street—but it didn't work in that room."

"Can you tell me what happened?"

He almost ra— Annabella stunted the thought. "A man came in my room in the infirmary. A soldier. He was acting all weird, but I could tell he was the wolf."

"How?"

"The way he moved. His eyes."

Custo nodded. "Continue."

"He said he was the hunter and that you and I had trespassed in his territory and that he wanted a bridge back." *Then he groped me, would have raped me if I hadn't nailed his disgusting stuff.* Custo went hot, but didn't interrupt as Annabella went on. "Talia came in, said she was a freaking banshee, and ordered the guy back to Shadow. 'Kay, then it got really scary, 'cause she made the room all dark. I hate the dark. And the hunter-wolf-guy exploded and uh, flew out the room. The whole thing is insane!"

Custo reviewed the details. "He said he was a hunter? I thought he was a wolf."

"Aren't wolves hunters?" *Duh.*

Custo ignored the thought-insult. "And he wants a way back to Shadow?"

The real question is, Annabella thought . . . "Why didn't light hurt him? It has in the past."

Custo could answer that. Before, the wolf was stuck in the Shadowlands. He stayed in the shadows because he had to. The divide between the worlds was inviolable. But in the brief altercation in the dark forest, when the three of them had clashed, the wolf had crossed over and fallen to Earth with Annabella's return to her reality. Just as Custo had fallen and been reborn. Shadow would always be the wolf's refuge, but he need not fear light on Earth. Not now that he was free.

All that was too much to explain, and Annabella was clearly too distraught to listen. The truth had taken Adam, his best friend and almost-brother, too long to believe, and they had a long history of trust. Annabella had no context to even begin the discussion. Angel? Banshee? Shadowlands? Custo settled for the simplest answer. "If he attacks again, I will handle him."

She laughed derisively. "We don't know what he looks like. He can change his shape. One minute a wolf, the next a man, the next a bunch of shadows. And you think you can 'handle' him? I doubt it."

"But he's made of shadow?"

"Weren't you listening? Light does not hurt him!" Her pitch went high and painful at "hurt him," but Custo didn't mind. If anything, an idea became clearer.

The more he thought about it, the more confident he became, his own panic replaced by new resolve. Talia had given him the answer. She was a child of Shadow, and she couldn't bear how "bright" he was in his current incarnation—angel. The wolf was also born of Shadow. The wolf might be able to challenge him in the Shadowlands, its primeval territory. Might be able to attack and to kill, if angels could possibly die twice (a disturbing thought). But on Earth it stood to reason that the wolf would be as repelled, as pained by him as the banshee daughter of Shadowman. Perhaps more, since Talia was half human and may have had some level of hereditary protection.

"Annabella"—Custo wiped dark strands away from her eyes—"we weren't prepared before, but we are now."

"He can change his shape. What if he becomes a lion? Or, or, a tiger, or—"

"A bear?" Custo finished with a smile.

She hit him again. This time it hurt. "Don't make fun of me."

Custo sobered. "Next time we'll be ready."

Annabella fell silent, though her breath still shuddered with each draw and release. She swallowed hard, her chin quivering for a second before she controlled the reflex.

Custo wanted to draw her closer, to comfort her, but he allowed her to push him away. One thing he was learning about Annabella—she liked to stand on her own two feet. As much as he admired her for the show of strength, it drove him crazy. Would it kill her to let him hold her—*really* hold her—for two minutes?

"He wanted me, or *us*, to bridge our worlds. Is that more of the Shadow stuff you and Talia have been talking about?"

Custo gave a short nod. "I don't know what Talia discussed with you, but for my part, yes. There are three worlds: Earth, the Shadowlands, and the Hereafter."

Her face contracted in a grimace. "So the wolf is a ghost?"

"No. Don't get ahead of me." Custo reconsidered his approach. "The Shadowlands is a place of possibility, of imagination, of inspiration. Yes, people pass through there briefly upon death; Talia is part of that, with her banshee voice, able to manipulate Shadow and force others to cross, like the wolf. But the nature of the Shadowlands is much more than that. Humanity accesses it during daily life for inspiration and insight. It is the source of magic, a well for talent to draw from, like yours."

"I don't know what you are talking about." She shook her head, denying everything that he was saying.

"Yes, you do. You of all people know," Custo said. Her chin came up, but he continued, "The first time I saw you was in the Shadowlands. You were dancing, bright and beautiful, all magic."

"I'm not magic."

"Your talent is a kind of magic."

She frowned, the sharpness of her gaze losing its edge as her thoughts turned inward.

"Why do you dance? How does it make you feel? What are you able to do that others cannot?"

The moment stretched. He tried to read her, but her mind was moving too fast, darting from one conclusion to another, her intellect traveling over the events and explanations, but never stopping in one place to realize it entirely. At last, she took a deep breath and exhaled, shaking her head. "So you're saying my dance puts me in both places. That I was, in fact, in his territory." *Does that mean I can't dance?*

Custo reached for her arm, but she pulled it out of his grasp, leaving his own extended, palm raised and empty. "Annabella . . ."

But she took a step back. "First the wolf, and now you. Where do you get off touching me? Getting all familiar? I don't know you from Adam. Not really. You offered me a safe place to sleep and so far—"

He had to interrupt her before she made a drastic decision. "This is still the safest place for you."

"Way I see it, nowhere is safe anymore," she said, voice rising. "I can't even dance."

"Of course you can. But now you know that you need to master the magic as you would any other movement. Now you know why the greats were the greats, and that you can be, too."

She put her hands over her ears and gripped her head. "I don't want to talk about this anymore!" *I can't.*

Custo swallowed back everything he wanted to say. The words burned in his throat just as his arms burned to hold her. He held his hands up in surrender. *No more tonight.*

She dropped her arms. "Now is there a frickin' bed in this place for me or not?"

He tried not to smile at her tone. "Yes. Adam has let us have his apartment while he's with Talia." Obviously, Custo would be sleeping on the floor his first night back.

He signaled the door to open and glanced out. The guards were in place. Everything still. No wolves waiting. He'd have liked to put his arm around her—they'd fit so well before—but he resisted the impulse. Annabella came up beside him, also peeking out into the tunnel. Her lips pressed together, probably summoning her courage, and then she stepped outside the lab.

"Elevator?" Custo asked the guards.

The guards led the way and would be stationed outside Adam's place for the night.

As they neared a conventional pair of silver sliding doors, Custo felt a hand on his elbow.

"Wait," Annabella asked, expression again filled with confusion, "what were *you* doing in the Shadowlands?"

Considering her last request, Custo went with the truth. "I was crossing them, heading back to Earth."

She stopped midstep before boarding the elevator, frowning while she tried to figure out what he'd said. He wasn't about to offer an extended explanation, not after she'd plainly said she didn't want to hear it.

"The Hereafter?" she asked.

Custo nodded, pulling her inside. "Heaven. I'm your guardian angel."

SEVEN

ANNABELLA ran, a pack of wolves snarling and snapping at her heels. Her mind's eye saw them clearly, though she didn't dare look back: bristling black fur, yellow eyes, sharp white teeth too long and jagged for any mouth—wolf or otherwise. Her heartbeat and footfalls combined to form a gallop of sound, the rhythm of the chase.

Somebody help me! she sobbed through gasping chokes of air.

But the forest was silent. She sprinted through widely spaced trees—*no place to hide*—their great trunks rising like columns to hold up the nonexistent sky. *Where was the sky?*

She pushed her body harder, faster, channeling all her fear and strength into her stride. She felt the distance between her and the wolves lengthen. Felt their interest suddenly shift, the pack swarming on a rise, ears pricked.

Saved?

Then, an infant's cry, a new-world wail made with a lusty first breath. A second cry signaled the twins' birth.

Annabella tripped and fell, gouging the earth, and turned her head in time to see the wolves alter their direction, a river of furious black rushing down the hill, making for the innocents.

No! Here! Not the babies. But she had no voice.

She clawed a tree trunk to stand and lurched to follow, but her muscles had hardened, betraying her, blood chug-chugging through collapsed veins. She pushed forward, crested the rise herself when a mother's scream pierced the air. A banshee's scream.

"Annabella!"

A low voice filtered through Annabella's darkened consciousness, but she refused to wake. *The babies, my fault.*

"Annabella!"

She felt herself gathered in a warm embrace, heat pouring into her shaking limbs.

"You're okay. It's just a dream," a rumble of a voice told her. "Wake up, Annabella."

The nightmare went gray, diluting, spreading into the absent sky. Her heart still pounded; her throat was raw.

Annabella cracked an eye and gazed dumbly at the gray-blue wall opposite her. The solidity was mundane, real. Yet a trio of imaginative paintings hung in the center of the flat expanse. Black tree trunks stretched across the foreground of the canvases like a wicked gate, but beyond was a magic swirl of indistinct figures, dancing. If she let her eyes blur a little bit, the picture seemed to move. The composition evoked ghostly *Giselle*, but was more mysterious than mournful.

Annabella triple blinked her bleary eyes. Where was she?

She shifted in place, turned to find Custo holding her. He smelled fresh, like soap and shaving cream, and his hair was spiky wet. He leaned against the headboard, her body across his lap. He smiled down at her like a lover who had beaten her to the shower.

"Morning," he murmured when her eyes focused on him.

She was tempted to curl into his chest and borrow the tempo of his heartbeat, slow and steady. His arms felt like the safest place in the world. So strong. A lick of desire had her core tingling as he nuzzled her neck.

"Everything's okay. You're awake now," he said.

And it all came crashing back: The dress rehearsal, Custo, the cab ride to some storage basement, her subsequent capture and imprisonment in that frightening cell. Sweet Talia, and her babies. The wolf.

Nothing was okay. And nothing ever would be again.

The world as she knew it had turned upside down. Monsters were just as real as she was. A nightmare stalked the shadows of her life. And the man holding her was not human. Or at least not anymore.

Angel.

Annabella sat up and slid off Custo's lap. The shadows in the corners of the room seemed to throb.

He let her go, and his expression sobered. "What time do you need to be at the theater?"

What on earth was he doing cuddling her like that? He was a frigging *angel*, for crying out loud. She'd stopped going to church a long time ago, but she was pretty sure getting intimate with an angel was a one-way ticket to hell.

Angel. The whole thing made her head ache.

"The theater, Annabella? It's past noon already."

Last night she hadn't been able to let the angel comment pass, so she'd pressed him into some half-assed explanation about how he'd died and his mission on earth: save her and save Segue. Seemed to her like he was making it up. If she hadn't seen his first clash against the wolf with her own eyes, she'd have never believed him. His fair eyes, dark blond hair, and olive-gold skin pretty much defined *angel*, but the way he moved—which in Annabella's opinion said more about a person than anything else—told a completely different story. His smooth prowl and tense bearing suggested a brute strength of sweat, blood, and violence. Not angelic.

She knew he wasn't telling the whole truth.

Now he was bent on ridding the world of her wolf. The one who'd killed Rudy and almost made Talia lose her babies. All because of her. She couldn't let anyone else get hurt.

The insanity of the situation burned through Annabella's body, scorching her dreams, destroying her hopes. This wasn't happening.

Reality was worse than her nightmare. Shadows were everywhere. In most light, she cast one herself.

Annabella dragged a twisted ponytail out of her hair to cover the return of her shakes. "I have to make a call so the director can make a substitution."

The gala was at seven. There wasn't a whole lot of time for the company to run through *Serenade*. Thomas Venroy would be angry she was ditching *Giselle* after she swore she could do it, and that would be the end of her time at CBT. The company would say she cracked under pressure. That she hadn't been ready. That she wasn't cut out for principal.

Principal.

Her dream of dancing *Giselle* evaporated. She went as dry and bare as a desert inside.

Dance. Ballet. Joy. All gone. She couldn't breathe.

Custo shook his head, as if reading her thoughts. "Annabella, you're thinking about this the wrong way."

"No, I've got everything straight now." His explanation last night had cleared up her questions about the Shadowlands, the origin of the wolf, and the role of her talent in allowing him to cross over into the world. Only one thing had gone unsaid, though she figured it out just fine for herself: Her debut as Giselle didn't matter when lives were in jeopardy. Therefore, she couldn't dance.

Custo nudged her chin up, and she reluctantly met his gaze. "What is our goal?"

Annabella shrugged a shoulder. She had no idea what he was getting at, and she was hurting too much to really try. Her decision was made, and she didn't want to think or feel anymore. Both were excruciating.

"Our goal is to return the wolf to the Shadowlands," he said.

Not at the expense of another person's life.

Damn. She needed a distraction before she broke, a way to disconnect her head and heart and be all body. A way to shut Custo up.

Her gaze traveled along the flexed length of his forearm to

where it disappeared inside the bunch of his sleeve, to the bulge of his biceps, over the boulder of his shoulder to where the muscle met his collarbone. She went warm and liquid inside.

A life without dance was hell. Why not dive in headfirst?

"Annabella? You have to dance." He'd gentled his bossy tone, but she didn't need his pity. She was too close to falling apart as it was. Why couldn't he just leave it alone?

"Annabella!"

Annabella watched his mouth move, the flick of his tongue on the *la* of her name. She'd never had sex with a near stranger before, but she was in the mood to be reckless. The wolf would probably kill her soon anyway. She had nothing left to lose.

She brought her gaze back up to Custo's eyes, now dark and slightly distracted from his original train of thought. He paused for a moment to take a controlled breath, his intensity doubling, but then continued, "Instead of isolating you, waiting for the wolf to track you again, I suggest we make you completely accessible. Perform in the gala."

She wasn't going to listen to this. Was he trying to hurt her?

"Dance. Allow the wolf to come close," he continued. "Lure him back into the Shadowlands."

He had to see reason, or he'd never stop. "You can't actually think I'd perform? That I'd go onstage with that monster after me? What if he hurt someone? Talia almost lost her babies. He *killed* Rudy."

"Not your fault. You couldn't have known."

Easy for him to say, but she wasn't buying it. He didn't have to live with the consequences.

"And the rest of the dancers, my friends, all the people in the audience! You can't actually think—"

Custo shook his head. "The wolf wants to get back himself. That's why he has followed you to Segue, isn't it?"

"What if he hurts someone to get to me?" She could not live with another death on her head. No. She wasn't going to change her mind. All this arguing was just making her hurt more. Why couldn't Custo shut up and kiss her? He'd been angling to do just that when he woke her. Why not now?

Now, damn it.

"Segue will be there to keep everyone as safe as possible. You dance. Give the performance of your life. Use your talent, your magic, to draw him into the Shadowlands. And then leave him on the other side. I will be there to give him a little extra incentive to go where he feels most in control."

"Onstage? For everyone to see? The audience will all run screaming . . ."

"Not necessarily. The Shadowlands are pure magic, pure possibility. Its inhabitants keep to darkness and illusion by nature. The public nature of the event is actually in our favor. It is more likely that the audience will see what they want to see—a spectacular performance." He raised a conciliatory hand. "But if the gala is ruined, Segue will take responsibility with a plausible answer. Your reputation will not be tarnished." Custo sighed. "The wolf may not even show up."

He made it sound so reasonable. But . . . "No. It's much better to set some sort of trap with me as bait and then kill the wolf away from people."

Custo's brows drew together. "I thought you understood."

"Understood what?" She couldn't take much more.

"Annabella," he said, voice lowered, "the wolf is a creature of Shadow. He is immortal, elemental. There is no way to kill him."

Annabella's heart lost its rhythm; one hard beat followed three rapid, skipping ones.

Custo placed a hand on her shoulder. "Without Talia, you're the only means we have to attempt a cross. You have to dance, open the way, and then we can force him back into

Shadow. If you think you can manage to open the way at another venue, I am willing to find a stage—"

To dance her best?

No. It had to be *Giselle* and with CBT. A different venue would be too distracting; her dancing wouldn't be the same. But with her company behind her, with Jasper as her partner, she might just be able to get to that strange moment where music and movement came together to create magic. Anything else would be too forced, too artificial.

"It wouldn't be the same," she said, sighing.

Annabella needed a minute to think, to process this new information.

She looked over at the paintings on the wall. Talia's? Had she glimpsed what lay beyond her shadows and put them on canvas? No. Each was signed Kathleen O'Brien.

"Her mother," Custo said.

"What?"

"The paintings. They were done by Talia's mother. Talia's father is . . . from there." Custo paused. Annabella glanced back to find he'd lost a bit of color. "From the Shadowlands."

Talia, the banshee. Right. Annabella had seen that with her own eyes, too.

Custo lifted his hand off her shoulder and tucked a strand of hair behind her ear. "So what time do you need to be at the theater?"

Could she really dance? Was it right to dance?

"And what if *you* get hurt?" she asked.

"Angel," he said with emphasis. He relaxed, at ease on the bed. "I already died; there's not much he can do to me." Custo gave a fierce smile.

"Oh, right," Annabella mumbled. Her guardian angel looked less angelic with each passing moment.

But . . . She had to be absolutely, brutally honest, just in case something *did* go wrong. "Custo, I want this chance so bad that I'm afraid I would do anything to hold on to it. I don't trust myself."

"You need to," he said, stroking her cheek with the back of his fingertips. "I don't think the crossover would work if you didn't embrace the dance with everything that you are. If you have reservations, the magic of your talent might not shine through." He frowned. "I am curious why it never happened before. Why do you think that is?"

Good question. It had been bothering her, too. "I don't know. Maybe because I've been pushing myself harder than I ever have." Her life was falling apart because of it—no dates, no girlfriends, no fun. "Maybe because I'm finally in the spotlight. That sounds bad, I know, but when you are in the corps, you always need to be watching others, keeping your lines—you're not completely free." There were times when she wanted to let go, jump higher, interpret the music her own way, but couldn't because she had to hold her place. "Or, maybe because Giselle is a ghost. She rises from the grave to dance in a dark forest, which sounds an awful lot like the Shadowlands to me."

"Maybe it's a combination of the three. Maybe with this performance you're coming into your full gift of talent."

She'd dreamed of this moment her whole life.

"The time?" Custo prompted again. "When do we need to get going?"

Okay . . . She would dance. *Dance!* The wild, careening spin of her world suddenly righted itself on its axis. Wolves might jump out of the shadows, angels might fall from the sky, but if she could dance, then she would be all right. She could breathe. She could live. The circumstances were far from ideal, but she'd take whatever she could get.

It was impossible not to smile. "Four o'clock would be good. I'm going to need a good breakfast. Or brunch. Starving here," she added with a huff. The choco-brownie mush hadn't lasted long with her athletic metabolism. "And we have to run by my place for my stuff."

"Good," Custo said, a devilish grin flashing. "Now that we've got that settled, let's return to another train of thought . . ."

His eyes lowered to her mouth, mimicking her earlier suggestion.

Oh boy . . . Her high excitement abruptly condensed and lowered to a tight, bright burn deep in her center. Custo.

She'd had one lover before, long over, but never, even at the peak of that passion, had she felt a fraction of the desire Custo evoked with the rake of his lust-hungry eyes. How could it be that an angel and temptation were one and the same?

Annabella's breath caught as Custo leaned forward and found her jaw with his mouth, whispering against her skin as he traced a line toward her lips. "Your mind is a jumble, but it's clear the direction you're going. Decide already."

The thought of her body under his, his muscles bunching, broad shoulders flaring as he braced himself over her had the burn coiling into a sublimely torturous, yearning knot. She was happy, celebratory, and, *yes*, she wanted it all. She wanted him.

"There it is," he breathed. He brushed her lips with his. The flame leaped at her core. Delicious, searing.

Custo's mouth settled on hers in a hot and hard press of heat and she was adrift in molten sensation. Angel, demon, she didn't care. She was near senseless with the smooth friction of his mouth, the way he surrounded and consumed her body in the furnace of his. Custo must have moved because his hand supported her head, the length of his arm at her spine to hold her close. Her sexy protector. His chest against hers was hard, strong, and packed with strength. Her muscles answered by loosening in some places and straining in others in a strange coordination that took no years of practice, just human nature.

She barely gasped for air when he darkened the kiss to taste her. He found her hip and drew her snugly against his thigh. The movement sent a deep, glorious thrum through her system. She squirmed against him, trembling—*yes, please, more!*—her hand finding and fisting in his hair. He eased his palm under her ass to move her onto his lap. She helped, straddling him, not caring that the bedsheet slid to the floor to leave her tank and underwear exposed.

Annabella reciprocated by pulling his shirt from his pants—too bad he'd been so neat and pressed before—and feathered her fingers over the ripples of his stomach to the defined mound of his pecs. His skin was smooth, hot, his nipple a flat patch of satin.

Her body was talking now, and she'd spent her life learning to listen to its demands, coaxing its limits higher, stronger, faster. Custo was about to push those limits further, his wide hands hot on the bare skin of her thighs. His thumbs fingering the elastic of her panties.

Yes, yes. Naked would be good. Naked would be very good. She squirmed to give him access, but he grabbed her hips with both palms to hold her still, groaning.

"Stop that, Bella. I've been two years dead . . . damn it . . ." His voice was gruff against her mouth, as if he were fighting himself.

The torturous knot in her pelvis pulsed, ached. She'd known him a single day, but she was certain that there was only one thing to do to a Custo on the brink: push.

The bunch of his shirt caught her wrist. She reversed her direction, sliding her hand down to the tight waist of his pants. A damn belt held them firmly in place, so she wrapped her fingers around the band and pulled at it with a whine.

"Not yet," he murmured as his mouth broke away to graze her neck. She tilted her chin up to give him the length of her. To give him everything.

Warm breath brushed her cheek and sent a chill down

her back, prickling her skin. Custo nuzzled the hollow below her ear. His teeth grazing, just *there*.

A sudden flash of the wolf's mouth on that very spot had her blood stalling, her muscles freezing up with poison cold and a memory of fear. Her nerves quivered, but not in a good way. The wolf had wanted to be inside her, too. Had touched her just like that.

Custo froze as well, his mouth on the bad spot.

Reality shredded the moment.

She focused her lust-clouded eyes and took in the foreign apartment and remembered why she was there. Custo was so fantasy-hot, but . . . *This is too fast. Too much.*

"I'm not the wolf, Annabella," Custo said against her skin. His chest heaved against her, their shared rhythm now at odds.

"I know you're not," she said. *But . . .*

One coherent thought allowed a line of others to intrude: She didn't really know Custo at all. Angel? Insanity. All she really knew, really trusted, was dance.

Dance. And not the bedroom kind. She should be getting ready.

The last embers of her arousal doused with a sick, disappointed hiss. She shifted back, away from Custo, easing herself first on the bed, and then scrambled to stand at the side.

She took a steadying breath. "I'm . . . uh . . . interested. There's just a lot going on . . ." Her feeble attempt at an explanation dribbled away to nothing. The air was cold on her almost-naked skin. With him glowering at her like that, a long-dead vestige of her modesty kicked in, shaming her. Heat scorched her cheeks while she shivered.

But if he had something to say, she'd take it before running and hiding in the bathroom. She owed him that much. She trembled, waiting, hoping she hadn't completely screwed things up. Yeah, he was going to help her, and he was physically delicious, but, well, she was starting to like him, too.

Custo inclined his head, jaw flexing. "Of course. I don't know what I was thinking. I'm sorry."

He didn't have to apologize. That made her feel worse. "It's just—"

"Don't worry about it." The side of his mouth slowly tugged up, but she could see the muscles of his body were still tense. He stood, approached—the smell of him had her aching again—and kissed the top of her head. "I have some work to do before we leave for the city. I better get to it."

Custo stalked from the room, casting a glance over his shoulder to catch Annabella dragging on a pair of sweatpants, blue washed to pale gray. Lovely, pale legs, quickly, furtively hidden.

As she'd kissed him, her body moving against him, he'd caught her single, stressed thought: wolf.

Anger had every nerve snapping. What was he thinking? Not twelve hours ago the wolf had assaulted her. Without the intervention of Talia, who knows what might have happened?

Annabella was coping with so much. The least he could've given her was a little space. A little self-control. Even now, the thought of her under him had him adjusting his pants.

Custo sat at Adam's computer console in the living area and touched the screen to activate the monitor. He stared at the list of credit card charges for gala ticket sales, but the names and numbers were a blur of black and white. He flexed his hands hard to burn away the memory of Annabella's satiny skin. Her sexy, slender body.

Besides, he had plenty of business to take care of, old and new, before he could linger with her the way he wanted— the memory would have to last an eternity. Soon he would be caught, if not by a seriously pissed-off Shadowman, then by some holier-than-thou avenging angels, and dragged out of this world. He had a lot of work to do before that happened.

Custo forced his concentration onto the screen, tabbing to the contact addresses and telephone numbers associated with the credit card accounts.

He put in an earplug so he could talk as he worked. "Tommy?"

"Here," Tommy's gruff voice buzzed across the line. "Good to have you back, man."

"Good to be back. I trust you've been brought up to speed?"

"Yeah, I got it. Adam gave a general security briefing this morning, told us that we were all at your disposal. Says there's some scary shape-shifting Shadow monster after your girl."

His girl? Not yet, but Custo didn't correct him. "I want to get Segue operatives into as many seats as possible. Put together a team. You have whatever funds you need to buy back what you can. I'm sending the credit card list to you now. Be discreet."

Custo ended the call and selected another file, the Segue personnel manifest highlighting staff members from before and after his death. One of these trusted people was a traitor, a wraith collaborator. Adam had gotten a head start on reviewing the profiles, tagging names with thoughts and background information.

The gala was the night's priority, but the traitor was Custo's past life's unfinished business. Spencer, the asshole who'd killed him, had been so smug with his ridicule about the traitor, so confident in the success of the back-stabbing shithead who wanted to bring down Segue. It had to be somebody close to Adam to get Spencer off like that.

But who? These were all trusted men: Tommy, Jens, who'd apparently lost a lot of hair in the past two years, Gomez, Jackson . . . The list went on.

Setting up a team had never been this difficult.

Maybe Tommy could buy up the tickets, but someone else should head the security around the stage. Tommy's smooth, affable style would have been perfect for the gala, but Jens could take point. Break up and overlap the duties for double coverage.

Custo himself would be with Annabella at all times.

And Gomez? Jackson? How much did he really know about them?

Damn it. Custo gripped his skull in frustration. He didn't know whom to trust.

EIGHT

CUSTO smothered a smile as Annabella chanted "lashes, lashes, lashes" while she tore apart her cubby of a bathroom.

*Lashes? Well, oka*y . . . but he restrained himself from commenting on his willingness to participate in *any* and *all* of her unusual sexual fetishes and surveyed her apartment with hungry interest instead. He wanted to know everything about her.

Her studio was a narrow space jumbled with colorful . . . stuff. The kitchen sink behind him was tidy, a short fridge snugged under the counter. A coffeemaker and hot plate cluttered the other side of the sink. A futon ran along one wall, reclined in sleep position, sheet in a twist, bold patchwork blanket still in the half-cocoon shape of her body. Pillows littered the area in deep reds, blues, greens, some with fussy tassels, and a small old TV-DVD combo unit took one corner. Clothes were everywhere, but mostly piled on one of her two chairs. The place smelled sweet and feminine, no one scent predominating.

Photographs sat on every surface, glass fronts glinting as the afternoon sun poured in her window. The one nearest was of her with a middle-aged woman and a young man wearing a graduation gown. The three shared Annabella's coloring, and the way they squeezed one another's shoulders, faces angling for space in the photo, told Custo they were her family.

For the first time in years he felt a pang of jealousy, the kind that used to precede a flood of bitterness when he'd been at school and heard the other boys going on about their family vacations. Not that he begrudged her a family where he had none, but he wanted to be in that photo, a day in the life of holding her tight, mugging for a camera.

Stop. But the want sliced through him anyway, cold and harsh. There would be no photos. Their relationship could not possibly end that way, and he'd learned a long time ago that fantasies only made reality worse.

"Yes!" Annabella shouted. He turned as she emerged, waving a small package in her hand, a set of spidery fake eyelashes. As if her natural ones needed any help. "Now just let me run the garbage down the hall, and we can go."

"I'll do it," he said. No need for her to carry the trash when he was there.

"No, no, I take out my own. But can you . . . uh . . . watch me from the door?"

Of course he'd watch her; he wasn't taking his eyes off her until she was out of danger. He'd have followed her, but his earplug beeped, and he let her drift down the hallway, plastic bag in hand, so she wouldn't be bothered by the security details for the night's performance.

It was a simple, but comprehensive plan: Annabella would dance, opening a way for the wolf to return to his Otherworld territory, per his wishes. Segue soldiers would be in the audience, backstage, and surrounding the building, exit strategy in place for Annabella, should anything go wrong. City Center personnel had been briefed about extra security posing as stage crew and were cooperative with Segue's measures. Custo would be side stage, prepared to give the wolf extra incentive should Annabella attract his interest again.

"Custo here."

"We're in place," Jens said. "We have the stage area covered and seventeen operatives with tickets for tonight's performance."

Custo stood in the apartment doorway while Annabella

ducked down the hall. He leaned out when she rounded the corner. With an abrupt clatter of metal noise, she was headed back toward him. She held up a finger, mouthing "one minute" and knocked on a neighbor's door.

He nodded to her, but spoke to Jens. "I want minimal disruption to the flow of things backstage."

Jens's com crackled again. "Where will you be?"

Custo thought that had been understood, but it bore restating so there was absolutely no mistake. "I'll be with Annabella."

Annabella stopped at her neighbor Peter's door and signaled to Custo that she needed a minute. *Yeah, right.* She needed way more than a minute; the way Custo looked at her had the liquid heat in her blood short-circuiting her brain. She got no relief since he had to stay nearby to protect her, to keep the wolf in the shadows. Her dependence was as unsettling as her attraction to him.

She had to concentrate on *Giselle*. The rest of the world, Custo-the-angel included, she couldn't entirely trust. All that was too different, too strange, too frightening to grasp. She had to focus on what she knew.

But, heaven help her, if not for the looming performance, she could easily do something very stupid. She almost had earlier that day. He'd just looked so good and smelled so good, and then he'd *felt* so good, better than anything she'd ever imagined with or without the aid of movies and steamy fiction.

Her sanity was hanging by a thread. Only dance could save her.

But first she had to deal with Peter.

She rapped on his door. Guilt had her gnawing on a fingernail, a habit she'd taken great pains to break. Talking to him was torture, but he'd worry if she didn't show up at her place for a few days without letting him know. She always had in the past. And he'd been so good to her when she first moved into the building, so green to the city that she almost backed out of her lease to live with a bunch of other dancers when she really wanted to be on her own.

Peter opened right up, his expression avid.

"Annabella." His voice was deeper than usual, almost gruff. He reached out a hand to touch her, but must have thought better of it because he dropped it back to his side to grip his thigh. And he was shaking.

"Hey, Peter . . . I just wanted to let you know that I'm probably not going to be around for the next few days. I'm . . . um . . ." Annabella heard Custo on his call, something about stage security, and glanced toward him.

Peter leaned his head out to look himself, and abruptly pulled back, wincing in pain. Yeah, Custo was hard to compete with, especially with that possessive lock his gaze had on her.

Peter's expression changed from excited to betrayal. "I don't understand," he said, almost a growl. "*We* should be together. You came to *me*."

Annabella flushed to hear him admit his interest. He never had before, though she'd suspected he was working up to asking her out.

What was with impossible men today? Annabella had never meant to lead him on. She had no idea when his feelings had gone past friendship to more. Maybe he'd always wanted more. He was attractive—tall, with dark-toned skin and expressive black eyes, though in his late thirties, a little old for her. And maybe there had been a window of opportunity somewhere in the past couple months when romantic feelings could have developed. But once Venroy had asked her to be Giselle, all her attention had abruptly shifted to the studio.

"I am so sorry. We just didn't work out that way." It was particularly awful that gorgeous, glowering Custo was standing in the doorway of her place while she tried to let Peter down easy. Talk about adding insult to injury.

"I could take care of you," Peter said. "Give you what you need."

She'd been about to offer the standard ongoing friendship, but his last comment, way too desperate, stole the words from her tongue. The conversation had just gone from uncomfortable to disquieting. Time to go.

"You've already helped me so much," Annabella said. "I have to go. I'm late for the theater already. I just didn't want you to worry if I disappeared for a couple of days. After the performance, I'm probably going back to my mom's." A lie, but Peter didn't have to know that.

"The performance?"

"Yeah." He should've remembered; she talked of little else for so long. "Tonight's the big night. My dream come true. I get to dance *Giselle* for CBT." She stepped back to signal a close to the conversation. She really did have to go.

"The dance is your dream?" He leaned forward to follow her, but pulled back with a hiss.

"You know me." She shrugged and took another step back. And another. "Everything is dance, dance, dance."

"I'll be there," he said.

Oh, no. The last thing she needed was more stress. Besides, if poor Peter tried to see her, or . . . or . . . come on to her, Custo was likely to wipe the floor with him.

"I'm pretty sure it's sold out," she said, turning to her apartment.

"It's your dream," Peter repeated to her back. "I'll be there."

Custo leaped out of the Segue SUV at the City Center's Fifty-sixth Street entrance and reached back for Annabella. What he got was her tackle box, retrofitted to hold stage makeup. She clambered out in jeans and an emerald green peacoat, wooly gray scarf at her neck, a massive duffel on her shoulder. Her hair was pulled back in a slick, tight ponytail that made her face teenage young, accenting her luminous skin and exquisite eyes. Her excitement brought faint, delicate color to her cheeks. The air around her crackled with energy.

"I'm late," she said, but she grinned.

She was hours early, so she had to be very nervous if she was worried about the time. "All you have to do is dance," Custo said. "I'll be just offstage, watching you every second. Everything is going to be fine."

"It has to be perfect," she corrected, and stalked toward the door.

Custo slammed the door closed behind Annabella and hit the roof of the SUV for the driver to move off. Other Segue vehicles crowded the street, but so far it seemed Adam hadn't elected to use his dispensation from the government to close off the block. If everything went as planned, the measure wouldn't be necessary.

Custo moved to follow Annabella, but a tingling feeling had him turning back.

Luca. The last time Custo had seen the angel was in a backward glance thrown at Heaven's Gate just before plunging into the water and making a break for the Shadowlands. Now Luca stood on the other side of the street. Come to fetch him, or worse.

Though traffic passed on Fifty-sixth, Custo met Luca's gaze and held it. The world disappeared for a moment; only Custo's heart, pounding furiously, and Annabella, thoughts full of dance, existed.

One night, Custo begged. He fisted his hands to control himself. He couldn't leave Annabella now.

Luca's hard expression didn't change, though Custo knew the angel had the same capacity to read minds as he.

One night. That's all I ask. I have to help her.

Luca frowned. *You never understood.*

Angels' minds were so much easier to discern than mortals'—clear, uncluttered, full of purpose.

One night, Custo repeated. He didn't wait for an answer—there was only one: he was staying. As he turned away from Luca, breaking the grip of his gaze, Custo could feel the shear of the universe, as if he were ripping himself out of its fabric to hurtle headlong into his own darkness.

So be it. Custo doubled his step to catch up to Annabella, who was just opening one of the building's brassy doors. He could feel Luca's eyes at his back, his condemnation rolling across the street. Well, Luca could chastise him for eternity, but later. After tonight. There was no way anyone was going to drag him away from Annabella's side until the wolf was back in the Shadowlands. This performance had to succeed.

And afterward? Annabella would have to develop a mastery over the magic, just as she had her dance. Talia could guide her, following the birth of her babies. This wasn't the way he wanted to leave. He'd wanted to help her himself.

Annabella hurried across the lobby. "Where's the warm-up class?" she asked a harried-looking woman carrying a frothy pile of white.

"Fifth-floor studio. They're starting now." The woman had a needle dimpling her blouse, thread cascading over a breast. Must be someone in charge of costumes.

"Thanks," Annabella said, hurrying to the elevator and hitting the up arrow.

"Class? You don't have time for a class," Custo said, utterly bewildered. He'd wanted to brief her on his team's assessment of the building's exits, introduce her to the team members she'd be able to turn to for help, take a moment to tell her that everything was going to be fine, to trust him.

But she was beyond that. The elevator *bing*ed almost instantly. "Oh, no no no." She shook her head as she unbuttoned her coat. *Class is essential.* "I have to warm up. I have to be ready."

"But Anna—"

She shoved her coat into his arms. "I can't dance well to-night without taking class. And we both know I need to dance well." She flashed him a smile. "So deal with it."

They took an elevator to a private dressing room, secured by Segue away from the other dancers for their protection. Annabella dropped her bag on a chair and started to strip. "Turn around," she said, but not before he caught a glimpse of her bra, shocking fuchsia lace, as she peeled off a snug sweater in cornflower blue.

He turned, but watched her anyway in the reflection of the dressing room mirrors, hungry like a man at his last meal: Pale, slender body, naked. Raspberry nipples soon covered by a flesh-colored insult to women's underwear. His gaze roamed down the long, flat flanks of her legs, which dimpled her ass as she bent over, and formed lovely, smooth planes to her knees. A swell at her calves tensed as she found what she wanted in her bag and stood. Beauty.

"Custo!" Annabella complained, though she smirked as her chest and face swept with color. *He doesn't seem mad about this morning*, she thought.

No, he wasn't mad. Not at her. He was looking for another opportunity.

It was a crime to cover that body with a dingy leotard, black tights, and faded sweats. She grasped some new shiny satin toe shoes and first-aid tape and took off down the hall to a studio. Inside, dancers gripped ballet barres at the walls and freestanding barres lined up in the center of the room. A woman was clapping a perfect, even rhythm to keep time for the dancers.

Custo tapped his earplug as Annabella took her position and joined in the deep squats, what the woman called pliés.

"Jens here."

"I'm on the fifth floor. She's doing some sort of dance class." As an afterthought, he added, "Adam here yet?"

"No."

Custo hoped Talia wasn't in labor. Those babies needed a little more time before they could handle this world.

"Everyone else checked in?"

"All except for Tommy," Jens said.

Custo cursed. "Find him. Now."

"Shhhhhh!"

Custo brought his attention back the dancers, who were staring at him. Annabella managed to roll her eyes from a very interesting upside-down stretch. *He's gonna get kicked out,* she thought.

"Custo out," he mumbled to Jens.

The class resumed.

The next fifty-five minutes were a revelation. Whatever fragility he might have attributed to Annabella shattered with the acute precision with which she "warmed" her body. The teacher, a fellow dancer, led the group through a series of rigorous exercises that outmatched any martial training he'd mastered, and then some. No show of tension betrayed the difficulty of the steps, though their feet were angled into tidy, unnatural positions. Their flexibility was nothing short of gymnastic, but the transitions between their movements had an ethereal fluidity that elevated mere training to art.

Annabella might not know the first thing about defending herself, but she was far from weak. She was flexible steel, personified. Her slight body, so trim and smooth, was primed for power. Not one ounce of ease remained on her frame, yet somehow she was still soft. Vulnerable.

"Annabella!" a pretty boy called to her. He had some muscle to him and moved with a cocky swagger. "You want to run through a few things?" His junk was straining his tights, but he seemed to revel in the effect, *yeah, look all you want,* which made Custo want to knock his mocking smile right off his face.

Annabella, breathless, walked over to him, wiping her

forehead with her wrist. "Yeah. Sure, Jasper. Let's hit the lifts first."

The pretty boy, Jasper, had the nerve to put his hand on her inner thigh, an inch from paradise, and lift her above his head. Annabella soared upward while Custo bit back a snarl. Too high, too intimate, too . . . much the wrong man touching her there.

Custo probed Jasper's thoughts, but they were all focused on the movement.

Jasper suddenly shifted, near dropping Annabella into a sweeping spin against his body, her arms embracing with a love-longing that made Custo's throat tight. He'd have looked away, but he was rooted, hands clenching, ready to tear them apart.

Jasper glanced over to gauge Custo's reaction, his stance cocky, his mind and body asking, *What do you think of that?*

"Leave him alone, Jasper," Annabella murmured. But Custo caught her own darted gaze, eyes bright with interest.

As soon as possible, as soon as Custo got her alone, he'd show her his version of the very same movements. Perhaps not as graceful, but infinitely more gratifying.

"Let's do the *sissonne* crosses." Annabella peeled off her shabby excuse for a sweatshirt and threw it to the side of the room. On her leotard, perspiration winged beneath her breasts, accenting her curves, while tiny droplets trailed down her chest, combining at the cleft of her cleavage.

Custo swallowed to wet his dry throat.

Annabella and the pretty boy moved to a corner. Jasper said, "Two, three, *and*," and she leaped, his hands high at her waist. The resulting movement was antigravity, the perfect union of strength and grace, male and female. They moved like their bodies knew each other, knew the rhythms of breath and blood without any reference to thought. Annabella didn't even have to look, and that pretty-boy bastard was there, holding her. Hands all over her body.

Custo was shaking, silent, by the time they finished their practice.

The curve of Annabella's lips told him she was pleased with herself. Her mind was full of possibilities for the night, with him, should the performance go as planned. Custo was in complete agreement.

"What now?" Custo said, his hands itching to touch her. He had so much to do, but all he wanted to do was shut himself in the studio with Annabella.

"Now I get ready," Annabella answered, sweatshirt flung over her shoulder. She sashayed out of the room, hips ever so slightly swinging. He wanted to turn her to face him, fill his palms with her backside, do his own lift, and demonstrate his own flawless technique.

She strutted to her dressing room. Custo followed, biding his time.

As soon as the dressing room door closed, he had her up against the wall. His body pressed into hers, her heart pounding furiously against him as she held her breath. She was hot, sweaty, and musky with it. But her eyes sparkled up at him, waiting for what he would do next. He was close enough for her breath to brush his chin. Her upper teeth scraped her lower lip, plumping it. She wanted to be kissed.

She'd been showing off for an hour, powerful and loving every minute. She obviously wanted to revel in her high a little longer.

He didn't kiss her. That was too easy, too expected, and they didn't have time to finish anything the kiss would start, which she had to know. This was a tease, a flirty taunt to both tantalize him and see if she could trust him to pull back. She could, but since he wanted her so bad, there was no reason she shouldn't want him back just as badly, just as acutely as he desired her.

Custo turned her to face the wall, trapping her in the confines of his arms. He held her tightly against him, her body just beginning to tremble, but he didn't so much as flick the thin strap of leotard from her shoulder.

He lowered his mouth to the slightly damp column of her neck, to the spot that had set her off before and spoke against her skin. "I don't know what the wolf did to scare you—you don't seem nearly as scared now as you were a few hours ago."

Her hips shifted in a feeble attempt to get away from him. Feeble for her; he knew her strength. If she really wanted to break away, he'd have let her.

"I'll answer your questions, though," he said.

"I didn't ask—"

Custo tightened his hold to shut her up. "Yes, I want you. And, yes, it drives me crazy to see another man touching you and holding you."

"He's *gay*."

"I don't care. I want that privilege." Custo exhaled a harsh breath, noting how her skin pimpled with goose bumps. He wrapped himself more fully around her to keep her "warm."

"But I won't force you. I am not the wolf."

She was utterly still now, hardly breathing.

"So think hard what you want when you look at me that way, when you sway those hips like that. I will take what's offered and damn the consequences."

Custo touched her mind and was surprised to find a very defined series of thoughts. She was scared he'd let go of her. Scared her knees would give. Scared they wouldn't have a chance to finish what they'd started.

He was a little shaken himself, but he forced himself on to other pressing matters.

"We need to talk about tonight, review the security plan."

Annabella was silent for a moment before answering. Finally, she shook her head. "No. I'm not going to think about that at all." Her voice was raspy, and she gave a little cough to clear it. "I can't, you understand?"

After seeing the mastery and grace of that dance class, he had to admit he did. Her focus had to be entirely on her performance. The rest was up to him.

Her weight shifted to her own feet, and he released her. He'd wanted to reassure her, show her that he had everything under control, to tell her that she could depend on him, but she was beyond that now. Had to be.

He attempted to follow her thought leaps. It was easier now that he was coming to know her better. She was retracing the steps of the story, and he could almost feel the veil between earth and the Shadowlands trembling.

By the time she sat at her dressing table, she was in deep concentration. He spent the next half hour checking in with his team—still no word from Adam—while Annabella transformed her girlish face into the ethereal appearance of a ghost. She pancaked her skin white. She lined her eyes black, adhering the lashes to her already thick, dark fringe. She shaded the hollow of her cheeks just so, then stood, holding her leotard over her breasts, and handed him a white-dipped sponge.

"Wipe me down, would you?" she asked his reflection in the mirror.

He didn't know what she meant, but would do anything she asked. So he took the sponge.

"My shoulders, neck right into my hairline, and my back," she clarified. Underneath her words was an implicit invitation. Among the complex movements of choreography filling her mind, she'd decided something.

Custo stepped close to her, their gazes locked in the glass. He couldn't act on his desires, so he bent to his task and stroked her with the sponge. Her character was the ghost of an almost-bride, so he swept the color from her skin. He erased the pulse of life from the curves of her back and arms. He stroked the white across her shoulders to the dip below her graceful throat and the valley between her breasts.

His head was bent, mouth at her ear, arms circling her waist when she spoke, her voice thin. "My costume is on the rack."

He could feel her heart pounding in her chest—his was, too—and forced himself to take a step backward.

She reached to take the frothy white dress from a hanger, and keeping her back to him, her face to a bland corner of the dressing room, dropped her warm-up clothes and donned the costume. Her hands molded the bodice to her frame and she backed up to him again.

"Would you?" she asked.

The back gaped open, lined with matching rows of tiny hooks and eyes, too small for his hands. He did the best he could with his clumsy fingers and when he brought his gaze back up, found Annabella utterly transformed into an other-worldly bride.

Someone knocked on the door, calling, "Ready in five," then moved down the hall.

"I guess this is it," she said.

"Don't worry about anything," Custo said. "Just dance."

She inhaled deeply and exhaled with a shudder. "Let's go."

From side stage, Custo could hear the rumble of the audience and the stray, discordant notes of the orchestra. The Segue team was either already seated or circulating until curtain.

Jens was on the opposite side of the stage. He'd simplified the Segue uniform to an all-black ensemble that might pass for stage crew. Only the jacket seemed unusual, but that couldn't be helped. He had to hide his gun somewhere. Everyone was in place. Everyone was ready.

The orchestra went suddenly silent and the audience muted to a murmur, then a general hush. The music began, each instrument weaving an eerie thread of the story.

The other dancers, brides in death, comprised the first movement. Then the stage cleared with a bustle and Custo's space was crammed with dancers heaving for breath, watching from the wings.

A new phrase of music began, mournful and romantic, and Annabella stepped into view, a maiden ghost, a wili. The light of the stage shifted slightly with her appearance, deepening with color, with compelling light, with magic.

Annabella. There could be no doubt; she was born to dance.

She mingled with the other wilis, and then exited to the other side with the group while cocky, pretty-boy Jasper took the stage.

Gay, Custo reminded himself. But he still didn't like anyone touching her.

Custo peered across the way, trying to get a glimpse of her and caught only a bit of white tutu. Not good enough. There were at least a dozen dancers in white tutus—could be her, could be some other woman. He extended his mind to see if he could glean her well-being from her thoughts: a shoe ribbon was too tight. Her throat was dry. The shreds of thought surfaced in the cacophony of mental chatter coming from the thousands in the audience and did him no good.

He touched his earbud. "Jens, how's Annabella?"

"She's fine," Jens answered. "Standing right here on her tippy toes to see over the—"

Custo's earbud crackled. "Oh, shit," Tommy's voice cut in, breathing heavy, shouts in the background, cars honking, a crash. "Wraiths."

Custo's heart lurched. "Say again?"

"A group of them! It's a trap!" A wraith screeched, high and painfully shrill in Custo's earpiece. "He can't hold them off for long."

Annabella joined Jasper onstage where he grieved at her grave.

"Who? Who can't hold them off forever?" But Custo already knew.

Onstage, the couple mirrored each other's movements—Jasper, strong and earthy, Annabella, light and ethereal, both utterly unaware of the nightmare unfolding outside the theater.

"Adam. He's out there alone."

NINE

GISELLE'S broken heart pulled her gaze to the dirt floor of the forest as she rose above from the freshly turned earth of her grave. She kept her hands folded on her breast, to hold the fragments of her love within her. Prince Albrecht would marry another, a royal lady, and not some peasant girl who knew nothing of the world. His betrayal killed her, yet she couldn't help but love him still.

But she wasn't a peasant girl any longer.

She was a wili, a ghost, and would dance forever.

Joining the host of other wilis caught in the midnight hush of the wood, Giselle tiptoed down the long diagonal sweep of dancers to bow to her wili queen, Myrtha.

Everything was as it should be, quiet and peaceful. Annabella's body felt strong, ready for this moment, though a chill of anxiety had her nerves snapping. The sensation went beyond opening-night jitters, beyond nerves, to fear.

On one side of her was the woodland backdrop; on the other, the black yawn of theater where the audience sat, voyeurs to Giselle's tragic love story. Annabella looked up and strained her eyes beyond the side curtains of the stage: A bright angel stood beyond the false trees, his pale green gaze fixed on her. He was her hope, her protection. With him watching, her dance would be lighter, her heart would be lighter.

If Custo were near, she would be safe.

Giselle rose from her deep curtsy and began the series of arabesque turns that marked her advent into the Other. Heart hammering in her chest, she stirred the air, spun her magic, and reached for a world beyond her own.

* * *

"Where are you, Tommy?" Custo bit out the words, keeping his gaze fixed on Annabella. She was dancing in the center of the stage, surrounded by the other dancers. There was no sign of the wolf. Yet.

Custo strode to the edge of the curtain. Should he grab her now? Stop the performance? Abort the mission? Would there be a second chance? *Damn it.*

"Why aren't you in your seat?" Custo stretched his mind to locate Tommy, found him quickly, by the rear, ground-floor exits. Custo invaded his thoughts: the soldier had made up his mind to join the fray as soon as he signed off the call. But on whose side was Tommy going to fight?

Using Tommy as a reference, Custo pushed slightly outward to the mental press of the city. Looking for Adam was like looking for a known star, but in an alien night sky. Nothing familiar, then—

There. Adam, burning with single-minded determination to survive.

Tommy buzzed in Custo's ear, answering, "I spotted a wraith and followed him rather than take my seat with the rest of the audience. Do you want me to pull the others from their positions?"

And leave Annabella unprotected and vulnerable?

"Recall only those in the back rows. Keep the stage surrounded and keep me apprised of the situation with the wraiths."

Custo listened in as Tommy called soldiers by name and directed them to the back of the building.

"Move fast," Custo added. Adam was out there. Talia and her babies needed him. If Adam died—well, there'd be one more angel—but a hell of a lot of good that'd do for the wraith war on Earth. Adam and Talia were mortality's only hope.

From his position, Custo had only a partial view of the audience. They were rapt, attention on the stage, but a few rose and sidestepped down their aisles. He assumed others farther back were doing the same. It would have to do.

Jasper caught Annabella in the first of their high lifts, the one Custo had seen earlier in the studio, with Annabella supported high in the air at her hips. The movement looked effortless, but all things considered—wolf and wraiths— Custo wanted her two feet on the floor.

Wraiths weren't in the plan, certainly not a coordinated public attack. They had to have been tipped off by someone inside Segue. The traitor. How had Adam survived so long with someone sabotaging every effort to fight?

Anger beat furiously through Custo's system. He clenched his hands—the last time someone betrayed Adam, they hadn't lived to regret it. This time would be no different.

A rustle behind Custo had him glancing back, but he saw only ghostly ballerinas in white waiting their turn to go back onstage.

The edge on his nerves had him looking closer, peering harder. There was no one unexpected, except . . .

In the blackest shadows, the figure of a man. He was dressed in black as well, his head covered by the hood of a sweatshirt, and bowed, difficult to see. His body seemed fit, a good 220 pounds and broad enough to have some muscle.

Not a stagehand. Not a Segue soldier.

Who was he? Custo extended his consciousness toward the man. Nothing.

He tried again, alarm sending a cold thrill of dread down his spine. His mind found only empty shadow, which left two possibilities: wolf or wraith.

Custo moved back, his stomach muscles tensing, his balance shifting to the balls of his feet, ready to fight. The dancers shuffled around him, filling his spot as he eased into the open area of the wing.

He was in full view of the man now, who had not so much

as twitched. The stillness around him was uncanny, unnatural, a vacuum.

If fae reacted badly to the presence of angels, as Talia had, then the man was not the wolf, or he'd be cringing. More likely, he was a wraith, part of the assault on the building, lying in wait until a prescribed moment when he would attack.

"Got one backstage," Custo said, alerting the Segue team. "Look for others."

Wraiths by definition were obscenely strong and couldn't die, characteristics that drew thousands of people to relinquish their humanity for eternal youth.

A series of "all clears" came from the rest of the Segue team inside the theater.

The fight was outside, except for this one lone wraith. Coincidence? Custo didn't care. The monster was getting a bullet to the head, then dragged out for transport and a lengthy wait in a cell until Talia delivered and could scream him to death.

In his peripheral vision, Custo marked the doorway that led to the outer hallway. He reached for his gun, not to fire—the report would disturb the performance—but to add stability to his fist. Then he'd force the wraith out and plug him in the hall. Several times.

The dancers aligned again, a commotion of silent white. In a blur they streamed onto the stage.

Custo stalked closer to his target, noting the subtle rise of the wraith's chest as he took an unnecessary breath. Strange. Why wasn't the monster moving? Why wasn't it ripping the air with its shriek?

Then his head came up, the hood dropping to reveal his face.

The blood in Custo's veins abruptly reversed its course. Not the wolf. Not a wraith. Those angry black eyes belonged to Death.

"Oh God," Custo said.

"Ironic you should call on Him now," Shadowman answered with a dark smile. He shifted away from the wall to standing. The planes of his face freckled with minute black splotches, burns, which fell in dust to the floor as the skin beneath rapidly healed.

The fae were harmed by angels, yes, but this was the lord of the fae, who had stood at Heaven's Gate too many times to count.

Shadowman advanced, and Custo stumbled backward, glancing quickly at the fae forest growing around Annabella, her gift blooming to the night.

Custo raised his hands to hold Death at bay. "An angel has already come for me. I've agreed to go when this is done. One night is all I asked."

"I am not concerned with the work of angels. Why would I be? I am nothing to them." Shadowman's voice was low, menacing. "I want only you. You who deceived me."

Custo planted his feet, flexed his strength to keep him in one spot. "I had to get out of Heaven. I had to return to Earth. Lives depend on me. Please, I have to stay."

Shadowman stalked closer. "How many souls, do you think, have pleaded before me? I have refused pain and anguish the likes of which you cannot begin to imagine. Spare me your sad tale of woe; I have heard far worse than yours and remained unmoved."

But . . . "One of the fae, one of your own kind, threatens that dancer. She is vulnerable, innocent. But look what she can do!"

Custo looked over to the woman weaving magic not ten paces from his position. Annabella glowed with the intensity of her gift.

A sneer curled Shadowman's lips. He didn't deign to look at the stage. "My Kathleen painted the unimaginable vistas of the twilight Shadowlands, and she still passed *beyond*, as all must do. You want to help your woman, yet you contrived to keep me from mine."

"I never said Kathleen was in Heaven," Custo argued.

"We can argue the subtleties of deceit on our way. I'm sure you know more on that score than most of your angelic host."

"I'm not going anywhere," Custo said, loud enough to get *shhhh*ed by the stagehand near the curtain. "She needs me. I won't desert her."

"I think you will." Shadowman laid a hand on Custo's shoulder. At the point of contact, burning cold spread through his body as filaments of Shadow threaded into his system, mingling with his blood. His nerves spasmed, and his marrow curdled when touched by the dark, shady tendrils.

"Come," Death said.

Custo fought the compulsion, his limbs, heart, and brain rebelling with every cell of strength. But still he moved forward.

"You should know," Death added with a mean slide of his eyes, "that I would not have any power over you if your soul wasn't dark and shadowed already. In the strange, ordered chaos of the universe, this is your choice."

Dark, shadowed, even ruined, yes. But not my choice. Custo tried to deny Shadowman's hold, but still moved a single step, then another. Custo's own hand reached out to open the side stage exit, and though his eyes strained for one more glimpse of Annabella, his legs carried him away from her.

Custo could breathe, but he couldn't speak. *What do you want with me?* he asked with his mind. His skin tightened with the thickening web of Shadow; he could almost feel himself grow dim as it leached vitality from his core. Somehow he didn't think Death was going to deliver him to Heaven a second time, not that he ever belonged there.

The music of the ballet suddenly muted with the close of the heavy door. The melody of the story was gone. Only the whine of the strings and the burr of the bass lingered.

"We made a bargain once," Shadowman said. They strode the back halls of the center, their footfalls hitting the floor in perfect time. "I intend to use you in another."

Custo made to respond, but couldn't even grunt. Shadow choked him. By now Jens had to know that he was gone. He'd adjust the coverage for Annabella, or maybe . . . maybe stop the performance because of the wraith attack.

Custo's hands cramped, so he knew he'd been reflexively trying to grip them. Even the clamoring beat of his heart was yoked in Shadow. *Where are you taking me?*

"If my Kathleen is not in Heaven, then she must be . . . elsewhere." Death's voice lost its loose sarcasm and took on bitterness. "She doesn't belong there. *I* broke the laws of Faerie, not her. I used my power to cross. What justice is served by sending her there?"

Custo had no choice but to remain silent. He didn't know anything about justice anyway.

"There is no justice," Shadowman concluded. "So I intend to make another bargain, this time with Hell. A simple trade, like ours at Heaven's Gate. You, for my Kathleen."

The Shadow kept Custo from shaking involuntarily. They reached the back doors that led to the street. From inside, Custo could hear a wraith screech, gunfire, screams, among sirens.

Shadowman slapped his hand against the door and stepped out into the melee. Leashed, Custo followed at his heels, the fetid stench of wraiths blowing up his nostrils, into a scene of chaos illuminated by the overcast hover of clouds reflecting city light back on itself. The street was unofficially cordoned off by abandoned cars. Bodies, human and wraith, littered the area. A cluster of wraiths had made human shields of two Segue operatives, while several other wraiths crouched like spiders on the building walls, ready to strike.

Adam, his back to a building on the other side of the street, his face crusted with blood, whipped to aim his rifle at Shadowman and Custo as they exited. The wraiths let out a quailing chorus, cringing from Death.

In the past, Shadowman had cut down the wraiths with great sweeps of his scythe. His duty for all time was to render the dead out of the mortal world, and none were more dead than the immortal wraiths. The smell alone was proof of that. Custo had witnessed Death's coming before, called by his daughter's banshee scream, at the West Virginia location of Segue. Shadowman had struck with a father's vengeance then, but he didn't seem to give a damn now.

Death descended the concrete steps, and Custo was compelled to follow.

Adam lowered his gun slightly. "Custo?"

Custo couldn't answer. Adam would know what to do for Annabella. Adam always knew what to do.

"Custo!" Adam repeated, louder. When he didn't get an answer a second time, he transferred his attention to Shadowman. Custo caught the dawn of realization on Adam's face.

"Shadowman, stop!" Adam glanced sharply to his side at the wraiths cringing from Death.

Shadowman halted and shot Adam a pained look. "Every moment I linger here is a moment of pain Kathleen endures in Hell."

"I need Custo to help me fight," Adam said.

"I need to trade him for Kathleen," Death returned, icy.

Adam's gaze flicked to Custo's face, but Custo knew Adam could read nothing from his Shadow-webbed expression.

"I'm sorry for her. For you," Adam said, looking back at Death. "But I cannot fight this war and protect Talia at the same time."

Custo noted the slow descent of a skinny female wraith dropping to the pavement at the corner of a building near Adam, but obstructed from his view.

"My daughter can protect herself." Shadowman turned, dragging Custo along.

"She can't do *anything*," Adam shouted after him. "She's pregnant. Every time she touches Shadow, every time she uses her voice, she risks both her life and the lives of our twins. We are besieged until she delivers."

Shadowman stopped again. The street's shadows throbbed around him.

"What would Kathleen want?" Adam asked.

Death bowed his head.

"Didn't she give her life to bring Talia into this world?"

"Twenty-nine years of pain in Hell," Shadowman ground out.

"That was her trade," Adam said. "Twenty-nine years for a daughter and two grandchildren. It was a *good* bargain. The *best* of bargains." Adam's eyes took on a strange sheen. "I need Custo to see that Kathleen's legacy is safe. Join us, help us end this war, and we can find a way to free Kathleen that much faster."

"You can't help me free her, mortal," Shadowman sneered. Then he threw his head back and roared to the sky. The air convulsed with his rage and ripples of power blew the windows out of the immediate buildings.

But Custo felt a contraction within him, a shudder of darkness, and then a scoring rip as the tendrils of Shadow released him. He fell to the ground in a heap, his head landing on shattered glass. Blinking through a haze of red, Custo saw Death continue alone into the night, then disappear beyond the strobe of police lights.

Custo planted a hand on the ground. His arm shook as he pushed himself to sitting. As he brought up his head, the female wraith darted toward Adam's turned back, her jaw unlocking, jagged teeth extending. Custo gulped free air and shouted, "Adam!"

* * *

Giselle drew Prince Albrecht to the side of the clearing as a line of wilis flew down the stage like a severe arrow of white. Myrtha stepped out from the trees, holding branches of rosemary to symbolize remembrance. Like Giselle, each of the wili spirits had died betrayed by a man who'd pledged to love them.

The music lowered with condemnation as Myrtha cursed Albrecht in the language of the dance. She pointed at him, *you,* she circled her hands over her head, *will dance,* and then she crossed her wrists in front of her, *until you are dead.*

Giselle rushed forward, placing herself between her love and her queen, stretching her arms out to the sides to protect him.

It was too late. Myrtha had no pity. The wilis rearranged themselves on the edge of the clearing, cold and indifferent to the lovers.

Giselle did not join them. If Albrecht had to dance, then she would dance with him. Together they would pass the darkest hours of night, and her love for him would see him to the dawn.

She tiptoed to the center of the clearing. The music deepened and the notes lengthened, a sad violin singing over the dread of the curse.

She began a slow *développé* to the side, stretching the limits of her ghostly form, then stroked the air and inclined into a melancholy, turning arabesque. The movements were effortless, boneless, as if, indeed, the laws of nature no longer applied to her.

Holding on to the moment, Annabella slowly focused her eyes on her surroundings. The stage, the two-dimensional trees, and the audience were all there, solid, but superimposed on a vast, darkening landscape of magic. The Shadowlands.

She'd done it again.

Her heart clutched. Her fear had the magic wavering, but

she steadied herself with the knowledge that an angel watched over her.

Albrecht supported a soft turn. Where before the promenade had been a negotiation of skill and balance, now the movement was easy. She didn't have to think or try at all. All she had to do was feel, and want, and the magic would comply.

It could be like this always, his voice said in her mind.

Their communication was suddenly just as easy as the movements they'd practiced over and over, just another level of their performance communion.

A dream. It can't last, she answered to herself.

Albrecht lifted her into a soaring spiral over his head. In the regular world, the lift was a difficult study in trusting her partner, but now she was flying. Gravity had no pull on her.

In the Shadowlands, anything is possible, especially forever. Let's linger a while.

Yes. There was a reason she needed to stay in this between place, though it was fading from her mind fast. All she had to do was dance, dance her best, and someone else—who?— would take care of the rest. Would see her safely home.

Her body arched to stretch the magic. To see just how high she could go. And Albrecht was with her, his caresses no longer performance-perfect, but sensual, a pleasure that stroked deeper than the surface clutches they'd rehearsed over and over again. His heat at her back sent a ripple of carnal desire over her skin, emanating from him but stirring her. Tantalizing her.

Join me, he coaxed, wordless. *Stay in this wood with me.*

It's not real.

It's as real as you choose to make it. The low timbre of his voice mixed with the hum of her blood. *Stay.*

Annabella sighed into the next lift, the worlds spinning around her. Hadn't she dreamed of feeling like this her entire life? Wasn't this what she'd worked for, punished her body daily to achieve?

Stay with me and dance.

Was it possible?

The first movement ended and the audience called their approval, the emotion shaking the tree branches of the Shadowlands. *"Brava! Bravo!"* The calls were both deafening and muted as the boundary between the worlds shuddered.

Annabella inhaled deeply to strengthen herself for the first of her solos. She opened her arms and gestured to Albrecht, as if giving him handfuls of love.

Albrecht met her gaze, his eyes roiling with desire. With Shadow.

Annabella froze.

Wolf.

Her sudden terror reminded her that she had a heartbeat, and that she was on a stage in the real world. She chanced a glimpse at side stage, focusing beyond the myriad trees to reality. No angel brightened the shadows. Custo was gone.

The orchestra waited on her while the audience applauded like thunder.

She whipped her gaze to the other side of the stage. Where was he? She couldn't do this alone. Had he left her alone?

Why do you look for him? He cannot possibly understand you. Understand this.

How could Custo abandon her?

Dance, Wolf begged. He had to be Wolf now, so much more than just any "wolf," after what they'd shared.

His request had her aching to move. He motioned to the crowd and took his place to watch her perform.

But how could she? *You attacked me. Would have raped me. You killed another.*

Wolf canted his head. *I didn't know what you were, or the ways of this world.*

The audience began to murmur, waiting for her.

Dance, Wolf repeated. *You want this; you want me.*

In a Shadow world where darkness shaded all certainty, she knew for a fact that she did.

Custo watched Adam spin, bring up his gun, and riddle the torso of the female wraith with a line of black holes in a cacophony of painful, echoing noise. The wraith trembled with multiple impacts, then fell in a heap to regenerate.

"What about Annabella?" Adam shouted.

Custo's limbs felt like jelly, but he managed to stand, bracing himself on the wall.

Annabella.

He lurched back toward the entrance. She needed him. Even now the wolf could be—

His vision blanked as something crushed him from above. A wraith. Disorientation had his head spinning as the wraith grasped him and clawed into his shoulder, taking him as a human shield.

Except Custo wasn't human.

Renewed strength percolated though his system, though his shoulder burned with the wraith's grasp. He didn't have time for this shit; Annabella was alone.

Custo reached behind him, grabbed the wraith by his open jaw, and heaved the stinking creature over his shoulder. Adam caught the thing midflight with another earsplitting round. The wraith was still moving when it hit the pavement, so Custo bent and broke the fucker's neck to extend its rejuvenation process. Custo wiped his hands on his pants, but the fetid smell clung.

Another wraith jumped on a car, tore off its hood with an *eeerch* of warping metal that would render any normal person deaf, and advanced down the street.

"Custo!" Adam shouted.

Custo kept his concentration on the new wraith. The hood would protect it long enough to get close to Adam. If Adam were disarmed, this fight was over. Hell, the wraith war was likely over, too.

The wraith swung the car hood like a misshapen Frisbee toward Adam. Custo darted into the arc of its trajectory, the metal crushing his ribs in a sickening, blood-wet exhalation that brought him to his knees. His mouth was coated in wet copper. Each searing, panting breath was like a drowning man's last.

Adam's gunfire filled the air again. "Custo! Look!"

Custo slowly brought up his gaze, but arrested on the first fallen wraith. His neck was skewed from Custo's break, but the rest of the creature's body had grayed to fleshy ash. Its bones seemed to be collapsing within the leathered skin. The smell coming off the thing had Custo fighting his gag reflex.

The wraith was dead. As in *dead*, never to regenerate again.

"How did you do that?" Adam yelled.

Custo inhaled, the pain diminishing to a general bitch of an ache as his ribs knit back together.

He had no idea how he did that. Probably an angel thing, but he couldn't stay to find out.

He hefted to standing and, wavering, wiped the blood from his mouth and temple with his arm. The remaining handful of wraiths on the street had frozen, looking bug-eyed and baffled at the corpse of their . . . friend.

"I've got to get to Annabella," Custo said.

A shot fired. Something bit him in his side. He glanced down as another fiery bullet took him in the arm and knocked him, spinning, to the ground again.

His vision blurred with dancing white spots. Warmth spread on the skin, plastering his shirt to his side, as a chill seeped into his bones. More shots punctuated the air, but he was insensible to their source or target. He concentrated solely on the burn that signaled regeneration.

It wasn't coming.

A hand at Custo's arm pulled him suddenly upward. His knees buckled so he ended up kneeling. A fight raged around him, a gun discharged, shouts. He caught Adam's voice, shouting, "Here!" but to whom he spoke, Custo had no idea.

Custo peered into the bleary sky, blinking rapidly to focus.

Luca looked down at him. "I thought we lost you. Well, pull yourself together and get off your lazy ass."

Custo was abruptly released as Luca dived into the fray. Custo stared, weak and stupid, at the street fight around him. Each movement was a strange rainbow arc of color in his vision. Each mundane shape was irregular and strange. He found Adam, expression fierce and joyful at the same time. That, too, was wrong; Adam was too perpetually worried to look that happy. Had Shadowman returned? Dead wraiths were stinking up the alley. The fetid smell made Custo's eyes tear.

No, not Death. Others had joined the fight against the wraiths. Their faces weren't familiar, but they were beautiful, skin perfect, eyes too deeply aware to be human. Custo knew them for what they were: angels. One held a wicked-looking short blade, its shaft subtly winging at its base like a trident. Custo could almost hear it singing though the air. The weapon was murder on wraiths.

Slowly the world solidified. The blurry colors collected in their rightful places. The shapes of building and body took on defined edges. And a blissful burn roared through his gut. He was healing at last.

Annabella.

Custo opened his consciousness to find her. He swept through the thousands in the audience, the bright specks congregated on the stage, the people waiting in the wings.

Custo searched for the glowing spirit that had brought him back to life, and found her flickering on the edge of hers.

TEN

A bell tolled the break of dawn. The music quieted, and the wilis delicately assumed listening poses, bodies leaning, heads cocked. The light on the stage shifted, yellowed, as the sun broke through the shadows of the trees. Giselle had seen her cursed Albrecht through darkest night. She clasped him one last time before returning to her grave.

Come. Now. Wolf pulled her toward a break in the trees, a deviation from the choreography of the ballet.

Yes, Annabella answered. All her dreams could and would be made real, and she didn't even have to try. She'd be miserable for the rest of her life if she denied Faerie and didn't embrace the magic with everything that she was.

Come, Wolf said again, this time with his sexy growl. The sound used to scare her, but now it excited. He knew her in ways that no other man could; he knew that her passions were hungry, just as he knew that nothing on Earth could satisfy them.

She belonged in the Shadowlands, dancing forever.

But . . . She glanced out into the audience—all the people were enthralled, spellbound, as if they collectively held their breath. The illumination of the stage lit their faces and had their eyes shining.

Just one more thing . . . one more moment, here . . .

Annabella wanted her applause. She'd worked hard enough for it. Seventeen years of breaking her body for ballet. She wanted the first bows with the company, then the curtain calls, the standing ovation, her arms full of roses. She wanted these people on their feet, shouting "*brava.*" If that made her a diva, so be it. If she were crossing to the Shadowlands, this was the only time her work would be recognized.

The orchestra sang the last strains of the love song. Albrecht was supposed to collapse center stage as Giselle disappeared into her grave, but Wolf stood, holding out his hand to draw Annabella into his world in a strange reversal of the story.

A happily-ever-after would have them exiting together, bound for the Shadowlands, but *Giselle* was a tragedy.

And Annabella wanted to take her bows.

Come, he said a third time, angry.

The ballet doesn't end that way. Annabella ignored his outstretched hand—she imagined the audience interpreted his reach as Albrecht's last hope, his longing.

The curtain fell. The audience was utterly silent. Then they broke into thunderous applause and shouts, no single word intelligible in the sudden storm of approval. The stage floor vibrated with their calls, thrilling through her body. It was . . . beyond wonderful. Worth the delay.

Venroy strode onto the stage, tears streaming down his face. He gripped her hands, saying, "Sublime, Annabella! Jasper! Perfection!"

Exquisite pleasure filled Annabella's chest, almost too much to bear. *The* Thomas Venroy. Crying. For her.

"Child," Venroy continued. "A *bravura* performance. You have exceeded all my expect—"

"Get back!" Wolf snapped, wrenching Annabella away by her elbow.

Venroy faltered. He swallowed his outpouring of emotion as if slapped.

Annabella frowned at Wolf. There was no call for that. And besides, she really wanted Venroy to finish.

"Of course," Venroy said, regrouping. "There will be time for this later. So much to do, to plan for . . ." He tapered off, waving for the corps of wilis to form a half circle upstage.

"I want my bows," Annabella said to Wolf, obstinate. It

had taken years of willpower to bring her to this point; she was not giving them up.

Wolf glowered, his discontent rumbling in his chest, but he stepped forward to clasp her hand. Tightly.

The curtain rose. The audience clamored with approbation.

Annabella shook off Wolf's clasp and swept into a *grande révérence*, a prima ballerina's thank-you to the audience. Every ballet class she'd ever taken had ended with a *grande révérence*, as was custom, but every performance until now she'd had to settle for the simple curtsey of the corps. Not anymore. She bowed deeply to the audience.

The applause was a gale wind through the Shadowlands. She could feel it caressing her skin, making her glow. The best of both worlds.

She rose and bowed again to the other side. How many times had she fantasized about this moment? Too many to count. She'd practiced in front of any mirror—studio, dressing room, bathroom, department store, even carnival fun house. *Thank you, thank you . . . and all you over there, thanks to you as well. And how could I forget the ones in the balconies? Thank you.* This was way better than she'd ever imagined. She could get used to this.

She glanced side to side to join the full company, and all together they bowed again. She gestured grandly to her partner to acknowledge his part; Wolf stared back at her, shadows a potent throb in his gaze.

Yeah, yeah. He'd just have to wait.

The curtain dropped again, but the shouts from the audience did not diminish. If anything the Shadow wind blew stronger. That meant curtain calls.

Sure enough, a stage tech signaled from side stage that he was about to stagger the curtains so that she and Wolf could step out and take another drink of the applause drug. *Thank you. Flowers for me?* A bouquet of two dozen long-stemmed roses, blood-scarlet against the wili white of her arm. Another deep dip. *Thank you.*

Annabella and Wolf backed up, and the curtain closed. She listened intently to the applause of the audience. Would there be another curtain call? And if so, how many? She'd bow all night if the audience would let her.

Annabella looked at the stage tech, waiting for a signal, ready, but Wolf grabbed her from behind, his hands digging into her shoulders. Those stupid Segue men rushed onto the stage. What did they possibly hope to do?

Besides, she needed a few more minutes. *Can't you hear them?* The audience wanted more.

But Wolf dragged her backward a few paces, his breath hot on her neck, the line of the corps breaking as he pulled her into the trees.

"Annabella!" a rough male voice called above the roar beyond the curtain.

Her attention snapped to Custo, emerging from the side of the stage. He stumbled forward, his chest heaving, his face white, blood smeared across his forehead.

Wolf growled at her back, his clutch on her shoulders increasingly painful.

"I won't let him hurt you," Annabella breathed over her shoulder. She sent a pained look to the confused stage tech.

"We must go," Wolf said at her ear. "Now."

"You can't have her," Custo said. His gaze fell to her left, on Wolf.

Oh, this was bad. Very, very bad. Maybe it *was* time to cross . . .

"It's okay," Annabella answered Custo. "I want to go. You don't have to worry about me anymore. This is what I want."

"You don't know what you're doing," Custo said as he stalked closer. He opened his arms wide as if to both tame and catch at the same time. "You can't trust him."

Wolf yanked her back against him, hard.

"He didn't know he was hurting anyone," Annabella reasoned. "He's not from here. He'd definitely never harm me."

"He's using you as a shield right now."

"You just don't understand." She looked at the gap in the curtain. The audience was louder now, expecting her appearance any second. Maybe just one more, if Custo would shut up and get out of the way.

"I do understand. I've been there." Custo's voice lowered with conviction. His body hunched forward unnaturally, as if he were in pain. But how could that be? He was an angel. Lines of strain formed at his eyes and around his mouth. "You can't trust anything about the Shadowlands, especially yourself."

Why was Custo ruining everything for her? It was her choice. Her life.

"Annabella?" Venroy said sharply. "What is the meaning of this?"

All the dancers were looking at her, too.

Come, Wolf said.

She had to cross now. It was the only way. Shame about her bows, though.

She gave Custo a look of apology—maybe he'd understand one day—and reached a hand back to Wolf.

"Where's Jasper?" Custo asked.

Jasper? Annabella felt him take her hand. No, that was Wolf. But it was Jasper's body pressed against hers; Jasper's voice asking her to come away with him. That wasn't right either. Jasper was gay and in love with his partner; he'd never want her. Had to be Wolf. But Wolf said he hadn't harmed anyone else. So the hand holding hers had to be Jasper's. But he growled like Wolf. So where was Jasper? Holding her hand—

Annabella's head hurt. She couldn't think. This had to stop.

Venroy looked wildly at the three of them and ushered

Myrtha out for the applause of the audience. "What is going on?"

Custo made a sharp cutting gesture in the air to shut him up. Venroy said something about security and stepped out of sight.

"That's right, Annabella," Custo said, tone insistent. "Where's Jasper, that pretty boy who likes to strut around with his package out there for everyone to see?"

An image of Jasper flashed in her mind—he stood in his signature stance, hip cocked to show off his body, a shameless and funny leer on his face whenever he wanted to make her laugh or put her at ease. The real Jasper—the one who'd stayed extra hours rehearsing with her to get the pas de deux perfect. The one who talked about hot, promiscuous sex, but had been a devoted boyfriend for over three years. Where was he?

If she could just think straight for one moment, maybe she could work it all out. Something wasn't right, but she couldn't identify what. All she knew was that her dreams were real in the Shadowlands, *dance* was real, but what kind of person would she be to think only of herself? What about Jasper?

She wrenched herself away from Wolf. The movement was like tearing herself in half.

Custo darted forward, shoving her out of the way, and leaped onto Wolf, who yelped.

Annabella fell as the acrid funk of burning flesh hit her nose, the smell beyond nauseating. The impact jarred her body into painful awareness, sweeping the glimmering magic of the Shadowlands from her eyes. Some Segue thug had his hands on her, keeping her back.

"No, not yet, Annabella! Hold the magic!" Custo yelled.

But her muscles seized, bones aching, and something was wrong with her neck. Her full-body euphoria dissipated in an excruciating hiss as she crashed brutally down from her faerie high. She felt tired and . . . and . . . old. What was wrong with her?

A panting brawl in front of her brought her eyes up. Custo grappled with Wolf, but in Jasper's form. The smell turned to bitter burning hair. The pair rolled toward the curtain, and pinned the velvet with their heaving bodies.

Myrtha almost tripped over them as she stumbled back to the stage from her bows.

"Anna," Custo gasped, "bring it back! We need the Shadows!"

How? It hurt to breathe. She'd be weeping if she had the energy. There was no magic left in her. Annabella saw the corps dancers chattering excitedly, but she couldn't hear them. What did Custo expect her to do—get up and dance again? She didn't think she could stand.

And besides, a sneaky little voice inside her pointed out, if she helped to banish Wolf, there wouldn't be a second chance for her to cross.

Struggling violently, Custo and Wolf rolled out in plain view of the audience. The audience audibly gasped. A sudden rise of shouts told her that they'd fallen into the orchestra pit. A metallic crash had her wincing, her ears ringing.

She bowed her head and the tears came. The Segue man pulled her to her feet and was dragging her offstage when Adam arrived.

"Orchestra pit," the guy holding her up said, as a second Segue person yelled, "Clear the way." But what he was talking about, and what they were doing, she had no idea. And she really didn't care. She was trying very, very hard to get a grip, but her reality kept slipping from her fingers.

Shadowlands out of her reach. Custo pummeling the wolf in view of the audience. And Jasper gone. Both her life and her dreams were disintegrating around her.

Annabella didn't trust mood swings. She'd just had the performance of her life. She knew as high and as happy as she'd been not ten minutes before, the opposite low was not far off. What had she been thinking? She was an idiot to believe she could've sustained that kind of euphoria forever. And she knew her low had not yet reached bottom. Not nearly. Bottom would be when they found Jasper's body.

"Where is she?" Custo said, shoving a Segue soldier out of his way. The idiot was rummaging through a first-aid kit to patch him up. He didn't need medical care. His body was on fire, healing on its own.

He wanted Annabella. He had to see her before Luca dragged him to who-knows-where.

Was she okay? Had she been hurt? Had she realized how close she'd come to disaster? His mind swept the theater but he was too keyed up to concentrate on individual people.

The sight of that . . . that *thing* . . . with Annabella in his clutches made Custo want to tear apart the wolf-turned-Jasper. At least Custo had hurt him, burned him bad, if the smell were any indication. Custo's touch had the same effect as Talia's voice—forcing the wolf back into the shadows. One moment solid, the next evaporating into absent light. What he would give to drive him all the way into Shadow itself.

He found Annabella in her dressing room, her expression stricken. Thin tracks of pink through her white makeup and twin flush-colored smudges under her eyes told him she'd been crying.

Stay back, she thought, but didn't voice, when she saw him. *Don't get near me.*

So Custo stayed by the door, while Adam sat next to her, a little beat up and bloody himself.

Adam rose and approached Custo. "The director, Venroy, has been by. He had some words about the 'lovers' quarrel' that took place onstage during the bows. There will be some repercussions for that, but he still wants Annabella and Jasper to attend the reception tomorrow night."

"Jasper's been found? Alive?" Custo couldn't believe it.

"He was out cold in his dressing room, but he will be fine. I told him that he had an amazing performance in spite of the drugs he was taking." Adam shrugged. "It was the best I could come up with, but he's taking congratulations now so I guess he's decided to believe it. There's a considerable ego on that one."

Custo flicked a probing glance at Annabella. Her head was full of *my-fault* grief. "But someone died," he said. "Who?"

Adam's expression grew serious. "A man named Peter Wells, Annabella's neighbor. I got a call from a contact in the NYPD, which is why I was late tonight. The police want to question her in conjunction with his murder."

"Coincidence?"

"No," Adam said, "I don't think so. I've started a Segue inquiry, heard the preliminaries from the police report at the scene. We're going to blame it on the wraiths and hush it up quick."

"I'm going to be sick," Annabella broke in. She made a grab for the garbage bin at her feet and dry-heaved.

Custo moved forward and stroked the column of her neck with the back of his fingers, then rested his palm on her shoulder and squeezed. "It's going to be okay."

"Not for Peter it isn't," she said and shrugged off his hand. *Don't touch me*, she thought as she turned away and started to pack her makeup in her tackle box. With her hands trembling as bad as they were, she wasn't making much progress.

"You have a team at your disposal to get her back to Segue," Adam continued. "I'll do the cleanup here."

If only it were that easy. Custo backed Adam into the hallway. "Adam, I don't know if I can. Someone is here to collect me, to drag me back where I came from. I'll try to reason with him, but I don't think he'll listen. This is probably it for me." He hated to ask, but he forced the words out anyway. "I may need you to take care of Annabella the best you can until Talia can destroy the wolf."

Talia wouldn't deliver for weeks. What protection could Segue possibly afford Annabella from a creature who could stalk her in the shadows?

Adam's frown deepened. "Your . . . cousin?"

Here it comes. Custo braced and nodded. Luca was a relation of some sort. Probably great uncle a couple times removed or some such.

"He asked me to give you this." Adam handed over a crisp white business card, smeared at the corner with blood. In small lettering, it read THE WHITE TOWER. "He said to meet him there tomorrow morning, nine A.M."

"Luca's gone?" Custo couldn't believe it. No address on the card. Probably wasn't in the phone book either. "And the rest of them?"

Adam shrugged. "They took off as soon as the last wraith was put down. Wouldn't answer my questions. Wouldn't acknowledge me beyond giving me the card."

Just hours ago Custo had begged Luca for one more night, and Luca was giving it to him. Should he have begged for a week? A year? A hundred years? Would it have mattered? What an excruciating, horrible thought.

And an irrelevant one.

Custo had a single night, but no way to track the wolf. Annabella was well beyond her strength, emotionally and physically. And he couldn't even lend his immortality to the wraith war, because he needed to be by her side in case the wolf returned.

He looked at the pristine, yet tainted card again. The White Tower. What kind of pompous name for a congregation of angels was that? This was exactly the reason he wanted nothing to do with them. Absolutely nothing.

Well, screw 'em. He wasn't going. He had a number of strikes against him already, what was one more? He'd lied a million times before; they should be prepared for it. He'd been a thief in his past life, too, always looking for an advantage. Well, he was going to steal every single moment he could. If he had to leave Annabella, she would know that he fought the sky to stay with her.

"He's like you, isn't he?" Adam asked, his intensity growing. "He and the others with him?"

"Yeah," Custo answered. But he didn't know what privilege permitted them to exist on Earth. *To exist on Earth.* He didn't know how to apply, or if his escape from Heaven (or the circumstances thereof) made him ineligible. As always, his decisions were tainted with regret.

"I'd like to go with you tomorrow," Adam said.

Of course he did. Big brother Adam always had to see things through.

"If nothing else," Adam continued, "I'd like to see if they'd be willing to cooperate with Segue to fight the wraiths. I'd give anything for Talia to be relieved of that duty."

Custo went cold. Talia. How could he have forgotten her? Talia had been saddled with an unimaginable horror. A life of rending the boundary between the worlds to force the crossing of the reeking dead.

He'd been too self-absorbed to track the direction of Adam's thoughts, but it wasn't so hard to guess their path. Adam had witnessed firsthand the ability of the angels to destroy wraiths without any threat to themselves.

Custo put a hand to his aching belly. An angel might risk pain and lingering discomfort fighting the wraiths, but little else. With Shadowman so clearly unwilling to help, what other recourse did Adam have? None. Adam needed the angels, and he needed Custo to help him find them.

The White Tower would be impossible for a mortal to locate on his own, even Adam with his untarnished heart and networks of information. For one time in Custo's life, he was in a position to help Adam, to give him the connections he so desperately needed in his war against the wraiths.

Movement from Annabella caught Custo's eye. She was using some kind of cream to wipe the makeup from her face. The skin under the white foundation was almost as pale. Her thoughts were a scatter of Peter, Jasper, and Wolf. The name Wolf was new, and Custo didn't like it, as if Annabella and the animal had become something to each other.

Maybe the angels could save Annabella from *the wolf*, too. Why hadn't they already? He'd like to have their response.

Custo cleared his voice, but his answer still came out tight. "I'll let you know when I've located the tower. Might take some . . . doing."

Adam nodded. "I need to go. I can almost smell the wraiths from here."

"I'll call you when I know anything," Custo said. He'd probably be combing the city with his mind all night, searching for the bell-clear thoughts that marked a host of angels.

Not the way he wanted to spend his last night.

Adam left just as the hallway thickened with people. Custo closed and locked the door—no gushing visitors for Annabella—then turned to size up her condition.

She'd managed to get most of the white off her face, and the spider lashes were gone. Though wrapped in a robe, a tuft of white at her knees told him she was still in her costume. All those hooks and eyes were too much for her, and she wouldn't have wanted to ask anyone else for help.

"Let's get you back to Segue and tucked in for the night," he said.

She nodded, passing a hand over her face, but he caught a hint of her face contracting with tears. She stood and removed her robe so Custo could help her out of her costume.

Applying his big hands to the little hooks, he considered what to say. It was pointless to tell her that she wasn't responsible for Peter's death. She'd only point out that it was because the wolf wanted *her* that he was dead. She might have been able to forgive herself if they'd managed to push the wolf back into Shadow at the end of the performance, but that effort had failed.

He'd have to try another approach.

"About five years ago—no, wait, it would be seven years now—" Custo kept his tone as flat as he could. He didn't want pity. "It was after the first rumblings of the wraith war. Some international arms-dealing scumbag put a hit out on Adam." He swallowed the stone in his throat and finished, "I hit him first."

Annabella's eyes widened in the mirror so that Custo could see the whites all around.

"His name was Heinrich Graf. I seduced his daughter into telling me his traveling itinerary, and then I made my move. But the first shot didn't get him. No, my first shot got an innocent bystander. A doctor, murdered in the street. The second shot got Graf. Adam doesn't know about any of this. I've been too much of a . . . *coward* to tell him."

"Why are you telling me?" Annabella croaked.

The last clasp came undone and the back of her costume gaped open. "The difference between you and me is that I killed those people myself, with my own hands, by my own actions. You haven't hurt anyone."

Her eyes filled again. "I could have stopped him tonight." *My fault.*

"We'll find another way. You know yourself better now." Custo turned Annabella to face him.

She put a hand to her breast. "It hurts to breathe."

"Try to remember that you were magnificent tonight. No, don't shake your head. Don't diminish what you have accomplished."

"It was Shadow . . . it was the magic."

"Annabella, that was *you*. That was all you." Custo grabbed her hand. If he could give her nothing else before he was dragged away in the morning, he wanted her to be aware of her power. "The wolf didn't learn *choreography*. The wolf took his cues from your imagination."

"He was supposed to go back," Annabella said. *But now he wants me, too.*

"I don't blame him for trying to take you with him." Custo fisted his hands to remember the burn of the wolf in his grasp. "Your talent, your gift, is amazing."

"You were so right to tell me not to trust myself, because I don't." She lifted her chin to meet his gaze, her eyes blazing, her thoughts begging, *Please don't hate me.* "I want the magic he offers so badly that in another weak moment I might take him up on it. Even now I want to feel the magic of Shadow again." *To go there with him.* "You have to promise me you won't let that happen."

"Annabella—"

The look in her eyes hardened to resolution. The fear clouding her expression cleared at last. No one had ever looked at him like that. Needed him like that. "Please. I don't want to lose myself. I won't if you're with me."

He'd been telling her to trust him from the moment he met her. Been telling her that he would be with her every step of the way. That together they'd push the wolf back into Shadow.

Now, Custo didn't have the heart to correct her.

ELEVEN

CUSTO tightened his arm around a sleeping Annabella and cursed the rising sun. Not that he could see it from Adam's underground apartment, but since the digital clock read 6:40 A.M., he figured the damn thing was lifting itself off the horizon. Truth was, he didn't want to move. His gut was still aching, wouldn't fully heal, and he didn't have time to have a doctor check it out—what could one do anyway?—before they left for the tower.

Instead, he'd spent his time the best way he knew how—keeping Annabella close while he could.

Her body was soft, fitted against his like a perfectly matched puzzle piece, her ass connecting with heat to his groin. She was supple and curved where she should be, though every bit of her was firmed with muscle. Almost every bit; his thumb had been stroking her rib cage under her breasts for the last twenty minutes. He didn't dare reach higher, or he wouldn't be able to trust himself. Only her hair, tickling his nose half the night and smelling of Talia's fruity shampoo, had been irritating enough to keep his mind from picturing the creamy, raspberry-tipped mounds.

Oh, hell. The tower. Think of the tower. No, that just made him want to have her more. The tower was a reminder that he was going away, probably forever.

Okay, then, cars. He pictured his first car, a stolen 1981 BMW 635CSI. Nice ride. Needed it for a date. Screwed the blonde from his university survey class in the passenger seat.

Annabella stirred. His dick tightened. The wound in his gut burned.

Who would have thought that mortality was Heaven and Hell combined?

He should be sainted for not having sex with Annabella last night. A monument should be erected in his memory for not accepting her invitation, exhausted though she was. Any other woman and he would have sated himself, and her as well, over and over again. He'd have screwed them both blind. Why not Annabella?

The trust in her eyes. Her belief that they would be seeing this nightmare through to the end together. How could he accept her confidence when he knew the very next morning he would betray it?

Somebody up there had better be taking notes.

Last night, he'd contented himself with stroking the long lines of her aching body, her front lounging on the many pillows littering the bed. His thumbs had worked the arches of her feet and had her sighing in relief. He had slowly ground the rocks of tense muscle from her calves. She'd shouted "ow, ow, ow" when he'd massaged the length of her thighs, then finally subsided into a grateful groan, wiggling her butt into his palms. The woman was not shy about her body, and with good reason.

As she drifted off, he'd watched her profile, her eyelids flickering in vivid sleep, and took sharp, smug satisfaction in knowing that the disjointed snatches of dream-thoughts were all about him. Not the wolf.

When the night deepened to utter quiet, he'd opened his mind to search for The White Tower. Its location had come easily, within moments. It was a beacon of calm order, a lighthouse in the confusing ocean of humanity. The only way he could have missed it before was because he was deliberately avoiding anything . . . angelic.

6:45 A.M. Time to be up. He was pushing it as it was. They'd need to leave in a little more than an hour and there was a lot to do. Too soon he'd be turning himself over to Luca. He didn't want to screw up Adam's chances of getting help with the wraiths, and he had to make certain that Luca would take care of the wolf. How long the wolf required to regenerate, Custo had no idea. A lot was riding on this appointment.

Custo brushed away Annabella's hair and kissed the spot behind her ear. He'd been planning to do that for hours. He turned his head, buried his face in her hair, and inhaled deeply. He'd found her too late, amid too much danger to know her—every slide of her skin, tone of her voice, draw of her breath.

"Custo?" she murmured. . . . *so warm . . . touch me more . . .*

"I'm here," he said to cut off her thought, and therefore, the temptation. But he couldn't help grazing his fingertips down to her smooth, tight stomach, memorizing her contours for later, when he faced the consequences of his actions. He barely managed to say, "We have to go soon."

"Five more minutes." She groaned, turning in his arms to face him, her eyes half lidded, and cuddled deeper into him. . . . *want more . . .*

More time to sleep or more . . . ?

She answered by twining a leg around his, knotting him close, pelvis to pelvis. She had to feel him rock-hard against her. The sensation was painful in its bliss, perfect in its fit. His blood filled with hungry greed, pounding out lofty intentions. He tilted his head back for clean, sane air. Didn't help.

. . . *wants me bad, too . . . why doesn't he . . . ?*

A better man wouldn't have his hand up her shirt. A better man would've never gotten into bed with her in the first place. A better man would have slept on the hard floor like a damn priest.

But he wasn't a better man. He was a bastard.

Annabella nuzzled closer, grazing her mouth against his neck. He clenched his jaw—there was a reason he couldn't sleep with her, but he had to think real hard to find it. All he could feel was warm, willing woman, the *boom boom boom* of his blood.

. . . touch me . . . why won't he touch me . . . ?

Oh, right. Because of the wraiths and the wolf, and a woman who trusted him to keep her safe when he was about to leave her. He tried to push her away, but ended up grasping her hips to bring her closer.

. . . oh, please, yes . . .

When she nipped him with her teeth, his control cracked. He skimmed his hand up again to cup her breast, stroking his thumb over the peaking nipple. Mouth dry, he barely managed to be lucid. "We leave in an hour, and I have to meet with Adam."

That was probably the most heroic statement he'd ever made. If it wasn't worthy of some wings, nothing was.

"Too soon," she pleaded. "Let's shut the world out for a while."

"I . . . oh hell, don't do that . . . Bella, please . . ." But her hand was already down his sweatpants. No blood was left in his brain at all. His last coherent thought: *Screw it.* He was going to Hell for sure this time anyway.

With an abrupt shift, he had her on her back. The burn in his side barely registered. It was hardly important considering the much more insistent ache in her grip. Her damn T-shirt got twisted around her chest. She released him so that he could kiss his way up her belly. He pried the cloth from her body and went facedown in the dip between her breasts, growling with dark satisfaction.

Annabella laughed out loud and seized his head by the roots of his hair. "If you don't kiss me soon . . ."

His mouth destroyed the last of her sentence, capturing her soft lips with his. Tasting her. He found her thigh and urged it up around his waist. Didn't take more than a tug and she had her legs around him, her exquisitely honed muscles pulling his hips down to hers. He resisted; any more friction in that area would probably disappoint them both.

The kiss started soft, but with an *ugh* of impatience at the back of her throat, she bit his lower lip to take the action deeper.

Custo pulled back, paused, forehead against her cheek while he strained for air. Wrestling with Annabella was well worth the ticket to Hell, but he didn't want to rush it. Levering from his elbows to his hands, he ground out, "Anna, slow down or this won't be good for you."

She scowled like a spoiled brat, her legs tightening around him to lift her hips off the bed. "You're the one who said we had to hurry," she snapped back, color high on her face and her breasts. "I've wanted you since you freakin' hijacked my cab. Now hurry."

He'd wanted *her* since he saw her dancing in the Shadowlands. All sleek and ethereal. She was a carnal, earthy woman now, and the devil in him liked her better for it.

"That's it," she said, fed up. . . . *have to do everything myself* . . .

Her hands went back to the waist of his pants, trying to simultaneously push them and his boxers down his hips from her ridiculous angle. Impatient, demanding woman. She wasn't making much progress; something was in the way.

He touched her mind, though it was obvious what she wanted. He caught an image of her straddling him, speared by him, arching like a glistening bow, every strand of trained muscle taut, her hands braced on her splayed knees.

Okay, he was flexible . . . they'd do it her way.

He shifted to give her better access to his pants. The pain in his gut stabbed him and he tumbled to the side, but he clamped down on his reaction before she could change her mind. He had to be on his back anyway, so it was all good.

"Shirt," she commanded, tugging the cloth up at his waist. He didn't mind the sharp jab when he sat up to pull it over his head. Not with that wicked, purposeful gleam in her eyes. He jerked the last of his sweats off himself.

No going back now. The only thing that mattered was this moment. Touching her, he was alive again, one last time. No, alive for the first time ever.

Her gaze darted to his and then held, her body wavering as she saw him, really saw him. This wasn't just sex. Couldn't be. Not when he traded the last of his honor to be with her before facing the angels.

Her expression sobered and Custo touched her mind. He had to know what she was thinking.

. . . *in too deep . . . in way too deep* . . .

So on some level she understood. Her thoughts went silent as tension hardened the long, supple contours of her body.

Why discover Annabella now, when he was past any hope of a life with her? Why now? He could think of only one answer: For all the order of the Heavens, there was no reason, just madness. It shouldn't be this way.

Annabella's breasts rose and fell with her labored breath. Her eyes were shiny, worry slowly darkening the blue of her irises.

Custo shuttered the thoughts that had revealed his ragged soul to her. She shouldn't have to see that. Not her. He was no good, but she didn't have to know it, at least not for another hour.

Besides, his blood was greedy. If there could be no reason, then they would be all feeling, all heat and sensation, and banish the rest. He was about to grab her waist and pull her down on top of him, to stroke and coax and tempt her demanding, delicious mood back to dominance, when the darkness of her eyes transmuted to raw lust, overtaking his own thoughts.

Damn, he liked her so, so much.

She extended one smooth leg, sliding onto him. She submerged him in her tight heat, her glorious body sheening with effort, arching with the satisfaction of deep contact. His hands gripped her hips to control their rhythm. He meant to go slow, really he did, but the sight of her above him and the mindless, rising drumbeat of sex drove him to rock her faster. To stroke her to high pleasure, then electric white ecstasy.

A charged bolt of shattering intensity shook them both, cracking, wrecking, sundering. His soul was in pieces, but as long as it was Annabella's doing, he really didn't care.

Heaven help him.

Wolf skulked in the deep, fallow shadows of the apartment. *They* were in the bedroom. In the bed. Together. Melded.

Wild yearning bristled his pelt and had him panting with harsh, bitter need. Yeasty scents had his Shadow-magicked body shuddering with the human emotion. It tainted his animal mind, filled his breath with new sharp words as his thoughts advanced to a darker, covetous violence.

The woman was *his*. She belonged to *him*. Hadn't he just shown her what they could be together? Hadn't he fulfilled her brightest dream?

Wolf drew his lips back over wet teeth, a growl rolling in his chest. That bed should be soaking with red. Annabella's soft body on her knees, back arching for him.

But he could not enter. The angel-light banished him. He was not strong enough yet. Not nearly strong enough to break their carnal communion. Mortality was diminishing him, darkness slower to amass his form, Twilight's Shadow less ready to feed his re-creation. His rebirth required *time*, the bane of human existence.

If not for his name, *Wolf,* the process would have been interminable. A name. *Wolf.* Power.

And she had given it to him. She had to know that she belonged with him. That together they could do great things, that *he* could exceed her every fantasy. She had to know.

And if she didn't, he would show her.

Oh, hell. What had he done?

Custo didn't have to reach in her direction to perceive the thoughts tumbling around her head. She kept telling herself to *relax, stay calm, to chill*—so her emotions had to be all over the place. He really should explain things now, tell her that he was leaving. Face her hurt and give her the opportunity to curse him to his face.

Custo patted Annabella's hip. "Better get up and get ready. I'll check in with Adam."

She frowned up at him, her bare skin rosy beautiful. "You're not telling me something."

That he was leaving her at her most vulnerable? That he was turning her scary wolf problem over to someone else? She'd never forgive him.

Custo managed to lift one side of his mouth. It was the best he could do. She'd find out soon enough. "Big day."

Annabella rolled her eyes, but crawled out of bed, magnificent and easy in her naked skin. She knew she looked good—slender, yet subtly curvaceous, sculpted by her art. That awareness had his blood heating again, his hands twitching to touch her. She stood and her breasts pinked slightly under his scrutiny, but she made no motion to cover herself as she padded to the bathroom, her ass sweetly swinging side to side. She glanced over her shoulder, eyes sparkling, to see if he was watching, then turned back, making the motions of knotting her hair behind her head to show her body off to its best advantage. Custo shifted in the bed to follow the siren, but a jab of well-deserved pain in his side reminded him about the day.

She left the door ajar, still afraid to be alone and trusting him to protect her.

Hell, he was a bastard, in all senses of the word. But . . . he'd do it again.

Custo labored into a sitting position and grabbed his mobile.

Adam picked up on the first ring. "Did you find the place?"

He must have been waiting for the call. "I did. I take it Talia's not doing well?"

Adam sighed. "She's hanging in there, but she can't engage wraiths or the wolf again before she delivers." Adam's subtext was brutally clear: Once Custo was gone, there was no way to protect Annabella, not without costing the lives of Talia and possibly the twins. Adam was telling him whom he'd choose if it came down to life and death.

Warring emotions rose in Custo: First, simple understanding. Of course Adam would put his wife and children before anyone else. Second, betrayal. Hadn't Custo given his life for Adam? And this was how Adam would repay him? This emotion, irrational, Custo pushed vehemently to the side. There were no ledgers between him and Adam; everything had always and would always be freely given. And finally, helpless urgency. If Adam couldn't help Annabella, Custo had to find someone who could.

That left Luca.

"Be ready to leave by eight," Custo said. "The sooner we get these women taken care of, the better."

"I'm ready now," Adam answered.

Custo glanced over at the cracked doorway to the bathroom. Something clattered to the tiled floor and Annabella cursed. It would be another minute or two on their end. "Have you ID'd the Segue leak yet? You know someone had to have tipped off the wraiths to your location at City Center."

The threat inside Segue was Adam-specific. Had to be. The wraiths could have caused far more destruction and mayhem by attacking the audience contained in the theater.

By blocking the exits, they could have fed and murdered with little opposition, then escaped when Segue finally organized enough forces against them.

Instead, the wraiths chose a concentrated attack on the area outside the theater. Why there?

Somebody had to have let them know where Adam would be stationed, ready to support Annabella at need. If they got Adam, Talia might falter, especially stuck in bed rest for the next few weeks. And if the world lost Talia's scream, the wraiths could attack and feed unchecked. Life as humanity knew it would be forever changed.

"I haven't got him yet," Adam said, "but I have a strong lead."

"Go on." This was the reason Custo had escaped Heaven, after all. If he had to go back (or to a warmer climate), it would be somewhat satisfying to know that the traitor was neutralized.

"Twenty-seven of the thirty-five soldiers survived the wraith attack. They were the only ones privy to the details of the mission. All are accounted for except one, Geoff, his partner murdered, but not by a wraith. Geoff logged on briefly to the Segue server during the cleanup, so it's unlikely he was taken by the wraiths for a little late-night snack. And it makes sense that he'd run, now that the pool of suspects has been narrowed from several thousand to only twenty-seven."

Sounded too easy. Custo didn't like it.

"But to be completely safe," Adam continued, "I've asked the rest of the team from last night to move to voluntary containment at the New York Segue compound for the duration of the investigation. I intend to question them all regardless."

That was better. Adam would be thorough, especially where Talia was concerned.

If there'd been enough time, Custo would've liked to have

performed the interviews himself. A couple of pointed questions would've yielded the man pretty quickly, even if he were lying. Mind reading was much more efficient than a lie detector test.

There were too many dangers from too many different sides. "Adam, I'm going to need a weapon. I don't want to be unarmed."

"Got your Glock right here."

Annabella emerged from the bathroom, leaving the light on, scared of the dark. Her hair was parted to the side and hung in soft, deep toffee waves around her face to her shoulders. She wore little makeup that he could see, except for a deepening of color at her lips.

"Good," Custo said. "We'll be right up."

Annabella looked from Adam's ashen sober face to Custo's. Neither was talking and the tension in the car was poisoning the air. The connection she'd shared with Custo that morning felt weirdly severed and distant, though just looking at his profile made her want him all over again. Wanting Custo was a fantastic distraction from the lure of the Shadowlands. That is, if Custo would talk to her or signify in some way that they were in this together. They were a team, weren't they?

But it wasn't as if she could ask while third-wheel Adam was right there, especially with Custo riding shotgun and her in the backseat. She'd just have to wait until they were alone again.

The mood heightened the sense that everything seemed shadowed today, the darkest places falling to impenetrable black. A prickly awareness told her that they were being followed. Flashes of adrenaline jumped her nervousness to paranoia. She hugged the fear close to keep her on edge, her mind sharp. Her anxiety, added to last night's aches, made her muscles and joints complain bitterly, but ballet had taught her to tell good pain from bad pain. Bad pain meant you were hurt. Good pain kept you on the top of your game. This was good pain, a centering pain; she couldn't afford to lose herself to Wolf again.

She knew they were going to meet others like Custo. She figured they were going to ask for help with their next try. The performance season would open in a few days, and this time she intended to get it right. They'd ask for help, make a plan, and get rid of Wolf.

The day called for proactive, forward movement. Custo and Adam, however, looked like they were going to a funeral.

"Anyone care to clue me in?" she asked. She kept her tone light to counter the oppressive mood.

After the horrible performance last night, and being duped by Wolf into almost going with him voluntarily, she couldn't stand any secrets.

Custo glanced over his shoulder at her from the front seat. "Nothing for you to worry about."

Macho bullshit always ticked her off. She countered it with a little bitch. "I need to know what's going on."

But Custo turned abruptly back to Adam. "No, over there. I can feel it, not more than a block from us."

He was ignoring her. Not one hour ago, he'd been *inside* her, and now he refused to answer.

Adam slowed the car to a crawl and glanced at Custo. "You ready for this?"

Adam was ignoring her, too.

"I want it taken care of," Custo answered.

Pigheaded men. "Someone needs to fill me in right now, or . . ." . . . or she didn't know what she'd do, but it would be extremely unpleasant for everyone.

"You already know, Annabella," Custo said placatingly. She didn't like his impersonal voice. This wasn't the man who'd just shared her bed and her body. He continued, "I've been called in to meet with some of the others like me. I hope to get some information about how to deal with the wolf." To Adam, he suddenly said, "Damn it! Here!"

"I don't see anything," Adam responded, but he pulled the car over to double-park.

Annabella peered out the window, though she didn't know what to look for either. There were no big churches, only a Manhattan street busy with morning traffic under an overcast sky that looked as chilly as it felt. Irregular buildings crowded the sidewalk, some fat and blocky, studded with small businesses—a Starbucks, deli, cleaners—while others reached into the sky, only to be blunted before they touched the low-hanging clouds. The street looked harsh, the sky menacing, and the combination of the two . . . wolfy.

She wrapped her jacket tighter around her. "Are you in trouble?"

As soon as the words left her lips, her uneasy feeling coalesced into certainty.

He was in trouble, and it was her fault.

The performance. If he were going to get reprimanded for the catastrophe of last night, she was glad she was here. Custo had done his best. She'd screwed up. She'd been so caught up in the moment, in herself, that she hadn't realized what was happening. And Wolf got away. If anyone had to answer for the disaster, it should be her.

Custo got out of the car without answering. Without looking at her. That was it then; she'd gotten him in trouble. Well, she'd just have to fix it.

Annabella joined him on the sidewalk with Adam, who had left the car in the street. Whatever they were going to do had to be *really* important not to take the time to park. A cab blared its displeasure at being stopped.

Yet Custo and Adam seemed only concerned with finding an address. Annabella kept glancing over her shoulder at the skulk of shadow near an alley, or the black-eyed face of a pedestrian, or the sudden growl of a garbage truck accelerating. Broad daylight and she was starting to shake again.

If there were such a thing as women's intuition, and recent freaky events led her believe that anything was possible, then something was watching them. Had to be Wolf. Tracking her movements. Stalking her.

"This way," Custo said, his face turned up into the sky in a grim kind of awe that confused the heck out of her and made her stomach clutch, too.

But he led them toward a grimy alleyway too dark for her comfort. Uh . . . Wolf anyone?

"Custo?" Adam asked.

Custo took a deep breath. "You don't see it?"

"See what?" Annabella asked.

"I see a tower," he said, "a narrow obelisk, smooth like a dagger cutting the sky. Its facade is some kind of white marble that seems to be absorbing the light of the day. There are no windows, except at the top, where there are two dark slits, like some kind of medieval castle."

Custo glanced over at them.

She shrugged. Nope, couldn't see nothin'. And people were beginning to stare.

"Well, you both are coming with me," he said.

Custo took her arm on one side, and Adam took her other. With his free hand, Custo seemed to turn the handle on an imaginary door. With his forward momentum, she stepped off the city sidewalk and into a blindingly bright hall. The transition was sudden and jarring. She stumbled for balance, gripping their hands to find her center of gravity, but gravity seemed to be pulling at her from strangely oblique angles. The sounds of the city—traffic, an occasional *pop-bop* of music, and a scrap of talk—were still audible, but distorted. The intense glow of the place had her eyes straining to focus, her mind struggling to sense depth and delineation in the glaring fog.

"They can't come in here," a male voice said. One minute the source was a distant smudge of color, and the next, he was in front of them. He was tall, a little lanky, with dark hair over black eyes. He dressed in jeans and a white T-shirt, his upper body fit enough to permit little loose fabric.

"Breaking all the rules already, Custo?" the man asked with a knowing smile.

When Custo didn't answer, the man shifted his attention. His manner seemed only politely interested, but his gaze looked right into her. He held out his hand, and Annabella took it out of habit.

"I'm Luca," he said. "Custo's great-great uncle. You'd think as his elder, he'd listen to me more often."

She didn't actually see much of a resemblance between the two. Their coloring, body type, and bearing were all different. And Luca was trying to be charming, a trait she'd yet to see Custo attempt to exercise.

"I'm here now, aren't I?" Custo cut in. Case in point.

Luca moved on to Adam, who took the outstretched hand and shook it firmly. "Adam Thorne."

Luca inclined his head and stepped back to address all of them, hands up in an apology. "I'm sorry. Annabella and Adam, you are not permitted within the tower."

Kicking us out just like that? Annabella glanced at Custo to gauge his response. When he didn't say anything, she looked back at Luca.

"I see your point," Luca answered.

What point? Did someone speak? The haziness of the place must have been affecting her brain.

Adam's stone cool broke with confusion as well, so she didn't feel too stupid.

Luca shrugged at Custo. "Well, they've come this far; I don't see why they can't wait here while we talk. Nothing can harm them within these walls. The hunter cannot tolerate this light, and the immortal dead, whom you call wraiths, don't know we exist."

These confines were giving Annabella a blistering headache.

"Actually, I'd like to talk to you about the wraiths," Adam put in. "It is the mission of my organization, The Segue Institute"—he produced a business card and held it out to Luca—"to destroy them."

Luca pushed away Adam's hand. "I know who you are. The wraiths at this time are not our concern."

Adam sputtered, then regrouped. "How can that be?" He took a step forward to command Luca's full attention. "They prey on people with impunity. No one is safe anywhere until my wife, the daughter of—"

"I know who your wife is, too. I wish her the very best in the successful delivery of your children. But the tower is not, at this time, working to eradicate the wraiths." To Custo he said, "If you'll just follow me . . ."

Adam wouldn't be put off. "Do you have the authority to make that decision? I want to speak to the person in change."

Luca smiled, somewhat ruefully. "You'll have to settle for me."

"I don't suppose you know anything about Shadow wolves, do you?" Annabella asked, though she didn't really expect an answer after Luca had dismissed the entire wraith war.

Luca shifted his smile to her. "I know there is one in the city."

Confession time. "Yeah . . . um . . ." she began, "about that . . . we almost had him last night, but I let him get away. It's not Custo's fault at all. I was too wrapped up in myself to do the right thing." Luca said nothing while she stammered through her explanation, so she summed up her point. "I don't want Custo held responsible."

Luca lifted a brow. "I believe he left you alone with the wolf for a period of time during the performance."

Annabella glanced at Custo. Yeah, actually, there had been that moment during the ballet when she'd looked for him, scared to be suddenly faced with Wolf. She'd forgotten in the aftermath and was still too chicken to revisit her part in her own seduction to recall that moment. But, yes, she had needed Custo, and he hadn't been there.

He'd have a good reason, she was sure. He wouldn't just leave her.

"I take full responsibility," Custo said, looking at her for the first time since they'd crawled out of bed. He turned back to Luca. "And I'm not going anywhere with you until I have your assurance that Annabella will be protected from the Shadow wolf, and that Adam will have the support he needs to fight the wraiths."

Luca gestured into the bright fog. "Let's go somewhere we can talk."

"No." Custo dropped the word like an anchor.

"Custo," Luca said, "you don't belong with them. You know this. You've done the right thing in coming here today, though I know it had to be difficult."

Annabella was totally lost now. Was Custo leaving them? She leaned over to Adam. "Are you getting any of this?"

Adam looked down at her. "Not so much."

"I can't abandon my friends for them to be preyed upon by monsters," Custo was saying.

Abandon them? That didn't make sense either. Custo couldn't very well stay here. Leaving might be hard on Adam, but it would be like throwing her to the . . .

Her chest was starting to tighten, breath more difficult to draw. Custo was leaving?

"At least follow me and get some information so you don't get yourself killed. Then you can decide," Luca said.

Annabella's throat constricted, too. This got worse and worse. "Killed?"

"Will you come?" Luca asked Custo. "Somebody needs to

dig that bullet out of your gut before you bleed to death internally."

Custo frowned deeply in response.

Bullet? Killed? *Leaving?*

Custo turned to Adam, including her with a darted glance. "You'll wait here? I'll be back as soon as I can and explain everything."

She wasn't budging without some answers.

With a quick tug on her arm, Custo kissed her, his mouth urgent, burning her up for all of three seconds. He drew back, his gaze hard on hers. "Do what Adam tells you."

Was that *good-bye?*

"I don't understand—" she said. Nothing made any sense.

"We'll be waiting," Adam said to Custo. The statement was loaded.

Custo released her, her vision blurring suddenly as he and Luca smudged into receding daubs of color, soon drowned out by the light.

Annabella's chest was so tight she doubled over.

"Deep breaths," Adam said, putting a hand on her back. She fought for air, and when her equilibrium returned, she straightened.

"I don't see a bathroom," she said to be funny, to cover the tears in her eyes.

"I think we hold it." Adam still grasped his rejected business card in his hand. His jaw was set with fury.

"Custo will work everything out," she said, though she wasn't sure about anything anymore.

She'd thought he was in trouble because of her, but he'd left her midperformance. The blame was just as much his as it was hers. Except he was an angel and was supposed to know what he was doing.

He'd also known he might be leaving, and hadn't bothered to tell her. He'd let her think that they'd banish the wolf together, when he'd intended to ask Luca to take over.

He'd let her climb all over him—oh no, she couldn't think about that. The mortification would burn her up.

Besides, sleeping with him was her fault. What had she been thinking? That he was gorgeous, that he desired her. Would be there to protect her. The fact that he looked and acted like a man made her forget that he wasn't one. She'd gotten carried away by fear and fantasy.

Here, now, confronted by these many revelations, she had to face the truth: She'd met him less than two days ago. He was practically a stranger. And he was different from her, set apart from the normal flow of life. Not a *man*, an angel. Her humiliation was her own damn fault.

It was all right, though. The thought razored through her hurt.

Screw-ups were important; she'd figured that out about the same time she got her first set of pointe shoes. It was the key to her success. That's how she learned to correct her balance, find her center, so the next time, she wouldn't repeat her mistake.

The intense glare of the tower might've been blurring her vision, but she had her bearings now. She knew up from down. Regular human being from angel. Trust from betrayal.

She wouldn't fall for Custo again.

TWELVE

CUSTO'S shoulders tensed with aggravation as he stepped away from Annabella. He didn't like to be away from her, especially when her mind was filling with hard questions. Bad things happened when he left her alone. Close calls that were his responsibility. He'd brought the wolf into this world, vowed to send the creature right back out again, and yet, he'd almost lost her twice now.

Except, she wasn't alone. She was with Adam, and in a tower filled with angels. She couldn't be safer.

The bustling room behind Luca promised some very interesting answers. Custo had glanced at Adam and touched his mind to see what he thought of the heavily armed men who'd passed the doorway beyond—*was that curved blade a sword or a saber?*—but Adam was insensible to anyone or anything but Luca. Annabella's thoughts were circling the same questions over and over again. His last kiss, intended to answer at least one, had only compounded her confusion.

Her mind was racing, and inevitably she would come to conclusions not in his favor, but he had no choice but to follow, to investigate that glint of sharp steel.

His interest rose exponentially upon entering what appeared to be a slick, modern command center. One wall was devoted to enormous sectional screens that displayed shifting images of cities around the world. Satellite input was overlaid with changing numerical data. To the right, screens tracked a developing weather system, while on the left screens flickered quickly though television news broadcasts in multiple languages.

The men and women, angels, were variably busy around

the room. All wore modern dress, some casual, some business-oriented, and still others wore combat gear as if they belonged in mortality. Several hovered over consoles, peering with concern into their screens. The thought-speak was rapid, direct, naming places of "breaches," conflicts, and instructions to angels in place to resolve them.

Grid C34, a man called near the periphery.

Custo startled, but realized they were pointing at a condensation of digital blue dots on one of the screens, identifying a location on a landmass surrounded by islands. Greece.

Get me Athens, another answered.

Immediately, a central screen displayed the face of a middle-aged man, his black hair threaded with silver, wrinkles fanning out from his eyes and rounding his mouth. Yet in spite of these signs of age, under bushy, graying eyebrows, the man's piercing gaze was unquestionably angelic.

An angel, aging? Custo definitely needed some answers.

With a sweeping glance, the man on the screen took in the whole of the control room, stopping on Custo. *The prodigal son?*

Attention in the room shifted briefly to Custo, a couple dozen all-seeing gazes zeroing in on his darkened soul. Custo felt his face flush with heat, but he clamped down on his irritation. "Not likely," he said. No mind talk for him.

You've got another breach near the coast, a man said from the floor, ignoring Custo.

The man on the screen centered his gaze. *We see it. Probably another one of the naiads trying to break through. Water is our most difficult medium. I swear, a week doesn't pass when some fool isn't tempted by the Otherworld and lost. Sex, riches, even food—with all the warning stories out there, you'd think humankind would learn a thing or two. But no, the stories pass into myth and the same mistakes happen again and again. Our thanks.* The man on the screen blinked out.

Custo turned to Luca. "What is this place?"

Luca smiled. "This is The Order, one form of the service you repudiated so passionately in Heaven. The tower is our North American Continental Division. Let me show you around. I don't think you'll be disappointed. Maybe you'll even want to stay."

Stay here? Custo didn't understand.

"Yes," Luca said. "The Order exists on Earth to help humankind. Lately we've been most concerned about the escalating breaches between the Shadowlands and mortality."

Custo took another look around. The place was charged with energy, intent, and work. The angels in the room had a forward momentum that echoed his personal restlessness. They were dedicated to a cause, tracking and fighting mythological creatures. It reminded him a little of Segue.

"This way," Luca said.

The control center occupied the greater part of the first floor. Beyond, a wide spiral staircase led upward like a shaft of light to the sky, the architecture contemporary and modern. In Heaven everything had been both primeval and overwrought with the ages, every surface telling a story. But the tower was spartan, pristine. A vessel for light.

Custo stopped midstep as the solid wall of the tower grew transparent. The street below was bustling with all the staccato pump of the city, a direct contradiction to the clean quiet within the tower's walls.

"They can't see us," Luca said.

Custo had figured out that much himself. "How's that?"

"The same way we read minds, we're able to manipulate perception. Dampen sensory acuity near the tower to the degree that only angels cross our threshold." Luca waved a hand in the air to concede an unspoken point. "That is, until today. If it were anyone but Adam Thorne, you'd have been stopped on the street."

And Annabella?

Luca didn't answer but continued up the stairs. Custo forced his eyes from the view of the city to follow.

A wide archway had Custo stopping in his tracks again. An armory. Custo entered, awestruck. A glittering display of blades, cuffs, bows, and other oddly shaped weapons were mounted in white-blue glass cases along the walls. Blades predominated. Swords—some thick, some slender—and wicked daggers. To his left, a display of body armor. Was that a breastplate? He knew instinctively that these were not normal weapons; they hadn't been crafted and honed by mortal hands.

Centered in the room were tabled exhibits. Slim drawers suggested more arms were tucked away. Curiosity had him stepping forward to ease out one of the drawers. Maybe he'd find the dagger shaped like a reversed trident, the dagger that had cut the wraiths out of the world last night.

The drawer opened soundlessly, but within lay varied tools, nested in molded blue velvet. Disappointed, he grazed a finger down the shaft of a raw-looking blacksmith's hammer. The wood was shiny with use, the head blunt on one side, rounded on the other. Not what he was looking for.

Custo's mind began to turn as he shut the drawer again. That blade would be damn useful at Segue, in Adam's hands. If Custo could get away from his guide for just a moment to search the room . . .

Luca's eyes narrowed at him; apparently, there'd be no stealing from The Order.

Custo hated angels in his head for good reason. At the very least he should be able to contemplate a crime, if not attempt to carry it out. Was it any wonder he didn't want to be anywhere near others of his kind? *Get out of my head!*

The only reason he suffered Luca's company was that Luca didn't try to sustain that annoying mind-to-mind conversation.

"What are these things doing in here when they could be put to good use?" Custo asked. In other words, *I know someone who could kill an awful lot of wraiths if properly armed.*

Luca raised a brow and answered the unspoken statement. "Adam will have to make do with what he's got. The weapons stay within The Order. Join us and you can have your pick."

"But then I'd have to be one of you."

Luca laughed. "You are already. I don't know why you fight it. Actually, I do, but I am hoping you'll come around."

"Don't hold your breath." To change the subject, Custo said, "I don't see any guns."

Luca leaned up against the entry, folding his arms. "There's a tedious, ongoing debate about acquiring modern tools of war. Most of the younger members are for it, but the administration of The Order is still very old-school."

"You've embraced technology in the control room," Custo observed.

Luca shrugged. "Many make a firm distinction between using satellites for information gathering and using semiautomatic weapons for violence. One life taken by accident is one too many."

Custo knew that from experience; it burned like the wound in his gut. Nevertheless, there was no denying the accuracy and utility of firearms when faced with a gang of wraiths.

"Over here," Luca said, exiting the armory for another minimalist archway. "Let's get that wound taken care of first. You can't heal with that bullet shredding your guts."

Custo followed, grudgingly. He'd have held back if his belly weren't so sore. "You said it was killing me."

The idea was more than bothersome. He didn't know his limits—he didn't know he *had* limits.

"It could," Luca answered. "If you were human, you'd be long dead."

The room they entered led to smaller, glass-walled spaces

resembling a hospital's operating room, banks of equipment tucked perfectly along one wall. Two white-smocked women were waiting near an elevated pallet. To the side of the bed was a narrow, utilitarian table with a tray of disturbing tools. And damn, a needle and syringe.

"I thought angels were immortal," Custo said. He didn't want to get remotely near that pointy thing. His belly didn't hurt that much. "We've already died, and we heal spontaneously. How can I, can *we*, be killed?"

Luca made an openhanded gesture. "Because we are in the mortal world. Everything, everyone, here is . . . *mortal*. On Earth, you are a mortal angel, and as such, you will age and can be killed."

That didn't make sense. "Just last night, I was hammered by wraiths, even shot a couple of times, and today, aside from this nagging pain, I'm little worse for the wear."

"Last night you were on the brink of death, and you know it." Luca lifted a brow as if to dare Custo to dispute him. "Had we not come to your aid, you would have died. You sustained and healed from those injuries because you have a *great soul*, a soul capable of much good, or evil, as you so choose. But taxed enough, your body can and will die."

Custo recalled debilitating darkness and the long wait for the welcome burn to signal healing. Yes, he'd come very close to something irrevocable last night.

"And what then?" Custo wasn't sure he wanted to know.

"You've already lost your life, so the only thing of yours left to give is your soul. You die a second time and you die forever. The choice to return to mortality is thus a difficult one, made with much forethought and deliberation."

Custo had jumped Heaven's Gate in a mad dash for the trees.

"Since the second birth is traumatic and painful, angels descend into the comfort and safety of the tower, to be cared for until they are strong enough and world-oriented enough to function without calling human attention."

He had endured the rebirth on a city sidewalk, naked and terrified, and then mugged some poor slob for his clothes and cash.

"Afterward, each mortal angel is assigned a task, a mission to complete for the benefit of humanity. Usually something small and manageable. And then another of greater difficulty and another, until the angel elects to return to Heaven, preferably long before sustaining mortal harm." Luca finished and made a show of waiting on Custo's next question.

But Custo was still stuck on the first. "So you're saying that I can die."

Luca's mouth twitched. "*Will* die, yes, if you remain long in mortality or don't get that bullet out of your side."

The table was ready, needle waiting.

No, no, no. "I'm fine for now." Translation: Someone else at Segue could dig the bullet out of him. His friends were waiting below, and he wasn't so keen on submitting himself to the tender mercies of the women in white.

You'll be asleep. Won't hurt a bit. The message came from the brunette.

"Don't talk in my head," Custo said, near growling. "And no thank you. I'm fine."

"You like to court disaster, don't you?" Luca said. "Very well, as always, it's your choice. This way . . ." They made another circuit of the wide stairway, ascending to the level above. Instead of the wide archways of the floor below, this upper level had several corridors branching off the landing. Luca stepped down one and opened a door, revealing a simple, colorless bedroom with a bathroom en suite. "Quarters," Luca explained.

The room was little more than a cell. "I'm not a monk," Custo argued.

Luca gave a long-suffering sigh. "Like I said, you like to court disaster. Your choice. These rooms are temporary anyway. Most get lodgings near their station in the world. Limits the coming and going from the tower, reducing the possibility of discovery. If you work in the control room, you stay here; if you're in the field, you get your own place."

So he could be part of The Order without actually having to put up with any of the Host. That was a consideration, especially if he had access to those weapons. There had to be a catch.

"No catch," Luca said. "Service. Dedicating yourself to the well-being of the world, a nonissue because you already have. You wouldn't be here, in mortality, if you hadn't."

Custo shook his head in denial. He was here on Earth because he'd jumped the gate and made a break for it.

"But why did you jump the gate?" Luca asked.

"Because no one up there would do anything." Custo's heart beat hard with sudden anger. "A war was going on, and no one would fucking listen to me."

"How many times did I come to you during your vigil at the gate? Think about that and answer me this: *who* wouldn't listen?" Luca tilted his head with subtle irony. "You're listening now. Join us."

Custo couldn't believe what he was hearing. All he'd been through. Pissing off Death. Diving into the Shadowlands. His uncontrolled crash to Earth. Bringing the Shadow wolf with him.

"You always did like to do things the hard way," Luca observed.

"Stay out of my head."

Custo had to think, and he couldn't think when every conclusion he came to was open to outside commentary.

"Why don't you come back downstairs, observe for a little while, work things out?"

"Don't patronize me either."

Luca held up his hands in surrender. "I'm just trying to help."

Luca turned then and left him alone in the cell. Custo could hear the soft pad of his tread down the steps. Luca was leaving him alone with his thoughts, giving him the most space he could to process this new information and come to a decision, one that Luca felt had already been made.

Had it?

Custo had no idea. Luca was persuasive, but then, Custo had been unprepared for this conversation. He thought he'd be taken into custody. Had feared that all his work would be left undone, his friends unprotected. Now, it seemed, those concerns were irrelevant.

The bright little room was claustrophobic. Custo exited and headed to the stairs. Maybe he should watch in the control room a little bit. Get a sense of The Order in action, then make his decision.

He passed the armory, remembering the dagger. It would be his to use, a compelling point in The Order's favor. Talia would be safe with the wraiths on the defensive once again. And the Shadow wolf? There had to be something in that glittering assemblage for him, too.

Okay: An apartment in the city, near Annabella preferably. A way to fight the monsters that encroached on his friends' lives. And all he'd have to deal with was the occasional interaction with The Order. Custo could almost see Luca's point.

If Custo was already going to fight, he might as well do so with the best tools, under the aegis of others like him.

He reached the main floor, hovering on the brink of change. Luca stood at the rear of the control room, his back to Custo. When Custo approached, Luca shot him a glance. "Decide already?"

Nearly. But still Custo hesitated. Something was bothering him, had been itching in his brain since the conversation started.

Right. His mood darkened. "You said to Adam that the wraiths weren't your concern at this time."

Luca shook his head. "The wraiths are trapped in mortality; they aren't going anywhere. Your Adam is doing an admirable job keeping them controlled while we fight active breaches in the barrier between the worlds. We have to repair them before any more dark fae can enter the world and wreak as much havoc as the one who created the wraiths in the first place."

"But you fought the wraiths in the alley last night. What makes today any different?"

Luca heaved an impatient sigh, as if Custo kept missing his point. "We weren't fighting the wraiths. That wasn't our aim at all."

"Uh . . . Looked that way to me."

"Then you are still a fool," Luca said. "We were fighting to save *you*. So that you can join us, add your great soul to our strength. There is more work to be done than you know. You are needed. Here. Now."

"I can't abandon my friends. I won't."

"Do you think the wraiths or the hunter are the only creatures to trouble the earth since Death cracked the universe open for love? Magic is again seeping into the world, and on the one hand we have art, beauty, and innovation with the makings of a great modern Renaissance—your Annabella is part of that, by the way—and on the other, we have every kind of dark fae testing the boundary to grasp the power of the mortal world. The repercussions go far deeper than the wraiths or a wolf on the prowl, and we are doing everything we can to stop it."

"You said that magic is *again* seeping in the world. This

has happened before?" Custo knew the answer before he'd finished phrasing the question. Of course it had happened before. Otherwise, where had all the stories, myths, and legends come from? The angel from Greece had said as much, too, that humanity had forgotten the old stories. Custo choked with the implications.

But the bottom line was . . . "You won't fight the wraiths? What if Adam and Talia decided to quit?"

"The wraiths would probably grow bolder. More people would die."

"And the wolf?"

"Similarly trapped here, and fixated for the moment on your Annabella. He is a lesser threat because, as a shapeshifter, he cannot hold his form indefinitely. Eventually, he will disperse into shadows."

Custo had seen that effect himself, the wolf's sudden contraction from beast to empty darkness. Problem was, the wolf could re-form again. "And in the meantime? What about Annabella?"

Luca's face was expressionless.

Angry frustration burned in Custo's blood. "So you won't help."

Luca met his gaze dead-on. "We are helping. You just won't see it. This morning a little boy in China called a dragon— that's right, a fire-breathing *dragon*—out of a storybook into mortality, and you want us to scour New York City looking for a wolf who will fade on his own?"

An exclamation within the command center set the angels in residence into a new flurry of activity.

Luca said, weary, "That would be Coyote, the trickster, and he just reassigned the flight numbers to all of the Southwest's airborne flights, and you want us to drop everything and hunt wraiths already pursued by Adam and world governments? Not to mention with Death abandoning his post, we have to guide the dead to our gate, or they would be lost to Shadow. We go where we're most needed. We fight the best way we can. And we need your help."

Custo was beyond caring. "If I can die in the mortal world, then the wolf can, too." After all, the wolf crossed to mortality, too, when he fell to Earth.

A long pause wedged distance between Custo and Luca.

"Sure," Luca said with a shrug of irritable defeat.

Custo's heart throbbed in a quick burst of bloodlust.

"But," Luca continued, waggling his head back and forth as if to argue a middling point, "as a shape-shifter, the hunter can return to a shadow-state, only to take on a live form again, man or wolf, uninjured. At least until whichever form is too difficult for him to hold."

Custo's blood cooled. Iced. So basically Luca was telling him that the wolf was immortal for the time being, while he himself could die. For the present, Annabella and anyone close to her would be at risk.

"There must be a way," Custo insisted.

"You already know it," Luca said. "The best way is to force him back into the Shadowlands."

Custo took a last look around the high-tech, gleaming fortress for angels. He thought of the sharp weapons in their cases above, and the conditional access to them.

Luca had said that as an angel Custo had earned the privilege of choosing his path. Okay then. All this was very interesting, and he sure hoped the dragon didn't burn up too many people. And he was near certain the well-trained people in the flight towers would see all those planes safely landed. But really, he'd made up his mind before he set foot in this crusty alley.

"I won't abandon my friends."

THIRTEEN

ANNABELLA was bent on keeping her equilibrium around Custo, but some things were easier said than done. Balance took practice. Her motivation: Self-preservation and, well, she was still angry, hurt, and humiliated. Good thing all three emotions, especially combined, were very useful.

She scanned the city street as soon as they hit pavement, not relying on the big protective men with her to spot Wolf first. Though she couldn't see him, the small hairs on her neck told her he was near. Watching. Waiting. Following. Anger strangled her fear long enough to get her across the sidewalk to the street. Custo tried to take her arm, murmuring, "We'll talk," but she neatly avoided his grasp. There was nothing to say, and she could stay close enough for safety without his hands on her.

She opened her own door and sat in the front passenger seat of the car, relegating Custo to the back. The fact that the vehicle was still waiting in traffic had to be divine intervention. At least the tower was good for something.

As soon as the car was moving, Custo reported the gist of his discussion with Luca. Basically, the divine intervention stopped with the car. They were on their own.

"That's not good enough!" Adam's knuckles were white from his grip on the car's steering wheel. It was the first time Annabella heard Adam raise his voice. The first time Mr. Control had come unglued in her presence. That vein on the side of his head looked about ready to burst.

Not that she wasn't a little ticked herself. Seemed Custo's cronies weren't keen on helping her either. But the performance season was ramping up. Another chance to get her life back was days away. The next time she danced, she'd keep her head on straight and use that Shadow magic to push the wolf out of the world. Things would never be normal again, but she'd be off this roller-coaster ride and back to reclaiming her life. Custo could go do whatever angels did when they were done with their work—fly away?

Whatever. She just wanted this over.

"They won't assist at all?" Adam pursued, though Custo had answered this question twice already.

"Luca says they have other, more pressing concerns," Custo answered. "Shuttling the dead across the Shadowlands, active breaches in the barrier between the worlds, and the dangerous creatures that have crossed. Says you're doing a bang-up job with the wraiths on your own."

"So quit," Annabella concluded on Adam's behalf. "If you quit fighting, then they will have to deal with the wraiths themselves."

"Talia can't quit," Custo said quietly behind her. "She straddles this world and the Shadowlands. And even if she could, she will always be a target because she destroyed the wraiths' maker. Adam is in the war to the very end . . . and so am I."

Annabella's gaze darted between them, but Custo was looking at Adam, who took a deep breath and seemed to exhale a lot of his fury.

"I know," Adam said, "and I appreciate everything you've already done. It's just that Talia has been through a lot, and it pisses me off that help was available but not rendered."

"So what now?" Annabella asked.

Silence.

Well, damn it, somebody had to make a plan. "Common sense says that we try again for Wolf with my next performance, and in the meantime, Adam stays close enough to Talia to protect her from the wraiths until she delivers."

There. Done. She turned around and sat back in the seat, making a mental note to call her mother when they got back to Segue, too. Her mom would be freaking out over missing her at the theater after last night's performance.

From the rear, Custo said, "Quit calling him Wolf. It's driving me crazy. Names have power. Don't give him any more."

Fine. *The* wolf. What about the plan?

"Your strategy would work if both the wolf and the wraiths act predictably, but I don't think they will. It isn't in their best interests. The wolf will try another way to gain access to you. And the wraiths are now aware that there are others capable of killing them. Because they are aggressive by nature, they won't run and hide. They'll attack first. And hard. We need to change things up if we are going to stay ahead of them."

Well, crap. Annabella looked over her shoulder to ask, "Then how . . . ?" and whipped around to grip the dashboard when Adam made a sudden U-turn.

"Abigail," Adam said. "She can't help Talia, but she might be able to see Annabella."

"See me?" Annabella asked. Adam made no sense.

"She's . . ." Adam began, "I don't know what she is. A visionary? A psychic? An oracle? Someone touched by the magic of Shadow, like you, but different. Abigail seethes with Shadow internally; you can see the darkness in her eyes, like there's a storm in her mind. It's sped her aging, taking decades off her life. She can foretell futures, what she calls possible futures because every choice changes the course of things." He fell silent, then added, "I don't know if she can help. The last time she saw a future for me, I wasn't able to change a damn thing."

Annabella wasn't sure she wanted to know what had happened, not by the tone Adam used or the misery that pulled at his eyes.

"That was two years ago," Adam said, his voice rough.

When Custo died.

Well, Custo was fine now, and Annabella had had enough

of him and the doom and gloom. Any more drama and she was going to lose it. Any more fear and she was going to start screaming. Any more Custo and she was going to fall apart.

A little food wouldn't hurt either. She could feel her blood sugar plunging. On an ordinary day, she was bound to get a little cranky. With all this insanity going on, the big men better look out.

"Maybe," she said perversely, "this Abigail will see my name in bright lights suspended over a theater, you know, bigger than the actual name of the ballet I am performing in. Maybe with the word *incomparable* in pretty cursive nearby. Or maybe *magnificent?*" Now she was just talking to herself. "Anyway, that's what I see when I look into my future."

Adam slanted a humorless glance her way.

"Really big lights," she added for Mr. Buzzkill.

She refused to peek over her shoulder at Custo again, though she felt him behind her like a warm sun on her skin. The sensation was impossible to block so she kept her gaze on the road, on the white license plates with their blue anagramlike letters and numbers. GKM rearranged could be gimmick, and SFR could be surfer, and AGL could be agile, but *not* angel. No matter how hard she tried, heat and comfort wrapped around her, embraced her. And she knew it was just as dangerous as the Shadow creature that stalked her.

The contradiction of Custo was pulling her apart and called for an exception in her once-a-year cheesecake rule. Just as soon as possible. And with whipped cream. She needed a binge and bad, the kind ballet rarely permitted her.

The building Adam stopped at was three stories high, one in a series of several similar buildings, on a seriously crap street that made her nervous in broad daylight. The brick was dulled to gray, except for the door, which was painted a clashing, crackling reddish pink. Litter clogged the gutter, and a couple of beer cans were lined up neatly against the building. Remnants of the night. A small sign was above the door, black lettering on a black background, so she couldn't read it until she was standing in front of it. AMARANTH.

Wasn't that a flower?

Adam pounded on the door while Custo stood to her side. He didn't try to hold her, for which she was grateful, though he kept shooting her sorry, troubled looks.

Yeah, well, deal with it.

"I don't want you to worry about whatever she sees," Custo murmured. "Adam said 'possible' futures. Just because he wasn't able to change mine, doesn't mean we can't change yours."

Her stomach had started to knot in spite of her determination not to worry. She lifted her chin an extra notch. "I'm not nervous."

"Liar," he whispered into her ear.

Adam pounded on the door again. "Zoe!" he shouted. "Open up!"

"I thought we were seeing Abigail," Annabella said.

"Zoe's her sister," Custo answered.

Adam turned, a questioning look on his face.

Yeah, Annabella wondered, how did Custo know Abigail had a sister?

"Angel," Custo answered them both.

Still didn't answer the *how* part of the question, but before she could press, the red door was wrenched open from the inside.

A cartoon character of a girl stood in the entrance. She was part Japanese anime, part Goth, with inky black hair, a blunt fringe of bangs at her forehead, the rest parted severely down the middle and woven in lots of thin, long braids. Her black makeup, heavy enough for the stage, exaggerated her eyes, while the rest of her face was ultrapale. A tight black crop top bared her midriff to show her belly button, and she wore low-riding black skinny jeans that fit like tights.

"I won't let you in," she said, snapping her gum.

"Tell Abigail I'm here," Adam said.

Zoe sneered and snapped her gum again. "She knows who's here, *duh*. Been up since dawn waiting with her visions. Got herself all dressed up and everything."

Adam planted a hand on the door to push it open; Zoe countered with her combat boot to the floor to keep the gap just so.

"But I'm not letting you in," Zoe finished in singsong. "She told me you'd pound and pound until someone answered, so I came down personally to tell you all to fuck off."

"Listen," Adam grated, "what Talia did to you was necessary at the time. You are alive and well, so get over it and let us—"

"Abigail is ill," Custo said, thoughtfully. "Dying."

Zoe's pale pout trembled. Her black eyes trained on Custo, wicked arched brows winging. "I don't know who the fuck you think you are, but forcing my sister to look into Shadow makes her even sicker."

Annabella blanched. She didn't want anyone made sick on her behalf.

Zoe's gaze hit her, too, her sneer turning her eyes into twin crescents. "That's right, you'd be killing her." She looked up, as if thinking really hard. "Hmmmm . . . Now, should I let my sister's killers in the door, or should I tell them to screw themselves? Hmmm. Gosh, it's just so damn hard to decide."

"Let me help," Adam said. "Let me bring you both to Segue. I have resources that might be able to . . ."

Zoe's sarcasm thickened. "Oh, I think you've helped quite enough, thank you."

Annabella lifted a hand to placate the girl. "They're here for me, and I am totally cool not bothering your sister about my future. I like to think that I make my own choices about my life, so I wouldn't really want to hear my fortune anyway. It would kinda destroy my illusions, you know?"

Zoe's black-kohled lids lowered halfway in an expression of acute boredom. Lovely girl.

"Okay, then," Annabella said. She leaned her weight into a step back to get Custo moving. No way was she going to kill some dying psychic today. Time to go back to Segue and work on Plan B. Or, uh, C.

Zoe rolled her eyes again. "Okay, fine. She might have said something about going to the party tonight. There. We're done."

"What party?" Adam asked.

"I don't know," Zoe returned petulantly. "*The party*. You figure it out."

Party, party, party . . . Oh, crap. Annabella had completely forgotten. "The reception for the company. It's tonight. I'll get out of it, say I'm sick or something." If Venroy wasn't already pissed at her, he was going to be livid about this. The new principal missing the start-of-the-season bash. Freaking fantastic.

At her back, Custo suddenly stiffened. Annabella felt his arm around her waist. It tightened as he lurched forward, then stopped himself. "Abigail is—" He halted for a second, his chest suspended midbreath. "—Adam, Abigail!"

"Move," Adam said, as he slapped the door to the side and pushed Zoe out of his way.

"Stop!" Zoe shouted. "What the fu—?"

A scream from above cut the air, then strangled into silence.

"Abby!" Zoe screamed back. All bitchiness dropped from Zoe's tone, leaving only gut-wrenching, frantic worry. She disappeared into the darkness after Adam.

Annabella tried to follow, but Custo held her back. "No, I think it's the wolf."

She bucked against the hard bar of his arm across her

middle. "Then you're the only one that can help. We have to go." She tried to drop her weight to escape him. "You can't let him hurt her."

His hold tightened further, but Annabella could sense a hesitation, a moment of deep, conflicted thought.

"Damn it," Custo said. "You stay with me. *Touching* me."

"Yes! Fine!" Her head flushed with the return of circulation as he released her, only to take her hand and drag her through the underbelly of the building.

They burst into a large, windowless room. Its walls and floor were painted drippy black, and a bar took up the far wall, lit with eerie red light. They hurried up a scarlet runner that led to a slightly raised dais. Behind the stage was a short hall, papered with cheap, neon flyers announcing disturbing rocker bands.

Not her kind of club.

Up a narrow flight of steps and down a horror-movie hallway, they found Zoe and Adam crowding another doorway. Zoe was half in, half out, her face fearful, as if she couldn't quite decide whether to go to her sister or run from whatever was in the room. Adam's jaw was set with grim resolution.

Their expressions sent a vicious, electric shiver up Annabella's spine that spread across the cold sweat dampening her body.

"Let her go," Adam said to whoever or whatever was in the room.

"So," a female voice trembled, as if in the throes of deep pleasure, "this is what it is like to be made flesh."

"Leave her alone!" Zoe shouted with a painful warble, her love for her sister stripping her naked.

The fear in her voice resonated painfully within Annabella. Her throat grew tight in sympathy, even as her belly quailed against discovering what was in the room.

Adam glanced over his shoulder, spotted Custo, and stepped back. Annabella stumbled after Custo as he slowly moved forward to take Adam's place at the door. She wrapped an arm around Custo's middle so the wall of his strength was between her and Wolf; then she stole a quick glance over his shoulder.

A woman sat in a rocking chair, gnarled hands clutching the armrests, aged beyond any believable sibling relationship to Zoe. Her thin white wisps of hair floated off sallow skin, colorless lips working into a parody of a smile. Her eyes were blackened with pulsing Shadow.

Annabella's blood ran cold.

The smile reached its grotesque apogee. "You can't hurt me," she taunted.

"Wanna bet?" Custo started forward.

From behind, Zoe yelled, "That's my sister!"

Custo halted again. "Release Abigail. She's not worth it. Her body is wasted, near death."

Annabella shuddered with a sudden realization, her fear turning sharp and cutting within her. Where before Wolf had simply assumed whatever form he wanted, the soldier and Jasper, now he *possessed*, sharing the old woman's body. The *how* was more than obvious: Adam had said that Abigail was so full of Shadow that her eyes were stormy with it. Now Abigail was full of Shadow wolf, the blackness of her gaze hungry, predatory, and . . . unnatural.

The union was wrong, but there was nothing they could do about it. Any harm Wolf took, the woman would as well, and by Zoe's account, Abigail was already weak and ill. Zoe had blamed them for killing her sister; it seemed her accusation was dead-on.

Annabella fought a tide of nausea. She thought of her mom and brother, safe at home. If Custo and Adam had come knocking, she would have barred the door, too. And then some.

"Yes, a joining of fae and mortal, less satisfying than I'd hoped"—the old woman's head cocked sharply; her nose twitched as she sniffed the air—"but nevertheless . . . potent."

One of her knobby hands uncurled, splaying its fingers, palm up in front of her. A condensation of light appeared above, while her eyes grew blacker still.

The magic pulsed, thrumming over Annabella's skin, loosening her joints and muscles, sending languid ease over her limbs, her core contracting with pleasure. The sensation was wrong, too. She didn't want to feel this, not here, not now. Not from *him*.

The magic within her responded anyway: It was pure possibility. Pure potential. The same kind she used to weave a story with her body and mind. Annabella couldn't draw her gaze from the shimmer above the woman's palm.

By nature Wolf could change his form, but he couldn't do more than that. He couldn't cross back and forth between the worlds, couldn't make or see or create like people in the mortal world, like she and Abigail. But now Wolf had discovered access to mortal power; they'd led him right here to Abigail's doorstep.

The wolf, Annabella corrected herself. Not Wolf. He already had enough power over her.

Annabella rose on tiptoe to whisper in Custo's ear. "Can we push him back into Shadow?"

Custo gave a short shake of his head. "He's anchored in her body. It's a refuge until she dies."

Annabella regarded the old woman's twisted expression, then had to look away from what she found there. "It's not a refuge. It's a rape."

She had let this dark creature touch her, dance with her, tap into her fantasies. The memory was both revolting and humiliating in the extreme, enough to really tick her off.

Annabella stepped out from behind Custo, channeling her fear and anger into action. "You said you wouldn't hurt anyone else."

"You said you would join me," the old woman whined. The light in her hand evaporated into the air. Her arm dropped like a stone into her lap, her palm spotted with blisters.

"Get that monster out of my sister!" Zoe was hysterical.

"I'll go if Annabella comes, too," the wolf offered, lips peeling back into a toothy smile.

Annabella shivered, recoiling.

"You can't have her," Custo cut in. "I won't let you."

"It's your choice, Annabella," the wolf said, "not his. Come with me and end this. I know how to make you happy in ways no one here can conceive. You have a body made for weaving magic; I am made of magic. Join with me."

Annabella's heart flooded her body with an *oh, yes!* wave of blood. She considered the offer for a split second, but the oily black throb of the woman's eyes decided it.

"I can't," she said, though Zoe's sobs turned her stomach with pity and guilt.

A hand roughly shoved Annabella away from Custo, as Zoe burst through. "Take me. Just leave my sister alone. She's been through enough. I'll do whatever you want."

Adam caught Zoe and dragged her back. Tears smeared black makeup down her cheeks.

"You can't manipulate Shadow," Custo said, "so that creature doesn't want you."

The talent was inborn, though Annabella understood that it took many forms—anything with vision, she imagined—but then the talent had to be nurtured and honed over years of sacrifice. Just look at Abigail. Her ongoing intercourse with Shadow had brought her prematurely to the brink of death.

"Annabella, please," the woman crooned, "you must come with me. Bide with me. You may not have set any traps for a wolf, but you have caught me just the same."

"Yeah, well, I'm setting you free now," Annabella returned bitterly. "Go away. Git."

Abigail cocked her head again, and with a little knowing smile made a gesture with her wounded hand. Shadow roiled into the room behind her, opening a moonlit vista of dusky purples and blues, of portent trees under a whirling cosmos possible only in story, myth, or magic. It was the landscape of Annabella's imagination, and she knew with one sinuous stretch of her body she could blow through the darkened forest and lick the topaz sky. The longing and want that filled her was excruciating. No amount of faking indifference could cover it.

The wolf belonged there, prowling beneath the darkened boughs, but the old woman's body did, indeed, anchor him in the mortal world. A single bloody tear snaked down the wrinkled cheek.

"Is she in pain? Is she suffering?" Zoe asked as she wept from Adam's arms.

Next to Annabella, Custo tensed.

"She's still with the wolf," he answered. "She's . . ."

Annabella looked sharply at Custo when he didn't finish. His jaw was clenched, nostrils flaring, his forehead drawing taut. Whatever he perceived was bad, real bad.

Zoe wrenched a sob. Her sister suffered. Shame made Annabella feel large and awkward and conspicuous. This was her fault, her problem. Maybe she *should* give herself up. Anything was better than the ache bleeding out of Zoe.

"Oh, just end it." Zoe begged. "Get that thing out of her." She hid her face against Adam's chest, her body visibly trembling as she clung to him.

"You don't have it in you," the wolf said to Custo, lifting the old woman's upper lip to bare her teeth.

Annabella went very cold and still. She knew that Custo did. He'd killed for love before.

He stepped forward into the room, putting her firmly behind him again. "This is your last chance," Custo said to the old woman. "Leave her now."

"You bluff," the wolf countered. "Are you going to break this weak neck with your bright hands?"

Custo's fingers twitched, but he said, "No."

Instead, he touched the old woman's brow. A slender hiss of smoke trailed upward from the point of contact.

Abigail reared back and thrashed her head to the side, but was trapped in the rocker. The wolf might be strong, but Abigail's human body was frail. Beyond, the view of the Shadowlands shredded, darkness fraying into ragged whips of magic, the incomparable tapestry of the fairyland dissolving. The wolf snarled and snapped her teeth near Custo's wrist, but with a backward whoop of black dust that had them all cringing, was expelled from the woman's body.

Annabella's terror seized her muscles, locking her in place. Was Wolf gone for good, gone for now, or not gone at all?

The cloud of black dust condensed, the grains whispering as they roiled, churning above the now-slack body of Abigail. The rocker pitched back and forth, creaking. Wolfish black specks melted and coalesced into an amorphous blotch of potent darkness, a shadow without a source.

Heart in her throat, Annabella caught Custo's wrist, her gaze tracking the wolf's movement. For a moment, the wolf blended with the deeper shades of Abigail's bedroom.

Her heart's wild pounding muted her hearing, which, in turn, seemed to confuse her sense of sight. Panic abused her reason. The wolf huddled in the shadows by the bedside table, then—*where?* Under the bed? Along the wall? Behind the door?

She couldn't see, damn it. Shadows were freaking everywhere.

Annabella's fear solidified into a stone in her gut, a chill prickling her scalp. With effort, she brought her gaze up to the ceiling, to the shadowy splay of the ceiling fan. Sure enough, the wolf crouched there, like a misshapen spider, once stomped but still living, its legs double bent under a nubby body.

Annabella stumbled as Custo hauled her to his side. With a tripping step, they fled to the far side of the room, opposite the door. Breath catching, broken into stuttering gasps, she backed to the wall.

The old woman stirred, whimpering. But oh, thank God, *alive*.

A flicker of movement brought Annabella's gaze briefly back to Zoe, as the sister wrenched free. Zoe twisted out of Adam's reach, driving forward to shield Abigail with her body from the predator above.

"Shhh, it's okay," Zoe said. "I'm here. Shhh."

Annabella gulped to clear her throat and squeezed Custo's hand. She hated spiders. *Hated hated* spiders.

"If you had angel wings, you could fly up there and squash him," she said, voice shaking, eyes tearing.

"I'd need a really big shoe to kill one that size," he answered. He was way more calm than she was, his attention focused on the ceiling. "Adam, add Big Shoe to Segue's weapon list."

Adam grunted.

Custo shifted beside her, and in one fluid movement brought a gun up and hammered the ceiling with a violent *pop, pop*. Adam was one second behind him with his own, *pop, pop*.

Annabella startled painfully with each report, as Zoe squealed and clutched closer to Abigail, hands protecting her head.

They had *guns*?

The shadow fell in a dark rain and landed on four paws on the other side of the rocking chair. A bristling wolf, the breadth and hulk of his shoulders too familiar. His ears were pinned, teeth bared, intelligent eyes glaring. Glaring, oh shit, at her.

Custo's shot was blocked by the huddled sisters. "Adam!"

Adam fired again, and the wolf dropped.

Annabella sucked in a shaky, hopeful breath, though she knew, *knew*, that the wolf could not be killed. She reached a hand to clutch the back of Custo's shirt.

Her high tanked as she spotted the sinewy twist of shadow easing toward her through the rungs under the sisters in the rocking chair.

Annabella tried to squeeze behind Custo, pressing herself against the wall. Wolf was never going to stop. Never never, until he had her. Never never nev—

Custo fired repeatedly at the floor—her body clenched sharply at the noise again—but he hit the thing, tight, smoky impact holes biting the snakelike body, but not slowing it.

The nearer it got to Custo and her, the more the dark Shadow of the creature hissed, foul steam rising as if Wolf, no, *the* wolf, were on fire. Yet it slithered closer.

Annabella kicked with her foot when it was inches away, but the Shadow branched, one tendril twining coolly around her ankle. When it hit bare skin she started to shake uncontrollably.

Custo dropped to his knees, grasping the dark body, and ripped it off her. The Shadow evaporated like smoke in his hands, and he redoubled his efforts as the snake reformed before Annabella's eyes.

A low moan, her own, reached her ears as rank terror gripped her. Custo couldn't stop it. Why couldn't Custo stop it?

The serpent insinuated itself beneath the hem of her pant leg in a sizzling caress, climbed her calf, and twisted around her thigh.

She screamed, near mindless, beating at her clothes in futility as the snake crossed her crotch, lined her like a fat G-string—*oh, please, no*—then tightened around her waist as he approached the cleft between her breasts. Her body quivered with its touch.

Custo was already at her pants, ripping the seams as he

tore the thing off her. The wolf's burn on her skin was hot, blistering, her body responding to his dark magic with a violent, unwilling orgasm. She throbbed with it, flesh, blood, bone. Her senses were subsumed with want and revulsion, Shadow and magic torturing and promising at once. Her scream gave way to choked weeping, and when Custo tore away the last of the wolf, she was certain her soul had been ripped away as well.

Her life, the world, was both wild and ravaged, reason and meaning torn ragged.

At last her legs gave, and Custo took her weight at his shoulder. Dimly she was aware of a subtle retraction of darkness, the retreat of the wolf. Part of her yearned to follow, to be satiated, obliterated by Shadow, even in an ecstasy of pain. But she was anchored in her body, too.

"Where is he?" Custo shouted. His chest felt solid, his arm around her secure. Which was good because she'd finally lost it. Custo would hold on to her. Custo wouldn't let her go.

"I can't see him!" Adam returned, but from a great distance.

Annabella's body went slack against Custo's, her head to the side on his shoulder, dumb to anything but the pump of his heart and the receding promise of magic. Her eyes burned and tears scorched her cheeks as they fell unchecked. The room grayed to static, the fuzz filling her ears.

Then nothingness swallowed her.

FOURTEEN

ANNABELLA was sleeping. Finally. She was tucked into bed, her shiny brown hair spilled across the crisp white pillow. Her breathing was deep and even, lips slightly parted.

Custo exhaled and scrubbed a hand through his hair. A shiver of fever racked him, though the wound in his gut was a hot throb. He was too angry to care. He wanted to hurt something, beat something, tear something apart with his hands . . . and make it stay dead. Was that too much to ask?

He stood up from the chair beside the bed, pain stabbing his belly, and paced the length of the mattress.

The fight at Abigail's place was the second time in as many days that the wolf had evaporated in Custo's grip, leaving him clutching at empty air. At least wraiths could be contained, but the wolf kept slipping away.

Why? Why attack and then retreat only to stalk and wait and watch? Why not attack and attack and attack, until all resistance was exhausted, all protectors dead?

Custo didn't like his answer. He'd spent the three hours since the fight trying to come up with a different one, but with no success. The reason was crystal clear.

The wolf wanted Annabella willing.

The wolf had already tried to seduce Annabella through her beloved dance. Like Custo had expected, he'd simply changed his approach.

Abigail, already filled with Shadow and ailing, required little effort for the wolf to possess. He could sample the mortality that he so craved in Annabella. If Abigail had been a stronger vessel, the wolf might have been satisfied, his menace to the world exponentially compounded, and the immediate threat to Annabella ended.

Abigail, however, was weak. And how wily of the dog to leave the old woman alive. That way, he'd deliver to Annabella a threat and a promise with the same act: Come with me, and no one else need be harmed. Then he slithered all over her to demonstrate how their union was inevitable. That he could give her carnal pleasure, however forced. That not even her "angel" could stop him.

The thought made Custo sit down again, sweating, clenching his hands, remembering the empty fistfuls of darkness as he tried to wrench the wolf off Annabella.

Custo gazed across the bed at Annabella's lovely profile. She'd awakened in the car, confused, blinking for memory. Then she'd sat up, spine stiff, yet shaking during the swift ride back to Segue. She wouldn't let him hold her anymore, and a touch of her mind told him she meant it. And she wouldn't eat, though he knew she'd been fantasizing earlier about food. Annabella had come to the same conclusions he had about the wolf's attack.

The wolf, the hunter, wanted her willing, and there was nothing anyone could do about it.

They had all returned to Segue, Abigail and Zoe included, as if Segue equaled safety. Nowhere was safe until Talia delivered and could deal with the wolf once and for all. Or until they could manufacture a new way to coax the wolf from the world, a long shot with the wolf growing so impatient. The only progress they'd made today was to learn that Custo was mortal, and the wolf, for all intents and purposes, was not.

Felt more like a step back.

. . . *idiot better cooperate* . . . The garbled bit of Adam's thoughts told Custo he was approaching. Sure enough, there was a soft rustle of noise in the foyer of the apartment, then a shuffle of multiple people crossing the living area. Custo stood in the bedroom, waiting for them to come to him. They'd better keep it quiet, too.

Adam had his "not taking any arguments" expression on as he entered. Dr. Lin arrived next. Short, round, and bald, he stood in direct contrast to the two accompanying muscle-bound male nurses pushing a mobile gurney and a trayful of tools and supplies.

Before Adam could get a word out, Custo mouthed, "No, thank you," and then turned his attention back to Anna-bella to dismiss the lot of them.

"Do you or don't you have a bullet in your belly?" Adam asked softly, with an unspoken *you poor bastard* tagged on.

According to Luca, presumably a trustworthy source, Custo did. Not to mention his gut on his left side ached like a motherfucker. So yeah, he wouldn't be shocked to find a bullet in there.

Custo frowned. If he let the good doctor dig it out, he'd be incapacitated for a while, even with his rapid healing. What if the wolf infiltrated Segue again? What if the wolf were in the room now? What if the wolf chose that very moment to attack again?

What if . . . what if . . . what if . . . ? That question was maddening.

"Or are you afraid of the needle?"

Custo gave Adam his best deadpan. Not funny. Besides, that was *years* ago, and there were extenuating circum-stances.

Adam shrugged. "You know you need to be in top form. Suck it up, and let Dr. Lin take the bullet out. I'm not telling you what's happened until you do."

What's happened?

Easy as 1-2-3, Custo reached with his mind, and Adam answered the question: Geoffrey, their suspected Segue trai-tor, had been found dead. Murdered by wraiths.

Custo scowled. He wasn't surprised. He had known that ferreting out the traitor wasn't going to be as simple as chas-ing the one that ran away. That left the twenty-seven in voluntary containment. He'd have to question them personally and see what he could uncover through more direct means. It had to be one of them; no one else was privy to their plans. With everything else going on, this one threat had to be eliminated, and soon.

They couldn't sustain another wraith attack with the wolf on the prowl.

But first, Custo had to take care of himself. Luca knew it, Adam knew it, and he knew it, too. Surgery was damn inconvenient, but his wound was a liability. And no amount of cursing or ignoring the pain would change that fact.

Custo would have preferred Gillian, whom he'd known for years as an excellent physician, but she wasn't leaving Talia's side. Which was good; Custo didn't want her pregnancy endangered because of him. He'd settle for Lin.

"Fine. We do it here." Custo turned to Dr. Lin. He kept his voice low. "Nothing fancy, just get in and out. I heal remarkably well." In case the man didn't get it, he added, "Wraith well."

"He's not a wraith," Adam countered, though Custo didn't think it necessary. "But he does have an extraordinary healing capacity impeded by the bullet."

Enough. Custo wanted this over. He grabbed the gurney, ignored his discomfort while he dragged it out of the startled nurses' grasps—pussies with muscle—and positioned it perpendicular to the bed so he could watch Annabella during the slice-and-dice. He peeled off his shirt. His hands went to his belt and he dropped trou. The skin at his side was hot to the touch.

Leaping onto the table and wincing with a roar of pain at his side, he said, "Ready."

The doctor and his crew were not.

"Now!"

Annabella whimpered and Custo bit back a curse. She had taken so long to settle down.

Adam came up alongside him while the doctor prepared. With a glance at Annabella, he said, "She seems better. Her color is good, and Dr. Lin tells me that she suffered no physical effects from the wolf's attack."

"She couldn't stop shaking for a full hour."

But yes, Annabella had been as shocked as he to discover that her skin was clear and smooth, unharmed. She'd commanded him to turn around while she checked out the more intimate parts of herself, and then sat grimly on the side of the bed making terrible, fear-based decisions about her life, none of which she'd uttered to him. He got the gist through his own means: if she stopped dancing, the wolf would lose interest in her.

At least she made a conscious effort not to call him Wolf anymore. Not to give him that power over her. Not to succumb to the seduction of Shadow. Even though she was withdrawn and quiet, she was holding her own in her head. Keeping up the fight.

"She'll get through this," Adam said. "Anyone can see how strong she is."

But she was human, too, and scared. Only her iron-willed determination kept her grounded. Though there was an exception. "She said the paintings were moving."

Adam's brows came together.

"Kathleen's paintings," Custo clarified. "Annabella said they were alive, that the trees were swaying."

Adam looked over at the framed images of the Shadowlands on the walls. "Was that just her perception, or were the trees really moving?"

"Is there a difference?" Custo answered. Annabella's unique perspective breached Shadow regardless, making the question of reality irrelevant. Adam should get that by now.

"Good point. I'll have them removed."

A nurse wheeled a tray up to the bed and Adam stepped

aside. A cold wash of something bitter-smelling was rubbed onto Custo's abdomen. The pressure, though light, hurt.

Then the damn prick, which wasn't as bad as Adam's lifted, mocking eyebrow. Still not funny.

Custo turned his head for a much better view. Annabella, asleep.

Custo's guts were wrapped, his belly on fire, as the first of the Segue soldiers entered the apartment under guard. He was held in the living room while Custo positioned two chairs in the corner of the bedroom, away from the still-sleeping Annabella. He wouldn't allow so much as a screen between them, and he would end anyone who remotely twitched in her direction.

"All of them passed the fMRI lie-detector test," Adam argued when Custo explained that he wanted to question each soldier himself.

Seemed Adam had gotten his hands on a new toy, a functional magnetic resonance imager, which was supposed to measure blood flow to the brain to ascertain truth from lies with more accuracy than the standard polygraph.

Custo wasn't that impressed with the results. The traitor had to be within this group of soldiers; only they had access to the intel that placed Adam at the back of City Center last night during the performance. Hence, Custo's own round of questions.

"You can tell truth from lies?" Adam asked.

"Sort of," Custo hedged. Not that he didn't trust Adam with his little secret about mind reading. In fact, he didn't know why he hadn't brought it up before, except that mind reading made him intensely uncomfortable. The whole angel thing still didn't sit right with him, and the telepathy made it worse. Reading thoughts was a handy tool, but he knew from personal experience how unpleasant it was to have someone else eavesdropping in your head.

Screw it. "I can read minds," Custo said. "It came with the wings."

He waited for anger, or at least annoyance, but all he got from Adam was, *Huh, interesting.*

Custo pushed harder at Adam's mind. "It doesn't bug you? Bugs the hell out of me."

Adam smiled slightly, saying exactly what he thought. "I'm used to it. Or kind of. Talia can sense emotion when I touch her. She doesn't get 'thoughts' per se, but she can guess them pretty easily based on how I'm feeling."

"But I am not your wife, and I can read your mind." Custo was incredulous. "That has to bother you."

"Nope."

"I don't believe you."

Adam's smile grew. "Then read my mind and find out. You know me too well for me to really hide anything from you, regardless. Anything important, that is. Just stay out of my bedroom." Adam's smile hit his eyes. "Or don't, if you need a few pointers in that arena. You never really could keep a girlfriend very long. I've wondered . . ."

"Oh, shut the fuck up." But Custo was grinning a bit, too.

The knowledge was more than welcome. Talia, a child of Shadow, could sense emotion. Custo, a denizen of Heaven (however unwilling), could glean thoughts from people's minds. The dichotomy made perfect sense considering the respective characteristics of each world. Magic and inspiration pervaded the Shadowlands, while order and deliberation represented Heaven. Mortality drew from both. No wonder the battleground was Earth.

"Does *she* know?" Adam tilted his head toward the bed. The question was weighted with Adam's opinion—he thought she should.

Custo ignored it. "Nope. She's pissed at me enough already."

"Chicken."

Chi——? No. "She has enough to worry about without feeling self-conscious about something as intimate as her private thoughts." Custo gestured to her. The woman had been attacked not hours ago. She needed a break.

"You like to learn things the hard way," Adam said, with a sorry shake of his head.

"Look, I'll tell her when I'm good and ready. When I think the time is right."

Adam shrugged, saying, "Your call," and motioned to bring the first Segue special operative into the room, but he thought, clearly and distinctly, *but be careful or she'll never trust you again.*

He was being careful, meticulously so. Adam just couldn't appreciate how difficult it was to respond to only verbal dialogue when the internals were much more telling. Like with the sequestered Segue soldiers—a couple of pointed questions, and bam, they'd have their traitor.

"Watch and learn," Custo said to Adam.

The soldier took a seat in front of him. He had a dark buzz, a swirl of tattoo inking out of the collar of his T-shirt.

"What's your name?" Custo had it on a card in front of him.

"Lieutenant Michael Joseph Parnham, Third Division, Segue Spec Ops." But in his head he said, *Mike.*

Time to get down to it. "Are you working in collusion with the wraiths?"

Mike straightened. "No, sir!" His thoughts echoed his exclamation, *No, sir!*

Annabella stirred. Hell, she was bound to wake up with twenty-odd soldiers going in and out of the room. But Custo wasn't about to leave her alone. It had to be this way.

"Are you aware of anyone working in collusion with the wraiths? And keep your voice down. Yelling your answer doesn't make it any more or less true."

"No, sir."

"Have you ever passed information outside your authorized unit?"

"No, sir." *Except for that one time I told Jeni about going overseas because I promised her I would let her know if I was leaving the country, but she left me anyway for an accountant because she wanted to have a baby and a minivan and a pretty house with a . . .*

This guy wasn't the traitor.

Next?

Annabella sat up during the third soldier's interrogation, after which Custo called a temporary halt. Adam was right—her color did look much better, though she kept her lips pressed tightly together, her body tense, startling easily. Still wouldn't eat.

She was debating in her head whether to call Venroy and tell him she wasn't going to the party, or to save herself the discomfort and blow it off altogether. She was leaning toward the latter, a very bad sign. She'd already discarded the impulse to call her mom.

A little more than twenty-four hours, and they'd come full circle. She was preparing to give up her dance. It wasn't right. It wasn't Annabella.

"What time is the party?" Custo asked.

"Doesn't matter," she answered. "I'm not going anyway."

Custo had been undecided until that moment, even though Abigail-the-psychic had said they should attend, per Zoe's report. He didn't like the idea of taking Annabella out in public again. Segue wasn't safe either, but at least they had the home-field advantage. The defeat in her eyes, however, was as perilous as the wolf itself. She had to live her life, revel in her accomplishment with dance, or the wolf's offer would become that much more tempting, her desire for Shadow that much more acute.

"We're going," he said.

"Custo," Adam said, "I don't know that . . ." . . . *going to the party is the best course of action at this time.*

"No, Adam," Custo said. Making allowances for her fear would only sap her energy and have her doubting herself more.

Adam shot him a look. *You said it yourself. She's been through enough today.*

Custo deliberately hardened his tone. "She doesn't have the luxury of wallowing in her self-pity. She needs to go to the damn party. She needs to find her spine again. Who knows what tomorrow will bring?"

Annabella raised fear-stricken eyes. Custo watched her fear transmute to recrimination and anger, but she didn't say anything. He touched her mind: Her thoughts were full of murder, but not for the wolf. She wanted to scratch Custo's eyes out.

Good. There was fire in her yet, though there was little chance he was ever going to get to touch her again. To move inside her. If that sacrifice weren't angelic, he didn't know what the hell was.

"Besides," Custo said, "the wolf *wants* to take you away from the life you've fought so hard to build. It would be one more victory for him if you didn't attend the reception. As one of the lead dancers, the reception would be in your honor, yes?"

He saw the delicate muscles of her jaw contract as she clenched her teeth, but she nodded, yes.

Her gaze darkened, and Custo knew that she was thinking about what he'd said. He felt the right decision form in her mind.

"Then we go," Custo confirmed. "We don't have to stay long."

"I don't have anything to wear," she said, voice thick, "and I'm not going home for my dress. I'm never going back to that place again."

"I'll take care of it," Adam said. "Custo, do you want my tux?"

After Peter's murder, Annabella was definitely going to need a new place to live.

"Custo?"

The tux. "The shoulders will be a bit tight, but it'll do," Custo answered by rote. It was an old joke between them, and a lame effort at lifting the mood.

It got a weak smile out of Adam at least, and a clap on the shoulder. Annabella turned sullenly away and climbed back on the bed. Adam brought over a laptop for her to pass the time during the soldier interviews. She downloaded a movie, *Dawn of the Dead*, so the sound of soft screams filled the room while Custo worked.

A more effective "screw you" he couldn't imagine. Very well played.

Twenty-four interrogations later, Custo was beyond perplexed. He'd asked questions from every angle, but a more straight-up, true-blue batch of men he'd never seen.

He was stumped, and he was man enough to admit it. He had to have missed something somewhere, but he'd have to think it through before taking another approach. And it was getting late.

A garment bag hanging on the bathroom door presumably held their clothes for the evening. A glance at his watch told him they'd better hurry if they were going to make the party.

Custo showered quickly, stripping off the now unnecessary bandage, while Annabella put on her makeup at the sink.

When he got out, Annabella used the open shower door to shield herself while she dressed, though he knew she had no problems whatsoever with modesty, notwithstanding the fact that he'd seen all of her lovely body just that morning. But okay, he could take it.

Adam's tux, classic in cut, was indeed a little tight across the shoulders, a fact Custo would point out at the first opportunity, but it looked good.

Annabella stepped out, devastating in a cobalt blue sheath, her skin a glowing contrast to the deep color and her rich hair, styled in a loose twist. Her eyes were luminous, her painted mouth set both to bitch and pout. When she turned to exit the room, she revealed a backless V that stopped at the last dimple of her spine, her supple, smooth body exposed, the cloth hugging at her waist and hips.

Custo's fingers itched to skim down her skin, to shed the fabric from her shoulders, to loose her hair, and graze the column of her neck with his mouth. That he couldn't made him deeply regret pissing her off quite so much.

It promised to be a hell of a night.

A slash of Wolf's claw shredded the bedsheets. Rage and want consumed him, blurring his vision until the hard lines of the room doubled, colors and edges shifting around him as his legs stumbled for purchase on the too-soft mattress. Pungent scents layered the room. Woman. Angel. Blood. And numerous other mortals, all masculine, but difficult to distinguish individually.

The sources of those thick, driving smells were gone now. The woman, too.

Shadow had offered him back to the world too late, too reluctantly, with too little substance to catch her and press his advantage. A little sooner and he could have compelled her acceptance, when she was too frightened and weak to fight.

Thus his own shadows betrayed him, but they had ever been variable, inconstant, like the shifting boughs of Twilight.

Wolf shook out his pelt. He had his form now. And the

woman might not choose to use his name, but she could not take it back.

What he needed was to set a trap. Not a cage like those on the lower levels of this massive structure, housing the life-charged corpses humankind called wraiths.

No, he needed a human trap fitted to a human heart.

And the banshee mother had taught him how.

FIFTEEN

ANNABELLA got another round of applause when she entered the reception. She smiled and bowed, this time with only a slight inclination of her head. She was seriously done with bowing. It was way overrated.

The reception was held at the extravagant Upper East Side penthouse of one of the ballet company's patrons. A champagne affair for the start of the season. The hosts boasted the kind of wealth her family had never dreamed of knowing, and they weren't subtle about it. An enormous, colorful blown-glass dewdrop of a chandelier warmed an entrance hallway several times larger than Annabella's studio apartment.

Talk about crossing over into a different world.

Custo's hand was warm at the small of her back, as if he were her date or something. She'd be damned, however, before she'd lean against him and get another of his remarks about her lack of spine. A nightmarish snakelike shadow had slid all over her today; the man could do with a little sensitivity.

Annabella's faith in the abilities of Segue or Custo to get rid of Wolf was rapidly diminishing. It would be much worse if he got a hold of her the way he'd gotten a hold of Abigail. Unimaginably worse.

Or better? In some very disturbing ways, she wanted what Wolf—damn it, *the* wolf—offered. Wanted it so bad that she hardly dared to admit the truth to herself, much less Custo.

She surveyed the crowded interior. The wolf was somewhere in this superstunning place, plotting how to ruin her life so much that she didn't want it anymore. Should she hide under the covers, afraid of the wolf (and herself), or live her life?

Damn it, Custo was right. She'd worked too hard to get to this glittering apartment, to receive that welcome applause.

Okay, back to basics.

Chin up, she commanded herself. The phrase was one of the most common corrections in the ballet classroom, especially for the youngest little dancers. *Shoulders back.* Another common correction. *Tummy in.*

One hour, Custo had promised. She could manage a little poise for that long. Heck, she'd go for two. Poise was her specialty.

A glittering assemblage of people halted her progress with congratulations and effusive compliments. "Magical!" "Transported!" "Inspired!" The fact that these comments were close to the truth dampened any pleasure she would have taken from them. But she was an actress, too, so she smiled and blushed and thanked the company's patrons for their kind words.

She double-kissed Jasper, who embraced her, and took a picture with Venroy, who was disappointed she'd missed company class that morning. Oh, well.

Custo steered her, unnecessarily, through the groups and into a gathering room off to the side. A large, gorgeous table was the only furniture in the room.

"Have a drink." Custo shoved a glass of wine into her hand. "This party is for you; it's okay for you to enjoy it."

Annabella frowned at him as the fruity smell wafted up from the glass and tickled her nose. Maybe not a good idea on an empty stomach. "I am enjoying it."

"Anna!" a familiar female voice shouted over the party din.

Annabella looked over her shoulder. Katrina beckoned to her. She stood with a circle of girls to one side, a group largely forgotten by the rest of the people at the party.

Annabella disengaged herself from Custo, though he grabbed her hand while some old cougar with obnoxious breasts purred at him.

"Hey," Annabella said, faking a smile, "drunk yet?"

"You weren't at class this morning. Everyone was looking for you." Katrina's eyes were bright, her face flushed. Yeah, a little drunk.

Annabella opened her mouth to speak, but Katrina continued, "Ohmygod! You have to tell us. Is there something between you and Jasper? We thought he was *gay!*"

The others shushed her, but Katrina went on, full voice, "And there he was fighting that hot guy over you—who is *he*, by the way?—as soon as the curtain went down. Venroy is soooo pissed, but somebody heard him on the phone singing your praises, so he can't be that pissed, if you know what I mean. What is going on?"

Damage control. Annabella mustered some calm to dampen Katrina's spirits. "Jasper is still gay, as far as I know. He just took something that screwed things up in his head. Some weird herb, I think. He's okay now."

"And him?" Katrina grinned stupidly at Custo's back. A couple others giggled into their glasses.

"A friend."

"A *good* friend," Katrina corrected.

Annabella shrugged. "I honestly don't know what he is."

"Look, if you don't want him—"

Custo chose that opportune moment to turn back and whisper in her ear. "If you are done here, you should probably do a little more face time with the big patrons, or we'll be here all night, *friend.*"

"I'm done," Annabella answered, but not because he said so. She loved gossip; she just couldn't stand to be on the exciting side of it. If she tried to tell them about the wolf, they'd call a bunch of men in white lab coats to lock her up.

Oh, wait . . . that had already happened, at Segue.

She and Custo moved beyond the hallway into a receiving room of sorts. Still no wolf, but plenty of moody shadows. The room had little furniture to accommodate the party, only a console table along the back wall and some trim, upholstered chairs. The walls held family portraits, tiny museum spotlights highlighting their faces.

"*Brava!*" a woman's voice announced as they entered. A small circle opened to admit Annabella, with Custo at her back.

"Thank you so much, but it's really the whole company—" Annabella broke off as Custo's arm circled her waist and pulled her hard against him. She could feel his heart pounding in his chest.

Oh, no. Something was wrong. Again. Where was he? Where was the wolf?

Her heart gulped into acceleration. She glanced over her shoulder at Custo to find the source of the danger, but his gaze was fixed on a man, not a monster.

The man was older, but not old. Tall and broad across his shoulders. Maybe in his fifties with dashing branches of laugh lines winging out from his eyes. He had a full head of salt and pepper, and the same strange mossy green eyes as— Oh. Small world.

"I thought you were dead," the man said.

"I am," Custo answered, dang cold for speaking to his father. If she ever dared answer her mom that way, there'd have been hell to pay.

"I went to your funeral," the man insisted.

Talk in the circle of wealth and congratulations halted completely.

"You shouldn't have bothered."

"Was it a ruse?" the man demanded. "Are you in trouble again?"

Custo seemed to attract trouble. And he was contrary and difficult, and sometimes outright mean. The man's conclusion that Custo might have faked his death did actually seem more plausible than the truth.

The man stared unblinking at Custo for a moment, a million disquieted thoughts in his eyes, but even she could tell that theirs was a conversation best saved for someplace private.

Custo's arm constricted further at her waist as the man's gaze shifted down to her. "I'm Evan Rotherford."

Custo pulled her back so that the man's outstretched hand was beyond her reach. Annabella leaned forward anyway. Her fingertips were grasped in a polite, old-fashioned nice-to-meet-you.

"Astonishing performance last night. You held me spellbound," Mr. Rotherford said. His voice had that flat New England inflection. Money. "I've been a ballet aficionado all my life, but I have never been so moved." He glanced over at Custo. "The appreciation for ballet must run in the—"

"We're done here," Custo said. He towed her back, and the connection between her and Custo's father was broken.

Custo assumed most of her weight as he propelled her toward the arch of the room's entryway. Annabella adjusted her bearing to make their partnered exit look as natural as possible, but it was a little difficult what with her feet barely touching the floor. A lifetime of dance classes for this? They pushed across the hallway into the opposite room, architecturally similar to the other, but with an open arrangement of sofas occupied by little old ladies nursing short, strong drinks.

Annabella tried to look back, but Custo gave her a rib-cracking squeeze.

Custo's father had seemed nice enough to her. He'd gushed over that cursed performance, which proved he had taste. Whatever had happened between him and his son couldn't have been *that* bad. He was genuinely shocked by Custo's appearance, though not by Custo's rude behavior, so it had to be old history. Weren't angels supposed to be forgiving?

"I don't want to hear about it," Custo said, preempting any discussion.

"But you're his son."

"I'm his bastard," Custo bit out. "He taught me the word himself. When I was four. When he fired my mother from his staff and kicked us out of his house."

Annabella ignored Custo's vise grip and craned her head over her shoulder to see if she could get another glimpse of the man. She had to have read him wrong. Someone that cruel couldn't look so handsome, so charming.

Evan was crossing the hallway in pursuit.

"Just make your rounds so we can get out of here," Custo said.

She couldn't very well say anything to anyone while he was holding on to her so tightly. And besides, the little old ladies looked like they were more interested in Custo than her.

"Hear me out," Evan said, as he caught up with them, "that's all I ask."

Custo ignored him, growling in her ear. "Who do you need to talk to?"

Uh . . . "I should probably check with Mr. Venroy again . . ." Annabella's answer trailed off. She didn't think Custo was paying attention to her anymore. Or looking out for the big bad wolf. Custo's eyes were unfocused, fixed on a blank wall, but his expression was hard.

"I don't have to listen to this," Custo said. He dragged her on, leaving his father agape behind them, an arm lifted, empty palm up.

Whatever Evan had done in the past, he was obviously very sorry.

Custo was having none of it. He plowed through the crowd to the door, dragging her with him.

Custo had said that she needed to attend the reception for an hour. She'd vowed to herself to try for two. And yet, here they were leaving not twenty minutes after arrival, and it was Custo who was running away. The irony was killing her, though with the current drama unfolding, she didn't have the nerve to point it out. Later, for sure.

She bit her lips in the elevator when Custo couldn't get a mobile phone signal to call their driver. He was cursing when he finally connected in the lobby and hauled her out of the building to the curb to hail a cab. "I don't care that you thought we'd be longer," he snarled into the phone. "I needed you here now. It's unconscionable that you would leave your post for a moment."

Cabs rolled down the street, but none stopped at Custo's wave.

Behind them, the door to the apartment building gasped open. Custo's father emerged. Tenacity must have run in the family, too.

"I was wrong," Evan said. "Even then, I knew I was wrong." His words had a gravity decades in the making, a note of pain that only profound loss could create.

Custo kept his face turned away, arm raised. "I don't care. Leave me alone."

"No. I left you alone for too long, and you died." That last little word ripped a hole in her heart. "Or at least I thought you had. If I leave you alone now, I know I'll never see you again."

"You made that choice a long time ago."

A cab finally took pity on Custo, and he wrenched open the door before the car came to a full stop.

Annabella didn't need the hard yank toward the waiting seat to know he wanted her to get in quickly. The combined smells of urine and cigarette smoke were bitter, but faint. She sidled over to make room for Custo, then leaned back toward him when he didn't immediately get in himself.

"—you stay the hell away from her," Custo was saying.

"Our family has been donating to the ballet since its inception. I'm not going to stop now. You'll just have to deal with it. With me."

"Get your hand off me." Custo's voice came out in a guttural rumble that had her cringing. His body jerked and he lowered himself abruptly into the cab, slamming the door.

Only Evan's dark suit was visible through the partial obstruction of the window.

"Go!" Custo shouted at the driver, who had to wait several beats for a break in traffic.

Annabella was glad Evan kept back. In the two days since she'd known Custo, he'd been beaten, distressed, angry, but never . . . undone. Near frantic. How was it that this strong man, an angel, could face all sorts of monsters but not his own father?

The car nosed out to the blare of a horn, and then bullied its way into the slow stream moving toward the traffic light.

"Where to?" the driver asked.

Custo didn't answer. His gaze hovered on the door handle, distracted. His shoulders and chest rose and fell with great, unsteady breaths. His skin, usually a very pale gold, had reddened with feeling.

Annabella sat forward. "Umm . . ." She had no idea where Segue was, and her place was definitely out of the question. She never wanted to go back there again. The wolf could find her anywhere, eventually, so why not . . .

"A hotel," she said. Give Custo some space to breathe and get a grip on himself.

The cabdriver scowled. "Which one?"

Her credit card had about $300 left on it. Her bank account had half that. "Somewhere inexpensive, but close."

In the corner of her eye she saw Custo shift. "Scratch that. East Thirteenth Street and Broadway."

"Where are we going?" Annabella ventured, sitting back.

"Nowhere," Custo answered. "I'm sorry about your party." His voice had mellowed, but he still wouldn't look at her.

"I didn't want to go anyway." Not the time to needle him about their length of stay. She needed him back in the present, ready to face whatever came out of the shadows. If the wolf were looking for a weak moment, this was it. Annabella glanced around nervously.

Custo shook his head. "You should be there."

"Yeah, well, I prefer to remain dramatically mysterious. I don't think my rep will suffer; the other dancers already think I'm a diva."

That got a wry, sidelong glance. "Diva?"

"I am very dedicated to my craft. Maybe too dedicated."

"I noticed," he said. "A little more balance might be in order."

Annabella let him change the subject for the moment. "Doesn't work that way."

"I imagine not," he said, then fell silent again.

She chewed a lip wondering how to help him. Passing street lamps were a slowly modulating strobe of sharp light, dazzling her eyes. "I don't want to meddle, but"—she took a deep breath—"seems to me like you have some family history that needs to be resolved."

Custo's expression turned sick. "Don't go there. My head is still full of him; I don't think I can take much more."

Annabella waited a beat, considering. No, it was too important. She knew from personal experience. "It's just that . . . It's your *dad*. Mine ran out on us a long, long time ago, but I'd give anything to sit down for coffee with him. I've been fantasizing about it since I was a kid."

He shook his head in denial. "I spent a lot of wasted time growing up imagining a happy future with my father. The kind of life that Adam had with his family."

"Seems like you have another chance now."

"I don't want it." His voice was rough. "And I don't want him meddling in your life either."

She shrugged. "I don't even know him."

Custo strained toward her. "He's going to find out everything he can about you. He's going to give your company more money. He's going to use all his influence to surround your life. He's going to try to talk to you to get to me." He swallowed hard. "Promise me you won't have anything to do with him."

"Why would I?" Though it wasn't like she could tell the company to give back the man's money.

"When he calls you tomorrow, promise me you'll hang up on him."

Custo was trying to save her from the Shadow wolf. Her side wasn't hard to pick. "Okay, fine. I'll hang up or whatever if he tries to get in touch with me."

It was too bad about his relationship with his father. Not everyone is so lucky to have a chance at reconciliation, and he was throwing it away. She'd give anything for five minutes to understand hers. Five freaking minutes, but no . . .

"He will," Custo insisted. "It was all he could think about when he saw you."

"I'm pretty sure he was thinking about you."

Custo put the heels of his palms to his eyes. "No. He's thinking about you as a way to get to me. About how he finally has a connection to exploit. I can't get him out of my head. Nothing my whole life, and now he's entrenched in my mind. He's already got a list of people he's going to contact tomorrow morning. He's going to talk to your director, Mr. Venroy, right now."

A chill washed over Annabella's body. Custo kept saying things like that. She hadn't thought much of it before, but now . . . "What do you mean out of your head?"

"I mean I can hear my old man in my fucking head." His hands moved to grip his skull. The muscles on his jaw rippled as he clenched his teeth.

Annabella darted a glance at the cabdriver only to see

him drop his eyes from the rearview mirror to the road. *Yeah, you just watch where you're going.*

She shifted closer to Custo. "You mean you can hear what he's thinking? You can read people's minds?"

"Some better than others."

Annabella was pretty sure she was part of the "some." He'd said, done, too many things to be merely observant. Damn it—she'd been practically begging him to touch her since they first met. Imagining his hands everywhere . . . No wonder they seemed to have danced right over the preliminaries and got right to the heavy stuff. Simple flirting was nearly impossible when all she could think about was—

Her gaze flew to his face, body rapidly flushing from chilled to heated embarrassment.

"You have nothing to be ashamed of," he said, voice rough and strained. "I've wanted you just as bad, and I showed as much this morning."

And did he know about the sick thrill she got from the wolf? From the Shadow magic?

Custo looked outside his window.

The burn in her face intensified. This was *not* okay with her.

She sat back against the door, putting as much distance between them as she could. She didn't want to be cold about his whole dad thing, but this was . . . was just . . . not okay.

The rest of the freak show stuff she'd handled, not well, but she'd handled. She'd seen and been told some scary shit, and she hadn't run screaming from any rooms or been drugged happy and drooling. Of course, the wraith thing she'd known about. They were all over the news and online. She'd never seen one, but the authority of the nightly news had, in a little way, prepared her for the idea of the existence of other spooky beings.

But still . . . People had the right to pick and choose the thoughts they shared.

He should have told her.

"Annabella, please . . ."

She didn't answer. Didn't know how. And, she didn't even know if he needed her to. Not when he could lift her responses out of her head.

"I can't help what I am," he said.

Me neither. I'm upset.

The cab pulled to a stop and the driver flung a number over his shoulder at Custo.

She opened the cab door and got out, leaving Custo to pay. She took a deep breath; the air here had the flat overlay of dust and concrete. The imposing buildings, facades quaint with old-world architectural details, were well kept, the street semiclean. A tall silvery block to her right looked over the rest of the neighborhood, all very gray and businessy, with little character in comparison.

Custo got out, paid, and joined her on the sidewalk. He looked up at the tallest building. "Come on."

If she decided to walk the other way, would he head her off?

He walked to the entrance and punched a code into a numbered pad. A tiny light turned from red to green. He pulled open the door, the inside a black rectangle of darkness, and looked over at her. "Whenever you're ready."

His sarcasm wasn't necessary. What choice did she have? Stick with the tortured, mind-violating angel, or be devoured by the obsessed wolf?

Her heels clacked across the sidewalk to the door, echoing off the nearby buildings. She didn't enter right away. What was this place? She gripped the doorway and leaned in, peering around. More dark. "Can't see anything."

Custo reached around her. She was suddenly enveloped in the sensual musk of his body. A light flickered on. "The motion detectors were off."

The entry was nondescript white, except for a small sign

that read ANNEX. No room for a reception desk. Anyone who entered here had to know where they were going. There were two choices: a plain door, or an elevator riddled with, dear God, bullet holes.

Had to be another Segue place.

Custo closed the outer door behind him and moved to the panel next to the elevator, inputting another code. A deep click, and the doors hissed open.

More bullet holes. She wasn't getting in there. "I think I could maybe manage the stairs."

Custo boarded. "Thirty flights?"

A long muscle in Annabella's neck, one that had been nagging her since last night's performance, chose that moment to twinge. Her feet, even out of her heels, would protest each step.

"We're not staying here. I just need to stop in real quick," he explained. The raspy tone of his voice did little to put her at ease. "I'd leave you down here if I could."

But she couldn't be alone. Only Custo kept the wolf at bay, and he was clearly going up.

"Okay." Holding her breath so as not to inhale any more violence, she stepped inside the metal box. Not like she had a choice or anything.

Her stomach dropped as the elevator lifted. Her lungs were screaming for air when they reached the top and the doors opened directly into a large, open space. She lurched out and took a shuddering breath of cold, stale air.

Custo's hand at her shoulder steadied her. "Maybe this was a bad idea. I didn't think . . . We can go."

She wasn't getting back in that elevator anytime soon. "No. Just do what you need to do."

Although, now looking around, she couldn't imagine why they'd come. The space was empty, scarred. No windows. The wood floor might have been beautiful once, and to her left, a stainless kitchen countertop seemed intact, a sink spout arching up. This was one of those trendy loft homes. Big and slick, worth millions. It only lacked natural light and a view.

"Where are we?" she asked.

"Adam's loft. Seems like he hasn't been here in a while." Custo looked around. "A couple years ago it was pretty nice. I guess he covered over the windows."

So there had been some. Without them, the place was too still, frightening. Way too many shadows. This better be worth it. "Why are we here?"

Custo walked to the center of the space. He cleared his throat, but the words came out tight. "I don't know. I wanted to see . . ."

Across the room, Annabella could feel his mounting tension.

Custo rolled his shoulders. "What with seeing *him* again . . ."

Annabella couldn't read minds. He'd have to spit it out before she understood what the hell he was talking about.

He turned toward her, eyes haunted. "I had to see the place where I died."

Wolf ran through the darkness of the night. His body stretched along shadowy planes, dissolving and reforming with each bounding leap. The air was sharp with cold, sweet with promise. He drove the wind, growling like thunder toward his quarry.

How *human* that the snare he would set was in the opposite direction of the woman he craved.

A tug in his awareness. *There!*

He prowled to a stop and peered across the darkness at his weak and unsuspecting prey. Lights glimmered within a structure, but they had no power to harm him.

He reached his nose to the sky and howled.

SIXTEEN

GOING to the loft was part knee-jerk reaction, part morbid curiosity. Okay, a whole lot of morbid curiosity. Once the address had left Custo's tongue, a sick tug in his chest demanded that he revisit the place, the moment he'd lost himself.

Meeting his father unexpectedly, being privy to his thoughts—something snapped inside him. His father was his beginning, and Adam's loft was his end.

Custo and Adam had held many strategy meetings here during those years when the wraith threat was growing from a pressing concern to imminent global menace. The creatures couldn't die; the only viable front to fight them had been through research. Hence, the careful founding of The Segue Institute. The search for Dr. Talia O'Brien, a specialist in near-death experiences. The discovery of her personal connection to Shadowman, aka Death. The rapid escalation to full wraith assault once her existence became widespread knowledge. The flight from the main facility in West Virginia. His capture and . . .

"You died here?" Annabella's already pale face turned ashen. She took a step back toward the bullet-riddled elevator, then stumbled away from the scars of violence, and wrapped her arms around herself uncertainly.

"I was caught by a bastard who sided with the wraiths." Bastard. Poor choice of words. "Spencer," Custo amended. "Bad timing, bad luck. Bad life."

A visible chill racked her body. Yeah, it was damn cold in here. Dead cold.

Bringing her here was cruel, but for some reason he needed her to see it. Everything else in his life had been borrowed or owed, but his death was his. He'd faced it alone, the one true thing he'd done with his life. A moment, a decision, without regret. Adam and Talia were worth it.

"Show me," she said. Her voice was falsely loud in the space, as if covering another strong emotion.

Custo didn't invade her mind to discover her motive. He didn't trespass into her private thoughts, though holding back took all of his control. She deserved that much respect for stepping into that riddled elevator, for trusting him.

If he could possibly help it, he wouldn't touch her mind again.

"Show me," she repeated.

Custo glanced toward the hallway at the other side of the great room. It happened on the other side of that door.

The bedroom was as bare as the rest of the loft. Hollow and empty, his tomb. He scuffed his foot over the place where he'd been tied to a chair, though he could never tell her about that. It would be too much to bear, even for him. He paced slowly across the room. A forest grew in his memory: the Shadowlands. Across time, the trees were still heavy with ominous magic, sighing with energy. A twitch of his inner eye and he could almost see it.

"Were you in pain?" Annabella's eyes shimmered, but the lock of her jaw told him she was furious that she'd been forced to endure this.

Custo smothered a heartsick laugh. Pain? "No," he lied, "it was quick."

He couldn't tell her how he'd pissed himself, and it didn't matter now anyway.

Swallowing to wet his dry throat, he said, "I wonder why Adam hasn't done anything with the place."

"I can guess," she said, her voice low, almost inaudible. She took a step back toward the hall, away from death. Louder, she added, her tone edged, "I can't read minds, but in case you're thinking of us staying here tonight, think again. This is worse than going back to my apartment."

Custo cursed himself for being an ass. He should get her out of here.

She swept a hand over her cheek to wipe away tears, her chin quivering. She turned on her heel, haughty spine ramrod straight, and stalked out of sight.

His gaze swept the room one more time, but he couldn't hear the rustle of Shadow trees. The place was gray and empty. Only a ghost remained—himself.

Being apart from Annabella sent a current of anxiety over his skin. The loft was rife with shadows, and he'd managed to piss her off enough that she might put more space between them than was safe.

Why in hell had he tortured her with his past?

He found her at the elevator, grazing her fingertips over one of the bullet holes. It was much better that she thought he bought it that way.

"I'm sorry," he said. "We can go now. We shouldn't have come."

She didn't say anything, wouldn't so much as look at him. Maybe she thought he was in her head again, stealing her thoughts. The suspicion wouldn't be too far off base; he'd stolen a lot in his life. He didn't have the kind of family money that Adam had access to, but he'd attended the same schools. Basic needs, and extraneous ones, had to be met somehow, and odd jobs here and there never remotely came close to paying for them. And he wasn't about to beg a buck from Adam.

He was a thief, but he wouldn't steal from her again. From this moment on, her thoughts would be her own.

She hit the button and the doors slid open. A charged silence carried them back to the night-soaked curb. He didn't try to hold her, but he stayed close and alert. Every living thing was a potential threat.

The cab had gone, but a black Segue SUV stood waiting.

The coded entry would have signaled a breach of the building at Segue. This particular building would have probably popped up as an alert. Damn Adam for knowing where he was, what he was doing, for making everything so easy by delivering a car when he needed it.

He needed one fucking Segue-free, Adam-free night, and this was it.

Custo opened the passenger door for Annabella, who climbed in with her stony silence. The driver shot him a questioning glance. "Out," Custo commanded.

"Sir?"

"Out," Custo repeated.

The driver climbed down while Custo circled the SUV. The man, Matt Becket, was security from the old days, before all the soldiers, the governmental cooperation. He didn't really deserve to be stranded in the middle of the city, but then, a lot of people didn't deserve a lot of things. "Tell Adam I gave you the night off."

"But, sir—"

Custo took the driver's seat and slammed the door on the rest of the question. The driver was still standing in the street as Custo pulled into traffic. Annabella was in a bad mood, he was in a bad mood, Matt might as well be, too.

Annabella was doing her best ice princess as he turned onto Houston and headed for Thompson. Alley Jack Bar and Club. Custo glanced at the clock on the dash, 10:43 P.M. Unless the wraiths had sucked the soul out of the club owner, Jack Stampos, then the Tuesday open mic would start in seventeen minutes.

If Adam and Segue had been Custo's home away from nonexistent home, then Alley Jack was his church, where he went to weekly meetings when the mood suited him. Attendance had been sporadic at best that last year before Spencer beat the life out of him, but no tour through the life and times of the bastard Custo Santovari would be remotely complete without a stop there. If he were lucky, Jack might even have a room for the night.

Custo had to park three blocks down from the club, and though Annabella was still giving him the silent treatment, he wrapped an arm around her as they walked in case the loitering groups of tall shadows got any ideas. The scents of ginger and Asian spices from the nearby Chinese takeout place reminded him how hungry he was, and that Annabella still hadn't eaten.

Annabella's profile in the streetlight was smooth and cold as marble. He liked a girl who could hold a grudge in the face of all the shit they'd been through. That kind of constancy took nerve and dedication. All those years of ballet discipline exercised to shut him out. Sucked for him, but good for her.

They reached the narrow concrete steps to Jack's. They were wicked steep for loading and unloading gear, and probably miserable on high heels. He'd just have to hold on to her some more. Good for him, too bad for her.

"I'm not going down there," she said.

"Sure you are." Custo gave her a little nudge. The street was bright with traffic, but he didn't trust the staggered blind corners of the buildings. A wolf lurked somewhere in this city, watching and waiting.

Annabella bitched all the way down, something along the lines of being dragged from one crap hideout to the next only to die by falling and breaking her neck on a freaking flight of stairs. When she wrenched open the door to the club, a rain of tenor sax finally drowned her out.

"It's too dark in here," she shouted, stopping in the doorway.

The wolf hid in shadows, so her fears were understandable, but the creature had no problem with light now either. She had to get over it.

Custo half pushed, half carried her into the comparable pitch of the club. The music was so loud, he could almost feel it vibrating on his skin. "We won't be down here long," he said into her ear. "It's a place where we can be off everyone's radar."

He waited for his eyes to adjust, the darkness taking on depth and variation until he could make out the block of the bar, to his left, attended by hunched men. Others sat at small tables crowding the long, crooked rectangle of a room. Various instruments cluttered the small spaces between the tables. The room culminated at a slightly raised platform where a trio played—drums, upright bass, and sax. Old cigarette smoke poisoned the air, leaving an acrid, bitter taste in his mouth. He took a deep breath of the wretched stuff, more at ease than he'd been since he'd scraped his bare ass outside that friggin' theater.

Custo was two years dead, but Jack Stampos was still at the bar. "Well, I'll be damned."

Custo dragged Annabella over to the bar and shook Jack's hand. "It's been too long."

Jack looked older: his hairline had taken two dips on either side of his forehead and the reluctant light of the club made deep creases of the man's wrinkles.

"This is Annabella," Custo said, yanking her hard up to his side, and just to tick her off some more, he added, "my sweetheart."

She gave an angry but cute grunt, grumbling "not likely," loud enough for Jack to hear.

"Nice to meet you anyway," Jack answered. He shot Custo a look that said, *You got your hands full with this one.* No mind reading necessary.

He was done with mind reading for the night anyway. It cost him too much.

Custo leaned into the bar, pitching his voice to both suggest and carry. "You still got that room upstairs?"

Annabella stiffened, then planted one of her pointy elbows in his gut.

Jack chuckled. "Yeah, I still got that room, but it'll cost you."

That was new, but Custo was willing. He reached for his wallet. "How much?"

"Put your damn money away," Jack said. He moved away to refill a drink, then stepped a bit farther, stooping, and drew out a guitar case from under the bar. "Play me a song, and I'll get you both supper as well."

"You've got to be kidding me," Annabella said. "I've got a monster after me and these heels are killing my feet. I want to go to bed."

"Oh, we will," Custo said, taking the guitar. The "we" had her scowling again. He was certain a whole new level of violence was added to whatever was in her head. Anything to distract her from the wolf. "Suppers, too, eh?"

"You were always hungry, if I remember correctly."

Jack referred to the days when Custo was just out of school. Adam had offered him a job in his father's company, but pride wouldn't let him take it. Another handout would have cost Custo way more than any paycheck could cover. It had been time to make something of himself, show his father what he'd thrown away so many years before.

He'd had only a few months of living hand to mouth when Adam called him, desperate for help. Jacob, Adam's older brother, had gone insane, turned into a wraith, and had murdered Adam's perfect family. The rest was Segue history.

"I am exhausted, Custo," Annabella said.

He was sure she was, but she would live. And if the wolf decided to . . . *engage* them, then here was just as good a place as any to make it clear that Custo was not giving up Annabella.

They took a table near the front. The back ones were

mostly filled with musicians ogling Annabella's dress, or depending on the view, lack thereof. Near the makeshift stage there was more light anyway, which should make Annabella less jittery. She settled herself into a seat. A glass of wine was set before her, another gift from Jack.

Custo popped the frogs on the guitar case while the guy on sax finished up his song. Opening the lid, a waft of sweet wood cut the stale air of the club. Nestled inside was a beauty of an arch-top jazz guitar, a Benedetto. Inlayed with abalone along the neck and constructed of a mix of exotic woods, walnut and curly maple most likely, it gleamed as he lifted it to his knees. Had to be a recent acquisition by Jack, at a pretty penny. It was an honor to try his hand at it.

Jack took the stage as the guy on sax accepted his smattering of applause. "We have a slight change in our lineup. When you hear him play, you won't mind the wait. Custo? When you're ready."

Custo took the stage, forcing himself not to look at Annabella, though he could feel her—he always felt her—simmering on his skin. She burned hotter just now.

The bass player, an old guy, held the neck of his upright, the knuckles of his hands enlarged. The drummer was college-young, with black bolts in his earlobes. A guitar cord snaked from the amplifier to the center and got tangled around the leg of a stool. Custo lifted the seat and planted it front and center of the stage. He switched the amp to "stand-by" to avoid a screech, then flipped it back to "on" after he was plugged in and ready to go.

He settled himself on the stool, glanced out over the group, and came to rest on his livid Annabella. "For you," he said.

Annabella gripped the seat of her chair as Custo put pick to guitar. Her insides ached, straining to control and compartmentalize the emotions that churned and surged within her.

The toxic air of this hole-in-the-wall of a jazz club was making her nauseated, too. She wanted to get out of there, but had no choice but to stay put.

They were tempting fate, dangling her like bait into the shadows. The wolf could, *would*, come any moment now. Why didn't he attack again? She was vulnerable.

A sip of wine burned her throat. She'd had enough of Custo Santovari. Enough. She couldn't think straight, *feel* straight, with him around. Angel? Demon? She barely even knew herself anymore.

Of course the song he chose would be depressing. The melody was one of those bluesy dirges in a minor key. She never really cared for free-form jazz anyway. Must be an acquired taste. The drum's soft rap counted the final grains of time at the end of a life. The bass's *doo-dow-dow-doo* was like a heart about to beat its last. And Custo had dedicated it to her. Well, thank you very much.

She clenched her hands on the wood under her thighs to stop her shakes.

Not that he could help the whole wolf thing. But still . . . Forcing her to go to that stupid reception, then bailing. Hypocrite. And she didn't need anyone tooling around in her head, picking apart her private thoughts. It wasn't like she could stop thinking to shut him out. Oh God, what awful things he must have learned about her. *She* was no angel.

And then to take her to that miserable loft.

What possible purpose could it serve to show her the holes made by the very bullets that ripped through his body? And how was it that those scars of violence still had the power to penetrate and wound? Because she was frickin' bleeding inside, and any second it was going to come pouring out her eyes in tears. Tears for someone already dead.

For someone she couldn't have.

He played the guitar in weeping notes, a lament of heartache for which she had no defenses.

How dare he mess her up like this? She bored her gaze into him. *How dare you do this to me?*

No response. Not even a flicker of his eyes as he picked the strings with one hand, while the other worked the frets.

Custo! Get me out of here!

She'd been shouting at him in her head since his big revelation at the loft. Why they were in the jazz club, she had no idea. Something about a room for the night. If they couldn't go back to Segue, she'd much rather sacrifice her credit card for the predictable double queens and bath in a hotel room. Something, anything, normal.

I'm tired. I want to leave.

Nothing. Just the wail of a note as he pushed a string high on a fret to tug at the melody. The guitar was a voice calling out into the club for attention, the last note crying, *Please!*

She didn't have to listen. She looked away, clenching her teeth so hard her jaw ached.

The song followed her, breaking away from the melody into a solo. The notes stayed low, quarrelsome, building to an angry, violent accusation, but laced with pain.

And then she knew Custo was speaking to his father.

All the things he couldn't say were translated into a medium where, like her dance, communication was visceral, pure. The music formed a foreign language, but like a gift of tongues, she understood.

With each pick of the strings Custo's story tumbled out, the specifics rounded by notes, but the layers of feeling pronounced in sheets of sound. Aggression predominated, but the intensity was strung together by hurt. The refrain passed away, and the song broke into a doubled melody, two lines of music in conversation with each other. One was regular, masculine, predictable, Adam. The other, its brother, was all improvisation, running headlong into a catastrophic explosion of notes, death.

If Custo's life hadn't been co-opted by the wraith war, she

knew what he would have become. The raw honesty of his music, coupled with obvious mastery over an instrument, revealed him. He couldn't keep his secrets while he played. This was his truth.

Annabella's heart was in her throat as she tried to keep the darkness of the club from shifting to Shadow while she resonated soul to soul with the weave of the song. Magic flickered at the edges of her vision, but she kept her attention fixed on Custo's bowed head. She stayed grounded in the club, breathing its smoke in lieu of the intoxicating air of Faerie.

Custo's playing reduced, and with a tilt of his head, he threw the song to the others for solos. The old man played as if he knew Custo's story, dribbling on the bass like a rapid heartbeat. The drums came up after with a snap and burr of a flight from danger.

When Custo rejoined them, his notes were higher, lilting, slightly eerie, and . . . threaded with the dominant melody of *Giselle*. Annabella flushed with the realization that he was playing *her* into his story. His improvisation wove the two songs together into one composition: soaring, mournful, full of impossible hopes. A love song.

She'd known him only two days of hell on Earth. And he was an angel, utterly beyond her.

But with his soul filling the smoky club, what could she do but love him back?

SEVENTEEN

GRIPPING the guitar by the neck, Custo stood to a smattering of applause. Not that he needed it. God, it had just felt so good to play. To channel his maddening restlessness into a medium that satisfied like a back-alley fight, but without the broken nose or bloody knuckles.

His hands had been itching for murder since the attack at Abigail's. The trip down memory lane hadn't helped either. Fucked-up life, fucked-up world. Now that the sensation had receded, he could think. He could be. That dark, angry part of him had finally gone quiet. Like absolution.

The darkness of the club had remained undisturbed while he played. Nothing had moved out of place. No wolf. Just peace. There had been so many opportunities for the wolf to attack, yet none were taken. The wait at Segue, his "outpatient" surgery, the party, the loft, now Jack's place. To what they owed this reprieve, he had no idea.

Maybe it wasn't a reprieve at all.

Custo had kept an eye on Annabella in his peripheral vision while he played. Ready to drop Jack's $20,000 guitar should she twitch in fear. Now he dared to look directly at her.

Annabella sat like a queen in her deep blue gown, always straight, never slumped and easy. She didn't look so angry anymore. Her eyes were shimmery with tears, which was never a good sign in a woman. But she didn't seem sad or scared either. He didn't like it.

He was glad he had already decided not to read her mind. At the moment, he was nervous about what he'd find there. He had wanted her to hear him play, but now he felt exposed. Uncomfortable in his own skin.

He discarded the feeling. It wouldn't take much to tick her off again. It was what he did best.

The bass player and drummer gave Custo a nod of recognition and Custo thanked them for backing him on the spur of the moment. He got a couple of sincere *anytimes*.

Then Jack was there. "At least you were playing these past two years, even if you weren't playing for me."

Custo hadn't touched a guitar for years. Somehow in all that time his fingers never forgot the intricate patterns of the song, and the music had obeyed. He probably owed the peak looseness and dexterity of his hands to his altered status, though he was still loath to own the title. Angel.

Jack held up keys and traded for the guitar. "Same room. I'll send out for dinner. Any preferences?"

A simple question would be a good way to gauge Annabella's real mood. "What do you want for dinner?"

She shrugged, expression transforming from shimmery tears to smug. "I don't care."

Also not a good sign. She wasn't that easygoing. Not remotely. She was the most difficult woman he'd ever known. And what was she so smug about?

"The usual, then," Jack said, "times two."

A sax player jockeyed for space on the stage. "Man, that was scary good. I almost don't want to follow you. Figure I better go up-tempo or out the door."

Custo thanked him and yielded the stage. He took Annabella's hand to lead her through the club. She held the skirt of her dress off Jack's dirty club floor with her other. She still hadn't said anything, still had a happy sparkle to her eyes. What did she have to be happy about?

The world was at war. She was being stalked by a wolf. Her life was at risk. And here she was about to tippy-toe through the club into which she had to be dragged in the first place.

Who got happy after hearing a blues song? She should be miserable.

They climbed a concealed flight of stairs to an upper level. The key unlocked the door to the apartment directly above the club. Jack's pad was another flight up. They'd have to sleep to the vibration of the music until two A.M., when the club closed. Not a hardship for Custo; Annabella would just have to deal.

He unlocked the apartment and held the door while she entered.

"Nice," Annabella said, appreciation in her voice. "Why is the club such a dive?"

Custo took a look around. Mismatched pieces of leather furniture were grouped in a small sitting area in front of an inset gas fireplace. The bedroom was visible through another door. Colorful art, mostly impressionistic renderings of jazz clubs and artists, brightened up the walls. The far side of the room had a brag wall, where Jack had hung black-and-white photographs of himself with music legends. None of the pieces really went together. No decorators. Stuff Jack saw, he bought. And his taste was usually expensive.

Custo threw his tux jacket over the back of the sofa and got rid of the damn cummerbund around his waist. "Club's the same way it was when Jack bought it. He's a little superstitious and doesn't want to mess with his luck—which has been very good since he took over the place. Dive or not, he has no problem bringing people in to hear music."

"He likes you," she said, peering into one of the photographs. Her skin glowed against the deep dip of blue, her spine curving deliciously toward her ass as she leaned forward.

"What's not to like?" Custo loosened his bow tie, and then left it hanging under his collar so it wouldn't get lost.

Annabella laughed. Not twenty minutes ago she was all nerves, now she didn't seem to have a care in the world. Custo didn't understand. The wolf was still a problem. Could be here, in the apartment, right now. What was up with her?

The floor pulsed suddenly with the start of the next song, the rhythm driven by bass and drums.

She turned back around. The dress clung to the curves of her waist and hips before settling. "What were you playing?"

"Civil rights tune called 'Alabama.'" The guitar felt so right, the song coming out exactly the same as he heard it in his head. He hated himself, but he had to ask, "Did you like it?"

Annabella's eyes filled with feeling. "I loved it."

The expression on her face made him take a step back, denying what he saw there, hating her choice of words.

A brow lifted. "Custo?"

He shook his head. "Don't look at me like that."

"Like what?" Her lips curved into a smile, so she had to know what he meant.

"Like that." He undid the top button on his shirt so he could breathe better, but still couldn't draw one good lungful of air.

"Whatever you want." But the happiness didn't fade. She brought her hands up to her coil of hair, and the mass tumbled down into curls on her shoulders. Again that smug satisfaction.

He wanted to kiss it off her face. Wipe away the knowledge in her smile.

She *knew*.

It had to have been the music that changed her. He'd gone too far, revealed too much. But that was the way with music; it demanded everything. No holding back. Denying what he'd played now was like trying to stop something that had already happened. Futile, wasted effort. And a lie.

He couldn't lie to her again. Wouldn't.

Fine, then. She knew. He loved her. He'd loved her since he first saw her dance in the Shadowlands.

It wasn't as if pride had held him back from telling her, or the stupid macho shtick played up on TV and in the movies. He didn't have the time or patience for any of that shit.

She had to understand.

He said, "I. Ruin. Everything."

The smile faltered, a dark glimmer of sadness far away in her eyes.

So she did understand. No matter how he felt, he was no good for her. He could play well and fight better, but that was about it. He was a thieving, murderous opportunist. Not too long ago he'd taken all he could get from her, and he would again tonight.

He dropped his gaze to get rid of Adam's cuff links. Everything borrowed, nothing his. Never his. He threw them on an end table, rolled his cuffs, and forced himself to look up again.

Her gaze was waiting.

"You'll have to tell me what you're thinking," he said. She was smart; by now she had to have guessed that he'd quit trespassing in her head.

She pinned him with dangerous intent. "Fine then. You ruin everything? Ruin *me*."

Heat and shock burned away his bitterness. If ever there were an invitation . . .

"You told me this evening, *who knows what will happen tomorrow*," she said.

He hated when people quoted him.

"For some reason, the wolf has left us alone tonight. I don't know why. Maybe you hurt him badly, or maybe he's plotting something more horrible than we can imagine."

Custo could guess where she was going with this. He should have kept his distance, kept his hands off her. There was no white picket fence in their future. Ever.

"I think we should dispense with any and all crap and tell the truth for once," she continued. "That way, neither of us needs to read minds."

No house in the burbs. No happily-ever-after. But some offers were just too good to turn down. He pulled his shirt-tails out of his pants and started removing the studs in his shirt.

"Now," she said, her voice wavering after her speech. "I think you should start."

Little coward. Custo caught himself from smiling. She wanted truth; she was going to get it.

"I hate your dress." There.

Her faced flushed, hands going to her flat, little waist. "Well, I—"

Custo flicked the last stud away as he strode over to her. Her scent, sweet and subtly flowery, filled him. He circled to her back and stroked a knuckle down the exposed skin. "It's been bothering me all night. It really should come off."

He lifted his hands to her shoulders and brushed away the straps. The blue fabric slid down her body and puddled on the floor. "Much better."

She turned her head to the side. "I saved for three months to buy that dress."

"This is much better, trust me." He skated over her waist to her flat belly to pull her back against his open shirt, skin to skin, then stopped at her breasts. He'd been certain a second ago that she was braless. He turned her to investigate.

Sure enough, a nude bra of sorts covered her breasts. Having no straps, the molded cups were held up by magic. He hated it, too.

"It's a stick-on," she explained, a shy version of her smile tugging at her mouth. She stepped out of her gown, stooped to pick it up, then laid it on a wing-back chair. He didn't stop her so he could watch her move in her high heels with her endless legs in thigh-high stockings and her itty-bitty G-string.

But his attention came back to the bra. "You're telling me that you have a sticker for a bra?"

Innovative. Brilliant. Somebody must be making millions.

Annabella laughed now. "A self-adhesive, yes. So my bra wouldn't show with my dress. You can't just yank it off either."

She began to apply herself to the task of slowly peeling the silicone from her skin.

"No, no," he said. "Let me. I thought I had mastered all women's underwear, but I seem to have missed this one. As always, Bella, you challenge me."

Her hands dropped to accommodate him, her weight shifting to sit in her delectable hip to let him know how exasperating he was being and how patient she was in return.

"Now let me know if this hurts, and I will kiss it all better." He tugged a little at the cup, gently, and kissed the bare spot anyway. The skin beneath was warm, dewy, and pinked. Salty. Her fingers threaded into his hair to keep him close.

Her touch had electricity charging his blood, beating in time with the pulse of the music below. Heat pooled in his groin, pulsing and insistent. The task required a tenderness that he didn't have. Never had. He wanted the thing off. He wanted her pinned beneath him. Pierced by him. So she would know, for certain, that no matter what happened tomorrow or the next day or the day after that, he was hers and she was his, and that's the way it was going to be forever.

The first breast sprang free, and he sucked hard on the nipple. She arched against him, yanking at his shirt, while he made short work of the cup on the other side. He had to touch and taste all of her. To learn her, memorize every lash and freckle. To *know* her. Not just for sex—they'd done that already—but for possession. So that every inch of her body responded to his, so that every nerve recognized him. Only him. No wolf.

He was sorry when she kicked off her sexy heels, but he shucked his shoes, too. His mouth grazed her shoulder, thumb sliding the G-string from her hip. She did a little shake of her perfect ass, which jiggled slightly in his hand, and the bit of fabric fell to the floor.

"Bed," she said. Demanded more like.

He was too far gone, ready to bring her to her knees and take her for the first time right there, stockings and all. Damn, he loved stockings. They made up for the maddening sticker.

She pinched him hard on his pecs. "Bed. Now."

Brat. The sooner he was inside her, the better. He circled her waist to pick her up and kicked open the bedroom door. He didn't mean to jar her with the doorjamb, but it was her own damn fault they were going in there in the first place. And he'd kiss that better, too.

He set her on her feet at the bed and worked the double clasp of his pants. By the time they were wrinkling on the floor she was crawling across the mattress toward the pillow.

Grabbing her ankle, he dragged her back toward him. The bed was the only comfort she was getting now. Pillows later, if she were lucky.

Annabella rolled onto her back as soon as Custo released her. She caught a flash of his green eyes, his full mouth, and his incredible physique before he came down on top of her, his tight, smooth skin rippling with muscle and incredible warmth. She expected him to ravage something—anything would be good—but he stopped, pinning her to the bed with his weight to drag a lock of hair from her mouth.

"You drive me crazy," he said. The vibration of his chest felt amazing against her body. She responded with a deep, petulant ache at her center.

"Right back at 'cha," she said, lifting her head to nip at his mouth. She wriggled a little under him to let him know she was impatient.

He ignored her urgency and brushed his lips over hers, the texture smooth, the pressure hard, as if finding just the right angle to settle in. Then he kissed her so dark and hot that she forgot to breathe. It made her heart pound harder. There was only Custo, his body, and the strange climbing rhythm of the bass from the club below. She was liking his music more and more.

When he moved to her neck, stubble rasping as his mouth worked her sensitive skin, she gasped for air. Her hands gripped his shoulders, her gaze blindly casting upward.

He lowered to her breasts, which by now she knew he liked a lot. He couldn't stop touching them. He nuzzled and sucked; the answering pull in her body was delicious. Her breath came faster as his hands traveled her contours, breast, waist, ass, thigh, branding her all over with finger trails of possessive heat. She blinked rapidly to clear her clouding mind, but his laves and strokes drove away coherent thought.

She couldn't lose herself yet; he hadn't admitted the truth out loud. With words.

Far off, a saxophone wailed. She grabbed hold of the sound as his mouth trailed down her belly. He climbed off the edge of the bed, hands sliding up her inner thighs, thumbs parting her.

The things the man could do with his hands.

"What's this song?" she asked as her vision fuzzed, his warm breath both liquefying her and sending hot sparks into her core.

Custo paused, then kissed her where she ached. "'Footprints.'"

The sax trilled up with his touch, as did the pressure rising within her. When the music fell to a lower register, she gripped the sheets, willing it to climb again. "I like it."

Custo echoed the rhythm, coaxing the music higher against her with his demanding mouth. His kiss was wet, and hot, and hard. Maddening. When the band came together to climax, she did, too, shuddering against him on the last waves of the melody.

Every joint and muscle in Annabella's body was happy-loose when Custo altered his hold on her, kissing her temple briskly.

"Up," he growled, pulling her out of her languid pleasure.

Not that she was complaining. She wanted his weight on her, him inside her, moving slow and deep.

He nudged her toward the headboard, lifting her to her knees like an expert dance partner, her back to him. He took her hands, braced them on the wall, and held them there. At her ear, he said, "Arch for me." His voice, dark with desire, had her coiling inside again. Heart pounding, she tilted her hips back for him, feeling his length behind her.

"More," he commanded, grasping her at her waist, forcing the curve of her supple spine deeper. Her stomach fluttered in anticipation.

She relaxed into the bend, and he filled her, his clever fingers building her pleasure again. Her hands dropped to the headboard, gripped, and rode the mindless, erratic rhythm from the club with him. The music was near form-less, held together by beat and voice, the sax a whine and bellow of wind, all topsy-turvy and endless. Custo wrapped his arms around her to pull her back, joined them hip to hip in his lap. She was protected and claimed, at the brink of something new and frightening, but not alone. He tensed, groaned, and sent an earthquake of dark bliss through her.

He held her when her body gave against him. She gulped for air, her head resting back against his shoulder. Solid, safe. His raw strength came in handy when he expertly adjusted their position, turning her to face him, stretching out on the bed, and tucking her against his chest, heart to heart, heat to heat.

"So are you going to tell me or what?" she said, and bit his earlobe for encouragement.

He grinned. "What? So you can be more of a pain in the ass?"

"You like my ass."

He touched his forehead to hers. "Yes, I must admit I do."

"So?"

"This can't work," he said, voice husky with emotion. "You and I."

"Yeah, yeah. We've covered that." But she kissed him quick on his lips, because the reality of their situation hurt her, too.

He lifted up a bit, so that their gazes joined. "I love you, woman."

She laughed. "Woman? Oh you smooth talker, you."

"My woman," he corrected, tone now deadly serious.

"You're mine, then, because I love you, too," she said, daring him to contradict her.

He sighed heavily, definitively, the movement a deep, changing wave upon her, and answered, "Body and soul."

Wolf gazed at the old woman sleeping on the bed. A false, cloying scent of flowers tainted her skin, near overriding the sour sweat that dampened her forehead. Her lids flickered and she strained restlessly against her nightmare.

Yes. Now. He growled low to rouse her.

When she gasped into wakefulness, he bared his teeth. Ready.

She had to see him first, had to break with fear, or the trap wouldn't spring.

The woman pushed up to her elbows, breathing harshly. Blinking to clear her vision.

Wolf felt the weight of her gaze settle on him and grinned more deeply, lowering his head and bunching his great hulk to spring.

The woman screamed. Loud and cracked and perfect.

Courtesy of Jack, the Chinese food showed up not too long after, eight neat white takeout boxes lined up outside the apartment door, smelling like Heaven should but didn't. Custo could always trust Jack. Chinese and a bottle of good wine.

Custo retrieved the food and they ate it mostly naked in bed. He'd found his briefs; she wore Adam's tux shirt buttoned once, the cuffs rolled up to her elbows. Her sitting position in bed was a ballerina stretch, one leg long to the side, the other crossed in front of her for balance, and blocking his view. He wanted to see all of her again, but he'd get to that later.

"I have one question for you," he said.

"Shoot," she said, picking at her chicken and rice with chopsticks. The smell was sharp with soy and ginger. Her lips were shiny with it, tongue darting intriguingly.

"Your feet." He lifted the one nearest him to examine her toes. They looked alien, knobby with calluses. With mock severity, he added, "Frankly, I'm concerned."

She giggled and kicked him. "They're supposed to be that way, or I wouldn't last ten minutes *en pointe*. I've worked very hard for my ugly feet, and I won't hear you say a word against them."

"In that case," he said. "I love them, too." Guitar players got thick calluses on their fingers, so he could relate a bit.

It was amazing, peaceful, to be with her like this. Happy, naked, laughing at inconsequential things.

Annabella was animated as they talked, her eyes shining, denying whatever hell tomorrow might bring, and he let her. They finished eating and made the bed their world, like a white island of happiness away from everything else. Annabella, sex, Chinese food. Couldn't be more perfect. He wanted these stolen hours to last forever, too, though the club had closed some time ago and once again he was faced with an unwelcome dawn.

Inevitably, Segue came up. Talia and Adam and the babies. Annabella lounged on the pillows, an arm behind her head, gazing at him with sleepy eyes, though neither of them wanted to actually sleep. "I was too mad to ask before, but what was with all the soldiers in our room?"

Adam's room. "I was questioning them, trying to get the truth about our failed mission out of them. One of them is responsible for the wraith attack."

"You were using your Spidey sense?" She flipped to her side, her hip and waist curving beautifully, tantalizingly, and she knew it. The shirt puckered and he could see her rose-tipped breasts, which by the gleam in her eye, she knew, too.

Custo shifted closer, parting the shirt. "Yes. There is someone inside Segue gunning for Adam. One of those soldiers had to have tipped off the wraiths to his position at the theater last night. Adam was almost killed."

"At my performance?" She looked horrified and sat up.

"The informant's actions are not your fault, Annabella," Custo said, tugging at the shirt to bring her back down. "The wraiths would have attacked Adam anywhere."

She resisted the pull. "Did you find him?"

"Nope. As far as I can tell, none of them went out of their chain of command." Custo sat up, too. Annabella obviously wasn't going to cooperate until she knew the whole story. He regretted bringing up the subject at all. "I figured it had to be one of them. There is no one outside the team who knew of our plans for the evening."

"Except Talia," Annabella said, a furrow of thought forming between her eyebrows.

"Okay, except Talia." But she didn't count. Talia would never betray Adam.

Custo put his hand inside the tux shirt to see if he could get Annabella's nipples to harden. A couple flicks of his thumb ought to do the trick . . .

"And her doctor?" Annabella persisted. "Did you question him?"

"Her doctor is a woman, Dr. Powell." Gillian had been

with Segue almost from inception. She'd seen firsthand what Jacob was capable of, and she'd been there when the wraiths attacked Segue en masse. If not for Talia, Gillian would have never survived the day. She, more than anyone, would know how critical Talia and Adam were to the wraith war.

"Okay . . . did you question *her*?" Annabella made an exasperated face.

"She wasn't privy to the details of the security for the night." Now could they move on to better things? And then much better things?

"Well, did Adam discuss plans with Talia? With Dr. Powell present?"

"He shouldn't have." But Custo could picture Adam at Talia's bedside, entertaining her, keeping her up to date on the goings-on of Segue, to which they dedicated their lives. Maybe he told her about the performance. Maybe he let slip his role in the night's security.

"But did he?" Annabella pressed.

"It would be a stupid mistake." Adam was always so careful. He was meticulous in granting access to information, everything coded and double coded with redundant measures on top of that. To speak freely in front of the doctor would negate all that, no matter how trusted she was.

Annabella smiled ruefully. "People make stupid mistakes all the time."

"You're saying Dr. Powell is the informant, the traitor within Segue." Alarm zapped down Custo's nerves. He'd have looked for a system hack next. Never in a million years would he have considered the doctor. Adam didn't make mistakes; he would be scrupulous where Talia was concerned. Maybe he thought Talia, with her gift to read emotions, would be alert to Gillian's intentions. But surgical gloves would take care of that. Of all the times for Adam to start screwing up . . .

"I think she should be questioned at least." Annabella sighed heavily, looking forlorn.

Custo wanted to stay, too, shut out the world and be content. But the thought of Talia, helpless on bed rest at the mercy of her doctor, had him scrambling for his pants to get his mobile phone. He had to ask Adam. Now.

Annabella rose and began picking through her clothes in the background, swearing at her bra. He wished he'd asked her before. Some things became so simple from a different perspective.

The traitor had inside information on Segue movements because Adam told her himself.

Custo punched autodial. It was well past four A.M., but he knew Adam would pick up immediately. Adam never slept.

"Here," Adam said. His voice was low, so Custo guessed he was with Talia and that she was sleeping.

"What about Dr. Powell?" Custo asked without preamble.

There was a long pause on the other end. Too long. Then, "Oh, shit."

EIGHTEEN

ANNABELLA knew how cold and frightening the concrete cells under Segue could be, especially with that smell, which now she knew was arrested decomposition, wraith. The stench was particularly gag-tastic in the interrogation room where Adam had incarcerated Dr. Powell until Annabella and Custo could arrive and take a minute to change their clothes. Dr. Powell, green in the face, kept adjusting her lab coat over her blouse and fidgeting in her chair, crossing and uncrossing her ankles. The woman seemed both defiant and terrified.

From within the adjoining observation room, guilt nagged Annabella: she'd basically put the woman in the cell herself. But Adam was right: caution first, apologies later. Which meant Annabella probably had to forgive him for her own heartless incarceration. Damn it.

Custo asked a few pointed questions and sent Adam a slight nod. *Traitor.*

Mystery solved. Now to get at why. This would take longer, an ordeal of careful questions. Annabella and Adam would just have to wait until Custo was finished before getting the real story.

Custo relaxed into a thorough interrogation, careful not to tip off Dr. Powell to the fact that he could read her mind, or the doctor would go to her "happy place" and he'd get nothing usable out of her. Apparently minds could be pretty hard to read. A very small consolation, as far as Annabella was concerned.

Annabella's stomach rumbled. If nothing else, her adventures with Segue were excellent for her dancer's diet. The Chinese had been delectable, but she'd burned through it hours ago and was back to starving. The gravity of the situation and Adam's rigid posture kept her from saying anything. Clearly not the time. And anyway, she'd been fighting her appetite's demands since she was fourteen. She could wait a little longer.

She concentrated on Custo's methodical disassembling of the doctor's thoughts. Custo circled topics seemingly at random—background, education, choice to join Segue— then darted in toward the wraith connection, which the doctor still denied.

"Custo told me that it was you who suggested Dr. Powell," Adam said, though he kept his gaze through the window. Even in profile, he looked sick and stressed and miserable. "I should have considered . . . but I thought . . ." He took a moment to regroup. "Couple years ago, wraiths attacked our West Virginia facility. We were made vulnerable by a traitor who stole our weapons and sabotaged our escape. I thought that Spencer was the only one involved, but it seems like he had a collaborator. Talia saved everyone's lives that day, including Gillian's. I am utterly shocked that she would try to hurt her." Adam looked Annabella full in the face. "Thank you. If she had harmed Talia . . ."

"But she didn't," Annabella put in quickly. "Talia is safe. The babies are safe. And you have your wraith informant. Everything's going to be fine."

Poor Adam, soon-to-be father. He had to be blaming himself for his mistake of blabbing while the doctor was present. Really dumb. He must love his wife a lot to lose focus like that, as if Talia were the only person in the room.

"Did you know Custo can play jazz guitar?" Annabella asked to distract him.

Adam blinked, gave a short nod. "Heard him play once. I had to hide in the back so he wouldn't see me. He was very good."

"He's incredible," Annabella corrected. No one in her

presence would ever get away with calling Custo's playing "very good." Talent knows talent: the man, her angel, was genius.

Adam's gaze narrowed, both scrutinizing and pitying. "You love him."

Annabella didn't want his pity. She wasn't going to dwell on the hopelessness of their situation. After all, love was made of hope, and her association with the Shadowlands told her anything was possible.

"He loves me, too," she said, defiantly. She didn't say it for Adam really, she just needed to say it. The wolf notwithstanding, was there a future with Custo? He hadn't said, and she hadn't dared to ask.

"He must love you if he took you back to the loft. I haven't been able to go there myself since it happened. I can see him right now, through this glass, but the pain is still too raw."

A lump formed in Annabella's throat. Adam was the only person she could probably ever talk to about this, and she might not have another opportunity. "The bullet holes made me . . ." She couldn't find the word. ". . . they were so ugly and hurtful. I can't imagine . . ."

"Custo would have been lucky to die by gunfire. Quick. Direct." Adam's jaw flexed, the little vein popping out at his temple. "But no, that Spencer piece of shit had to torture him. Ruin him first. Grind him down. And, of course, Custo would take it, stupid selfless bastard, so that Talia and I could get away."

Tortured? Her chest constricted.

Annabella studied Custo's face, his gaze drilling Dr. Powell. When he was done with the doctor, she was going to have to love him all over again, until the intensity of this revelation was blunted.

"He's had my back from the first day we met," Adam said, "taking the worst of everything. Fighting my battles."

Annabella smiled a little. "He said something similar about you."

Adam was silent, staring into the room where Custo pinned the doctor with question after question. Finally, he said, "Anyway, thank you. Anything you ever need, ask."

Annabella's stomach groaned again, but she wouldn't bother him for that. Since the wolf was still absent, she might as well call her mother and get her tongue-lashing over with.

"How about your phone?" Hers had long since died without the charger and was a shiny rock in her dance bag.

Adam handed her a slim mobile. She stared at the face trying to figure how to turn on the super-techy screen . . . then maybe she could dial. That is, if she could get a signal way down here. Adam reached over and flicked something. The gadget lit up.

Yep, Adam's phone had a signal. Probably cost a fortune.

Coward that she was, she dialed her messages first. There were four.

The first was her mom, worried about missing her at her dressing room after the performance and alarmed that there had been a wraith incident behind the building. Thank goodness no one had been hurt. Then she circled around to Annabella's "date" the day before and wondered aloud if she was going to be able to meet the boy. Translation: how much do you like him? Annabella liked the *boy* a lot, but her mom wasn't getting details anytime soon. Delete.

There were a couple messages from Venroy, a reminder about the reception, then a reprimand about leaving so early. Nothing much to do about that except apologize and grovel. Smooth everything over in time for the next performance in two days. Delete.

The next was her mom again, laughing and saying, "You've got to hear this!" There was a rustle of static, a bump, then a faraway whine, which broke off almost immediately. When the sound began again, it was unmistakable.

A howl, a high, extended note that finally fell off slightly, only to climb and hold again.

Annabella grasped the ledge of the window in front of her. All the oxygen in the room had disappeared. Her head pounded. The room tilted wildly.

Her mom came back on, laughing. "It's been doing that for hours. Got all the other dogs in the neighborhood going crazy. Sounds like it's right outside my window, but I can't see anything. I called animal control, so I hope I can get some sleep tonight. Anyway, call me when you can. Love you."

A monotone female voice asked Annabella if she would like to delete, save, or replay the message.

"Are you okay?" Adam asked.

"Just have to call home." Annabella fumbled to hang up on her messages, her fingers suddenly stupid, and dialed her mom.

One ring, two rings, three . . .

"Hello?"

Oh, thank God. Tears pricked in Annabella's eyes. "Mom! Are you okay?"

"Tired," she answered. "Did you get my message?"

"Yeah," Annabella croaked. The wolf. At her mom's house. Howling. Got it.

"Damn dog kept me up all night. Remember yours? The one that followed you home from rehearsal?"

"Yeah," she said again. It was the same dog. The wolf. He'd ceased stalking Annabella and had paid a visit to her mother. To Mom.

Annabella needed Custo. She looked at him through the glass, but he didn't raise his gaze. His attention was wholly fixed on Dr. Powell.

Her mom went on, "I must have dozed off because I saw him in the house, in my bedroom, but he wasn't a dog."

Wolf.

"I haven't had a keep-the-light-on nightmare in a long,

long time. Didn't know I was capable of it anymore. All my nightmares changed when I had you kids. Nothing was scarier in my imagination than the reality of making sure you kids were safe and healthy. When your brother first got his driver's license . . . I still get ill thinking about it. But you won't understand until you have your own."

"I think I get it now, Mom." That kind of fear extends to anyone you love.

"Anyway, animal control never showed, but the dog's gone now. And your brother stole the last of my good coffee, so I'm going to have to kill him."

The wolf hadn't been recovering from the fight with Custo last night. He'd been busy harassing her mother. The meaning was simple, though Annabella didn't want to see it: the wolf would kill again, and someone she loved, until she gave in. Custo couldn't be everywhere at once, and if he tried, he'd get himself killed. His bullet wound proved that. There was no time to search for another way to contain the wolf, or to drive him back into Shadow.

"Oh, and Marne from Pretty Ballerina Dance called to ask if you'd come by and talk to her advanced classes. She says you're an inspiration." Her mom's voice brightened with pride.

To sacrifice dancing to end the threat of the wolf was excruciating, but conceivable.

"Honey?"

To allow the wolf to hurt her mom or her brother or Custo . . . There wasn't even a decision to be made.

Annabella cleared her throat to keep the emotion out of her voice. "Yeah, Mom, I'm here. Listen, I have to go . . ."

Custo had given himself up for Adam, the closest thing to family he had. Annabella could give herself up for her mom and for him. Easy. No matter how scared she felt—and her terror was mounting steadily—she just had to shove it into the back of her mind. Let part of her brain go crazy screaming, which it already was, while the rest of her did what was necessary. All she needed was endurance, and she'd been training for that all her life.

"But what about Marne?"

"Tell her yes, Mom," Annabella answered. It wouldn't matter one way or another. "Really, I have to go. *Love you.*"

The trick was getting away from Adam and Custo, and both at the moment were distracted by Dr. Powell and her increasingly agitated answers:

"I don't know what you're suggesting by . . ."

"I'll have to look in my notes . . ."

"No, I have never passed information out of . . ."

There was no better time. Annabella stepped back, silent on her sneakered feet. The exit was open.

Hesitation would cost her the opportunity, so with three soft steps, Annabella was out the door and into the corridor.

Any moment now Custo or Adam would realize she was missing. She had to get out of Segue, find a dance studio, some place familiar, and then maybe she could ignite a bit of talent to attempt a cross. She should have gone with the wolf the night of the gala performance and ended this nightmare before it started.

Video cameras followed her as she ran down the underground tunnel. She heard a shout, but didn't stop.

Not even when she sensed the hulk of the wolf at her side, running with her.

Of course the wolf would be there, with her, waiting for the moment when his trap would spring shut. He had to be there when she realized that he'd found the bait that would decide her, that would have her leaving the safety of her protectors.

She'd forgotten about the enormous, code-locked exit, and was astonished to find it open, the thick metal door ajar. She ran through it, just as the door began to close again. The wolf leaped through in a haze of Shadow.

Zoe stood on the other side, alone in the cavernous tunnel, looking bored and put-upon, and very strange without makeup and dressed in the same oversize Segue sweats that Annabella herself wore.

Annabella stumbled to a stop. The wolf crouched, growling beside her, ready to rip Zoe's throat out.

The girl didn't seem to care. "Through there," she said, pointing sullenly. "Abigail says it's the only way. Any other direction and lots of people die."

Zoe pointed toward an unmarked concrete doorway.

"Is that the way out?" Annabella asked. She thought they were deep underground. The big yellow lift to the surface was on the other side of Zoe.

"Storage," Zoe said.

"Abigail wants me to go to a storage closet? Why?"

Zoe shrugged. "Code is 852137. Took her all night to figure that out, by the way, while you were off getting some nookie. Abigail saw that, too; she liked the 'arrest' position the best, says it was damn hot, but the one where Custo put your leg up . . ."

The wolf growled low in his chest.

Annabella's face heated. The idea that she and Custo had had a voyeur last night made her sick. But if Abigail had seen that . . .

"Off you go," Zoe said.

. . . then maybe she knew a way to get out of Segue.

How Annabella remembered the code, she didn't know. But the little light turned green and the lock clicked. She grabbed the lever and pushed. The wolf brushed by her to enter, and she followed him into pitch.

The door closed with a devastating soft snick, triggering her fear. Alone, in the dark, with the wolf. She felt his bristling fur brush by her body, his nose at her crotch. His rapid panting and her choking breaths filled the void. A scream pushed its way up her throat. She clenched her teeth to keep it from escaping, her body breaking out in a cold sweat.

Light, a half-sane part of her brain suggested.

Shaking, she fumbled for a light switch, found it, and flicked. Then collapsed against the cold concrete wall behind her, trying to draw on its solidity to bolster her caving nerves.

The wolf backed a pace, regarding her, then barked. It was a formless sound, but she understood the command. *Dance!*

"I can't here. I'm trying to find another way out," she said, brushing away wetness on her cheeks. Custo had told her she needed to learn to control her magic. Now there was no time left to learn.

Anger rolled from the beast's chest as she looked around the room. It was packed with stuff, leaving little space to move. No way out. The smell was metallic and dusty-old at the same time, but far better than the wraith cells. White sheets covered narrow panels closest to her, obscuring the boxes and crates beyond. Maybe if she climbed up, there would be an escape. Otherwise she was trapped. Custo and Adam would find her any second. And the wolf would attack.

Putting as much distance as she could between her and the snarling wolf, Annabella inched by one of the panels to get to a box. She climbed a couple crate steps upward, but couldn't see anything other than more crates, and the wood didn't look very sound. Where was the way out?

The wolf barked again, and she whipped her head around, fear trembling her body.

He was facing one of the larger panels. The sheet had fallen off.

Annabella angled her head to see what bothered him. It was a canvas, one of Kathleen's, depicting the great Otherworld of the Shadowlands.

Annabella scrambled down and ripped the coverings from the other panels. All were Kathleen's art. A stack of three looked very similar to the ones that hung in Adam's bedroom apartment. She inspected them closer; they were the same paintings. Had to be.

Why were they here? Why was Kathleen's art shoved out of sight, locked in the bowels of Segue?

The wolf's body pressed at her legs, urging her forward. Its tail brushed her thigh, its growl vibrating on her skin. A shudder ran through her at what was to come, her body tightening with deep apprehension . . . but not desire. The realization was quick and sharp. She didn't *want* the wolf anymore, not that way. Not any way. She loved *Custo*. The wolf might have tricked her into going with him to Shadow, but he'd never be able to really reach her now. Not after the night she'd spent with Custo. The satisfaction of that knowledge gave her the strength to go on, though her stomach clenched, shakes mounting.

Annabella turned back to the large painting. It portrayed a shadow-laden copse, ageless trees stretching upward, exceeding the boundaries of the canvas. Though darkness saturated the area, the trunks, gnarled branches, and hanging purple leaves had their own illumination, a shimmer of magic imbued by Kathleen's imagination and rendered by her brush. If Annabella allowed her eyes to lose focus, she could almost see the boughs moving.

Oh.

So Abigail *had* shown her the way out. The one with the least amount of violence, just as Zoe said.

Tears burned Annabella's eyes; she didn't want to go. Terror gripped her, white and cold. A part of her wanted to hide behind Custo or her mother, like a child. But it was her turn to take care of them. To do what was necessary.

The wolf's growl grew louder, rolling toward the strike of his bark.

Hot, wet drops ran down Annabella's cheeks. There was no need to dance; a medium of transport was right there. All that was required was a shift of perception, a mental blurring of reality and fantasy, and the trees took on depth, heady scent, texture. Shadow was always that close.

For Mom. *Custo.* And everyone else.

Annabella laid her shaking hand gently on the canvas, and yearned for passage. The gift for magic opened inside her, thrilling in her blood as it raced over her body.

An impulse glimmered bright in her chest, and she allowed it to propel her forward. The wolf was panting at her side. One moment she was at Segue, the next she was . . .

Custo leaned back in his chair and shook his head at Dr. Powell. "Gillian, you're not telling the truth, not the whole truth. We have proof that you contacted someone outside of Segue."

He wasn't interested in her verbal answers; his concentration was fixed on the mental scramble of the doctor's mind, which like her allegiance to the wraiths was confusing and backward.

He can't know about . . . I was so careful . . .

He was not letting her go until he'd wrenched every last morsel from her mind. But damn, it felt good to sit in the same room with this woman and know her for what she was. The informant, the elusive insider. For her, he'd come back to mortality.

Custo leaned forward again, elbows braced on his knees, hands clasped so as not to shake the answers out of the woman. "Look, Adam trusts you with Talia. He'll understand if you were manipulated or coerced into relaying information." That was a lie. Custo was pretty sure Adam intended to see Dr. Gillian Powell locked up for the rest of her miserable life. He might even be tempted to throw one of those stinking wraiths a doctor bone. Give 'em both what they want.

Dr. Powell's lips pressed together, holding her secrets inside.

"How did you contact the wraiths?"

Talia's phone. "I just said I have never been in contact with the wraiths."

Adam would have to search Talia's phone records. "What do you stand to gain?"

The last cup of wraith immortality. Don't want to die. Came too close once. "I've answered that already. I refuse to answer again. I want a lawyer."

Immortality? Was that still possible?

Adam had told him about the demon bile that granted living death in the guise of perpetually renewing life, a perversion of the Holy Grail. Seemed like there was still some left, scraped off the floor of the ship the *Styx*. Anyone would be tempted; who wouldn't want to be young, to live forever? Apparently, Spencer had gotten to her at Segue, charmed her. Her brush with death had done the rest. She seemed to have overlooked how ugly the reality of the wraith alternative was.

"We're almost done here," Custo said. "I know this is difficult, but these are all questions I must ask. Standard. I interrogated a unit of soldiers just this morning."

She squirmed in her seat.

"What do the wraiths want?"

Dr. Powell examined her nails—*Talia's babies. The wraiths want Talia's babies*—then brought her gaze up with an innocent little no-idea shrug.

Custo turned his head to the side to hide his revulsion. The woman was a menace, worse than the wraiths, because as a person she should still have a shred of humanity. Talia's babies were bound to be special, like Talia was, but to prey on infants was beyond obscene. To facilitate their capture was no less reprehensible. At least now the threat to Talia and her unborn children was revealed.

Custo gave the doctor a half smile. "When was the last time you contacted the wraiths?"

Yesterday. Tower location. Had to tell wraiths. But she said, "I have never initiated any kind of contact with the wraiths."

Custo went very still, a mercury-cold fear creeping up his spine. "And why did you inform them about the tower?"

Dr. Powell set her jaw and folded her arms, locking herself down. Her eyes were full of suspicion.

Right. She hadn't spoken that last part. He'd just screwed up. Shit.

Custo scrubbed his scalp to get the blood flowing. He needed to think, find a way to recoup. Probably have to double back to other topics and approach from . . .

An alarm sounded, deafening and painful as it echoed off the concrete.

Custo's concentration broke. His gaze flew to the observation window, though he couldn't see through that way. Then he sought Adam's mind to find out what had happened.

But Adam wasn't in the observation booth. He was outside of the holding area, thinking hard, *Annabella. Gone. Annabella. Gone.*

Custo lurched off his chair, pitching himself toward the open door. He scrambled around the corner, and when he hit the main corridor, ran.

How could he have missed Annabella leaving? There'd been no shouts of alarm, no sounds of a fight. Those would've attracted his attention. Had she been overpowered? He'd been too distracted by the interrogation, the only thing, the only person, that could have absorbed him to the degree that he might disregard the rest of the world for a moment. One lousy moment.

He passed a soldier and shouted, "Dr. Powell. Hold her," and kept running.

Each footfall sounded, *anna, anna, anna, anna,* in time with his laboring heart.

Custo reached ahead to Adam's mind so he would be prepared to face the situation. Adam was near unintelligible, reminding himself that a man did not hit a woman.

Custo understood why when he entered the great cavern and found Adam arguing with Zoe. The yellow lift was lowering, a unit of armed soldiers responding to the alarm.

"You say the wolf was with her?" Adam asked, voice harsh.

Zoe twirled her hair around a finger. "Yep."

"But you won't say where they went?"

"Nope."

Adam's voice rose, sharp with anger. "Why? Annabella's life is in danger."

"Ya know, I don't think I like your tone," Zoe said while she closely examined the ends of her hair.

Custo wanted to strike her, too, but he clenched his hands and forced himself to gentleness. "Please. Annabella is everything to me. Tell me where she went."

Zoe heaved a sigh. "What time is it?"

Adam answered a precise, "Seven fourteen."

"I guess that's close enough," Zoe said. She looked at Custo, but pointed to a gray door. "She's in there."

Of course it was coded. Custo fought frustration while Adam tapped in a number.

The door opened. The light was on, the room packed with crates and miscellaneous storage, but empty of Annabella and the wolf.

In front of him, Kathleen's paintings were alive, the Shadowlands vibrant, potent in every exposed canvas. The largest one depicted the dark forest, a hollow of undiluted danger throbbing with power. Like Shadow, the trees were shifting, changeable, the place where every uncertain traveler lost his north and disappeared.

At least she was with the wolf and not lost alone in the forest. Bitter, though, to hold on to *him* for hope of her safety.

Custo turned quickly to Adam. "The wraiths want Talia's babies, but I wasn't able to find out why. I do know that Dr. Powell told the wraiths about the tower. You have to warn Luca."

Adam's eyes cooled, his jaw flexed, but he gave a short nod. "Go get your girl."

Custo was already reaching through magic, breaking the surface between the mortal world and the Other. Frightening euphoria swept over his body as his senses grew indistinct, his mind's ability to reach and read others going dark.

The forest was endless, without trail or boundary.

How would he ever find her?

NINETEEN

DARK forest surrounded Annabella. The crossing had changed her sweats to the long, classical tutu of *Giselle*, but whether that choice came from her or the wolf or some other Shadow power, she didn't know. At least she wasn't naked.

The wolf pushed her through the trees, the branches snagging like fingers at her tulle skirts until the netting hung in ragged shreds down to her ankles. The bodice was tight and far more ornate than it should have been for the peasant girl of the story. It was diamond-crusted and sharp, scoring her arms as the wolf ran her through the forest. Toward what, she couldn't guess.

All around, the leaves chattered, the individual sounds collecting into almost-words that had Annabella looking over her shoulder, wary of what lurked in the deeper shades between the ancient trunks. She could make no sense of the rhythmic, running syllables.

—*doesn'tbelong, doesn'tbelong, doesn'tbelong*—

The air was thick with the scent of earth and plants, underscored by an exotic fragrance that confused Annabella's senses and burned in her mind, making her exhaustion and hunger sharper, and an already bad mood, worse.

She hated nature. Hated dirt. Hated *hated* the crawly things that inhabited such places. But she would deal.

The wolf had gotten what he wanted—they were in the Shadowlands, together. She wouldn't give him anything more, and didn't want to. She belonged to Custo now. The wolf was trapped and that's all that mattered. Everyone she cared about was safe.

—*doesn'tbelong, doesn'tbelong, doesn'tbelong*—

The hushed voices followed them into a clearing, a starlit

meadow flickering with colorful butterflies, which burst upward when she and the wolf entered the field.

At the center was a tall and slender figure, nearly human, but not. She was pale as moonlight, with fine long hair past her waist. Her cat eyes were large and black, and she moved with a regal bearing and strange grace, her gown floating oddly around her. A queen. Her jealousy was palpable, barely suffering Annabella's presence. Annabella could sense it like a dissonant sound or a bad smell or an ugly touch.

"She does not belong here, Hunter," the woman said, her voice a sigh on the wind.

The wolf morphed into the figure of a man, naked, but covered in hair, and hunched, his snout shortened. Seriously not her type.

"She's mine," he growled. "My mate."

Like hell, Annabella thought. But the loathing coming off the woman was too dense for open sarcasm, and the wolf seemed too defensive at the moment to annoy. Much smarter to keep her big mouth shut.

"She's a danger to us all." The fae woman's gaze settled on Annabella, cold and piercing. "You know what she can do."

"I'll control her," the wolf said.

"And if you can't?"

"I will." His tone was all confidence. "It will be so simple."

Custo had called her the most difficult woman alive. She'd have to count on that.

The woman narrowed her gaze. "If you can't, I'll have your pelt. She doesn't belong."

—*doesn'tbelong, doesn'tbelong, doesn'tbelong*—

Annabella understood now. They, whoever "they" were, didn't want her here. The fae woman feared and resented Annabella's gift. *You know what she can do.*

What can I do? Under the right circumstances, as in a stage with costumes and a very appreciative audience, she could dance her heart out, maybe make something happen. Open a way. But that was a secondary, passive effect. She was in the Shadowlands. It wasn't as if she could click her heels three times and say, there's no place like home. First, she didn't have magic sparkly red shoes, and second, the ice queen in front of her sure didn't look like Glinda, the Good Witch of the North. Seemed pretty certain that she was stuck in Oz.

—*doesn'tbelong, doesn'tbelong, doesn'tbelong*—

Even if they didn't want her here.

Only when the faery woman turned and moved back toward the dark trees, floating more than walking, did Annabella notice glimmers of midnight light following, as if attending her. A court.

Annabella turned back. Alone again with the wolf.

The whispers didn't stop: *doesn'tbelong, doesn'tbelong, doesn'tbelong*. Maybe they would help her, eventually. If she could ever see them. Speak to them.

Suddenly, the trees reached their boughs into the sky like great skeletal grasping hands. Annabella threw her arms over her head, crouching, and only stood when she realized that the branches formed an arched ceiling. She stood in a wide, open room, a medieval hall of a fairy-tale castle. The trunks became the walls around, adorned by great murals depicting the first act of *Giselle*. The peasant girl is wooed by Prince Albrecht, though he was already bound to marry another. Giselle dies, becoming a wili, when he breaks her heart by honoring his first engagement. Not exactly a romantic story.

"Dance with me," the wolf said, shifting. Now he wore Prince Albrecht's costume and looked ridiculous. He had Jasper's face again, too.

Whatever face he wore, Annabella knew him for what he was and had danced with him for the last time.

Annabella wasn't about to playact his fantasy. She looked away.

"You loved me once."

She didn't dignify that with a response. She'd been performing at the time, the Shadows making her judgment questionable. Her judgment was just fine at the moment.

"What about now?" Jasper morphed, took on height and broadened, and became Custo. Annabella's heart tripped in her chest.

A low-down, dirty, rotten trick. Very wolfy. But at least her anger got the best of her fear. She dared to ignore that, too.

"You will forget him," the wolf said. "Memory doesn't last long here. Eventually you will be mine."

Not going to happen. Not in a million years. She already belonged to someone, and she wasn't giving him up in her heart. This new reality she would endure, moment by moment, until . . . Until what? The end of the world? Until the little voices said, "exit this way"? Didn't matter. They were both in for a long wait.

The wolf bowed like a prince in a ballet, like Albrecht, and then split into creeping darkness, his shadows, leaving her alone.

If he meant to scare her, he got it wrong. Alone was wonderful. Alone she could think, steel herself for what was to come. She hoped he left her alone forever.

She blinked, and a banquet was laid before her, the rich table filled with every kind of delicious food she could conceive.

She double-blinked. The food was still there.

The feast before her was every holiday dinner, roasted meats and their accompaniments, as well as great baskets of perfectly ripe fruit—oranges, pomegranates, thick bunches of grapes. These were circled by baked delicacies, her favorites, the rich, creamy desserts she forbade herself for dance. Napoleons, éclairs, and, hooray!—cheesecake. The smells were tantalizing, intoxicating.

Annabella's mouth watered, her belly ached, and her body complained with deep fatigue.

The spread looked so dang good.

But it was *his*. She wasn't touching the food. Something wasn't right about it.

Except, her mouth watering . . . the immortal fae might not need to eat, but she was human. If she didn't eat, she would die. And she wasn't quite ready to cross that boundary yet. The Ice Bitch had openly acknowledged that Annabella was dangerous. Could do stuff. And the freaky voices seemed to agree.

Maybe there was hope yet.

So how was she supposed to keep her strength when she was hungry? How could she fight the wolf with her blood sugar plunging? Low blood sugar always made her cranky and weak. How could she be ready for anything if she did not eat? She needed nutritious sustenance.

Annabella reached for a chocolate nub, but the whispers stopped her.

The voices were faint, timid, and many layered.

—*persephonee persephonee persephonee*—

They made no sense this time. Annabella popped the chocolate into her mouth. The morsel melted in delicious ecstasy, the texture smooth as velvet, the taste dark like sin and sex. It made her tingle all over. Why had she been dancing all her life when she could have been eating?

The voices whined, redoubling, as if in warning.

—*persephoneee persephoneee persephoneee*—

Annabella didn't care. Could they say, "delicious"?

She dipped a finger into the edge of a napoleon and licked the cream. Scrumptious. Her heart was thundering in her chest, a pleasurable coolness crawling over her skin. The silvery sensation hit her blood and had her cells singing, her vision slightly blurring. Yeah, baby.

—*persephoneee*—

What she needed was a fork and a plate. No sooner than she thought it, they appeared, the utensil made of heavy gold, the plate edged with it.

—*lost lost lost lost lost lost*—

Annabella set to work. The feast was delish, every taste decadent. And no matter how much she ate, she never became full, another happy wonder of the magical dinner. She worked her way down the table and finally collapsed— *almost* satisfied, but not quite—in the large chair at the end. The cool air on her skin grew cold, icy, prickling over her scalp. Her mind dulled pleasantly with the glut of food, though that fruit still looked sweet and luscious. Maybe one more bite—

Reaching toward the heaping basket, she noticed a set of doors beyond that came together in one great arch.

What was through there?

She forgot the fruit and rose, the simple movement thrilling her muscles, bones, her nerves that crackled along her skin. She exited into the forest clearing.

But where she was, and why she was there, she had no idea.

She didn't feel right either. Her body had no weight, as if the air carried her in its subtle currents, eddies tugging at her and floating her skirts.

Forever midnight filled the sky. In the trees, soft glows flitted behind the tall trunks. She almost made to follow them, but her gaze was captured by a grave, heaped with flowers.

So sad. Whose?

She tiptoed forward, skimming along the grasses, to examine the marker.

Giselle. The grave was hers.

Grief welled in her heart, and she crossed her arms over her chest. Love, life lost. An eternity consigned to an existence as a wili, haunting the night.

A sound behind her, and she turned.

It was Albrecht, her love, coming to bid her farewell.

Perhaps the stars would stretch the moment, and they could dance, one last time, until dawn.

A tree was stalking him, or Custo had passed that gnarled trunk for the third time. Either was possible, so he kept going, straining for any sound or movement that might lead him to Annabella. He saw only great, luminous forest stretching out of layered shadows and heard only hushed whispers taunting his course. What he wouldn't give for a bagful of bread crumbs. He was getting nowhere, and sick to death of it.

"Annabella!" he called at regular intervals. If he attracted some other Shadow creature, he'd pin the thing down and demand directions, but except for the indistinct voices, the wood seemed unnervingly uninhabited.

Deliberately doubling back on his path, he caught his first flash of movement and leaped toward it, scrabbling over a root-bumpy rise for a better view.

He called through the trees. "Annabella!"

But instead he found a man dressed in mottled green-gray combat gear, armed and ready for action. Custo tripped to a stop. It was Adam, his face set in his I-know-what-to-do expression, eyes direct, jaw tight.

"What are you doing here?" Custo asked, half excited, half concerned. Adam was supposed to be warning Luca about the wraiths.

"I came after you to help," Adam said, "and I found her."

Custo's heart leaped. Trust Adam to be able to navigate in these shifting woods. Anyone else and he wouldn't believe it. "Show me."

"This way." Adam took off at a wary jog, careful to slow at blind spots along the way and test uncertain ground before moving forward.

Custo kept close behind. "How did you find me?"

"You were making a racket. Anyone could find you." They moved deeper into Shadow, the variegated shades growing less distinct. Adam slowed marginally, but seemed to have no problem with the pressing darkness.

Which was good, because Custo could think of little more than getting to Annabella, and quick. And all he had to do was follow.

"Does the wolf have Annabella?" Custo asked. He could guess the answer.

"Yes, but I couldn't get to her without help."

They hit a deep ravine, and crossed via a thick, fallen tree trunk, a black void yawning on either side. Sweat dampened Custo's body by the time they hit the forest wall again.

"How much farther?" Custo asked. If Adam were following a trail, Custo couldn't see it.

"Just ahead," Adam answered.

But "just ahead" seemed like more of the same passionless trees.

And damn if that one didn't look exactly like the gnarled trunk from before.

The gnarled trunk.

Shock halted Custo in his tracks, dread icing the blood in his veins. The whispers rose around him and, out of the corner of his eye, he could see slender figures watching, darting behind the ancient trunks. They'd probably been there all along.

Adam pressed forward a few steps, then turned back. "What's the matter?"

Custo swallowed hard. "What are you?"

He would have followed Adam for hours, forever even.

Stupid.

The man in front of him couldn't be Adam. Custo should've known right away. Adam would have never stepped through the painting into the treacherous Shadowlands, leaving Talia and his babies behind. Not for anything or anyone. Adam was going to warn Luca about the wraiths, even if Luca had denied him aid before.

The whispers rose to loud chatters, like chirping cicadas hidden in the leaves, near deafening.

"Come on," Adam said, making to start off again. "The wolf has her."

Custo steeled himself, doubts crowding his mind, but turned the other direction. Leaving Adam. Denying his presence. The fragrant air resisted his change of course, sheering at his body as he tore himself away from years of friendship and trust. The act was excruciating, every cell in his body rebelling.

Not Adam. This was a ploy, a game, or a test. Not Adam.

Custo pressed on. The direction didn't matter, not with the trees and fae messing with his mind. The only thing to do was continue searching. Annabella was here, somewhere. And he would find her if he stayed his course, in his mind, if not in the forest itself.

The trees opened somewhat, and Custo upped his pace, only to come to a second tripping stop.

His father. Evan Rotherford, standing in his fine suit, his white sleeves peeking out, the Rotherford family cuff links that Custo would never own glinting where there was no light.

Custo knew his father for what he was, another test, but it still took a deep breath to form the question, "What do you want?"

"I want my son back," his father said, extending his hand.

Years of resentment and anger condensed into a bitter rebuke that burned on Custo's tongue, *No.* His father had denied him for years. He wasn't allowed to change his mind. Not now, not ever. His father could go to hell.

Custo closed his eyes, clenching his teeth. His hate would keep him rooted in the same spot, and the roots went deep. Soul deep.

But this was not his father, just like Adam had not been Adam. It was a trick he had to solve, or he wouldn't be able to move on.

Think of Annabella.

Annabella, his future, as this man was his past.

The air took on that uncompromising quality again, the kind that resisted change, insight, and clarity. With effort Custo inhaled a lungful of the stuff, and like swallowing a mouthful of shit, Custo worked his tongue and teeth to transmute the *no* into something different. His "Yes" cut the air with a sharp hiss as he grasped his old man's hand for the first time in his life.

His father, surprised, tried to flinch back, but Custo held tight. The illusion failed, and a fae woman trembled in Custo's grip. She was pale and lovely, her skin washed in moon glow. Her long hair fell in a veil over her lower face, but her eyes took on a shape of pain.

He didn't buy it. He'd caught a fae, and he wasn't letting go.

"Where is she?" Custo demanded.

"She doesn't belong here," the faery said, staring with anguish at her clasped hand. He would not allow himself to be moved by it.

"Well, stop fucking with me and show me where she is," Custo returned. The woman's fingers were slight and cold, her contact numbing.

"It is not our nature to reveal," she said, turning haughty.

"Even if you want to get rid of her?" The contradiction was just like Shadow, eschewing reason for madness.

—*doesn'tbelong, doesn'tbelong, doesn'tbelong*—

"She dances with the wolf and belongs to him now." The fae woman's lowered lids and the cruel twist of her mouth said she didn't like the union one bit.

"She belonged to me first," Custo argued, "and I'm taking her back. Help me find her."

"I can't," she cut back, as though she hated it herself.

The heavy air stirred, blew, rustling the branches of the trees with a high whine not unlike . . . violins. Another breeze took up the lower notes and formed the opening measures of Giselle's ghostly dance.

Annabella.

Custo's heart lurched. He squeezed the fae woman's hand. "Is this another trick?"

"Perhaps," she answered, with a sneer.

Custo peered into the dark trees, which stood like great sentinels blocking his path and his view. The Shadowlands defied logic, so he had to follow his heart.

His heart was through those trees.

He released the faery. She pulled her hand from his grasp with lightning quickness, her nails cutting a deep, long gash across his palm.

Pain lanced through Custo's hand and his blood flowed thick and free onto the forest floor. Looking up, he found the faery woman gone. She'd exacted her revenge and disappeared. He gripped his wrist above the wound, waiting for the burn of healing to start.

—blood, blood, blood, blood, blood—

No burn came in Shadow's domain. Custo's blood fell in slick, fat drops to the ground. Ripping a misshapen band of cloth from his shirt, he bound his palm tightly to stop the gush. He didn't have time for this. Annabella was just through there.

Custo ran toward the music. When he saw the first flicker of movement, he slowed, creeping forward to hide in a dark copse and watch Annabella dance with . . . Jasper? The blond hair, lean body, ridiculous tights, and near-feminine shirt all belonged to Jasper. Custo couldn't get a good look at his face, but he was sure it had the pretty boy's features.

It took no effort to recognize this lie, though Annabella seemed lost to it. The man, the creature, holding her could only be the wolf. His hands were all over her, lifting, spinning, embracing Annabella. The wolf had just set her down again when he cocked his head, sniffing the air. He held Annabella's waist, but his nose lifted, sniffing again. Distracted. Scenting something.

—*blood, blood, blood, blood, blood*—

Custo looked down at his bandage and recalled the scoring rip of the fae woman's fingertips. She'd helped him after all, the best way she could. She wanted Annabella *out*.

Custo buried his wound against his middle, willing the wolf to pass him in favor of the blood-soaked forest dirt. With a great leap, Jasper changed into a slavering, yellow-eyed beast in pursuit of fresh game. When he disappeared into the trees, Custo rushed forward to Annabella.

She had settled into a delicate position, forlorn, awaiting Albrecht's return. She was stone pale, her marble skin lined with a spider-fine webbing of Shadow, lips gray. When she raised her eyes, Custo found her blue irises and pupils were full black, unfocused, with the distraction of blindness.

He approached carefully. "Annabella?"

She gave no answer.

"Annabella, it's me, Custo." He grasped her shoulders, gave a little shake. There was no time. She had to work her magic and get them back. The wolf could return any moment.

"Annabella, I know you're in there," he said. "Come on out, love. Fight. I need you."

She didn't seem to hear a word, lost in some fragile, internal dream world.

His hands went to her face, thumbs stroking her cheeks, so cold. He brought her to him, kissed her passive lips with everything he had. Poured his hope, love, and guts into her. No response.

"Bella, I love you. I need you here. Please." He was tempted to slap her, but something told him she might break, rather than come to her senses.

"Sweetheart, remember Jack's place? Chinese food? I told you that you are mine."

Her eyes twitched slightly.

"That's right. Come back to me, honey," he said, voice gritty. A universe of feeling filled his chest to near bursting. "Come back and make an honest man of me."

Just that faraway look again. So much for professing undying love. *Damn it.*

Okay, think. He brought their foreheads together and exhaled roughly.

—he'scoming, he'scoming, he'scoming—

Custo's voice turned stern. He shook her, harder. "Wake up, Annabella. You can control this. It's your gift. Your talent to draw from Shadow. Use it to get us home. Get us home, Annabella. Fight for life. Don't you want to dance?"

At that her head turned softly.

"That's right, *dance*," Custo said.

"I danced with Albrecht, but he broke my heart, and I died."

Custo recognized the story of *Giselle*. Now he understood: she was lost in the ballet, a refuge and a trap. His mind raced to recall the details. Giselle rose from the grave as a wili, a spirit. When Albrecht came to mourn her, the queen of the wilis commanded that he dance until he died. Giselle chose to dance with him, to see him through the night to the dawn of day.

Oh, that cunning wolf.

—he'scoming, he'scoming, he'scoming—

The Shadowlands were perpetual night, perpetual darkness. A night that lasts forever. And Annabella was trapped in it.

Very clever.

But Custo could do the wolf one better: he knew the difference between Giselle, the character in a ballet, and Annabella, the storyteller, the magic-maker.

"You've already danced with Albrecht, Annabella," Custo said. "What happens next?"

No wonder the fae woman was so keen on getting rid of her. Annabella's power was beyond formidable. It was frightening.

"What happens next, Annabella? Tell the story."

—*he'scoming, he'scoming, he'scoming*—

Annabella lifted her head, listening as morning bells jangled loudly through the forever night-darkened trees.

—*he'scoming, he'scoming, he'scoming*—

Custo didn't bother to look over his shoulder, his body electric with hope, even as he heard the wolf's rapid footfalls pounding across the clearing.

"That's right, honey," he said, eyes tearing with fierce pride. "Bella, tell the story: raise the sun."

TWENTY

THE ground rumbled beneath Annabella's feet, bells clanging loudly in her mind. She held on to the sound with everything she was, lashed her heart to the story, and heaved, lifting the blazing orb of the sun to the horizon line.

Tell the story. Raise the sun.

Pink washed the sky, drowning out the diamond glow of the stars. A sudden, monstrous gale blew through the Shadow forest, denuding the trees of their leaves, the trunks rising like skeletons from the trembling ground in the wan glow of dawn. A keening wail lifted all around, the dark inhabitants quailing under the revelation of light.

Annabella clung to Custo's solid shoulders to borrow his strength, sought his eyes for courage, and coaxed the hot sphere higher. Morning in the Shadowlands. Salvation.

Like a blotch marring the burgeoning blue, the wolf leaped behind Custo. The wolf's rage crackled in the air and raised the fine hairs on Annabella's skin.

The ground lurched, lost its solidity, churning under their feet. The Shadowlands, expelling them.

—*doesn'tbelong, doesn'tbelong, doesn'tbelong*—

The three fell back to Earth, to Segue, and the confines of the open storage room in an airborne brawl, Custo gripping the wolf's jaws.

The concrete was brutal, crushing, but Annabella rolled immediately to her feet—she could handle a little pain—and threw herself on the huge bristle of black grappling with Custo.

She wrapped an arm around the beast's neck and used all her muscle to force the jaws away from Custo's throat. Riding the wolf's hump, she grabbed a fistful of coarse hair and yanked it back. The wolf smelled like a dog, dark and beasty and a little bit foul.

"Run, Annabella," Custo ground out, red-faced, shaking with effort to restrain the crazed wolf.

"No," she managed, locking on to the wolf's back with her thighs. Thank God for pliés.

A shout brought her gaze up to the door. She ducked her head just as a soldier fired, hitting the wolf between the eyes. Adam must have been prepared for this very contingency.

More men filed in behind him, guns trained through the doorway, ready to unload on the beast. Custo reached out a hand toward them, and the soldier scuttled forward to hand him a mean knife.

Which the wolf knocked away.

Annabella scrabbled to get it and cut her fingers on the sharp blade before grasping the hilt in a slippery hand. She stabbed while she could, where she could, in his shoulder. The knife hit bone and glanced to the side, slicing across the wolf's flesh and not down into it, hot red spilling across her arm before it cooled and evaporated into Shadow.

The wolf bucked and threw her, hard, into one of Kathleen's paintings, cracking the frame and tearing the canvas. Stars of pain exploded in Annabella's vision. A soldier dived for her, grabbing her arm to drag her out of the fray. She was passed into the concrete cavern, through a line of soldiers, and laid on the ground.

The soldier, a square-faced man whose eyes were too close together, demanded, "Is this your blood?" but he stalled in his examination, staring openmouthed at her face.

"I cut my hand," Annabella answered. Not enough to take her away from Custo.

The soldier touched his ear. "Sir, we've got a medical emergency. Need immediate evac."

"I'm not going anywhere. It's just my hand." And even

that wasn't too bad. She pointed in the direction of the storage room. "He's the one who's hurt!"

Another volley of shots echoed in the tunnel, battering her eardrums. She cringed, covering her ears, but the report kept ricocheting in her skull. To her right a masked soldier was donning a small tank of a backpack attached to an oddly shaped gun. Had to be a flamethrower.

"Yes, yes, yes," she said, "fry him."

"Ma'am, it's not safe here." The first soldier again. "You look *very* ill. You need a doctor."

"I'm not going—"

There was a sudden shout, a break in the line of guards, and a cacophony of violent gunfire. Custo was pulled through, blood everywhere, his right arm hanging limp, bloody, and broken at his side. At least he was on his feet.

Now they could get out of here.

The gunfire let up. With a loud pause in the action, the soldiers fell back. Then the cavern was filled with a roar of tremendous heat and the smell of fire. The gunshots had hurt the wolf, but the fire would consume his body. That would give Annabella and Custo time to run while the wolf remade himself out of Shadow and pursued.

Someone grabbed her under her arms, and Annabella was carried toward the yellow lift, though her legs worked perfectly fine. She'd have fought it, but Custo was at her side, his good arm slung over another soldier. The lift engaged and they ascended with agonizing slowness to the upper level.

"I need a helicopter," Custo said. "Now."

"Sir, you both need serious medical attention," a soldier responded. He seemed to be the head of the unit, a little older, his buzz so short that he was shiny bald.

"I'll heal on my own, and"—Custo shot Annabella a worried look—"I don't think there's anything you can do for her. She needs specialized care, and I intend to see that she gets it."

That was the third time someone hinted that something was wrong with her. "What the heck is everyone talking about?"

Annabella caught a couple sidelong glances, but no one answered her. The lift screeched to a stop. One of those funny army-styled golf carts was waiting.

Custo helped her into the back bench and jumped in beside her, squeezing her hand to comfort, and shouted "Go!" to the driver.

Annabella blanched when she got a look at her arm.

Under the smears of blood, she was pasty-pale, with fine lines of black scribbled along the surface, like minute burst capillaries. She angled her head to get a glimpse of her face in the rearview mirror, and then wished she hadn't. She'd officially joined the freak show.

The shape of her face was the same, her features recognizable, though speckled with blood, but the rest was just wrong. And ugly. The centers of her eyes, pupil and iris, were black, as in voodoo-witch black. Her complexion was waxy, way beyond the stage white of Giselle. And now that her adrenaline was tanking, her body had that getting-sick feeling, everything achy and extra cold.

She dropped her eyes. "What's happened to me?" Was she going to die?

"I don't know, sweetheart," Custo said. He inhaled, then held the breath.

"What?"

"Did he hurt you? Did he . . . ?"

She shook her head, fighting tears. "We only danced, but . . . I did kinda lose myself in it for a while. Until you came." A thin trail of hot wetness skated over her cheek. "Am I going to be okay?"

"Absolutely. We're going to The White Tower and we're

not leaving until Luca fixes you up. The Order must know a way to cure you. We're not leaving until they do."

Sudden fear knifed through Annabella. "My mother. The wolf will go after my mother."

"Is that how he coerced you to go with him?"

Annabella nodded. "And he'll follow through on his threat, especially now that I've run away from him. We have to get to her first."

Custo caught her gaze with his. "I'll send an extraction unit for your family, but we are going to the tower."

"No. This is my mother we're talking about."

"Bella. Take another look at yourself in the mirror."

Annabella kept her gaze on his face. She wasn't budging.

He shook his head, no. "We have to find out what's happening to you and if it's reversible. My hunch is that the wolf will follow you, especially now that you are infected with Shadow, rather than make good on any threats to hurt your family. Remember what happened to Abigail?"

Annabella's argument stuck in her throat. The memory of Abigail's possession was vivid, horrifying, an invasion of body more complete than she could fathom. But she wanted her mom and brother safe and sound.

"Decision's made, Annabella," Custo said. His tone brooked no further disagreement. "We need to get you help before the wolf catches up with us. I don't think we have much time."

The army cart burst out of the concrete bunker. A helicopter was waiting, its propellers beating the air into a deafening hurricane of small debris that stung Annabella's eyes. At Custo's direction, the driver helped her inside, though she still didn't need it. She looked like a freak, but she wasn't helpless.

The helicopter lifted off before she was fully strapped in, nose angling toward the city. Annabella stared at the skin on her hands, while Custo yelled into a headset.

"Adam, repeat!" Custo's forehead and eyes strained as he listened. He rubbed a hand over his face and told her, "I can't get a clear signal."

He asked the pilot, "What's our ETA?"

"Seventeen minutes."

Custo looked back at her. "How are you feeling?"

"Fine. The same." Which wasn't quite true. She was bitterly cold.

Annabella watched Custo's arm heal as they flew, the flesh knitting together from the inside out as the minutes ticked by. The bone looked straighter, too. She tried to control her shivers while she listened to Custo make a series of calls. Her mom had been picked up, and though spitting mad, was fine and in transport by her city's police to rendezvous with a Segue unit, which would really piss her off. Her brother had likewise been detained by campus security. Annabella could do nothing but wait and hope they were safe.

"Oh. Hell." Custo was looking out his window to the city below.

Annabella leaned over to see for herself, but couldn't immediately make sense of the chaos. A narrow building was in near rubble, its street-side wall collapsed, the interior floors and rooms exposed. Great white pieces of stone littered the sidewalk and crushed two unlucky cars. Other cars were abandoned helter-skelter in the middle of the road as in a disaster movie.

The helicopter lowered, and people became visible: a line of army soldiers crouched behind debris, protecting the remains of the building, firing upon an encroaching armed throng who obviously weren't scared of guns.

The helicopter banked toward a rooftop landing, and from this new perspective, the street became more familiar. The destroyed white building below had to be The White Tower, occupying the space of the alley where it once had been concealed from human eyes. Now it was in full view.

The soldiers protecting it and the fallen angels were led by Segue, holding off the invading wraiths.

"Adam was too late," Custo said.

"Or just in time," Annabella answered, unbuckling her belt. "We've got to hurry."

Custo put a staying hand on her arm. "I'm not taking you down there."

"Ha! I'm not asking permission." She opened the helicopter door and pushed against the wind, her hair flying in all directions.

Custo climbed out after her, expression fierce. "Annabella—"

She cut him off, lifting her Shadow-veined palms for him to see. "There's nothing down there scarier than what the wolf will do to me. He's got to be close behind us—nothing can hold Shadow—and the next time he attacks we won't have a flamethrower to stall him." She pointed to the melee below. "The Order has answers and they need your help. I'm going whether you like it or not."

Annabella took off across the roof toward a set of red metal doors, and Custo had no choice but to follow. Joining the fray was madness, suicidal, something for him, but definitely not for her. Besides, they were on the wrong side of the fight; they'd have to cross through the wraiths to get to Adam and his defense of the fallen tower. And though it was plenty cool that he could kill wraiths with his hands, as he and the other angels had the night of the gala, there were far too many of them for him to take on alone. But Annabella wouldn't think of any of that.

As always, she seemed determined to be a pain in the ass.

The doors opened to a flight of utility stairs, which led to an upper floor of the building, housing what appeared to be a series of small, independent businesses, little gold plaques to the side of their doors. They took the main elevator to the lobby. Custo avoided the main entrance and barged through a very sketchy-looking staffing business to exit out the rear to a parking lot off the main street.

He hid her behind a Dumpster and assessed the thick army of stinking wraiths held back by Adam's gunfire. Had to be upward of a hundred converging on the Segue men defending the broken tower.

No way to get through. The wolf could catch up at any moment, and then they'd be beset on all sides. They had to keep moving. Maybe if they circled around—

"Who's that?" Annabella nudged him.

Custo's attention focused on where she pointed, a blind spot some ten yards from their location at the juncture of a low concrete wall and a building.

"He was right there a second ago," she said.

Against the age-whitened concrete, a lash of rippling, smoky darkness whipped into existence, and a wraith was propelled backward from the press of the throng. Midair, the wraith halted, and though partially obscured by Shadow, Custo saw his head suddenly torque, and then the sack of wasted flesh fell to the ground. The kill was over before Custo could blink.

Two nearby wraiths turned at the sudden motion, teeth thick in their mouths. With a bloom and jut of Shadow, the lower jaw was knocked off one, and the other crumpled, head lolling after a blur of movement.

Darkness crawled across the lot. A third wraith suddenly threw himself onto a rusty stake.

One by one, wraiths were picked from the back of the throng.

Had to be Shadowman, come to Adam's aid. And he'd said he didn't care.

Near a vertical cement post, the Shadows came to a roiling stop. Only Death's stern face was visible in its depths, expression pitiless, eyes stirring with deep black. He looked over to the Dumpster and spoke, his words clear though he seemed to only mumble across the distance. "Don't trouble yourself to help."

Sarcastic son of a bitch. Custo had jumped Heaven's Gate to help rid the world of wraiths; if he could have been wrenching the necks, he would have.

"I can't. I've got a human woman here," Custo replied. He couldn't, wouldn't leave Annabella alone for a second. "She's been infected with . . . something."

Shadowman tilted his head, forceful gaze intent across the debris and cars in the parking lot, assessing. Custo would have guessed from context that he was examining Annabella, but she was hidden by the gang-tagged Dumpster.

"She's lost anyway," Shadowman concluded, returning his attention to the throng of wraiths.

Custo straightened. "Over my dead body."

"Don't be a fool. You're already dead." Shadowman's darkness contracted, and he was revealed completely—tall, broad, strong beyond imagining, and cruel. His trench coat, black leather from the look of it, seemed to absorb light. With a wicked whip and twist of darkness, Death's long hair was bound effortlessly behind him. "The body you now hold is a choice, made of your soul, and thus mortal. Be careful with it. She's gone regardless."

Shadowman left his cover, stalked up behind the press of the immortal dead, and tapped one on the shoulder.

The creature turned, opened its mouth, and got its neck broken for his hesitation. The nearest wraiths hurled themselves back from the presence of Death, trampling a few that fell to get away from the one being that could kill them, but wouldn't die himself. At least Shadowman had killed a few before revealing himself.

The wraiths scattered, a good many pelting for the Dumpster where Custo hid with shivering Annabella. A wraith leaped over the Dumpster with a great hollow thump. Custo altered its trajectory and brought it head first into the pavement, then stamped its neck to the side. Dead.

Two others rounded the side. Annabella tripped one, was slapped back, which gave Custo enough rage to break its back with his knee, then its neck with a midair strike that nearly ripped its head from its shoulders. The second wraith missed Custo's face and locked onto his shoulder with his teeth. It jerked when Annabella stabbed it with something, releasing him. Custo jabbed his elbow in the wraith's face, crushing its nose, and hurled it over his shoulder to stomp its trachea, then break its neck.

They'd be safer in Shadowman's wake. No wraith would get near enough to hurt them. Taking Annabella's hand, he made a break for the tall, dark man parting the wraiths like Moses at the Red Sea. Bodies of wraiths littered the street, the smell so foul Annabella vomited as they passed the worst of it, but stumbled alongside of him.

Beyond was the white wreckage of the tower and the ragtag group of Segue soldiers who'd held the wraiths at bay. Adam was midcommand, organizing a triage to save what injured angels he could. He glanced over, noted Shadowman, Custo, and Annabella's presence, but continued with his work. Time was critical. A pitiful few others, angels, dug in the rubble for survivors. They called with their minds, seeking responses, but got only flickers of consciousness.

Hold on. Help is coming.

Custo wrapped his arms around Annabella as cold certainty ran through his blood.

The tower was a refuge no longer. No help for Annabella's condition could be found there. The angels couldn't save her when their brothers and sisters were buried, their mortal souls at risk.

In one minute, or ten, or thirty, the wolf would come again for Annabella. She was trying to hide her mounting shakes but not fooling anyone. Custo would have to fight him again. And again. Since Custo was mortal, the wolf would eventually prevail.

Which left . . .

Shadowman set his cold gaze on Annabella, and she visibly shivered.

"Please help her," Custo said.

"Did your elders teach you nothing?" Death asked Annabella with disdain.

"I don't know what you mean," she said.

Shadowman lifted a pitying smile. "Long ago, a girl such as you came into Shadow. Her name was Persephone, and she ignored warnings, as you likely did. She ate four pomegranate seeds, and in doing so, bound herself to spend a season each year in the Otherworld." Death made a show of looking Annabella over. "How much did you eat at the hunter's table?"

Shadowman's tone was as awful as Annabella's expression, and Custo almost intervened. But she lifted her chin, returning the bastard's cold glare, and said, "I think I started with the chocolate, and then an éclair, no wait—" She inclined her head dramatically to remember, then continued, all brat, "I think I hit the comfort food first, some cheesy au gratin delicious dish I can't name, but my mom would probably love the recipe if you wouldn't mind getting it for me—"

Custo grabbed her hand to shut her up, but she brazenly continued in Death's face, "And then the chicken pot pie, with the *best* spring peas I've ever—"

"Point is she ate the wolf's food," Custo cut in. "Could be worse, right?"

"Look at her. She's bound to Shadow, and yet as a human, even one with a gift to draw from Shadow, she cannot tolerate it indefinitely. Eventually she will weaken, and the wolf will overtake and possess her."

"Is there a cure?" Annabella asked.

"He has to release you," Shadowman said, "but I don't know why he would with your power. I think he'd bring you to heel"—her chin went up again—"or let your body die, and keep you from passing into the Hereafter."

The set of her jaw and the intensity of her black eyes told Custo she'd use every atom of her contrary spirit to make her submission miserable for the wolf. If she had to go, she wouldn't go easy.

Custo was ready to beg. "Is it in your power to help her, to force his cooperation? Can you kill him?"

"The hunter is elemental, immortal. I can order him back to Shadow, but Annabella would eventually have to follow. He set out to capture her, and that's exactly what he has done. There is no 'cure' for a choice. Even one so seemingly insignificant."

So, better to fight now, when Annabella was at her strongest, than to run and be hunted again and again until they wished for an end. Any end.

"I like a good fight," Adam said, coming up beside Custo. Adam was already beat to shit, his pretty, aristocratic nose swelling under blackening eyes.

Luca joined them. His face was scabbed with blood, eyes heavy with losses from The Order's ranks. *I'm with you, too.*

Hell of a way for Segue and The Order to come together, but at least some good was coming out of the nightmare.

Annabella was shaking her head. "This is between the wolf and me. Has been from the beginning. I can do things with Shadow. Magic. I can make him hurt."

But eventually he'll overpower you, Custo added mentally to himself. Not good enough.

There was no way he could bear Annabella submitting on her own, alone. At the very least, he'd be by her side, even if it cost his embodied soul. It wasn't worth much without her anyway. They'd fight, and they'd pay for their mistakes together, in blood and pain, which was nothing new for him.

But they couldn't win.

Last time he died, he had nothing to lose but his regrets. This time . . . everything.

Someone had to win.

Adam had Talia and their babies. Custo couldn't allow him to help, and in so doing invite more loss and misery into the world. Or Luca, whose end would be as final as Custo's.

And Shadowman?

"I tricked you once," Custo said, "and I am sorry. Is there anything I can do to make it right before . . . *he* comes?"

"I can't exactly trade you to Hell now, can I?"

No. "Other than that."

Shadowman's eyes slanted to the ruin of the tower. To the arsenal now littering the white stones. The weapons would have to be carefully tucked away until The Order could rebuild.

"I need the hammer," Shadowman said.

"Take it," Custo said.

Death's nostrils flared. "I would have already, if I could touch it. But I need an angel to hand it to me."

Luca bumped Custo's arm. "No. It's forbidden. Don't add this mistake to the others."

"Who are you to talk?" If Luca had listened to Adam in the first place, the tower would still stand. If the hammer would bring Kathleen and Shadowman together, then so be it.

Custo climbed the steps of rubble and found the hammer in the dust, the same one he'd handled in the tower's armory. The shaft was solid, a dark wood rubbed smooth by handling. One side was wide and blunt, the other a rounded knob. A blacksmith's tool. Custo had no idea what Death would do with such a thing when there were some awesome blades littering the area, and he didn't care.

When he turned back, his heart stopped.

The wolf was padding slowly across the street, his bunched shoulders rolling with the stealth of his advance. The wolf barked once, and Annabella fell to her knees.

"Hunter," Death said, "there is no need for that. You've leashed her already."

Custo leaped down from the white rubble as the wolf morphed into an almost-man, naked, hairy, potent, and vicious. His body was built for power, muscles thick and corded. His expression was feral, but had lost that rabid craze that had cost him the fight at Segue. He was back to cunning, to searching out and exploiting weakness.

He'd set traps, and one had sprung. He was here to collect his prey.

Custo helped Annabella to stand and, handing Shadowman the hammer, said, "I won't let you have her."

"You can't stop me," the wolf said. To Annabella, he barked, "Come."

The blackness of her eyes seemed to throb, the thin lines on her skin growing thicker. Annabella swayed, but obstinate as ever, said, "No."

"Come!"

Annabella blurred, the Shadow within her hazing toward the wolf in obedience, but the rest of her was rooted in the rubble. Custo put his arms around her waist. Her slim frame trembled, every trained muscle overriding the compulsion of Shadow.

How long could she keep it up?

An hour? A day? And yet, what else could she do but refuse and endure? She'd fight until her body broke. Annabella was made of willpower, had honed it, like her body, for most of her life. She was by nature a fighter.

"Come. Now," the wolf growled across the war zone that was the street. His disgusting stuff was getting hard as if he anticipated dominating her.

Rage pounded in Custo's head. He put Annabella behind him. That monster would not touch her while Custo was living.

Annabella reached around Custo's body to flip the wolf the bird. God, Custo loved her.

Adam's thoughts filtered through Custo's worry. *I've got six guns trained on him, waiting for your signal.*

To fight the wolf with conventional weapons was to prolong the inevitable.

Luca added, *I can think of three of The Order's blades that would cut him out of the world.*

That might take care of the wolf, but what about Annabella? The Shadow was making her ill. She'd have to return to the Otherworld eventually to survive, and the wolf would be waiting for her.

No. Shadowman had stated the only possible way: the wolf had to willingly release her. But what circumstances would compel the beast to do such a thing when Annabella's power was almost in his grasp?

The wolf needed a better offer.

Custo slanted his gaze toward Luca. "You said my presence on Earth, my body, was a choice?"

"No." Luca shook his head. So he'd thought it, too. *You have no right to offer your body, your great soul, to a dark fae. Annabella would give him free access to Earth, but with you he could breach Heaven.*

Hence, a better offer. It was a simple solution: Convince the wolf to release Annabella in exchange for him instead. A mortal for an angel.

A sharp pinch brought Custo's attention to Annabella. Her eyes were huge in her face, the lines of her skin like old, cracked china.

"I don't know what you're thinking," she said, her voice strained with threat, "but I know I don't like it."

Custo had to smile at that. The world needed someone

with her kind of spirit, her talent, her light. He would not stand by and watch her grow dim.

To Luca, he said, *In my body, the wolf would be mortal, as I am. Adam has six guns at the ready and you have three swords to choose from. Kill him as soon as he overtakes me.*

You'd be giving him your soul.

Custo had given his life for Adam. He'd easily give something as inconsequential as his soul for Annabella. And all he'd have to do is control the wolf within his body long enough for Adam or Luca or even Death to do what needed to be done. To kill him—gunshot to the head ought to do the trick—and thus kill the wolf. There was a way after all.

Decision made, sweet peace swept over Custo. He kissed Annabella on her head and then forcibly guided her to Adam for safekeeping.

Her feet were damn stubborn. "What are you doing?" she cried, resisting him.

The wolf growled, lips peeling back from canine teeth. "Annabe—"

"Forget her," Custo interrupted over his shoulder. "I've already had her anyway. Find yourself a more faithful mate."

"I'm going to be sick," Annabella said as Custo delivered her to Adam's hands and left her without a backward glance—better that way—to approach the beast.

"I want her power," the wolf answered.

Custo shrugged. "Release her, and you can have mine."

TWENTY-ONE

ANNABELLA twisted and yanked her arm out of Adam's vise grip. She caught the glances he exchanged with Luca. They were up to something, and since no one saw fit to clue her in, the plan was probably very, very bad. She couldn't hear clearly, but Custo had offered something cryptic to the wolf, which the wolf seemed to understand and be considering.

Whatever it was, the answer was, "No!"

Custo turned back. "Baby, trust me, it was meant to be this way."

"Don't 'baby' me!" Annabella yelled. She wasn't a child. "Stand by me. Fight with me."

She really didn't think she could handle this if he weren't by her side, and she couldn't believe he was pulling this macho crap on her now. Actually, she could believe it. This pigheaded behavior was just like him.

Custo murmured to the wolf. "Yes, they'll try to stop you, but my body will heal on its own if you can get away."

"You're suggesting that I possess an angel?" The wolf grinned, toothy and cruel.

Annabella's heart stopped beating. She should have known Custo would attempt a stupid but impossibly sweet thing like that. Trade himself for her.

But what then? They'd still have a power-hungry, crazy-ass wolf on the loose, just inside an impossibly gorgeous body. And as far as she knew, they didn't have a way to restore Custo afterward, unless the angels and their Order had some extra power no one had shared with her.

Movement caught her eye: Adam flicking his fingers. A signal, but to whom? For what?

Annabella scanned the area, saw the black tip of a rifle braced on white stone. And ten feet away, another weapon came up, carefully aiming at the wolf and Custo. A third soldier knocked the decaying remains of a wraith off a wall and took up position.

They better be careful where they fire, because even though Custo could heal supernaturally well, he could still be . . .

Oh. God. No.

The plan became clear, and as she'd suspected it was stupid and horrible and she didn't want any part of it: The wolf would possess Custo, an angel, and therefore an offer way better than her comparatively frail body. The wolf would take his chances with the guns for this perfected form, while Adam shot his friend in cold blood in an attempt to kill the monster. A gamble on both sides.

'Kay. Now she was pissed.

Annabella whirled back to the wolf and Custo, but it seemed they'd already come to an agreement.

The wolf spread his fingers toward her, and the marionette strings that had been tugging relentlessly at her limbs and mind released. The Shadow within her fell away like a breath exhaled, leaving her raw and sore, and heavier than ever.

She pushed away her exhaustion; the show wasn't over yet.

"Stop!" Annabella yelled, lurching toward the wolf and Custo to prevent whatever insanity Custo had proposed.

But it was too late. As she lunged toward them, Custo took a simple step forward, and absorbed the wolf.

At once the day dimmed, clouds boiling out of the blue and grumbling over the sky. The edges of the world became grittier, its sounds harsher. The air grew sullen and bitter to the tongue.

Annabella cast her weight forward as Custo whipped around. Black bled through the mossy green of his eyes, obscuring the color. The veins in his neck, forearms, and the backs of his hands darkened, as if his heart now pumped

Shadow. His expression took on a mask of barely controlled rage.

"Stay back," he said, his voice a low rumble of effort.

She dodged his outstretched arms and wrapped herself around him anyway, gripping her wrists around his back so she couldn't be shaken off. If Adam's men were going to shoot, they'd have to shoot her first. She wasn't going anywhere.

"I can't fight him long," Custo ground out, his cruel hands prying at her wrists.

"You should have thought of that before," Annabella answered, holding on tight to spite him. A sob formed in her throat, but she swallowed it back. She could cry later. "How dare you change places with me? It's not right. Everyone here knows it's not right."

"Adam!" Custo called. "Take her! Please!"

In her arms, Custo was changing, his chest broadening. His breath came in labored pants.

Two Segue soldiers crouch-walked into position at Custo's back, guns trained on him. Out of the corner of her eye, she spotted Luca holding a long blue blade.

Even the angels were against them.

"Annabella, I don't want to hurt you." Custo sounded like he was speaking through clenched teeth.

"You won't," she answered back. "You love me."

"I do, but the wolf wants you"—Custo shuddered—"bad."

"Sucks to be him."

"This is the only way," Custo said. His voice had taken on a disturbing bestial roll, but she wasn't giving up.

"Listen to me, Custo," Annabella said. "I don't want you to die for me. What kind of crappy gesture is that for someone you love?" The worst.

"Annabella . . ." Bones cracked in his shoulders.

"Besides, you already died for someone once," she continued, "and look how that turned out."

He growled in her ear, breath hot on her neck.

"Try something different." Her sob broke free anyway, and she spoke through her tears. "Live."

Custo gripped Annabella's wrists so tightly the bones moved. She squeaked, but she wouldn't let go. Twining voices filled his head, but they couldn't agree: *Kill her. Love her. Use her. Fuck her. Protect her.*

Where was Adam when he needed him?

Annabella raised her face, expression stubborn. The blue was back in her irises, her skin clear and perfect. She was normal and whole again.

She returned his scrutiny. "Not your best look," she said.

In the glass storefront across the street, he was unrecognizable. His bones had altered to accommodate more muscle and tough flesh. His cheekbones were prominent, eyes wider, blacker, deeper. Shadow pulsed through his veins and sparked along his nerves. The power surging within him was thrilling, giddy, and slick.

Custo turned slowly, assessing the street. Soldiers crouched in a wide circle around him, poised to shoot. Luca's knuckles were white with his grip on the sword. Shadowman's disinterest had given way to pity.

Adam's gun was loose at his side. He'd taken a step toward Annabella, ostensibly to retrieve her, but stopped himself.

"Adam!" Custo shouted.

Adam moved no closer. Made no attempt to rescue Annabella.

Custo looked at the sky for help, but the heavens were closed. The storm above swallowed the tops of buildings and snapped with electricity, agitating the dark boulders of the clouds to knock hollowly into one another.

A growl shuddered through his mind, hungry and impatient for the storm to break. For the street to run with red.

He took Annabella's arms and forced her grip to break,

knowing he'd leave bruises. Her hold on him loosed with sobbing shakes. "Not letting go" ran together in a *notlettinggo* chant forced through the clench of her teeth. She slid down his body to her knees, her forehead hot against his hip, arms locking again elbow to elbow.

Insensible to anything but holding on to him, she'd just given Adam and his soldiers a clean shot. Custo's head and chest were in plain view. There was little danger of hitting her.

The time was now.

He glanced down to stroke her hair in a last comfort, but his hands were altered, fingers thick, mottled with gray, and tipped with wicked-sharp, curling black claws. They itched to gouge, crush, and tear, incapable of gentleness.

Custo fisted them tightly, his heart fisting, too. He would not lay those hands on her head. Would not touch Annabella with violence while a shred of his soul remained intact. His love for her condensed into a bright *will not* that roped the beast of his rising bloodlust.

He lifted his arms open to the side in a wide arrest position, his nails cutting into his palms. He'd come full circle, ready again to face death. This time a final, endless, consuming darkness.

No sniveling allowed.

Custo sought Adam's gaze, found it waiting, his brother's face lined with grief and pain, mouth curling downward as if to spit a bad taste out of his mouth. And yet, it was so much better that death come at his hands, than it had at that piece of shit Spencer's. A mercy and a gift.

Custo nodded, quick and short, *shoot now,* as the wolf snarled within to fight. To use the woman as a shield, and if she still lived when they'd fled this place, to mount her and fu—

He brought his hands to his head to smother the impulses.

Hunger clouded his mind, voracious as a killer. His will burned with a lust to kill, hunt, to rut. His sight darkened,

the day churning with a spitting and cursing storm, obliterating light and all sense of time. The streetscape was heavy
with gray, the wind whipping the dust of the tower into
spinning devils, awaiting the break of violence.

Shoot. End this.

His vision sharpened, and the darkened world edged with
keen outlines of the men, his prey. He could almost scent
them individually, their blood and sweat a dark bouquet. He
touched his tongue to a sharp canine tooth, elongating in
his mouth. How easy it would be . . .

Hot tears snaked down his cheeks as small fissures cracked
his strength.

Adam, please! Custo couldn't voice it. Annabella, whose
sobs had gone hoarse, would come to her senses and stand.
Protect him with her life while he fantasized about murder.

Adam worked his lower jaw, coming to a decision.

Make it quick. No time. Custo waited for the bite of the
first bullet. Welcomed its relief as lightning sliced the sky.

Waited. But nothing happened.

"Stand down," Adam said, dropping his weapon and his
gaze to the rubble.

"Sir?" a soldier asked.

"I said, stand down."

Custo gaped in disbelief. His gaze flew to Luca, who must
know the horrors crowding his mind and the weak grasp he
had on his will.

Please! He could hold on until Luca walked ten paces
forward and impaled him. He'd *have* to hold on that much
longer.

But Luca's eyes went dull and he dropped his blade. A
puff of dust-smoke lifted. *I can't. I won't.*

So much for family. Custo was abandoned, alone, and
made a bastard all over again.

At least Death, callous as stone, would not discriminate.
Shadowman?

Death lifted the hammer Custo had given him from the ruin of the tower. "We're even now." With that, he folded himself into Shadow and stalked silently away.

Custo was alone with the rising beast, Annabella, and an audience. They'd betrayed his trust when he needed them most. Did they want to see a monster?

So be it.

Custo threw back his head and howled to the sky. The sound was a mix of wrath and soul, a curse to God and a prayer for deliverance. Lightning flashed in answer and black Shadow lifted like mist from the pavement, dark trees growing in the midst of the city, his hunting ground, prey packed into buildings like cages. Their myriad thoughts would both betray their locations and their intentions. So easy. Too easy. A glut.

The air filled with layered fae voices: *Anna. Bella. Anna. Bella. Anna. Bella.*

Annabella stood, eyes blazing with her formidable temper. She assumed a position, arms outstretched, to create a circle around them into which she allowed no curling dark tendril of magic to pass. Shadow seethed behind her, cold and silky, but she wouldn't let Custo have it.

The beast in him roared.

"No," she said. Her magic kept Shadow from feeding Shadow. She'd found the shift of mind that permitted her to draw from or deny the Otherworld. He'd helped her learn that trick himself, and she raised the sun.

How dare she?

"Custo or . . . or Wolf . . ." She shook her head in irritation. ". . . or whoever you are. You want Shadow? You deal with me first."

Custo almost laughed. What did the puny woman hope to do?

Her hair whipped in the rising foul wind. She was graceful

and strong, but tactically ignorant. With one swipe, he could drag his claws across her belly and end this.

But that would be too easy. He went for her neck.

Annabella flinched as his large hand closed around the pale, slender column. Her stubborn chin dimpled as she glared at him, unafraid. Angry. Willful. A tight bundle of passion daring him to do his worst.

If it hurt, she didn't signify. But then, endurance was second nature to her.

Teeth bared, he snarled in her face. She was a pain. In the ass. She'd been this way from day one. Obstinate. Irritating. Intractable.

Before he did anything else, he would break her, body and spirit.

Hand around her neck, he forced her backward toward the ground. She had to know, had to learn, who was master once and for all. And then he could be finished with her. If she cracked her thick head on the pavement when her legs gave and she fell, so much the better.

But her legs didn't give. Her body bent like a willowy bow, the epitome of supple strength. The kind that weathered hurricanes. And she made it look easy. The arch of her spine into the brace of her legs was the antithesis of submission. The satisfied smirk on her lips told him what he knew already. That her soul was made of the same stuff.

Her face was getting red. He could kill her, easily and with pleasure. The storm thundered its approval, echoing the primeval growl in his head.

—*Anna. Bella. Anna. Bella. Bella. Bella. Bella.*—

He could squeeze and squeeze and squeeze the breath out of her, until she collapsed from suffocation. The action required only the slightest contraction of his hand.

But that wouldn't satisfy him. Not remotely.

Why wouldn't she break?

Custo's animal mind sought an answer, the means of her

undoing. There had to be another way, and with it the secret to human will, the power of mortality.

Lightning flashed, illuminating the area. The bolt was caught in an eternal moment, the scene laid bare to Custo's hungry eyes: On one side of the wreckage stood Adam, his dark, brooding eyes watching in expectation. On the other was Luca, his expression equal parts worry and faith. They were beacons of purpose—one from his life, and one from his death—their thoughts willing the man to overcome the beast.

In Custo's grip was Annabella, the axis of his existence, his name in her mind while her throat was silenced.

The three of them created a strange geometry, an Order beyond his complete comprehension. But without doubt or reservation, he knew it was an equation calculated to save his soul.

Like a searing bolt from the sky, love fractured him.

Custo and the wolf were two again, inhabiting the same cursed body, but this time Custo was ascendant. A second chance. His life had been ruled by bitterness and regret, by clear paths scorned for darkness; now he could make a different choice.

The beast in his head roared denial and frustration as Custo forced his joints to open and release Annabella; the storm above cracked in protest, but he was in charge now. For the moment at least.

The air took on the uncompromising solidity that resisted a change of course. Annabella was right: He'd died before; now he wanted to learn something new. He wanted to live.

She straightened slowly, her gaze wary, guarded, as she gulped the thick air. "Custo?"

Her chest heaved and her skin shone with a determined light, offset by the pressing darkness at her back. Though she trembled with weakness, she again put her hands against the throbbing wall of Shadow to keep it from touching him, from nurturing the wolf.

And good thing, too, because the beast had started to prowl in his mind, wildly hungry, primitive, immortally strong, searching for a human weakness to exploit. Custo knew there were a lot of them: anger, violence, sex . . .

A wolfish growl rumbled in his chest—*Found one!*—and Custo's tainted, pounding blood raced toward his groin.

Skin so smooth. Body so tight.

Custo clenched his teeth. He blinked hard and dropped his gaze from sweet, brave Annabella to the hot pavement. No. Not going to happen.

Strip her. Lick her. Take her in the trees.

Custo's vision burned, the concrete rippling with dark mist. "Custo?" Annabella repeated.

Every time he'd tried to resist her before, he'd failed miserably. Every single time her best interests would be served by not touching her, his wants had overruled judgment. How long could he resist? He wasn't stupid, not long at all.

Custo had to be fast. Had to be prepared for even greater personal darkness.

His mind's eye turned inward; he could sense the hulk of the wolf within him, in the most obscure, twisted corner of his mind, slavering with hunger. There was no way to kill the beast and Custo knew he could not sustain this dual existence much longer. Eventually the wolf would control him as it had Abigail.

There could be only *one* mind, *one* will, that ruled this body.

And the beast was so damn hungry. Custo grasped on to that singular lust, stoked it higher, denying the rest.

He let the hunger of the wolf inundate him, felt the appetite commingle with his gathering intent. The wolf responded, crouching as if to spring and overtake his consciousness again. When the wolf leaped, Custo braced and with a great, inner gulp . . . *consumed* him.

Custo swallowed, the burn a fierce roar of agony that overwhelmed his senses, sharpening them to brutal clarity. He took in the wolf, forced him thrashing into his blood and bones and the sizzling snap of his nerves. He absorbed and digested the raw, animal power, the dark identity. Made it his own, while obliterating the wolf's personality in his head.

The burn intensified, beyond pain to shock and wonder. Custo arched with the agony of it. His body was changing again, always changing. This second life would not let him rest. What he would become this time, he didn't know. How much of himself would he lose? Would there be enough left to protect Annabella?

He threw back his head, reaching up with his Shadow-touched hands to part the threatening storm, and found the stars spinning in the black above. The sounds of the city blended with the whisper of voices, the chatter of faery voyeurs to his transformation. The scent of sweat and blood filled his nose, but what direction it came from he didn't know.

He reeled, his sense of direction confused. This way Earth, that way Shadow, over there Heaven, and down this dark path, Hell. Which way to go? Who was he: wolf, man, angel, or all three? Where did he belong?

A thought reached him. It sounded like a prayer. *Please be okay.*

With a snap, the erratic swinging of his internal compass found north and the needle stilled, telling him true in this place of utter uncertainty. Annabella.

And then it didn't matter what he was.

"Custo?" Annabella said. Her chin was up, shoulders square, hands fisted to fight.

Not if she could love him.

He put out a hand to calm her. She didn't have a timid

bone in her body, but he was different and ugly. He startled to find the claws had reverted to human fingernails, which was a good sign. His skin was slightly pale, still tinged by his mother's olive, but his veins were a deep gray. Not so good.

"I won't hurt you," he said, trying to keep emotion from his voice. He pulled his hand back; suddenly he wasn't so sure what the rest of himself looked like. "At least, I don't think I will."

There was only his own voice now in his head, but if the physical change signified anything, the power of the wolf was in him, was *his*, thrumming in his blood. The air snapped with static crispness, singing along his skin. So strange. Maybe Adam should lock him up for a time, just in case. He didn't dare trust himself, especially with Annabella. Yes, much better to wait and see what—

With a flash of movement, Annabella's arms went around his neck. She held herself in midair, her hot, soft lips pressed hard to his. Custo gasped, surprise bringing him to his knees while he clutched her from falling. She exhaled a hoarse laugh against his mouth at the jarring pavement, and . . . damn it, he had to kiss her back.

Trial by fire, then.

Custo parted her lips with his tongue to take the kiss deeper. Annabella answered by tightening her arms, a hand in his hair, gripping him close, and—*have mercy*—a little painfully. His body burned with the touch, her closeness, and a dark wave of lust swamped him. Darker, more primal than he'd ever known. Near wolfish. Her scent was stronger, muskier than he remembered. Her skin, smoother; her mouth wet. He needed her on the ground, beneath him, or on her knees, arching for the moon.

By the way her legs wrapped around his waist, she seemed in agreement.

A catcall from the other side of the city street brought dim awareness of his human audience. The street, the ruined buildings, the stink of fallen wraiths. It would not do for his Annabella, who now hid her face in his shoulder.

Custo. Luca's voice invaded his mind. *Are you all right?*

Custo sighed heavily. If he could hear someone else's thoughts, he was probably still an angel. Not his preference either, but he was getting used to it.

Luca would have to wait for an answer. Privacy, please.

By instinct, Custo reached for Shadow, and it obeyed like a curtain drawn on the world. Which meant he had a little wolfish fae in him as well. That's the one he was most worried about.

One moment he and Annabella were Earthbound, the next transported, surrounded by ageless trees, the primeval layering of dirt, undergrowth, and heady, magic-filled boughs filling his nose. He sensed the interest of his faery observers, and banished them with his mind, too. This was for him and Annabella alone. This new Shadow-magic was going to be damn useful.

He cupped Annabella's ass with his palms—*perfection*—and left it to her to hold on tight as he made for a tree trunk, a little leverage and support to strip and plunge and pump . . .

Wait. Custo pulled back and shuddered through a deep breath.

Not like that. She deserved gentleness. Soft strokes. A forever show of thank-you and love and how-did-I-get-so-lucky?

He put his forehead to the rough bark of the tree. Hell, he was shaking. And panting like a dog, too. This was going to be a problem. He squeezed his eyes shut and gave her the truth. "I don't know if I can control myself, sweetheart. Not near ready to trust myself with you."

Annabella bit his earlobe in answer. "If you can ask the question, I'm safe enough."

Annabella felt Custo's weight shift. He'd pinned her deliciously to a tree. Her body tingled with awareness, sore muscles loosening, strengthening in preparation. The embrace was familiar, the pressure and fit all Custo. Her heart thumped hard with relief. They'd survived, somehow. And he was still hers. The rest she didn't have the strength to care about.

Custo started to draw back, hesitated, sighing deeply, then allowed her to look him full in the face. The green she'd seen in his irises had not lied—he was back, his expression more tortured than ever, waiting for her reaction. His coloring had altered, the lines under his skin telling her that he was permeated with Shadow. Which would probably get very interesting. But it was still him, still Custo, just having a very bad day.

She blinked back prickling tears and with mock severity, threatened, "Don't make me seduce you again."

His eyes smiled slightly, underscored by deep rue. Against her body, she could feel the vibration of a growl in his chest.

"I try to be good, really I do," he said, as if very tired. His thumb smeared a tear across her cheek.

She had to grin now, in spite of everything, and lifted her face to kiss. "Don't try too hard."

TWENTY-TWO

"Mom, I know I've only known him a couple of days," Annabella said, phone clutched between her shoulder and ear as she rummaged through one of the boxes the Segue soldiers had packed from her studio. Apparently, Adam took her "I'm never going back there" very seriously.

The apartment she shared with Custo at Segue was jammed with brown boxes smelling like cardboard and packing tape. The place was a disaster with spills of clothes and random junk piling everywhere on the floor from Annabella's search. And now that she and Custo had decided they were moving, she'd just have to pack it all up again.

If she didn't find her stash of pointe shoes soon, she was going to be late for rehearsal, and Venroy was already ticked at her for leaving the reception early two nights before. Good thing the news broadcast of the battle in the city had been blurry where she was concerned. The video capture from mobile phones was less so, but Adam was working on that before she was publicly recognized.

She'd stayed in bed all day yesterday "recuperating" with Custo, but now it was time to get back to work. She had a name to make for herself.

"Then it's clearly too early to move in with him," her mom said. "You barely know the man."

Annabella knew Custo was good and strong and soulful. In his keeping, she was safer than anywhere else in the world . . . or beyond it. He would help her master her gift, just as she would help him master his new abilities. Then, when she wasn't dancing, they'd combine their efforts to help with ongoing breaches between the worlds.

"I told you, I am not staying at his apartment." Which

was the truth. Custo didn't have one. "I'm staying at his friend's home until I can find somewhere to live. I won't be able to sleep at my apartment knowing a murder took place next door."

"Are you sleeping in the same bed?"

Dang, her mom was smart. Annabella had thought for sure the murder thing would get her all excited again and have her going off on the dangers of the city.

"That's none of your business," Annabella said a little primly.

"Then you're living with him." A long silence. "Annabella, it's not like you to fall so hard so fast. I'm worried. I don't want you to get hurt or jeopardize everything you've accomplished with your dance."

"He's a good guy, Mom. I'm crazy about him, and I bet you will be, too."

A pang of worry in her heart told Annabella that the question of her future with Custo did bother her. The fact that he aged like a human person was weirdly comforting, but they still had to figure out how they could share their lives, especially with his slightly abnormal appearance. They'd have to make up a halfway plausible "condition" to explain the dark lines on his body. That he ate a Shadow wolf wasn't going to cut it.

Another silence, a little longer. Then a huge sigh. "Bring him to dinner Sunday."

Her mom was her best friend; she couldn't keep Custo from her for long. "I have performances. What about Tuesday?"

"Tuesday's fine. I'll call your brother so that he can give your Custo a hard time, too."

Annabella smiled. It would be fun to watch Custo squirm. And more fun to make it up to him later.

A rustle behind her. Annabella turned to see Zoe crouching by one of her boxes. The tape hissed as Zoe pulled it off.

25

~~PINK~~
PINK
white
✓Blue

Showldice-

LEN 102

552089

ACCH acexa

the drop

Medical
University
Caribbean
ACCH acxe

SGU St. Georg

AUC — Americ

Saba ⟩ 40-50%
Ross ⟩

Cay St. Math

T – 6:30 – 9:

Jeffrey

"Uh . . . Mom, I've got to go to rehearsal. See you Tuesday. Love you." Annabella disconnected the call. To Zoe she said, "That's not your stuff."

Zoe looked up, the black fringe of her bangs hanging in her eyes. Still no makeup. She looked like a grumpy kid without it.

"I don't have any stuff," Zoe said. "I need clothes. I won't leave Abby here alone, and I'm not about to ask Adam or Talia for a damn thing. That leaves you."

Abigail wasn't making as much progress as Dr. Lin would have liked, but she was holding stable. Zoe must have been worried out of her mind. In a strange place with no friends and a heck of a lot of scary monsters, no wonder she was in a foul mood.

Zoe rummaged through the box. A flash of pointe-shoe pink made Annabella's heart leap. Bingo! Now if she could find Custo, she might make rehearsal on time after all.

"Clothes are in those boxes," Annabella said, snapping up her shoes. "And my makeup in is the bathroom. Help yourself."

"I don't know why you're so happy," Zoe called after her. "It'll never work out for the two of you."

Annabella looked back, feeling sorry for her. No one could know the future with any certainty, not Abigail and certainly not Zoe. The girl just had the uncanny ability that other unhappy people have to sense and tweak the deepest fears of others.

It'll never work out?

Ha! "The hell it won't."

"You're looking better," Adam said, turning away from his computer monitor. "Less ugly, but still . . . disturbing."

Custo grinned as he dropped into a chair opposite Adam, glancing over his friend's blackened eyes and the swollen bridge of his nose. "You still look like shit."

"Yeah. Talia's mad at me for getting hurt. Almost put her back into labor when she heard about it."

"She knows you fight wraiths for a living, right?"

Adam chuckled. "She doesn't want me doing it without her. I'm hoping with you and The Order around she won't have to do much of it at all, but she's still angry."

Which reminded Custo . . . "About Talia and the babies . . . what are you going to do with Gillian?" Custo asked. "You can't exactly let her walk."

"Why not?"

"She knows too much about Segue, about Talia. And the wraiths were keen on getting a hold of the babies, probably to harness whatever gifts they have. The woman needs to face the consequences of her actions." Custo had half a mind to go down to her cell and strangle her himself.

All humor dropped from Adam's face. "The wraiths aren't getting near my children. And for the audacity of threatening my family, I will hunt each one down and kill it. I have the manpower, if that term reasonably extends to The Order, to launch a full-scale offensive now." Adam leaned forward, his eyes narrowing. "As for the good doctor, I leave her to the tender mercies of the wraiths. Without her connection to Segue, all she's good for to them is food."

"So you're letting her walk," Custo repeated. Gillian would be running scared for the rest of her short life. Inevitably, the wraiths would catch up. "Does Talia know?"

"Yep. I can't keep anything from her. She wanted to gift wrap Gillian for the wraiths with a shiny red satin bow. Her words." Adam smiled slightly. "Impending motherhood has, shall we say, intensified her temper."

"Sounds like it." Talia had always been such a quiet, studious thing. Except when she screamed, that is.

Adam put his elbows on the desk, his expression clearing. "Luca and his Order wouldn't stay here, so I've put them up in the Annex building. Unless you have any objections, I'd like to give him the go-ahead to renovate the loft on the top floor. Neither Talia nor I want to live there, and it could be a usable space again."

Custo shrugged. If anyone could excise the memory of his death from the loft, it was The Order. "That's fine. It's past time for that place to get a new paint job." And windows. And elevator doors.

"You could have gotten all this from my head," Adam said. "So what did you come to talk to me about?"

Custo heaved a sigh. The air became thick to breathe, but he forced it in and out of his lungs. It was past time for this, too. "I'm leaving Segue."

The silence filled the room.

"I guess I knew that was coming," Adam said, but he looked tired. Older.

Of course Adam knew. Custo was joining The Order. With his new abilities, the scope and strength of which he'd yet to fully explore, he was needed now more than ever. Plus he had a lot to learn.

"Are you going to become as unreasonable as the rest of them?" Adam asked.

Custo smiled, playing along. "No, you cannot have access to their . . . *our* . . . arsenal. The weapons have supernatural properties, and it would be inviting trouble to permit humankind to use them."

"You let Shadowman have the hammer," Adam pointed out.

"And I will have to take responsibility for whatever chaos he creates with it." But if Shadowman could use the tool to retrieve Kathleen, the exception was worth it. Custo didn't have to read Adam's mind to know that he would second that opinion.

Adam shook his head. "Unreasonable."

Since Segue and The Order would be working together a lot, Custo figured he'd be hearing that same complaint from Adam often.

Adam lifted his eyes just as there was a soft rap at the door.

Custo turned to see Annabella. She had her enormous dance bag over a shoulder, her dark hair pulled severely back into a tight ponytail. Her eyes were fairy-tale big and bright.

"Rehearsal starts in an hour," she said with a token "sorry" wince.

Custo knew the expression was fake. She wasn't sorry. She wanted to go right now. The light was shining in her eyes; she wanted to dance.

"You coming back here tonight?" Adam asked.

Annabella darted a look to Custo. He guessed that meant, *No. We'll find a place in the city.*

A nice hotel, with all the luxuries. After the last couple of days they more than deserved it. Later he'd have to scout out some place for them to live. A comfortable, but secure apartment not too far from The Order's new headquarters and her ballet company. When Luca had mentioned living discreetly among humankind, Custo didn't think he meant living with a human woman. But then, Custo had never lived by anyone's rules before. He wasn't about to start now.

Custo stood. He didn't have the words for everything he wanted to say to Adam. For being there most of his life. Saving his ass over and over. "It's been . . ."

Adam cleared his voice. "Yeah. It's been."

They clasped hands over the desk and held. Custo's chest tightened uncomfortably. He would still be seeing Adam regularly, but this was good-bye.

Outside the office, Custo dropped his arm on Annabella's shoulders while they walked down the long hallway. She squeezed him around his waist. Perfect fit. He moved away from his past and headed toward his future.

"So . . ." Annabella began.

Custo hit the elevator button to take them to the exit level. The drive would take an hour into the city. He'd drop her off at rehearsal, then hit the Annex building to tell Luca how the renovation should be done. Whoever dictated the construction of the tower had relied on the angels' ability to mask the place from humankind's perceptions. These were dangerous times; the Annex building's security needed to go beyond illusion. And, of course, their policy against modern weapons needed to be challenged. If the wraiths were armed, The Order needed to be as well.

"Custo! You're not listening to me."

He kissed Annabella's head. "Sorry. You were saying . . ."

She made a face, then said, "You know in the Shadow-lands . . ."

"Yes, I'm familiar." And growing more so.

Annabella shot him a cool, narrow-lidded glance.

Okay, she wasn't kidding.

She bit her lip, taking a deep breath. "Do you remember when you said, 'Make an honest man of me'?"

Custo groaned inwardly. She was quoting him again. "Yeah?"

"Well . . . did you mean it?"

He frowned. What was she getting at? She had a cute worry line forming between her eyebrows, which he smoothed away with his thumb. She had nothing to worry about but her performance. He'd take care of everything else.

"Of course I did," he answered. Annabella was the best thing that had ever happened to him. The truest. Recent events proved that.

"What I mean is . . ."

Custo sighed. This would be so much easier if she'd let him read her mind.

"Well . . ." She blinked rapidly, but he caught the shine of tears.

Oh. She wanted the happily-ever-after. Marriage, a home,

and little babies like Adam and Talia were going to have. In his head, he was already married. She was it for him, and no piece of paper would make that more or less true. And the home? Would have to be centrally located. But, yes, every night he was remotely able would be spent in bed with her. Could he even have children? He had no idea. Good thing he believed in miracles.

Annabella was wringing her hands, still hedging around what she wanted to say. "The phrase is usually associated with *'til death do us part* kind of scenarios."

Scenarios? Custo almost laughed aloud. He gathered her in his arms, fitting her into the Annabella-shaped spot against his body. She was soft and smelled fresh from her shower. He'd fight for the rest of her . . . scenario, but of one thing he was absolutely certain.

"Death can't part us."

INTERACT WITH DORCHESTER ONLINE!

Want to learn more about your favorite books and authors?
Want to talk with other readers that like to read the same books as you?
Want to see up-to-the-minute Dorchester news?

VISIT DORCHESTER AT:

DorchesterPub.com
Twitter.com/DorchesterPub
Facebook.com (Search Pages)

DISCUSS DORCHESTER'S NOVELS AT:

Dorchester Forums at DorchesterPub.com
GoodReads.com
LibraryThing.com
Myspace.com/books
Shelfari.com
WeRead.com

Dorchester Publishing is proud to present

⊰ PUBLISHER'S PLEDGE ⊱

We GUARANTEE this book!

We are so confident that you will enjoy this book that we are offering a 100% money-back guarantee.

If you are not satisfied with this novel, Dorchester Publishing Company, Inc. will refund your money! Simply return the book for a full refund.

To be eligible, the book must be returned by 9/27/2010, along with a copy of the receipt, your address, and a brief explanation of why you are returning the book, to the address listed below.

We will send you a check for the purchase price and sales tax of the book within 4-6 weeks.

Publishers Pledge Reads
Dorchester Publishing Company
11 West Avenue, Ste 103
Wayne, PA 19087

Offer ends 9/27/2010.

"An exceptional literary debut." —John Charles, reviewer,
The Chicago Tribune and *Booklist* on *The Battle Sylph*

The Shattered Sylph

L. J. McDonald

SHATTERED

Kidnapped by slavers, Lizzie Petrule was dragged in chains across the Great Sea to the corrupt empire of Meridal. There, beneath a floating citadel and an ocean of golden sand, lies a pleasure den for gladiators—and a prison for the maidens forced to slake their carnal thirst.

Despite impossible odds, against imponderable magic, three men have vowed Lizzie's return: Justin, her suitor; Leon, her father; and Ril, the shape-shifting but war-weary battler. Together, this broken band can save her, but only with a word that must remain unsaid, a foe that is a friend, and a betrayal that is, at heart, an act of love.

"Wonderful, innovative and fresh. Don't miss this fantastic story." —#1 *New York Times* Bestselling Author Christine Feehan on *The Batle Sylph*

ISBN 13: 978-0-8439-6323-6

To order a book or to request a catalog call:
1-800-481-9191
Our books are also available at your local bookstore, or you can check out our Web site **www.dorchesterpub.com** where you can look up your favorite authors, read excerpts, glance at our discussion forum, and check out our digital content. Many of our books are now available as e-books!

LEANNA RENEE HIEBER

With radiant, snow-white skin and hair, Percy Parker was a beacon for Fate. True love had found her, in the tempestuous form of Professor Alexi Rychman. But her mythic destiny was not complete. Accompanying the ghosts with which she alone could converse, new and terrifying omens loomed. A war was coming, a desperate ploy of a spectral host. Victorian London would be overrun.

Yet, Percy kept faith. Within the mighty bastion of Athens Academy, alongside The Guard whose magic shielded mortals from the agents of the Underworld, she counted herself among friends. Wreathed in hallowed fire, they would stand together, no matter what dreams—or nightmares—might come.

The Darkly Luminous Fight for Persephone Parker

ISBN 13: 978-0-8439-6297-0

To order a book or to request a catalog call:
1-800-481-9191
Our books are also available at your local bookstore, or you can check out our Web site **www.dorchesterpub.com** where you can look up your favorite authors, read excerpts, glance at our discussion forum, and check out our digital content. Many of our books are now available as e-books!

□ **YES!**

Sign me up for the Love Spell Book Club and send my
FREE BOOKS! If I choose to stay in the club, I will pay
only $8.50* each month, a savings of $6.48!

NAME: _____

ADDRESS: _____

TELEPHONE: _____

EMAIL: _____

□ I want to pay by credit card.

□ VISA   □ MasterCard.   □ DISCOVER

ACCOUNT #: _____

EXPIRATION DATE: _____

SIGNATURE: _____

Mail this page along with $2.00 shipping and handling to:
Love Spell Book Club
PO Box 6640
Wayne, PA 19087
Or fax (must include credit card information) to:
610-995-9274

You can also sign up online at **www.dorchesterpub.com**.
*Plus $2.00 for shipping. Offer open to residents of the U.S. and Canada only.
Canadian residents please call 1-800-481-9191 for pricing information.
If under 18, a parent or guardian must sign. Terms, prices and conditions subject to
change. Subscription subject to acceptance. Dorchester Publishing reserves the right
to reject any order or cancel any subscription.

GET FREE BOOKS!

You can have the best romance delivered to your door for less than what you'd pay in a bookstore or online. Sign up for one of our book clubs today, and we'll send you *FREE* BOOKS* just for trying it out... **with no obligation to buy, ever!**

Bring a little magic into your life with the romances of Love Spell—fun contemporaries, paranormals, time-travels, futuristics, and more. Your shipments will include authors such as **MARJORIE LIU, JADE LEE, NINA BANGS, GEMMA HALLIDAY**, and many more.

As a book club member you also receive the following special benefits:
- **30% off all orders!**
- **Exclusive access to special discounts!**
- **Convenient home delivery and 10 days to return any books you don't want to keep.**

Visit www.dorchesterpub.com or call 1-800-481-9191

There is no minimum number of books to buy, and you may cancel membership at any time. *Please include $2.00 for shipping and handling.